PAMELA FRANKAU

(1908-1967) was the younger daughter of the prolific novelist Gilbert Frankau and his first wife Dorothea (Drummond-Black) Frankau, who divorced when she was a child. She was educated at Burgess Hill School, Sussex and thereafter lived with her mother and sister in Windsor. Declining a place at Cambridge she decided to devote herself to writing. Her first two fictional attempts were rejected and, forced to find employment because of her mother's illness, she took a job at the *Amalgamated Press*, making use of the journey to write.

This time she found success: *The Marriage of Harlequin* (1927) appeared when Pamela Frankau was nineteen. The next few years were prosperous —she was promoted to sub-editor on the *Woman's Journal*, found a ready market for her articles and stories, published three more novels and became friends with Noel Coward, John van Druten, G.B. Stern and Rebecca West. This halcyon period was short-lived. The story market slumped, Pamela broke off an engagement and, ill and unhappy, retreated to the South of France to finish *She and I* (1930). She later recorded these differing fortunes in an autobiography, *I Find Four People* (1935).

In 1940, Humbert Woolfe, whom she had loved for nine years, died suddenly. Devastated by his death, she travelled to America for some months. On her return she worked for the Ministry of Food — where she became a great friend of Lettice Cooper — and later the ATS. In 1942 she converted to Catholicism. Three years later she married an American professor, Marshall Dill Junior, and moved to California. Their child died in infancy and the marriage collapsed after seven years.

The best-known of Pamela Frankau's thirty novels include *The Willow Cabin* (1949), *The Winged Horse* (1953), *A Wreath for the Enemy* (1954, also dramatised for television) and *The Bridge* (1957). She also published non-fiction, three collections of short stories and was a critic for BBC radio.

For the last decade of her life, until her death from cancer, Pamela Frankau shared a Hampstead house with the theatrical producer Margaret Webster.

VIRAGO
MODERN
CLASSIC

NUMBER
293

PAMELA FRANKAU

The
Willow Cabin

WITH A NEW INTRODUCTION BY
SUSANNAH YORK

Virago

Published by VIRAGO PRESS Limited 1988
20-23 Mandela Street, Camden Town, London NW1 0HQ

First published in Great Britain by William Heinemann 1949
Copyright © Pamela Frankau 1949
Introduction Copyright © Susannah York 1988

British Library Cataloguing in Publication Data
Frankau, Pamela, 1908-1967
The willow cabin. — (A Virago modern classic).
I. Title
823'.912[F]

ISBN 0-86068-950-6

Printed in Great Britain by Cox & Wyman of Reading, Berks.

INTRODUCTION

"You've got your forebears beat," said the literary agent to the author. Winter, 1926. The author was Pamela Frankau, eighteen years old, her novel *Marriage of Harlequin* had been accepted by the agent sight unseen on the strength of those forebears, chiefly her father Gilbert Frankau, a prolific novelist and short story writer, and her paternal grandmother Julia Frankau, who, writing as "Frank Danby", was a successful Edwardian novelist. Now the book was read, publication date set; and in the glorying author's head (she later wrote) there was a noise of bells, as there had been a couple of summers ago when, with a sense of dread (had she not after all, wasted that whole year, cramming only in the last five days?), she had opened the telegram bearing her School Certificate results. "Frankau — First — Honours" she'd read.

"There was never" Rebecca West much later declared, "a family which so indefatigably furnished material for phd. theses." A Christmas pudding of a family, rich in charms and wit: besides Gilbert and her novelist grandmother, there was Pamela's great-aunt Eliza, Mrs Aria, a distinguished journalist who had succeeded Ellen Terry in Henry Irving's affections, and in whose salon Pamela was to meet contemporary luminaries like Michael Arlen, G.B. Stern, Sybil Thorndike and John Van Druten. There had been "Owen Hall", a great-uncle who wrote lively musical comedies in the 1880s, there was Ronald Frankau, her father's brother, a popular stage and radio star; and Pamela's older sister Ursula, as well as her young cousin Diana, were to become admirable novelists in their own right.

The sisters were children still when their parents, Gilbert and Dorothea divorced. The girls lived with their mother, "a woman of plaintive charm and wit", attending a good Anglican school in Burgess Hill where Pamela became a star, if erratic pupil. Schooldays over, Ursula looked unsuccessfully for work, and Pamela (later to regret not following up her scholastic achievements by going to university) applied herself enthusiastically to writing two novels. Both were rejected. Then Mrs Frankau fell seriously ill:

money was tight, and Pamela got her first job as "sub-sub-editoress" with the Amalgamated Press at 37s. 6d. a week. *Marriage of Harlequin*, her third novel, had been written in a third-class carriage of her daily train between London and Windsor — "You've got your forebears beat"! The bells were ringing, ushering in her season of "oysters and champagne".

Nine years, twelve novels, many short stories later, aged twenty-seven and prompted perhaps by a short spell in hospital, Pamela Frankau followed up her early precocity with an autobiography. In *I Find Four People*, rather as an actor might slough off his parts, she recognises, salutes, and divests herself of the four people she has already been — P. Frankau at school, Miss Frankau at the Amalgamated Press, the author fêted with oysters and champagne, the author-in-love-and-in-debt, turned copywriter: greeting the fifth for whom "two of the most important factors in my life are work and travel". These were always to remain. So of course was her Jewish ancestry, less a factor than a fact of life.

In England between the wars, anti-semitism ran deeper than is commonly recognised. To her famous ex-Etonian father brought up in the Church of England, the discovery of his origins may well have been a shock; but for Pamela this "fact of life" only became necessary to examine with the rise of Hitler in the 30s and the floodlight thrown once again by all Europe on the Jewish question. In *The Devil We Know* published in 1939, Frankau explores what being Jewish means to Philip Meyer, an ambitious young screenwriter in the burgeoning British film industry; following him through five years and an obsessive love which turns to hate, the largely self-induced fall in his fortunes, and the travail of soul which brings him out of the angst, sense of persecution, and hatred of his own race to which he has always been heir, to that moment when he can quietly declare "I love my race and I am proud of it". The book is dedicated to her mother and her sister, "my earliest memories of peace, kindliness, and freedom"; perhaps it was also a gift to her father . . . Jews, things Jewish, were to remain a minor theme throughout her work. "The racialist would do well to remind himself that our Lord was a Jew", the young Don Bradley in *A Wreath for the Enemy* answers his father; but Pamela had already richly addressed the question, and Jewishness stayed for her a fact of life like her writing arm.

When one comes to *The Willow Cabin* written ten years later, one is hard put not to see — with what immediacy, intensity, *tangibility*, does that central relationship unfold — in Caroline Seward's love for Michael Knowle the enshrinement of a passion Frankau herself had experienced. The ingredients are there — the wilful, life-loving, excessively gifted young woman, that authentic English wartime background: the common social/theatrical backdrop, time served as an officer in the ATS, the experience of post-war California (Pamela had married an American university professor in 1945, and lived there for seven years). There had also been Humbert Woolfe, the distinguished civil servant and poet, whom she had loved for nine years, and who had died in 1940.

And yet . . . would Pamela ever for long have regarded "the world well lost for love"? The pattern of her life belies it: unlike Caroline she worked whole-heartedly throughout this, the central love-affair of her life, and there is a robustness, a "bounceability" that sings out in the author's autobiography which her heroine, for all her courage and tomboyishness, is denied. Pamela's early and lifelong dedication was to her work; her genius one suspects, was for life. Caroline's dedication is to life, and life takes the shape of one person. Only when that person is gone will life include her work.

One reconsiders. Rather than an "enshrinement", was this an extension, perhaps, the *development* of a passion, a route through it Frankau took on paper alone? But if we discount that grand passion as a third "most important factor in her life", another presents itself — perhaps born of it. Her conversion to Roman Catholicism in 1942.

The mind lingers over the timing . . . The "Jewish question" was then concentrated in Nazi Germany alone, and she was serving with the utmost seriousness in the ATS for love of her country — for that particularly ardent love which as she herself pointed out, is felt for England by many English Jews. For Frankau, at ease with her bloodstock though raised like her father in the Church of England, why this, now? "He made a compromise of prayers, having long deserted his own religion." When Frankau wrote these words of Philip Meyer in 1939, she might be writing of herself.

vii

Since he did not serve God in any church, he refused to ask a benefit from Him. He would kneel for a long time, thinking confused thoughts, fingering the crucifix he had brought from France. At this moment he would search for words as though an immortal phrase now denied might one day be spoken for his consolation.

Humbert Woolfe had died in 1940. By 1942 was Frankau, long searching herself, at once too at ease, and yet too far from her never-practised Jewish faith?

"'Mysteries. Well, I do like them.'" Caroline Seward tells Jay Brookfield half-way through *The Willow Cabin*.

"'There are none,' said Jay.

'There's God,' said Caroline."

This, from the girl who three years earlier had told the man she was so passionately to love.

"'I've no use at all for God. I'm an atheist' . . .

'Could you spit in His face?' Knowle asked negligently.

She winced. 'What a hideous thing to say' . . .

He was laughing. 'As I thought. You are no more an atheist than I am. No artist worth twopence can be an atheist.'"

The catalyst for Frankau was surely Woolfe's death, yet one feels there must always have been a way for her conversion to happen. A sense of religion, of its mysteries, delicately but deeply seams even her early writing and perhaps her entry into the Roman Catholic church was in the end, simply the profoundly natural furthering of her way that obeyed its own laws of when.

Questioning force that she was, it must have been hard for her to reconcile her newly-found faith with the tragic accidents of the coming decade. The death in infancy of her only child; the painful and premature deaths of three more of her dearest friends: the dissolution of her marriage, the lacerating illnesses of her later years . . . Love, death, the death of love. But it was that very faith which sustained her; in *A Wreath for the Enemy* (1954), it emerges as the dominant theme quietly, as if by accident, ineluctable – in the mouth of the youthful Penelope a huge question, but for Pamela a question no longer. Beneath the announcement of her death in 1967 was written "She served God right merrily." Married to that unquenchable wit, her faith shaped her work and her life to the end.

In *The Willow Cabin* we find much of the diversity, the gaiety and complexity, the richness and underlying seriousness we read into Frankau's own life. It is the story of an obsessive love. Caroline Seward, a young actress already dubbed a "genius" by the cognoscenti, falls in love with Michael Knowle, a brilliant surgeon nearly twice her age who is married to the exotic, liberated Roman Catholic Mercedes. Caroline lets drop her career for him with less than a backward glance, but as the years of joy, terror and passionate surrender unroll, Mercedes takes on for her the aspect of a dark avenging goddess. But is it indeed Mercedes, or is it actually Michael who clings to the permanency of the marriage? And what are Michael's true feelings for Caroline? The fragile-seeming structure deceives. The book, with a love at its centre that grows in depth and subtlety, combines such diverse and unexpected qualities as to make it something of a psychological thriller too — above all, a *quest* — as these questions begin to haunt, and then obsess the actress. Until they are answered, in a final, long slow movement when Caroline in an astonishing *coup de théâtre* brings herself face to face with her "rival", and discovers at last the true nature of the beast . . .

Frankau gives us prose which is lively and elegant in its sometimes archaic use of English, and apt, precise dialogue often of great wit uttered by people who yet manage to speak in their own language; a strong feel of the times (the novel spans sixteen years, 1932-1945), and of time as we are sprung back and forth across the years with no jolt. Equally, of locale — one after another, as various as they are authentic, places and their atmospheres are realised. We *smell* the interior of the lush, faceless Rufford Hotel where Caroline lives, the theatres, "star" and grottier dressing rooms, the smoke-filled Casino, dry Californian hills, sweat and talc of the ATS platoon-huts, the good cheap meals of The French Horn; keep pace with her through pre-war New York, the Riviera, wartime London, post-war America "the country of a dream"; and with Michael too, leaping and living the years with him, with Dorothy his sister, with Caroline's's childhood friend Joan Bridges, and the hapless Vera Haydon. And finally, with Mercedes as Frankau effects her most daring twist, the thrusting into prominence three quarters through the book of this hitherto shadowy character, this wife who holds such a different view of

Michael — and with whom against all expectations, we come to empathise. For what ultimately gives *The Willow Cabin* its resonance and power is the depth of Frankau's understanding of her characters, particularly Caroline, of whom she draws a strong, funny, tender and highly intelligent portrait of a young woman in love.

Released on the public in 1949, Caroline was resoundingly dubbed by the critics "an original", an epithet due perhaps above all, in those post-war years when masculine and feminine were so strongly defined, to her androgyny, a quality not new though never so successfully realised, in a Frankau heroine. But one that was to be pursued. In *The Bridge* published in 1957, Linda Platt, archetype of Frankau's "boy-woman", tells David Neilsen whom she is later to marry, "All intelligent people are bisexual." Towards the end of the book Linda attributes her own bisexuality to "a failure to grow up", and yet . . . and yet. Neilsen, the "grown-up" person in her life is to fail her, from — if to be grown-up is to take responsibility —a lack of that very quality. Caroline Seward in *The Willow Cabin* is briefly not immune to the emotional appeal of the young ATS cadet Vale, but her love is focused, single-mindedly and forever, upon Michael Knowle. It is nevertheless that quality of androgyny which makes her seem, nearly forty years later, so astonishingly contemporary. In fact, she is *hors de temps*, a timeless, intensely individual creature. What remains original for all time about her is the quality and kind of her loving . . . And there is Michael. And there is Mercedes, fascinating reflections of each other. Or the clear side of each other's moon.

It is to Mercedes that are granted some of the most penetrating perceptions of Caroline herself; it is Mercedes who recognises this "believer who cannot identify her God; she has only the habit of loving". Without Michael, she tells Caroline during that long moment when the sun seems to freeze mid-sky ("A bereavement" Pamela had written of Humbert's death, "that had power to put out the sun"), without Michael "'Everybody matters to you a little; nobody matters supremely. You have work and fun and the illusion of company'". And it is Mercedes who recognises in the not-so-young-any-more actress the dedication which once belonged to Michael, but which Caroline is now turning outwards, towards her work and her public. Beside these two women

Michael Knowle, their catalyst, remains an enigmatic figure, likeable, yet somehow incomplete. Philip Meyer, Crusoe and Don Bradley in *A Wreath for the Enemy*, Levitt in *The Winged Horse* are as real as any of Frankau's women, but in *The Willow Cabin* she has concentrated her imaginative powers on her heroine, and in that rare *coup de théâtre*, on her "rival". And if Michael has remained so long elusive, when we finally come to grips with Mercedes we begin to understand why: "So much that Caroline had loved in Michael and learned from him had its origins here; in the mind of the woman who looked like a tired marble statue." And as the discovery comes that marks Caroline out a true lover forever — "Logically she supposed it should diminish Michael in her mind, but it did not" — we understand that she must come to love Mercedes, too.

The book stands or falls by the character of Caroline. In 1935 the bouncy twenty-seven-year-old autobiographer had issued the dictum: "Repetition of the physical characteristics of persons in fiction is unnecessary and irritating." Fourteen years later Frankau overburdens her heroine with references to characteristics both physical and mental — the huskiness of Caroline's voice, length of her legs, wide green eyes, blunt nose, boyish gait: her "Slavic"ness, "Bryonic"ness, "strickenness"; above all by the bandying of the word "genius" (albeit in the mouths of other people) to describe her. "Prove it!" I hear a mocking voice cry, mine; and of course it cannot be done. Has any actor of genius leapt quite satisfactorily off the page? Lorraine Barry, perhaps, in Noel Coward's *Star Quality*, but then we know she was based on Gertrude Lawrence: Donata Genzi in Pirandello's *Trovarsi*, but that is a play and she was modelled on (and first acted by) Marta Abba; and with each new production the actress playing her will give us, through her own vibrancy, the measure of the fictional actress's genius.

Here we have no such touchstone. To be taken through Caroline's Viola on the written page does not quite do, however freshly the performance reads. And could any actor worth their salt, denied their chosen form of expression for seven or eight years, feel so *little* sense of conflict, so little anguish, so little *missingness* no matter what the prize? That Caroline's art is of so little importance to her makes one less ready to grant her the great talent she is ascribed. That said ... much contradicts.

Caroline is not actressy, but splendidly the actress at certain moments in her private life — as rapturously imitating to herself a Boston matron, "My, this wash looks dingy", or sighing in the direction of an imaginary French lover, "*Cheri, tu m'enivres* ..." Her relish is deeply infectious, and as the book develops and she with it, moments like these begin to persuade one she is indeed an actress *manquée*. Certainly as it draws to its close and through Mercedes' eyes we preceive this freshly-hewn Caroline, "As variable as a stream reflecting images while it flowed, the liveliness and ardour changed their source continually, and she changed with it", Frankau shows a rare understanding of the being that is an actor. "From every encounter of the day, she emerged wearing some of the colour of the person she had met ..." Frankau continues, concluding, "One might say she was insincere, only an actress after all. Or that her unprotected energy and warmth made her so available to every one of them that their preoccupations could enter her bloodstream at any time."

And that understanding too was inevitable. At first through her family connections, later her choice of friends — she numbered Noel Coward and Sybil Thorndike among them, and lived the last ten years of her life with Margaret Webster, daughter of actress Dame May Witty, and a theatrical director herself — Frankau always had strong sympathies with the theatre. But more important still to her understanding was that ability which every serious writer has in common with any good actor, to take on the life, lives of her characters. To *become* them.

In our last glimpse of Caroline, "a moment of solitude", Frankau roots the actress for all time, giving her to us not as a filter for other people or for other emotions, but as the rich accumulation of human emotion, being, experience, which is entirely and uniquely Caroline herself. Roots her, and arms her for the future. Now, paradoxically, the actress may fulfil her promise. And if in the guise of a great actress *manquée* Caroline Seward has not always convinced, as a character she wins us from the start. Funny, idiosyncratic, brave, full of thought, horrendously truthful, appallingly vulnerable, she is generous with herself to a fault. Never for a moment do we doubt the passionate sincerity and depth of her love, and this is the book's great *raison d'être*.

"You write what you are", it's been said. Of Frankau it might be said "She was, therefore she wrote, therefore she was", for she was always "becoming", always affirming herself, writing — as in George Bernard Shaw's words, Ellen Terry acted —"to realise herself". And in the process she grew, as all good people do, simply "more so". What *has* been said of Frankau is that, good as her novels were none are as good as she was. *The Willow Cabin* is considered by many to be her best, though she herself preferred *The Bridge*. She got her forebears beat, but perhaps she could not quite beat herself . . .

Susannah York, London, 1987

To the memory of
D. M. F.,
H. W.
and
M. V. W.

CONTENTS

PROLOGUE
(1936)

"Mine own escape unfoldeth to my hope."
Twelfth Night, Act I, Scene II

PROLOGUE

THE curtain rose upon the company standing in line. From the third row of the stalls, Margaret Radcliffe-Preston observed her daughter Caroline, who was giggling at some private joke with the young man who had played the part of the detective. This was entirely to be expected of Caroline. Obviously she was not in the least impressed with her good fortune.

"At twenty-two," Margaret thought, "with her small experience, it is something to have a part in a Brookfield play. And a part that is not unimportant. She looks as though she doesn't care. She isn't even bowing with the others. She just goes on giggling at that boy; her manners are terrible."

She tried to excuse the girl on the grounds that the success of Jay Brookfield's intellectual thriller might not be apparent from Caroline's side of the footlights. Yet surely, this solid applause, these rocketing shouts of "Author!" must make it plain. "It will run a year," said the man on Margaret's left. "And if it did," Margaret thought, "Caroline would still be unimpressed."

"Here he comes," said Margaret's husband.

Jay Brookfield stood quite still, facing the crescendo of sound; a young man with a pale, triangular face, black hair and a long thin body, a sexless harlequin of a young man. When he bowed he bent so low that you could see the back of his neck and the top of his high white collar. He straightened himself and spread out his hands on either side of him, to include the company. His face was unsmiling; set. His voice, hard and clipped, said, "All I can say is that if you have enjoyed watching it as much as we have enjoyed your reception of it, you must have had a very good time indeed." He ducked again to kiss the leading lady's hand, fondled the leading man's shoulder, bowed so low that he

3

seemed about to turn a somersault and strode into the wings. The curtain fell. "Now," said Margaret, while her husband folded her chinchilla wrap across her spare white shoulders, "we must find Caroline."

"Is she coming to supper with us?" Leonard asked; he was a large red man with china-blue eyes and a stubbly moustache.

"I imagine so," said Margaret. Leonard's attitude to his step-daughter was unfathomable; she did not know what he had thought of Caroline's performance. This was not his kind of play. Leonard's idea of the theatre was like Mr. Van Koppen's idea of Paradise, "something with girls in it," something called a Show. He seemed more at home when they had followed the crowd through the pass-door. There was an atmosphere of the Stage-Door-Johnny about him now and he should properly have headed for one of the two main dressing-rooms, whose open doors with the sycophants pouring through showed spectacular glimpses of flowers, of coloured greeting-telegrams stuck aloft on walls and mirrors. Only a few people went the way taken by the Radcliffe-Prestons, down a long tunnel of corridor and up three stone steps.

"Hullo, you two," said Caroline; she shared this restricted space with the young woman who played the part of the maid. She was already in her dressing-gown, with a white cloth tied over her hair; she was smearing off the last of the make-up, her fingers tipped with gouts of cold cream.

To Margaret there was about the small dressing-room an atmosphere at once embarrassing and raffish, two adjectives that she often applied to Caroline. She found it hard to look straight into the glass at her daughter's reflection. It was impossible to see whether the girl were hideous or beautiful. She had Margaret's high cheek-bones; not Margaret's arched nose, blue eyes and tiny mouth. Caroline had greenish eyes that slanted, a short blunt nose, a mouth that was large and square. She could look like a deer or a Mongol or a decadent nymph; at the moment she was just a shiny mask. Then she pulled off the white turban, shook her short, brown, curling hair and turned from the glass to grin at them

4

both. "We're a hit; blow me down; what a thing. . . ." Caroline said, in her deep, resonant voice that was, Margaret thought, so much more cultivated than its pick of words.

"You are indeed. Congratulations, Caro," said Leonard heartily. "You were very good," said Margaret, hearing herself sound more temperate than she had intended. This was Caroline's inevitable effect upon her.

"I don't think I was," said Caroline, "I loused up the last speech; and that was Bobby's fault for making me giggle. Know what the bastard did?" she asked. "When he handed me the photograph—and my line, get it, is 'But she's exquisite' —it was just a picture of a baby hippopotamus."

She passed the powder-puff across her nose and chin, dabbed at her eyelashes, painted her mouth carefully and stood up, saying: "Do have a drink; there's some whisky left, isn't there, Jenny?" "Ooh, rather," said the other young woman, appearing from behind the screen. "May I introduce Miss Webster? My mother and my stepfather." "How dew yew dew. Dew let me give yew a drink"; her refinement was pressed down firmly over a Cockney accent; she had flashing teeth.

"No thank you, really," said Margaret, "I never drink whisky. And we're just going out to supper. You're coming, aren't you, Caroline?"

"Me? No. Thank you kindly, but I'm going to Jay's party."

"To *Jay's* party?" Margaret was impressed in spite of herself.

"Well, to be accurate, it is his sister's party. She has a mansion off Sloane Square."

"Do you mean Mrs. Alaric Forrest's house?"

"Et's roight," said Caroline in exaggerated cockney; she disappeared behind the screen.

"Is the whole cast invited?"

"Couldn't say. Kate Forrest came in to watch some of the rehearsals and gave me my summons. She is fun. *Almost a* bitch, if you see what I mean."

"Caroline, must you use that language?"

"I don't know; that is what I ask myself," the deep voice

5

grumbled. Leonard yawned engulfingly. He said: "Well, better be getting along." Margaret hesitated; it seemed that there was something more to be said, something gracious and friendly, but when she spoke she found that she had asked: "Will you be late back?" The corollary: "You must be tired," she did not say, and the question sounded hectoring, fussy.

"Probably; and probably drunk."

Leonard said: "That's the stuff," with another attempt at heartiness.

"Good-night, Caroline. And many congratulations."

"Thank you, Mamma."

Margaret said to Leonard as they walked toward their car: "At Kate Forrest's house she will certainly meet the right kind of people; the people she affects to despise."

"Alaric Forrest's a good chap," said Leonard. "Can't say I care for Kate; none of those Brookfields appeal to me much. That Jay. . . . They're Jews, aren't they?"

"I believe there is some Jewish blood. But Jay and his brother both went to Winchester. The brother owns the Brookfield Art Galleries, you know."

"M'm," said Leonard, who obviously did not know. He opened the door of the car and Margaret settled herself; for once she could feel a little courageous about Caroline's future. She could see it only in terms of marriage; the rich, respectable marriage that so often appeared a forlorn hope. In her mind she began to conduct one of her periodical arguments with Caroline's father. "You see . . . the Forrests invite her. That is because of me; Kate Forrest wouldn't invite just any little actress who had a part in her brother's play. I have given Caroline something; something more than this absurd passion for the stage, inherited from you, with everything else that is awkward about her."

"Didn't give her a name, though, did you? I see that she appears on the programme as Caroline Seward, bless her. . . ."

"By adoption, her name is Radcliffe-Preston; and from the fuss that she makes about calling herself Seward, anyone would think that you were Gerald du Maurier instead of a third-rate performer in concert-parties."

The image of Caleb Seward was quite clear now. She saw the laugh, the hat-brim, the cigarette that clung to the lower lip. The battered gentleman-of-fortune was laughing at her.

"You'll never forgive me, will you?" the phantom voice murmured. "Not as long as our brat continues to shape like me."

She blinked his image away. Beside her Leonard was saying: " 'Must say, Caroline takes it all pretty calmly."

"She's spoiled," said Margaret. "Everything has come too easily. Thanks to you." She patted Leonard's arm; he said: "Oh, I don't know," embarrassed as ever by any reference to what he had done for Caroline.

ii

Caroline decided that she liked the party. She saw it as on a motion-picture screen; she had no sensation that she belonged to it; it was something to be watched. Jay's harlequin face came near; he was carrying a glass in each hand. He said: "Hullo, puss. Would you like one of these?"

"Thank you kindly. Aren't they bespoken?"

"One for me; one for you. You were *very* good to-night," he said, emphatic, unsmiling, ramming the point home with deadly seriousness. "You looked almost as lovely as you look now and you made that problematic young woman quite dazzlingly clear. But I *don't* want you always to play problematic young women."

It was flattering, she supposed, that he should be standing here, having his drink with her; there was a circle round them now; still he talked to her alone. This would please her mother, she thought, and at once began to sneer at it inside.

"In future, you will come to me before you decide anything at all," said Jay. "Is that a promise? Even your choice of lovers should be submitted. That reminds me," he said: "I promised my brother Dennis that he should meet you. He admired your photograph. Where is he?" Jay began to look wildly round the room; somebody else caught him and took him away. Kate Forrest, wearing a *Cinquecento* gown, darted close to her, saying:

7

"Don't you want food? I am driving people to the buffet. Where has that squalid Jay got to? I know he's had nothing to eat since breakfast." She had a pretty, surprising head, with blue-white hair and a forehead childishly smooth; her black eyes had the amused look that was in Jay's eyes.

Caroline would have liked to go on talking to her, but Bobby was clutching her arm. "Come *along*, Caro; there is the most wonderful supper. Have you forgiven me for the hippopotamus?" She allowed herself to be led. "Such a chic party," said Bobby with his mouth full. "Far above our station."

"Have you a station? I don't think I know which mine is."

She liked Bobby, whom she classified as a comrade-in-arms rather than a chap; but there were moments when she found him naif and thrusting, as now when he said: "I saw you being singled out by the maestro."

(" *'Chic'*; *'Maestro'*; why are those words so offensive to me? I suppose this is the way that other people feel when I say '——'.") She said: "Yes, well. It would appear that he wants me for his brother Dennis. Which is Dennis, Bob? Do you know?"

"I've no idea. I heard that the brother was rather stuffy and Blimp-ish, and didn't approve of Jay."

"You may be right. I can't care much as long as there is this lobster-salad."

She did not, she decided, want to waste too much of the party with Bobby; she wanted to prowl and stare. People were her favourite study; although, as her mother complained, she was devoid of social ambition, she had endless curiosity. She wanted to watch the animals, store up their tricks, record their voices in her excellent memory and imitate them all, in front of the looking-glass to-morrow. She passed a happy fifteen minutes while nobody claimed her. She was deflected by the discovery of a plate of small caviar patties all by itself on a table in a corner. She was gobbling these whole-heartedly when the *Cinquecento* gown swept past and Kate stopped to gobble them with her.

"I starve," said Kate. "You must hear about my Society for the Protection of Starving Hostesses sometime. Jay says

8

you are the-most-talented-newcomer-to-the-London-stage."
Her rendering of his clipped voice was accurate. Caroline
gave it back: "All-I-can-say-is-that-if-he-has-as-much-fun-
directing-me-as-I-have-acting-for-him,-he-must-have-a-very
good-time-indeed."

"Cocky little speech I thought," said Kate. "Curious to
have one brother so conceited that he'd give you his auto-
graph if he were dying, and the other so modest that he's
barely audible."

"Dennis?" said Caroline. "I haven't met Dennis."

"Oh, you'd love him. He's not a bit like Jay. But he isn't
here to-night; he had to go to Paris in a hurry, to sell some
tapestry to a Maharajah. I don't see the point of leaving
just three of these, do you? Are you greedy? I am very
greedy."

"What is so nice," said Caroline. "Is that I am always
hungry as well as greedy. It would be so sad to be one without
being the other."

As Kate broke the last patty in halves, showering pastry
flakes on to the carpet, a man wearing a dinner-jacket halted
beside her. He stood observing their behaviour with apparent
distaste.

Kate said, "Oh, Michael . . . how very unexpected of you.
You haven't met Caroline? Mr. Michael Knowle; Miss
Seward."

Caroline knew the name. She looked at him thoughtfully.
"The bloke who operates on Royalty," she reminded herself
in her vulgar vein. "The Brilliant Young Surgeon. Harley
Street's Boy Wonder. He doesn't look all that young." Kate
flashed away and he was left staring at her, his expression
gentle and mocking.

"You were saying," said Michael Knowle, "that it was nice
to be hungry as well as greedy." He took a silver case from his
pocket. "And now perhaps you are ready for a cigarette?"

"Yes. I have all the appetites," said Caroline.

"May I get you a drink?"

"I've got one, thank you. There is an untouched one here
that could be for you." She gave it to him.

"Thank you. All the appetites," said Michael Knowle. "Well, well."

His formal looks and manner were contradicted by the extreme liveliness of his large grey eyes. "Barrymore type," thought Caroline. "Except for the squareness of the chin. A profile and a manner and a rock-like confidence beneath the manner. He must be at least forty. I wonder why I like middle-aged men."

"You don't look greedy," Knowle continued; he had a caressing voice. "You look as ethereal as a fountain."

"Now I know all about you," she decided. "You're one of these heavy-deliberate charmers—the sort they always say are the best to go to bed with at the beginning. Indubitably and irrevocably married."

"I was in front to-night," said Michael Knowle; she wondered what he had been doing between the play and the party, to arrive so late. "Your performance was quite lovely."

"Thank you. I thought I bitched it."

"You thought *what?*" He looked outraged.

"I said I thought I bitched it."

"You did say it. And I couldn't believe my ears. To hear a vulgarity spoken in that voice of a—a baritone thrush."

"Look," said Caroline. "Please don't start about my language. Everybody does and it only makes me worse."

"Do you not care for words?"

"Of course I care," she said violently.

"Then why don't you do them more honour?" asked Michael Knowle.

She said, "I don't know"; she was suddenly miserable.

Somebody greeted him and he turned away. At first she felt snubbed and small; then defiant and out-at-elbows. She was noisy with Kate and Jay and a crowd; she did not expect Knowle to speak to her again. While she was saying good-bye to Kate, she saw him out of the corner of her eye; set in a group and looking absorbed. It surprised her that he should detach himself and follow her to the door.

"Was I horrid to you?" he asked. The adjective, with its old-fashioned or childish overtone, was endearing.

"No. Yes, you were; but you were quite right."

"May I drive you home?"

"Oh. . ." She was pleased. "I was going with Bob Hammond."

"Well, don't."

"All right," she said after a moment.

He had a solid, expensive car and he drove fast. She collected from him, between Knightsbridge and Marble Arch, that his main interests were poetry and crime; that he divided his holidays equally between the English countryside and the French Riviera; that he was only thirty-nine. She said, "You seem older; I mean it as a compliment."

"It shall be taken as such. May I know your age?"

"I am nearly twenty-three."

"Oh, dear," said Michael Knowle. "You are quite improperly young, aren't you?"

"Yes, well . . . I shall grow out of that."

Once again she brooded upon the adventure of first acquaintance, when you could be so easily and entertainingly yourself; light-hearted and wise for a stranger, as never for those who knew you well. She had discovered this before, on homeward drives; the atmosphere the same; the lighted empty city moving past the window; on your right a profile and a white silk scarf and a black coat; words above the noise of the car's engine. "Grown-up," she thought contentedly. He talked to her now as though she were grown-up; as though she were already a person of achievement.

"I should like to see you play Shakespeare," he said.

"Which?"

"Cleopatra," said Michael Knowle. "Why do you live in Bayswater, darling?" The lightly-brushing quality of the endearment made it a new word; not the old worn exaggeration that they all used without thinking. She said to herself, "I like that."

"It isn't quite Bayswater, is it? I suppose it is. It is my mother's house."

He climbed out with her and stood looking up at the pillared portico while she searched for her latch-key. "Heavy; impressively respectable," he said; there was now a more youthful atmosphere about him; he was standing with his head tilted back, his hands in his pockets; he began to whistle *Loch Lomond*.

"Would you like to come in and have a drink?"

"I oughtn't to, but I shall."

She went ahead of him through the dark-pannelled hall and turned up the lights in the small study at the back; she disliked this room less than any other in the house. It had green walls and the furniture was haphazard, not opulently correct, like the furniture in the other rooms.

Michael Knowle came after her, looking about him with an expression of placid interest. She said, "There is whisky and there is beer."

"Beer for me. May I help you fetch it?"

"No; stay where you are; I can manage." She wanted to do a little scouting; a prowl halfway up the stairs assured her that they had gone to bed. She went into the dining-room to collect the bottles and glasses. When she came back, Michael Knowle had pulled a book off one of the shelves and was reading devotedly. Without looking at her, he began to read aloud:

"With a host of furious fancies,
     Whereof I am commander,
     With a burning spear and a horse of air
     To the wilderness I wander——"

"Lovely," she said. "Read the verse that begins 'I know more than Apollo'." She decapitated the beer-bottles with her teeth. He stared at her comically: "Where did you learn that low trick?"

"From my father. When I was eleven."

Michael Knowle said, "Surely nobody who lives in this house takes the tops off beer-bottles with his teeth."

She giggled. "How right you are. This is my stepfather's house. I don't like it; it is a mixture of a prison and a well, don't you think? Sometimes I have to walk halfway round Paddington before I can bring myself to open the front door. Do read about 'the stars at mortal wars in the wounded welkin weeping'."

He was still staring at her. "Do you have to go on living here, if you dislike it so much, or is that an impertinent question?"

Caroline said, "A bloody astute question, I'd say. Do I have to?" She thought about it. "I suppose the answer's yes. Because it is generous of my stepfather to keep me; I am a bastard."

There were other ways of saying this thing; she had tried them all. " 'I was born out of wedlock'; 'I am subject to a bar sinister'; 'I am illegitimate'." As Michael Knowle took the glass that she held out to him, she saw that he was not embarrassed by the confession; he continued to look gentle and interested.

"I hope," he said, "that it isn't your stepfather who insists that he is being generous."

"Crumbs, no," said Caroline. "He's one of those Etonian, Stock Exchange sorts who wouldn't dream of mentioning it. That's my mother's theme-song. Look, the sofa is the most comfortable thing to sit on."

Knowle sat on the sofa. Under the lamplight, she saw him in sharp detail; the greyish hair looked white, the delicately-boned face pale as water; he had an exceptionally smooth skin. She summarised the neat lines of the eyebrows above the large, brilliant eyes, the high-bridged nose and the deep curves of the mouth. She saw how the upstanding shadows from the collar sharpened off the square chin. "He is decorative," she thought. "And I like this stillness, this calm. That is an interesting hand, too," she added, watching it lift the glass. "He isn't tall. He has wide shoulders and a narrow waist, but I expect he would have liked to be tall." She saw him begin to laugh. "Will I do?" he asked.

"I'm sorry; I like to get peoples' faces by heart."

"I shall never get yours by heart," he said. "Or your mind either. I thought that when I was watching you on the stage. You refuse to be labelled. It is rare, by the way, for a very young woman to walk as you do."

"How do I walk?" she asked, fascinated. She expected a pretty simile; Michael Knowle said, "You keep your body still and move from the hip."

13

"I suppose I could say that my father taught me that too. He was always training me for the stage at the time when we used to meet."

"You don't meet any more?"

She shook her head. "That was when I was at boarding school; I went to my aunt for the holidays. She's a kind, silly one and she could never stand up to Caleb; so he always came to see me, but when I left school my mother stopped all that. At the time of the great stipulation," she said; it was comfortable to talk to Michael Knowle.

"And what was that?"

"Well, it was an edict. I wanted to go on the stage and my father backed me up, but he couldn't pay for my training. He hasn't any say in the matter, because my mother adopted me by a deed. But he did get them to agree that I should go to the R.A.D.A., paid for by Leonard. And their pound of flesh was that he shouldn't come here or try to see me. He drinks and only gets jobs in concert-parties and pantomimes; and he does hang around when he's out of work, and my mother has become so thunderingly respectable, what with all Leonard's money and his stuffy chums. In fact she always *was* respectable; county-snob and quite good family. It was only an error, going to bed with Caleb. In Weston-super-Mare, I understand; what a thing. Where was I?"

"At the time of the great stipulation."

"Yes, well. . . . We all agreed and said Here Is Our Hand On It, when what I really wanted to say was 'Oh stink and drains and nuts and run away'."

She saw the beginning of the compassionate look, and although she had resented it from others, she did not resent it now.

"Are you fond of your father?"

She tried to answer honestly. "I get on with him better than I do with my mother. He can be sweet. But the drink is tedious; I'm quite happy not to see him. I just despise the principle behind the stipulation. It belongs to the creed of the Spoilers-of-the-Fun."

"Is that what you call your mother and your stepfather?"

14

"Not only them. They're a whole race," she said. "When I was a child I used to call them No-Glasses-of-Water, because there always seemed to be somebody who said, 'You don't want a glass of water now', when you did. I suppose they're really Puritans; joyless and correct and suspicious of anything unusual; they persecute. And they all wear mackintoshes, even if it isn't going to rain; and they think of indigestion before they think of food, and the morning after ahead of the night before; and anything that is highly-coloured or extravagant or luxurious hurts them. And they are always underlining the most boring details; like 'Don't forget to turn out the lights in the hall'. And they always perform sterling actions and always have a poor vocabulary; give me a murderer who says the pretty thing at the moment you want to hear it." She heard her voice beginning to shake. "This house," she said, "I think of as their headquarters; it gets me so low that I behave much worse here than I do anywhere else. Damn their eyes."

Michael Knowle set down his glass. "Well, why don't you go?" he said mildly.

"Because I'm a coward. I can't face the fight. It would be a fight. Unless I got married. There is a chap who wants to marry me."

"Which isn't the answer," said Knowle.

"No, I think I know it isn't."

"Marriage for that reason, and marriage at the beginning of a career, can be the most fatal mistake. I made it and I know."

"Are you still married?"

"Unfortunately, yes; I have to be."

"Can't you have a divorce?"

"Not as the position is at the moment."

Caroline drank some more beer. "I can't imagine your being intimidated," she said.

"Intimidated?"

"If you want a divorce and your wife doesn't, you must be intimidated."

He smiled, "It isn't quite like that. My wife is a woman of whims."

"Do you live under the same roof?"

"No; she spends most of her time abroad. She is half American, and she was brought up in France. She hasn't much use for England nowadays."

"What is her name?"

He said, "Why do you want to know?"

"I just do."

"Her name is Mercedes. Next question."

"Do you think I ought to run away?"

"Heavens!" said Michael Knowle. "You say that as though you would act on my advice. I talk too much; I always did. And there you sit, on a low stool, hugging your knees, looking so lovely that I want to embrace you. It wouldn't be a tiger's embrace. I should like you to put your head on my shoulder and I would hug you gently and say 'It's all right'."

"Well, that would be very nice," said Caroline primly. She thought, "I am enjoying this more than anything that has ever happened to me." She stared at him and saw the re-assuring quality in the smile. "It is all right, you know," he said. "You will do what you want to do. I'm not worried about you. I should like to be there to hold your hand from time to time, that is all."

"Please do be."

He leaned forward and touched her cheek.

She said, "Did you escape from your family?"

"Oh lud, yes." The word "lud" was not unexpected; she was beginning to see him as an eighteenth-century character. "In my case," he said, "it was a tougher proposition. I owed mine something. My father was a country doctor. He wanted me to take on his practice. I wanted to be a surgeon. And the poor darlings had spent every penny they possessed on my training, so I did feel obligated. But I got away. I married and got away."

"Hence the Cassandra-like warning about my taking marriage as a way out."

"Yes; don't do that. You don't need to. What do you owe to——" he looked about him—"to these people anyway? I am sure they're very nice, but——"

"They're not," said Caroline, "they're hell."

"Once you have got away, you will establish quite a new relationship with them. Then they will seem infinitely less hellish; that is the way it goes." He looked at his watch. "Do you realise that it is after three o'clock?"

"Have you got to operate on somebody highly distinguished at seven?"

"No, my child. I shouldn't be sitting here if I had."

She said, "Do you get jitters before you operate? I should."

He stood up, shaking his shoulders: "No; I never get jitters about anything. But I have a nightmare that comes when I'm tired. I don't sleep well at the best of times, and when I'm really tired I dream that I am on a complex job and that my hand won't stop shaking." He laughed: "Why do I tell you these things?"

"Well, I told you things."

He bent forward and touched her forehead with his lips. "Thank you. God keep you," he said.

"I've no use at all for God," said Caroline. "You might as well know it first as last. I'm an atheist."

"Rubbish," said Michael Knowle.

"I tell you I am. I had enough of God from my aunt and my school. I abandoned Him as soon as I grew up."

"Could you spit in His face?" Knowle asked negligently.

She winced. "What a hideous thing to say; and you've complained of *my* language."

He was laughing. "As I thought. You are no more an atheist than I am. No artist worth twopence can be an atheist; and you're an artist worth considerably more than twopence."

She said, "Yes, well . . ." sulking now because he had won again. She helped him to put on his coat. In the gloomy, ponderous hall, she felt that their acquaintance was suddenly spoiled, cut short; that she would not see him after this. She opened the front door and he paused on the steps. She expected to be kissed now, but it did not happen. He said, "What is your telephone-number?"

"It is in the book. The name is Radcliffe-Preston."

"Is that what you always say when you don't want gentlemen to ring you up?"

17

"No. I'd love you to ring me up."

"Would you?"

She nodded vigorously. He touched her cheek again. "Good night, darling," he said and ran down the steps to his car. It was a youthful speed; he looked like a young man leaving in a hurry. The engine made a roar and the car shot away into the dark. She stood looking at the place where it had been.

iii

Coming into the dark-panelled hall from the gloomy February afternoon, Margaret Radcliffe-Preston found two letters on the table. One was for Caroline; she glanced at the envelope; it was light brown in colour, an expensive and slightly affected type of stationery, addressed in small, intelligent handwriting; a man's handwriting. She carried it upstairs with her and Caroline came out of the drawing-room as she reached the first floor.

Until this moment, Margaret had been feeling charitably towards her daughter. Three days had passed since the play's opening. The problem of Caroline looked as though it would presently solve itself. The press-notices and the personal congratulations were making it clear to Margaret that there might be a future wherein the girl would cease to be an agonising liability and emerge, in contradiction to all previous theories, as an asset.

There was nobody to whom her mother could confide the sudden relief. There never had been anybody. Leonard hated to talk about Caroline; he had made his gesture long ago and he blinked at the size of it; he had settled in his mind for the fact that in taking on Margaret, he had taken on also a step-daughter, who might have been the child of a previous marriage. Being a man, she thought, it was easy for him to assume that if a problem were not discussed, it did not exist. He was too simple a creature to know the dark ways that she had walked for twenty years; he never guessed that she drank off a mixture of guilty responsibility and self-justification every morning of her life. This was the secret place; nobody shared it. Her sentimental younger sister might have understood. But

18

Margaret had never found it possible to talk to Evelyn, who was liable to burst into tears about it all, and make wet, flowery protestations until her sister stepped with disgust into a mood of cold sarcasm.

She was as lonely now in the beginning of peace as she had been for years in guilt and anxiety.

Yet, as always, the sight of Caroline put peace away. Margaret would not face the truth, that they were antipathetic to each other; that their personalities in contact made for discord; that they were two people who had no meeting-ground. That was not to be borne; that was an additional weight thrown into the scale on the side of guilt. Mothers must love their daughters; daughters must love their mothers. And loving, for Margaret, meant liking. Yet here she was, jarred by the sight of Caroline and receiving an atmospheric retort of cheeky hostility before either had spoken a word.

The girl must have been sitting in the drawing-room; but she had not turned up the lights and stood now on a back-ground of shadowy gloom. For some reason known to herself, she was dressed in a green sweater and a pair of brown corduroy trousers. Peering at her, Margaret saw that she wore no make-up and that she had a glass in her hand. It was early to be drinking, not yet five o'clock.

"Wotcher," said Caroline, "I want to talk to you."

"Come up to my room, then. I must change. We are going to a cocktail-party."

"Okay," said Caroline, "I'll just get myself a refill."

"Isn't it rather early for that?"

The girl stared at her. "Is it? I don't know what the time is."

"Not five o'clock yet. Here is a letter for you."

Caroline took it, examined it for a moment, then put it unopened in the pocket of her corduroys. The gesture was annoying. Margaret went up to her room, the Louis Quinze room that always reassured her and made her feel safe. She was comfortably swaddled in her satin dressing-gown and sitting before her mirror when Caroline returned. Caroline sat down on the bed.

"Please, Caro—how many times must I tell you? *Not* on my bedspread."

"Oh, sorry." She slithered off and threw herself into the chair beside the electric-fire, sprawling, long-legged, with the glass in her hand. She took a drink from the glass, put it on the floor, sat up and crouched forward, with her hands on her knees.

"Look——" she said and stopped. In the glass Margaret saw her frown. "I have a thing on my mind. . . ." She hesitated again. "I do wish I knew why it was so hard for us to talk to each other."

"Is it hard?"

"You know it is."

"I wasn't aware of it."

"There you are," said Caroline. "Nothing I say ever gets through."

Margaret sighed. "You haven't said very much yet, have you?"

Caroline cocked her head on one side. "I wonder just how much you dislike me," she said thoughtfully.

"Are you drunk?"

"No, Mamma. I can absorb three of these without becoming at all drunk; and this is only my second."

"*Dislike* you. . . ." Margaret repeated.

"Look," said Caroline again. "This is it. I must go away."

Margaret stared at the reflected face; it was pale.

"That's all," Caroline said. "Except that it won't be all; we shall start arguing."

"What on earth are you talking about? How can you go away? You're in work; this play will run for months."

"I know. I don't mean that. Oh dear, oh dear, oh bloody dear, how difficult this is. And it oughtn't to be. I've got myself into such a private mood about it that I don't think I'll ever be able to talk."

(A private mood; a secret place that nobody shares; yes, Margaret thought, I know about that. But why should you have this thing?)

"I want to go away from this house and live somewhere

else," Caroline said; she was shivering so much that her teeth chattered on the words. She raised the glass to her lips. "I'm sorry. Don't be hurt; don't be cross. I just can't stand it any more." She put down her glass and began to pace across the room and back; one of her most irritating tricks, Margaret thought mechanically.

"It isn't your fault. And I think you'll probably like the idea once you get used to it."

Margaret said, "How very thoughtful of you to take my views into consideration at all."

Caroline halted by the window and stood looking out. She said, "Oh, hell."

"Why have you got yourself into such a state? What is the matter with you?"

Caroline said, "I can't explain. It's been going on for ages. You could say, if you liked, that my integrity has been taking a wallop."

"Now you're talking Double Dutch."

"Well, the plainest way I can put it is that I've taken a room in an hotel and I propose to move there on Sunday."

"Caroline, will you please turn round and look at me; don't go on talking to the window."

The girl turned slowly; she looked ill and ugly now, narrowing her slanted eyes, pursing her lips together.

"All I propose to say for the moment," said Margaret, "is that when you make a decision of this kind, it is better to face the issues involved. And you are not facing them."

"I don't think I know about Issues," said Caroline. "People are always talking about them and they seem to me a lot of——."

"That is a filthy word."

"Yes, well. . . ."

"The issue in this case is your own future. Putting aside questions of gratitude and family-feeling, you must realise that it is very important for you to have a home and a background; more important for you, perhaps, than for most people."

"Why? Because I'm a bastard?"

Margaret said, "You gain nothing by this language, my

dear. I wasn't thinking of your birth. I was thinking of your character, of the sort of person you are."

"Do you know what sort of person I am?"

"Unfortunately, I do." This was not the answer that she had meant to make; the baffling demon was at work, giving her the lines.

"Then you'd better tell me," said Caroline roughly.

"I don't think we'll talk about it any more now."

Caroline's voice cracked. "Don't you see, if we don't talk about it now, we never will? I'll go to-night and that'll be the end of us."

Margaret shivered. She despised herself for asking the question that had been in her mind since the beginning:

"This idea of yours, is it because of some man?"

Caroline hesitated. She took two paces and said, "No; not in the way you mean. Would that matter?"

"Of course." (How small my voice sounds; and now she is looking at me as though she were sorry for me; I never saw her look like that before.)

"It wouldn't be the first time, for me," Caroline said.

Absurd to think that she was going to cry. She took a cigarette quickly from the box on her dressing-table. The flame of the match blurred, broke into small pointed rays of light. She could not speak.

"You do mind," Caroline said slowly and thoughtfully. "But you knew, didn't you? You must have known. It isn't a thing one talks about. I thought you——"

"Stop," Margaret said. "All I want is for you to go out of this room and leave me alone."

The blurred figure before her eyes lifted its hands once, then dropped them. It shrugged its shoulders and went.

iv

The lounge of the Rufford Hotel was decorated in lush taste. It reminded Caroline of an hotel in Paris. There were tapestry curtains, gilded and padded furniture, a dark red carpet and two crystal chandeliers. At each end of the room there was a marble mantelpiece. There was nobody here and she could pace undisturbed. She walked backwards and forwards, trying not to look at the fat French clock on the farther mantelpiece. She did not really need to look at it. She knew that the time was past midnight and that he might not come.

In the outer hall she heard the night-porter lock the doors; then he went back to his small office behind the glass screen. She was straining her ears because the switchboard was in the office and if a call came through she would hear the whirring buzz and the night-porter replying in his sing-song voice, "Rufford Hotel." This had happened twice; the first time the porter had said, "He's not back, I'm sorry," and the second whir had been made by somebody calling down from one of the rooms to ask for some cigarettes.

Caroline was light-headed with hunger; she had not dined before to-night's performance and she had hurried back here to await the telephone-call. The porter, she was sure, would be able to make her some sandwiches; but she seemed to be shut up in the mood of impatience, denied all action except this steady pacing, incapable of communication with the world outside. She lit another cigarette and drew the letter from her pocket; it was the only solace for the moment and she had read it so many times that the words ran ahead in her mind before she turned the brown pages.

"When you know me better—as I hope that you will—you'll become acquainted with my habit of writing letters. It is a vice with me, particularly when, as now, I cannot sleep.

"I loved our interlude. A little of you has gone about with me for forty-eight hours. It is good company, bless it, but my sense of middle-aged guilt predominates to-night; and I sit here thinking that I had no right to talk to you as I did. It is, in any case (and according to the book of clichés), idle for the not-so-young to try to impart tabloid wisdom to the young; who must discover and prove the formulæ for themselves. Is that too pompous for you? Anyhow, please believe that most of my wisdom has been acquired unsuitably, *and* I haven't yet learned to be wise when I meet somebody as young and as heartbreakingly lovely as you.

"I read these lines lately and they seem to be yours:

" 'To be young is to have expectation, to await.
      There is no gift like that gift afterwards.'

"Do wait. Don't marry the 'chap who wants to marry you' as a means of escape from that grim home of yours. And don't hurry your decision to leave it. That is where I feel most guilty, not because I think that it would be bad for you to go, but because timing these things comes naturally; you will know when it's time to be going. Nobody else can tell you, least of all I.

"Incidentally I leave for the North to-morrow (only it's to-day) by a horribly early train to perform an operation on a rich, frightened gentleman who will soon be feeling much better and regretting my fee. I shall be back Friday afternoon and will telephone at the week-end to suggest a meeting.

"Blessings,

"MICHAEL"

Caroline looked at the fat clock. Twenty minutes past twelve. The secretary had sounded fluting and refined. She had said, "Mr. Knowle went straight to an appointment at the hospital as soon as he got here. I will give him your message."

"She must have gone long ago. Perhaps she forgot to leave this number. Then he would ring me at home. That is what has happened. I wonder what Mother said to him. 'Caroline walked out yesterday afternoon.' Not she."

For a moment her thoughts were deflected as she tried again to realise that the thing was done; that she was in fact alone and free. But that was impossible to realise. The walls of the house were still there, shutting her in; there was still the panting urgency of escape and the knowledge that she never could escape, the foolish prisoner who sat in her cell and pitied the warder. "Stop this. Don't look back. It is over; you're out; you have got away."

There was only one authority who could tell her whether she had done right or wrong; whose sanction she needed now. "Why do I still think that he will come? Because I cannot imagine that he would ever fail me or hurt me."

24

She threw away the cigarette half-smoked; it joined the other half-smoked cigarettes, in the august steel grate below the marble mantelpiece.

The porter came into the lounge. He had taken off his jacket and he was pushing a vacuum-cleaner. He smiled at her. He said, "I have to do a bit of cleaning up now. Anything you'll be wanting, Madam?"

She shook her head. She wanted to say, "Oh, do stay by the switchboard."

"I'll start in the bar," he said and pushed the glass door open and was gone. She heard the faint roaring of the vacuum-cleaner begin behind the door. "Now if the telephone does ring, he will not hear it at all and I haven't the least idea how to work a switchboard and while I am fetching him Michael will get tired of waiting and hang up."

A bell rang; a low, purring bell. She stopped in her pacing. While she hesitated, wondering whether the porter could hear it, whether it were the front-door bell, it rang again. She went into the hall. She shot back the two bolts on the door and unlatched it. Michael Knowle was standing on the step. He wore a light overcoat, no hat, a black silk scarf folded under his chin. Her first thought was that he looked tired to death. Then he smiled at her and the reassurance of the smile was still there.

"Are you acting night-porter?" he asked.

"N-no." She had never stammered before. "Th-there is one. But at this time of n-night, he appears to take the vacuum-cleaner down to the other end of the lounge."

"How purposeful that sounds; as though he had his way with it when he got there," said Michael Knowle.

Caroline giggled. He came into the hall and took off his overcoat and scarf. She saw that he was wearing a dark blue suit, a light blue shirt and a bow tie; unexpected brown suede shoes. These things were very important. He passed his hands over his hair.

"I am sorry to be so late. To-night was full of trouble." He fished in a pocket, found his wrist-watch and put it on his wrist. Again she noticed the shape of his hands.

25

They went into the lounge. Here he stared at her medically under the light from the chandeliers.

"My child, you look as pale as a ghost; no, paler; the ghost of somebody's ghost. What is that about?"

"I'm hungry," said Caroline, "I didn't have any dinner or any supper and my stomach is touching my spine."

"Then we had better go out and get some supper. Or can your porter find us some food?"

"I should think he can. I'll go and ask him."

"You will not."

He pushed her gently into a chair. She sat still, with her head in her hands. Michael came back; she felt his hand on her shoulder. "What have they been doing to you?" the caressing voice asked.

"Nothing. Nothing at all." She raised her head and saw him seating himself in the opposite chair, crossing his knees, folding his arms. "That is how he would sit in his consulting-room." She felt like a patient. The porter came from the bar, carrying a tray with a bottle of whisky and a siphon of soda-water. He said, " Just be a few minutes cutting the sandwiches, sir."

"All right. Thanks very much. I'll pour these." The porter set the tray on one of the small, marble-topped tables. "Don't drink it all at once," Michael said, as he put the glass into her hand. He stood looking down at her.

"Is it awful of me to drag you here at this time of night?"

"You didn't drag me; I wanted to come." He went back to his chair. "Just drink that and be quiet for a minute."

"I don't want to be quiet. I have to explain."

"You needn't explain anything."

"I believe that's true. I don't believe you'd ever require it. Which is one of the things that I like." She said, "But you're the only person I can talk to; if you say it's all right, I shall stop feeling guilty."

He looked at her affectionately. "What have you to feel guilty about?"

"Running away."

"Yes; I thought it might be that."

26

"I tried to discuss it with my mother, but it wasn't any good; so I thought it was better to stop talking and go."

He was silent.

"I had made up my mind before I got your letter. I see what you meant, about not wanting me to do it because of you. But,"—she stared at the floor, "I'm afraid the letter only made me more positive that it must be done."

"Somebody ought to cure me of writing letters," he said.

"Why? It was a lovely letter. It was the nicest letter I ever had from anybody."

The porter returned with a small mountain of sandwiches on a plate. "Those aren't all for you, so don't you think it," Michael said. "I did dine, but it seems a very long time ago." For a few minutes Caroline found herself entirely concerned with the food, posting down one sandwich after another; then she became aware of his eyes; their expression was rueful and tender.

"Why do you look at me like that?"

"All the appetites," he quoted.

"Yes, well. . . ."

"At least you begin to look a little better. Tell me, do you propose to live here?"

"I thought I would. It only costs four guineas a week; and I didn't want a squalid bed-sitting room. Nobody but me seems to know about St. James's Place. I found it on Tuesday, all by myself."

"You won't be lonely?"

"I don't think so. I have always been alone a lot. That is why I talk to myself." She stretched her arms and said, "Oh, this is lovely."

"Euphoria," said Michael, "the result of sandwiches and whisky."

"You're different to-night."

"I know I am."

"Do you *not* think it's all right? Would you rather I had stayed at home?"

He said, "Is my approval so important?"

"Yes."

27

"Well, then, I think you had to do it. But I feel a little as though I were standing on a railway-platform seeing you off on a journey that you aren't really fit to take. I don't know yet why they had such a violent effect on you; your mother and your step-father. But they have done your nervous system a damage."

"Have they? What have they done to it? Do you think I am queer in the head?"

"No, darling. But I think you'll take a little time to readjust. And possibly living alone in an hotel isn't the best regime for you. Do I sound like a Spoiler-of-the-Fun?"

"You remembered that. You? You're *less* a Spoiler-of-the-Fun than anybody I ever met." She set her chin in her hands and stared at him, learning the face by heart. He took his cigarette-case out of his pocket. She said, "That's a different one, isn't it."

"Different from what?"

"Different from the one you had on Friday." She leaned towards the flame of the lighter.

"Do you always notice details with such alarming attention?"

"Usually I do. Look—I'll be all right if I can go on seeing you occasionally; I promise not to become a nuisance." Her heart had begun to beat violently. "You see——" she stopped.

"Go on." For the first time, the note in his voice was rough; he looked heavy and solemn.

"Well, I know that ladies should not make declarations unasked, but it isn't any good my trying to be reticent; I never can keep that sort up for long." She turned the glass in her hands.

"Don't try, then." The voice was gentler now. She went on turning the glass and looking into it.

She said, "I haven't thought about anything but you for six days. And if I hadn't seen you to-night, I think I should have died. I felt as though I were dying while I waited for you. And please don't say that was because of not having had anything to eat."

"I wasn't going to say anything of the sort."

She said, "I have fallen in love with you."

He got up and bent over her, holding her close to him. He kissed her forehead. After a moment he sighed and let her go. He wandered away from the circle made by their two chairs and the table. She watched him, afraid of his silence and of the words when they should come. He stood in front of the marble mantelpiece.

"When one is handed a gift like that," he said, "however old and capable one may have thought oneself, one goes straight back to school."

He sounded so solemn that she said, "Yes, Michael," lightly and obligingly.

"Caroline, I am serious. I want you to listen to me—I can give you nothing."

"I don't expect you to give me things."

"Hush. So, I have no right in the world to take your gift. I am hopelessly involved; I can never be free. And I am approaching forty and you're twenty-two; you haven't begun to breathe yet. You're a very young twenty-two, despite your efforts to appear a sophisticated person."

"Please," she said. "I knew you'd talk about our ages and I wish you wouldn't."

"Be quiet. I haven't many morals, but I have a very decided opinion of married, middle-aged gentlemen who go about making love to young women; and a very rude word for them."

"You needn't get a conscience about me. I have had a lover already."

The expression of his face was baffling; he might have been shocked or relieved. She seemed to have silenced him. She said, "Look; it wasn't important. It was done partly out of curiosity and partly as a gesture against my mother. I suppose that does sound very low. Do I disgust you?"

"No."

"I only told you so that you wouldn't have a conscience."

He was still silent.

"Oh, dear, now you're cross."

"I am not in the least cross. I am wondering just how

completely they've succeeded in setting you against all rules; all standards."

"I would take rules and standards from you. You wouldn't make them into restrictions."

He said, "Will you please answer me one question and answer truthfully. Would you have run away if we hadn't met?"

Caroline frowned over it. "I don't think that's a fair one; or an easy one. Obviously it would have happened sooner or later." She looked up at him. "Oh, all right, the answer's No," she said, "I wouldn't. You decided me. But that doesn't make me your responsibility."

"It's a responsibility I should like very much."

"Are you being polite?"

It was surprising to see him look helpless. He shook his head. She said, "If you want to know, I decided to run away at the exact moment when I fell in love with you; which I clearly remember. It was when I'd just told you I was a bastard; and you said that you hoped Leonard didn't make me feel that it was generous of him to keep me in the house."

He said, "Why did that please you so much?"

"Because it was grown-up and kind and it sounded as though you cared about me."

He came over to her chair, pulled her out of it and stood holding her hands.

"If I were really grown-up now. I should say good-bye to you and walk out of your life. And yet I cannot bear to go. And, oh Caroline, I would give my soul to be twenty-two again, d'you see?"

She put her arms round his neck. He said with his mouth above hers, "I will always look after you. I will always be there. I can't love you your way. Do you think that you can ever be content with mine?"

She said, "Now and forever."

BOOK ONE
(1939)

TIME STOLEN

"In your denial I would find no sense,
I would not understand it."

Twelfth Night, Act I, Scene V

BOOK ONE

CHAPTER ONE

THE lights were going down as Dennis Brookfield and his companion reached their places. The theatre was dark when Dennis opened his programme. He had a moment's fear that he might be making this gesture uselessly and that the leading lady would be restored to health.

Probably he was the only person here who suffered such an emotion. He could imagine many whose spirits would droop as they detached from the programme the separate leaf of paper announcing that the part of Viola would be played at this performance by Miss Caroline Seward. The all-star production of *Twelfth Night* had a life limited to six weeks ; nobody wanted to see the understudy; the role of Viola belonged by right to the most talented young woman on the London stage. He would have liked to think that her illness marked an upward change in Caroline's fortunes; more, he was determined to precipitate this change, and that was why he had dragged Rokov here to-night.

He owed his acquaintance with Rokov to his illustrious brother Jay; who would have little sympathy for any project that might favour Caroline. Already Dennis felt opposition in the air; not from Jay, conveniently attending an opening in New York; not from Rokov, who was a spectacular novice to the London stage and who had never heard Caroline's name until now. Rokov, casting his new play, was in furious search after the right young woman for the lead. Rokov would bless him if Caroline turned out to be the right young woman. The opposition came from one person only; from Caroline herself. He had an inkling that none of this was going to work out as he had planned. He was arguing indignantly in his head while Orsino's spell-binding baritone demanded,

"How will she love, when that rich golden shaft
Hath killed the flock of all affections else?"

"*How will she love?*" Dennis sent the question pointing after
Caroline and flung the answer back at Orsino: "Like a fool."
So that he was already reviewing and condemning the whole
unhappy business when the curtain rose on the scene and he
saw her standing there.

He tried to see her through Rokov's eyes. In the trailing
dark clothes she was, he thought, at a disadvantage. One of
the most characteristic virtues of Caroline's appearance was
her long-legged grace. When he thought of her, he thought
first of her walking to meet him or walking away. There was a
beautiful smoothness in that stride, in the straight back and
the carriage of the small head; now she was drooping like a
sick bird and Rokov would have no hint of it. Nor, since the
dark cloak muffled her about, could he get the look of her
head. It was amusing, this; it was like presenting Caroline to
Rokov in a parcel, waiting for the wrapping to come off and
for Rokov to say, "How did you guess? It's just what I wanted."

The voice at least he could judge. It was a strong and vibrant
voice, without a smile in it; the pitch was perfect. Framed by
the dark hood, the face with the high cheek-bones and the
slightly hollow cheeks looked as though made for grief. He
did not often find this thing in Caroline's face; he was saddened to find it now.

He listened with infinite pleasure to the words spoken
stripped of all lilting affectations and traditional Shakes-
pearian overtones. It fascinated him to hear that Caroline
could say, "Thou shalt present me as an eunuch to him," with
the same thoughtful, twentieth-century inflexion that kept
other phrases alive in his memory: ("It would help enormously
if I could borrow five pounds till the First"; "I think I could
lunch to-morrow, if that's all right with you.") And as she
said, "Only shape thou thy silence to my wit," he heard
another urgent appeal: "If anybody asks, for heaven's sake
say that I was with you."

34

" She's unusual," said Rokov's thick voice in his ear.

"Like her?"

"I am not sure. Do you?"

"No," Dennis thought; "I love her, but that's something else again. '*Ein Jüngling liebt ein Mädchen, Die hat einen andern erwählt.*' The hell with it." He saw none of the neat fooling of the next few moments; he was sitting in judgment on the man who had invaded Caroline's solitude.

He wished often that he had known her before Michael knew her; he could imagine that mixture of steadfastness and perplexity, when it was directed towards no person and no creed; he could picture it when it was merely the quality of youth; the questioning spirit in a body that was consumed by more than the usual fires. Knowing her then, he guessed, it would have been difficult to distinguish between her animal and her spiritual needs.

Perhaps, of all the foolish sentimental games that he played in his mind about Caroline, this was the most foolish, the most sentimental; this hankering for a knowledge of her lost virginity, for the times and the places that he could never share with her. It still irked him that so simple a fact should have robbed him of the chance. He had been unable to attend a party at his sister's house and it was at this party that Caroline had met Michael; just over two years ago, in the winter of '36. So that when he did meet her, she was already Michael's property.

It was curious in this hour to remember for how long he had been Michael's friend; a shareholder in the family affection felt by the three Brookfields for Michael and Mercedes Knowle. Dennis knew that, of the three, he was the only one who had waned in affection when the marriage broke. Kate and Jay were on Michael's side; they thought Mercedes an impossible person. He himself had never spoken in defence of Mercedes; he had continued, resentfully, to see Michael; to lose his resentment and become used to Michael alone. Now that old grudge looked remarkably like a prophecy of the time when he would meet the young

35

woman whom Kate called "Michael's girl" and stare at her and know that he was in love.

He could not see Michael as a person any more, he could see him only as a shadow fallen upon Caroline's life. If they met in her dressing-room at the interval ("but it would be more like him not to be there") they would talk as friends. Perhaps they would all three go to supper together. Dennis described himself frequently as a natural third; he looked back along the years and saw tables where he sat with Michael and Michael's wife; with Michael and somebody else's wife; with Michael and any one of the casual, short-term acquaintances who had ranged between Mercedes and Caroline.

There was a " take-it-or-leave-it" attitude about Michael. Dennis had seen it at the time when the marriage broke; he was aware of the same challenge now, concerning Caroline. "And, like an idiot, I take it," Dennis thought. "Do I like him more than I realise? Am I afraid of him? At least I'm not here to-night because of him; I am here because of her. Determined to fight them all, Jay included, with my conviction that she's a genius; that however badly she may have damaged her own career so far, she has a chance of achieving greatness. And this conviction has nothing to do with loving her. Hasn't it, though? Am I not aiming for two targets? If she became an established success that would be one in the face for Michael, who is the sole cause of her failure."

He forced himself away from the sour sadness to look at the stage; feeling guilty because so much expensive talent was waving itself before his eyes unheeded. He thought that he liked the stylised set, that was all bluish columns and draperies of deep red; yet, as soon as he was aware of this he was again in danger, because Michael's wife had amused herself for some years by designing stage-sets and stage-clothes, and this scene had a touch of her idiosyncratic method about it. Unnecessary, he knew, to assure himself that the set could not be Mercedes' work. In all probability, the likeness was to be found only in his own mind, another signal that all his thoughts were now fixed and forever running along the same rail, like the electric hare at the White City.

The clowns pranced away. Caroline walked between the bluish columns. For a moment Dennis let himself be still and contemplate her without pain; it was not difficult to do this, he thought, when your love was playing Viola in a black and silver doublet.

It was always easy for Viola to look like a principal-boy in pantomime. He tried to see how Caroline avoided that look; perhaps because she had truly boyish legs, growing thinner above the knee; her buttocks did not curve at all; she was flat as a board behind. Nor did she move with the traditional swagger; it was her own smooth, loping walk; and her head, for all the tight sheen of the short curls, remained obstinately Caroline's head, as he saw it on other backgrounds.

Rokov hunched forward. "What does he make of that face now?" Dennis wondered. "I know what I make of it; the narrow face and the wide eyes; that loose lock falling on the forehead; always the shadow where the cheek thins, and the straight blunt nose, the jut of the square mouth. It is—what? A touch Slavic; a touch Byronic; impossibly gay when the laugh slants her eyes and impossibly stricken when the light goes out of them. She is an exaggeration in all that she does."

He was impatient with the scene, because it kept her hanging around ("as Michael keeps her hanging around; oh stop this——"). He listened hardly at all to Orsino, the outsize West End lion; he sucked the loveliness of her voice out of the few lines allotted her, and saw her go and could not tell what impression she left. Rokov said nothing. The clowns took over; Dennis was bored until the moment of Olivia's entrance with Malvolio. The actress playing the part was one of his early stage-loves. She looked magnificent in the variation of black and silver that clothed each of the cast; she had a high tranquil forehead and her hair was red. After a few lines he began to find her dull also; she had acquired too much polish and too much tinkle.

Olivia veiled her face and was seated. Caroline strode

across the stage. He liked the gruff, shy growl with which she brought out, "The honourable lady of the house, which is she?" There was an exquisite satisfaction afterwards in hearing the half-gay, half-melancholy notes begin. He thought. "Only when she has been talking a little while do you become aware of her clear, pure diction. At first there is always that roughness in the voice, as though it had been silent a long time and were grown rusty.

"How good is she? Rokov will tell me. I can't tell; I am nervous for her now; too much with her; reading genius into every syllable that she speaks and every movement that she makes. Or is it really there? Surely it is there."

He watched her draw in her breath when Olivia lifted the veil; it was a palpable and natural gasp of astonishment, and he thought that it was a trick of genius to put what was almost a stammer into the hackneyed, copy-book words:

> " 'Tis beauty truly blent, whose red and white
> Nature's own smooth and cunning hand laid on."

She said it as an amateur courtier might have said it, marvelling and transfixed. Then the bewilderment in the voice was the sulky bewilderment of a boy.

> "Lady, you are the cruellest she alive,
> If you will lead these graces to the grave
> And leave the world no copy."

As one who had suffered from an overdose of school Shakespeare and from many platitudinous productions around London and Stratford, Dennis shook a puzzled head at his own rapture. He did not want to look at Rokov, in case he saw too clearly that this enthusiasm was his private affair. He heard the voice, now grim and rebuking :

> " If I did love you in my master's flame,
> With such a suffering, such a deadly life,
> In your denial I would find no sense,
> I would not understand it."

"*In your denial I would find no sense.*" The phrase formed in his imagination her own challenge to Michael; the spearhead of her love; the hopeless crusade.

Now as Olivia asked, "What would you?", Caroline lifted her chin and stared into space. As though sighting her own hopeless destiny, she let her lips droop in a small and rueful smile; it was a look whose sadness wrung his heart. ("Terrifying," he thought, "when a cliché becomes true; there is an actual pain stabbing at my ribs.") He did not know for how long she held the mask of sadness before her face. He saw her smile suddenly and differently; as she spoke, full-voiced, a flaming conviction seemed to run after that sorrowful fear and grasp it by the throat and throttle its life out. The words rang triumphantly:

> "Make me a willow cabin at your gate,
> And call upon my soul within the house;
> Write loyal cantons of contemned love
> And sing them loud even in the dead of night;
> Halloo your name to the reverberate hills,
> And make the babbling gossip of the air
> Cry out 'Olivia!' Oh, you should not rest,
> Between the elements of air and earth,
> But you should pity me!"

No, he was not alone in his belief; he could feel that the magic wind blew to the ears of all the dullards round him; blew and stirred their hair.

When Olivia spoke, she sounded abashed:

"You might do much."

It was damnably coincident; it was everybody's condemnation of Caroline; it was his own. He lost the rest of Olivia's speech because Rokov leaned close and said in a harsh whisper, "God!—you were right about this girl."

ii

After that, he expected that Rokov would accompany him to Caroline's dressing-room in the interval; the producer said, "No; I'll go to the bar; see your later," and forbore to explain. Dennis edged through the pass-door with the small, privileged crowd. It was a safe assumption that they were none of them going to see Caroline. He had made several back-stage visits to her; to the cramped dressing-rooms that she had shared with lesser lights. It was remarkable to find her alone and temporarily installed in the spacious sanctuary where the leading actress should be. She met him at the door and before he could speak he saw her looking past his shoulder.

"Is Michael with you?" were her first words.

"No," he said, "I came with Leopold Rokov."

She did not appear to be listening; at close range, in these clothes and this make-up, she seemed a stranger, tall and glittering, with blue eyelids that moved quickly. This was all the more odd because behind the footlights she had been the essence of herself. She stood with her fingers lightly touching his arm, looking down the corridor.

She said, "I suppose he had a call from one of his bloody patients. It's sad, because I shan't be playing to-morrow night." She appeared to wake to the fact of Dennis: "Come in and have a drink. Isn't this elegant?"

He looked round him, at the flowers and the gold baskets, at the mosaic of greeting-telegrams on the wall. There was a low couch beside him and he sat on it while Caroline poured out the drink; she gave herself a glass of soda-water.

"Palatial, I call it," said Caroline, "and pretty decent of her to let me move in." He saw that her hand shook as she lifted the glass; the brilliant mask of make-up seemed to stand out from a face that was in fact pale and suffering. She grinned at him.

He raised his own glass, looking at them both in the large mirror; he thought that he did not often look at himself for fun; he saw his face while he was shaving, but that was a business-acquaintance, as when he gave a last look at his total reflection before he left his bedroom. Now, perhaps because there was so little amusement to be had from his

encounters with Caroline, he found diversion in the sight
of his smooth dark head, his hawkish profile, the conventional
evening clothes, with the glittering shape of Caroline beside
them. It looked all right; it looked like a man sitting in an
actress's dressing-room, with a drink in his hand, having a
good time.

"Am I going to take you out to supper, Caro?"

At once she looked hunted. "Oh, dear, I don't know. You
see, Michael was coming and now it's all got loused up."

"You use more cant words than anybody I know," he
said peevishly. "It is a sin to hear them spoken in that
voice; by somebody who can do what you've just done to an
audience out there."

"What did I do to an audience out there?"

"Don't you know?"

She hesitated. "I thought I knew; but I'm no judge; how
can one be?"

"You're good," he said. "*So* good. Oh, darling, don't be
in any doubt about it."

"I felt good," she said, still sounding abstracted and
glancing at the clock on the dressing-table.

"Will you concentrate? Stop thinking about whether you
will telephone and where you will telephone. I told you I
was with Rokov."

"Yes, well . . ." she said flatly.

"If he's coming to supper, you'll jolly well come."

"M'm." Then she woke and snapped, "What's the point
of Rokov being here?"

"To look at you."

She frowned. "Look, Dennis, forgive me, only I must go
to the lavatory and it means I shall have to cope with these
tights."

"Oh, really. . . ." Dennis thought; jarred and angry, he
waited for her. "Does that thrusting vulgarity—or simplicity—
enrage Michael? Nobody can make such violent swoops
between good taste and bad taste. At twenty-six surely, one
ought to have the beginnings of dignity." When she came

41

back, he said, "Go on; get your telephoning over and tell me if you can come to supper. Ask him to join us if you like."

"I was thinking; Rokov won't want to have supper. Particularly if he's looking at me with a view to casting. That isn't the way he works."

"How do you know the way he works?"

She shrugged her shoulders.

"Well, what does he do?" Dennis asked.

"Pompous stuff; affairé; secretary asking if you could step round to his office at thirteen-and-a-half minutes past eleven on the twenty-second of next month."

"I don't see how you can know. Will you, at any rate, promise to come if he does?"

"I hate promising."

"Caroline, I don't want to bully you."

"But——" she said, grinning widely.

"Damn it, how you like to spoil things; your own things."

"What am I spoiling?"

He said, "Listen, silly. What you're having to-night is a triumph; and Rokov knows it. And he's got a play with a leading part that they'd all give their eye-teeth for. *All* of them, do you see? From——" he named the owner of the dressing-room—"downwards. Every one of them has read it and he's still not satisfied. You don't realise what a break it is to have him here to-night; what work I put in to get him. I doubt if Jay could have done it."

"Put your mind at rest on that point, darling. Jay wouldn't have done it. Jay hates my guts."

"Miss Seward, please——" chanted the voice outside the door.

"Damn," he said again.

"Sorry, Dennis. Look," she said. "Come round afterwards."

iii

He felt smaller when he came a second time to the door with the star's name on it. There were a few visitors ahead of him and she was calling to them from behind the screen. Among them he saw the frizzy-headed, pink-cheeked girl who was a surprising friend for Caroline to have, the plump, hockey-playing type called Joan Bridges. She was talking in a breathy voice about First Folios.

Dennis loitered outside the group, reviewing Rokov's speech. Rokov had said, "I'll see her to-morrow," and then, cramming his black felt hat over one eye, had added lightly, "If it weren't for her reputation." "Reputation? How?" "Unreliable," Leopold had grunted, steering his short, bulky shape across the foyer, trailing words over his shoulder, "Tricky; can't be found at the end of a telephone; cuts rehearsals; that's the snag. Still, I'll see her; grateful to you. Good night."

"Now where," Dennis wondered, "did he pick that up? He said he knew nothing of her." Caroline came round the screen, wearing a narrow dark suit and a lime-green shirt. She greeted the others and said to him demurely across the drinks, "It's all right; I can come to supper."

He thought that she was about to ask what had happened to Rokov; then he saw her being embarrassed on his behalf because she had been right and he wrong. His mind went on searching: "Did somebody talk about her in the bar? Is that why he went there? To spy; to get reactions?"

Caroline was talking about Orsino. "You know, when I see people doing their own job really well, I fall in love with them. It's true. I fall in love with ski-instructors and jockeys and dressmakers." "And surgeons," thought Dennis bitterly; although he doubted whether Caroline had yet put on a mask and a white coat to stand by the table while Michael did one of his brilliant performances on a cleft palate. Perhaps she had watched him operate. She was always talking about it: "I want to, but I know I might be sick. I must do it some-time; not because it is Michael, but because it frightens me. You must always do the thing that frightens you; no, I don't mean that everybody must; I mean that I must. It is one of the rules."

43

Against that violence, this chatter, he still caught the current of the magic wind:

> "Oh, you should not rest
> Between the elements of air and earth,
> But you should pity me."

Only when they were free and walking out of the dingy little doorway together did she say, "Rokov not coming?"

"No; he wants to see you to-morrow. I gave him your telephone number."

He saw that the autograph-seekers let her pass unmolested. The cold night air of early spring made her shiver; he glanced at her ironically as she stood by the car. "For how long," he asked, "may I count upon your company?"

"Till twelve-thirty." She was seldom so definite. "He left a message for me. There was an emergency job at the Clinic."

"And do you propose," Dennis asked pontifically, as he turned the car towards the Strand, "to have a second supper at twelve-thirty?"

"Oh, don't be cross." He saw that she was now in the mood of relaxed good-humour when she could afford to be kind to everybody in the world.

"I'm not. I am only wondering how you'll feel if Rokov wants to see you at twenty-seven-and-a-half minutes past nine to-morrow morning."

"Terrible," said Caroline comfortably, "and look worse. Gosh, I'm hungry. Haddock Monte Carlo. No, corned beef hash; only that takes so long. In America—it would be ready, wouldn't it? Quite an ordinary thing on a menu?"

He glanced sideways at her. "What is this about America?"

"Nothing," she said innocently, "except in terms of corned beef hash."

He wondered; he knew that Michael was on the edge of departure for the United States. "But that is a professional journey; a medical conference. He couldn't take her along."

She was staring out of the window.

44

"I've told you a dozen times," he said, "I'll take you to America and you can eat corned beef hash all day."

She said, "Lovely" in a far-away voice.

"Nice place to be, for the war," he added.

"Oh, don't; '*the* war'."

Yes, he thought; better to look away; we shiver in our little lighted tent, with the dark piling up outside.

They were caught in the fussy jam of cars and taxis packing into the Savoy court-yard. "Silly to come in by this entrance; I wasn't thinking. Hop out here, Caro; I'll drive round and park on the hill. Order us some drinks." He had to wait, though angry horns screamed behind him, for the pleasure of seeing her walk. When he came into the lobby of the grill-room she was seated at a small table by the door, with Leopold Rokov bending over her. Rokov turned, said "Hullo" off-handedly to Dennis and went to join his august chums.

"It isn't twenty-seven-and-a-half minutes past nine," Caroline said, "it is twelve-o'clock-say-ten-minutes-to. What a funny creature; an animal; what sort of animal? A bear? Smaller than a bear. A badger? I ordered you a whisky-sour, was that right?"

He said, "Well, you appear to have brought your pigs to market. Pleased?"

"Of course I am pleased. Thank you, Dennis, very, very much."

"I don't want to be thanked. I want you to be a good girl."

"Well, I will be——" she said, sounding hurt. He debated whether he should tell her now of Rokov's reservation. Not yet, he thought, but it must be told before we part. He swallowed his drink rapidly. "We'd better go in if you're hungry. You haven't much time."

As he followed her to the table, he looked possessively to left and right. They were all here; they always were; the celebrated faces, the known alliances; he watched the waiters placing them, driving the smaller fry to the outer circles behind the pillars and inwards to the back wall; while the

45

tables from the aisle to the plate-glass windows received the people with names. There was a hierarchy of waiters, just as there was a hierarchy of names. It was the maître-d'hotel who guided Dennis and Caroline. "In my case," Dennis thought without rancour, "it is a matter of being Jay's brother; of having the money to keep up that position." But he thought that he had been humble long enough; that anybody other than Caroline might well be content with his company.

He looked at her while she read the menu with the kind of devotion more naturally inspired by a breviary. The bent curly head wrung his heart again and so, when she looked up, did the blue hollows of fatigue under her eyes.

He did not raise the subject of Michael; she gave it him just as he was beginning to be soothed by her gentle, inconsequent mood. She had said, "I saw a *monk* getting on a bus in Oxford Street; what a thing," and when he replied "Nothing odd about that. Last year I saw five nuns driving along the Croisette at Cannes in a Bentley," she giggled and wrinkled her nose and said, "You are nice when you are like this; when you don't go *on* so about Michael." Then the rainbow round them broke and he said heavily, "Even if I didn't love you, I should still go on about Michael."

The skin seemed to tighten across the bones of her face. She said, "It has nothing to do with anybody but us."

"My dear Caroline, nobody lives *in vacuo*."

"Who are we hurting?"

"*Whom*. He is hurting you. You are hurting yourself; and your family; your mother."

It was a feeble thrust. She said, "Don't be an ass. My mother and I would have declared war anyway."

"All your friends——"

"How I hate that expression. It suggests a circle of bright-eyed vultures murmuring, 'Isn't it a pity about Caroline'."

"Well, it is a pity about Caroline."

"——," she said. "And in any case there are only two friends I care about besides you. One is your sister Kate and the other is Joan Bridges and they have both settled for it.

Why are you like this, Dennis? Is it because you used to be a friend of Mercedes?"

"She is another person whom you might be hurting." This, he admitted, was worse than feeble; it was thoroughly reprehensible; another cliché coming true; love, like war, packed up all obligations to play fair.

"Well, why won't she let him go? Silly rich bitch," said Caroline. She repeated. "Rich bitch" and giggled. "And a French name into the bargain," she said with her mouth full; "I think I could put up with anything but that. And both their names beginning with 'M' is stupid. Mercedes. How it minces."

"I think it is a pretty name."

"Look—" said Caroline. "This isn't one of my evenings for wanting to talk about Mercedes. I admit I have them, but I'm not having one now."

"All right. I withdraw that anyway, Caro. You couldn't hurt her if you tried." He saw the flash of authentic anger and said, "I'm thinking of you; only of you. Even if my feelings toward you were those of brotherly indifference, you couldn't expect me to approve."

"I haven't asked you to approve."

"If you weren't a genius," he said, "I wouldn't mind. Or perhaps I would. Even if you were just a nice bright girl, I'd think it a pity."

"But why?"

"Darling, you know why. If you could live with him, under the same roof, all right. You'd be one of the mistresses; what an old-fashioned word that is."

"Well, better than one of the whores," said Caroline, peeling a peach.

"And nobody in our neighbourhood would care. But this situation is just plain silly. It isn't a love-affair; it's an obstacle race. Lunch; supper at midnight; week-ends at hotels; you waiting outside in a car while he completes his public obligations. Sham respectability; keeping up appearances."

"But surgeons have to be slightly respectable," said

47

Caroline. She added mournfully, "At the beginning, you were on our side."

He pushed that away and went on, letting the savoury grow cold on his plate. "It is an endless strain on you. What is the fun of being always tired, always worried, always looking over your shoulder, listening for the telephone?"

"That," said Caroline, "is my business, not yours."

"You have nothing of your own; and you never will have, at this rate. No home; no money; no background."

"I don't want them. I'd hate to have them. No, I lie," she said. "I should love to have money. But only for peace of mind. I shouldn't buy anything with it, except taxis and drinks and railway-fares and just enough clothes not to have to think about them. Never solid things; houses or silver tea-sets or furniture. If I were rich I'd go on living at the Rufford; the only difference would be that I'd pay the week's bill regularly."

He stared at her. The words were hers, but something of the philosophy belonged to Mercedes. He had heard Mercedes curse the tyranny of things, confess to finding property tedious, declare that she wished to live always as a traveller. He had seen the plaint as a protest against her manifold possessions; a protest that Caroline, in her poverty, had no need to make. No two people could be less alike; it was curious to find them in agreement.

"What are you thinking? Something odd and abstruse, that you don't care for."

Her mind-reading trick always disquieted him; he said, "I was thinking it was time that you grew up."

"Look——"

"I wish you'd get out of that maddening habit of saying 'Look' with every third sentence——"

"Your manners——" said Caroline. He was silent, seeing the way that it would go now, as it always did. Better, he thought wearily, to be done with this and not see her any more. He clutched at the thought of Rokov and tried to build on that foundation a future wherein Caroline redeemed her past failings, crashed the gates of West End triumph overnight, became solvent and arrogant and threw Michael away. Now it seemed the wrong moment to warn her of Rokov's private information. He looked at his watch.

"It is twenty minutes past twelve," he said.

"I'll finish my coffee and then I'll telephone. Give me a cigarette, would you, please?" she asked wistfully.

She was adept at this sad, bewildered attitude, making him feel in the wrong and liable to apologise humbly.

He called for the bill. "Would you like to be dropped?" he asked when she came back from the telephone.

"Dropped?"

"I meant at Michael's."

"Oh, no; thank you. It would be out of your way. I asked the porter to call me a taxi."

"Very clever of you." Yet it was not done, he knew, in a desire to avoid further lecturing. She had never, in the length of their acquaintance, allowed him to leave her at Michael's door. It was a delicate scruple and he did not know why he respected it.

At most of the tables, people with leisure were still eating their supper. When he stood beside the taxi, she leaned out at him and thanked him again and said "I really am excited about Rokov," in the way that she always over-played her gratitude for any present that he gave her.

"Will you call me at the office after you have seen him?"

"Yes, of course."

"And we might lunch."

"That would be lovely."

He waited on the pavement until the taxi was out of sight.

CHAPTER TWO

CAROLINE reminded herself, in an imitation of Michael's voice, that there was no need to sit forward on the edge of the seat in the taxi. "The process, my sweet, does not in any way affect the speedometer or the traffic-lights," she echoed as she let down one window with a slam, straightened her back and continued to sit on the edge. "I can't unknot myself yet," she explained to the image of Michael. "This is the best kind of being tired; when one's muscles are made of electric wires and one's thoughts go feathery and one says something funny and well-shaped before one has recognised the intention of saying anything at all."

She stared at the lighted streets; north of Oxford Circus they were empty and somehow disapproving. She was talking to herself: "Here are the respectable streets; the narrow, flat-faced houses; all full of doctors and gynæcologists and radiotherapists, and heaven knows what practitioners in parts of people; with Baker Street for a boundary; such a dull boundary. I wonder whether anyone likes Baker Street," she thought and was instantly sorry for it. Here was the square, and the house on the corner. It stood out from the others by reason of its new black-and-white brick façade, its pale wooden door, the antique, wrought-iron lamp on the railing at the foot of the steps. "A smart-alec of a house," Caroline thought, not for the first time. "How I used to hate it. I used to think it was against me. But I've got the hang of you now——," she said to it. "That was before I ever slept under your roof; when I thought I never would."

She knew that he was waiting, for the light went off at the ground-floor window as she walked up the steps. She heard him whistle on the other side of the door; she whistled back. He opened the door. He pulled her into his arms and hugged her close.

"D'you hate me?" he asked brusquely, letting her go.

"Whatever for? Oh, I see, for not being there. Ass; of course I don't."

"Why do I have to fail you?" He sounded so cross and grim that she said, "Oh, dear; oh, dear; it isn't such a tragedy; and I don't imagine that you could help it. Was it your lady with the osteomyelitis?"

"It was. She blew up just to spite me. Perishing woman," he said.

"Did she perish?"

50

"No; I avoided that issue for her. I only just got back,"
he said; "I hope Dennis fed you."

"He did; what about you?"

"Banfield has left some rather odd-looking cold things on
plates in the study." He put his arm round her waist. "Come
and have a drink and tell me how good you were."

"I was so bloody good you wouldn't have known it was me.
Much better than last night."

She sat by the fire in the study upstairs, drinking beer
while he ate the cold supper; she talked about the play,
wondering why she could sing with excitement for him as
never for poor Dennis. "If I live to be a hundred, which
God forbid," she said, "I'll never have anything better than
that. It felt like ski-ing on champagne. Oh God, how I wish
you'd been there; I'd just got used to your not being, and
now it has all come back to me. Too sad."

He shook his head exasperatedly, pushed his plate away
and lit a cigarette.

She said, "Leopold Rokov was in front; he wants me to
go and see him to-morrow."

"Has he got something for you?"

"Dennis says he has."

"What sort?"

"According to Dennis, a leading part for which all the
girls are fighting; to no avail because he doesn't like any of
them. But when I get there I shall probably know different.
Dennis was in a crusading mood."

Michael's eyebrows lifted. "That sounds all right. You
know what I'm going to say to you now, don't you?"

"Yes; and I'm not paying the slightest attention; you have
been warned."

He sat very still; the profile like the profile on a coin was
sunk in lines of weariness; below the chin, she thought, there
was an air of crumpled officialdom about him, in the wing
collar, the black jacket and striped trousers.

"Darling; if it is a job, and a good job, and an immediate
job——"

51

"Oh stink and drains," said Caroline, "I wish I hadn't told you at all; I thought of not; but for me to decide to dissemble is enough to guarantee that it will come bursting out at the earliest opportunity. Look—whatever the job, it can't stop my coming to America with you."

"Yes, it can. It must."

"Michael, it won't."

He said, "There is no point in our arguing. Now that you know my views, let's leave it until the job materialises." He smiled at her.

She said, "That is about the most irritating and grown-up attitude that you could take."

"I'm sorry, Caro."

"Are you dead tired?" she asked. "You look it."

He said, "Rather less tired than you, my love."

"I doubt that. I'm still treading champagne." She went to sit beside him on the sofa, with her legs tucked under her, holding his hand. She thought that a blind person would know that this hand was unusual, feeling the shape of the bones.

"You're my authority anyway," she said. "So you have the advantage that Dennis lacks."

"It is not the only advantage I have that Dennis lacks."

"We fought," she said.

"About me?"

"Yes."

Michael said, "I wish he'd leave you alone. Which—I suppose—is what he wishes about me. He is a good friend, but he isn't always wise."

"Is he your good friend, do you think?"

"Oh, lud, yes," said Michael. "You wouldn't hear him say a word against me if he hadn't fallen in love with you. Come here."

She lay cradled against his shoulder, her mind still made light and lively by fatigue, her body beginning to be at rest; she was aware of the room rather than of Michael, as though she sat here waiting for him. It was a room walled almost completely with built-in book-cases; its colours were blue and grey. The sofas and the chairs were large, square, modern things; all the ash-trays were uniformly big, made of heavy glass; there was a solid, curved desk, built out from one wall, at an angle to the window.

Over the fireplace, the portrait of Michael carried on the pale colours of the room; it was a cloudy, youthful portrait, more a decorative panel than a picture. In it he was wearing a white coat, whose shadows were blue. It looked casual, unfinished, the likeness fleeting, the young, dramatic head barely sketched, the hands traced as lightly as skeleton-leaves. "It is like the ghost of you" she had said when first she saw it.

She had gone through the phase of hating the portrait because Mercedes Knowle was the artist, and now she was merely puzzled by it; it made a point of uncertainty in the room, a wispy threat, somebody else's secret.

"Come to bed," said Michael.

There began for them the urgency from which they could not escape, the obsessing appetite; she knew that it haunted him as persistently as it haunted her. There were the first minutes, when tenderness remained distant and apparently impossible, when there were only two bodies, each greedy and alone. This changed, until she said, "I love you so." (And more than you, she thought, I now love what your body does; your own desire driving you, while you resist, because, until the last bearable moment, you will make sure of my delight before you meet it with yours. . . . Over the top of the mountain; and here the mind dies and I am all body. . . . And now we fall like stones and are the two other people who never knew that ecstasy, the tumbled, friendly people with heavy limbs.)

Presently she turned up the lamp to see whether he slept. When she spoke to him, he gave a small sigh and his eyelashes fluttered. Perhaps he would not wake again to-night. His insomnia was still a worry to her; a mysterious, adult affliction. She could sleep for nine hours, no matter what time she went to bed. For the moment, she was wide-awake.

53

"And what is more," she thought guiltily, "I am hungry." She climbed out of bed and picked Michael's blue-and-gold dressing-gown off the chair; she turned out the lamp.

In the study, the fire had burned low, but the room was still warm and she curled up in one corner of the sofa, grabbing from the plate of biscuits and cheese. She smoothed her fingers on the prickly brocade of the dressing-gown. "What a beautiful, solid feeling it has; but it is too Burlington-Arcade for Michael; he doesn't entirely suit it, any more than he suits this house or this room. He is simpler than all his possessions. I can imagine him so easily when he was a shabby student."

The end of hunger meant that she must smoke. She put her plate from her and lighted a cigarette, reminded at once of their first encounter when she had claimed to have all the appetites. She could remember every word of the dialogue. Sometimes she liked the accuracy of her verbal memory; sometimes it was a demon that plagued her furiously with the sad things.

To-night it was set to conjure the ghost of her quarrel with Jay Brookfield and her abrupt relegation of her stage career to a secondary importance. This had happened in July of '36, when the intellectual thriller was still playing to capacity.

She sighed, unwilling to recapture that afternoon. But because she thought that a similar decision might await her to-morrow, she went back to there in her mind.

She was alone in her dressing-room, after a matinée. It was a hot afternoon in the middle of the time of doom. Mercedes had arrived in England; she had come for the express purpose of quarrelling with Michael about Cold Ash, the country house that was their joint property. But it felt like doom. Nothing was safe; London was changed and Michael, when last seen, had been more than usually grown-up; calm and balanced and businesslike, saying, "This happens from time to time and is soon over." Now, every day brought her one of his long, talkative letters; sometimes two came in one day. He was staying in Sussex, in his father's house, five miles from the bone of contention, the property. Mercedes was at the local inn, with a

French maid and, according to Michael, a mood that would try the patience of the Heavenly Hierarchy.

Caroline drank neat whisky, sitting before her looking-glass and annotating aloud a paragraph from the evening-paper on her knee :

"Mrs. Michael Knowle (the well-known Rich Bitch) who is (of course) the only daughter of the late Sir Lewis Barry, our former Ambassador to Paris and Washington (uffle, uffle, wuffle). Mrs. Knowle (who persecutes for a hobby) has lately been visiting the United States (tactful way of saying that she hasn't lived with her husband for years). She is a person of various talents (blow me), has studied art in Paris under Depuy (what a thing), is well-known here and in America as a stage-designer. (And if she doesn't clear out soon and exercise one of her bloody talents a long way off, she is likely to find herself with her throat cut from ear to ear.)"

"Hullo, puss; talking to yourself?" said Jay. She looked up and saw him leaning against the door. He wore a pale suit and a dark shirt; he looked like all his photographs, fragile and cynical and sure of his ground.

"Hullo," said Caroline gloomily. "Would you care for a drink?"

"I would not. Nor do I care to see my little girl lowering four inches of whisky between performances. Put that down *at once.*"

"Certainly," said Caroline, tilting the glass at her lips. Jay shook his head and made a clicking sound with his tongue. He said, "In order to prevent you from sitting here drinking yourself into a stupor, my pet, I am going to take you to my flat and feed you with chicken-sandwiches."

"Thank you kindly." She was flattered; she leaned towards the looking-glass, adorning her face. She saw that she looked shabby; it was a listless black silk dress that would do so long as Michael remained away. She was in debt and she had begun to hoard her better clothes carefully. As she rose, she saw Jay looking her up and down.

"Thin, aren't you?" he said.

55

"Too thin?"

"Yes, I *think* so." He appeared to be giving it serious consideration.

Jay's flat was in Fitzroy Square; he was said to delight in the shock received by his public on hearing that the boy who held the mirror up to Mayfair should live in Bloomsbury. The flat was entirely Victorian. There were antimacassars, heavy dark pieces of furniture, red curtains, shell boxes and steel engravings. It was an enormous room and in the tired evening sunlight it semed to Caroline a cool and ghostly place, as though he had taken her with him into another time. He rang the bell and his manservant, who wore side-whiskers, wheeled in a table that held sandwiches, coffee and iced orangeade. Having settled Caroline in a large plush chair beside the window, Jay threw himself into another large plush chair and put up his feet on a beaded footstool. The table was between them.

"Change is coming into your life," he said. "I want you to take your holiday next week, Caroline."

It was an order, spoken in the clipped voice. She stared at him.

"I know you weren't due to take it until the end of August, but that's out of the question."

"Why is it?" She felt that her stomach had shut like a box: the sandwich was now completely undesirable.

"Because you're coming out of the play and going into another. My new comedy," said Jay. "You're a very lucky little girl. I am going to read it to you to-morrow afternoon; here. With——" he named three current lions—"who compose the rest of the cast. Two o'clock here? All right? The script isn't back from the typist yet or I'd let you have a preview to-day."

She said, "Look——" Jay went on imperturbably, "I want to begin rehearsals by August the sixth, latest. We shall open in Edinburgh towards the beginning of September. You're playing the second lead; in fact more interesting than the lead; you're rather a tart, dear. Will you like that?"

She said, "Jay, I know I'm going to make you cross, but I can't do it."

"Pardon?" said Jay in Cockney. " 'Didn't quoite cetch."

"I said I couldn't take the part."

He looked winded. He said, "Oh, *don't* tell me you're going to marry Dennis and leave the stage. You can't marry him, dear; you'll be so bored. If it's a question of marrying my brother, leave all that to me."

"I am not going to marry Dennis."

"If you're going to have a baby——"

"I am not going to have a baby."

He took his feet off the beaded stool, rose, stood in front of her with his hands in his pockets and said crisply, biting off each word, "Then would you mind telling me precisely why you cannot play the part?"

"I am going to Italy with Michael Knowle."

Jay's harlequin face sagged in bewilderment. "Forever, d'you mean? To live there? To get evidence for a divorce, or something?"

She hesitated. She recalled a maxim taught by Michael: "When you're using what seems to you a weak argument, leave it as bare as you can; don't bolster it up." She said, "No. For a holiday. For two weeks at the end of August. He can't get away before."

Jay said, after a pause, "Are you serious?"

"Yes."

"Then you're insane."

"Yes, well. . . ."

He took three paces along the carpet, stopped and came back, flinging himself into the chair.

"Now look here, Caroline. As chap to chap. For God's sake—I know about being in love."

"It isn't any good your talking, Jay. We have counted on this holiday for months—I'm not going to do anything that would endanger it."

"Oh, my poor deluded girl, will you use your wits?"

She said, "I'm sorry; I am bloody sorry. If you can postpone the rehearsals——"

57

"I-am-trying," said Jay with his eyes shut, "to-maintain-a-modicum-of-self-control." He screwed up his face until he looked like a Chinese. "Apart from that piece of supreme impertinence, which I should not have expected from a whipper-snapper like yourself; *quite* apart from that——" he gasped.

"I'm sorry if——"

"Shut up. Please shut up. Let me do this. Do you imagine for one moment, for one single moment, that anybody as intelligent as Michael would countenance such imbecile behaviour?"

"It simply doesn't arise. I shan't consult him."

"I shall, though," said Jay, with his eyes tightly shut.

This possibility had not occurred to her. She said, "Look —if you do, you'll be everlastingly sorry. I'll never forgive you. Just the sort of ——ing interference that I used to put up with from my mother. If you go to Michael about this, I'll break my contract and walk out of your company."

"*Caroline!*" He was now quite green. "Listen to me. You are a very obstinate, moronic little girl and you don't make yourself any more attractive by flourishing threats. Who the devil do you think you are? *Quiet*, please. I shall ring up Michael to-night and tell him that I want you for a part that will make your career. And if you don't want me to throttle you here and now, that is the end of the argument."

She was frightened of him and this was somehow stimulating; a David-and-Goliath situation, the challenge to make the most of her feeble weapons. She said, "I repeat that if you do that I'll walk out of the company to-morrow; and I'll never speak to you again."

Beside the dying fire in Michael's study, Caroline made a sympathetic grimace towards that gesture of defiance. It had proved useless. Jay had telephoned to Michael in the country; Michael had written her four pages of placid, understanding persuasion. For him, she had climbed down, suffered the tortures of defeat and rehearsed the play. Six weeks later she had found herself the possessor of good notices in the otherwise unanimous abuse that greeted Jay's comedy. It ran for two weeks in London and the end of it saw the end of her friendship with Jay. They had been limping along in an uneasy armistice ever since that afternoon; throughout rehearsals he had behaved as though he were an acid governess and she the stupidest pupil in the class. She thought that the failure of the play gave her, in his mind, a belated, undeserved victory. At least she had never worked with him again; Dennis and Kate were still her friends; Jay was her enemy.

"And it is curious to remember how many things went wrong, from the moment that Mercedes came. As though the bad luck stayed even after she had gone. Nothing but flops and quarrels and people calling me unreliable. I suppose I was."

By then, she thought, the theatre had ceased to be her profession; her profession was Michael.

"And I didn't do so well at that one, in the beginning."

She was reluctant to let her memory take over at this point. The path of these thoughts would lead her into dark places; past all the betrayal of that first confident assurance that she could love him forever and be content with his way of loving. She must pass by vows and recantations, by pain that was as violent as toothache; past unreasonable jealousy, humble withdrawal and the sterile suffering that went on throughout his absences. She must taste again the pure hatred of Mercedes, who was less a target for jealousy than an ultimate obstacle, the wife who was adamant, the arch-priestess of the Spoilers-of-the-Fun. She must see herself swayed like a person under a spell; with Michael standing by, always courteous, patient and truthful; the rock of strength on which, in her darkest moments, she could feel that she dashed herself to pieces.

"When did it begin to be all right?" she asked herself bewilderedly. "How? Did I learn to behave, or did he learn to love me more? Or both?"

Because, lately, she could feel that she had won; that in patient bondage to the hopeless thing, she had builded better than she knew; that in contradiction to all theories of love, she had tied him to her by simple devotion. Was that too pretty a translation of the truth, she wondered, staring at the last gleam of red among the coals in the grate. "Oh, you can make it look any way you like. You could say that you had made yourself necessary to him." (And if you looked at it in that light, you would see that it was a severe and exact apprenticeship, whose training had left no time for any other.)

Slowly, she had learned to rage in secret and to weep alone. She had learned to hide from him the small worries that he begged to be allowed to share. She had discovered early that she could make him laugh, and it became an obligation always to make him laugh, to save the funny things for him and hand them over, as toys to a child, at the day's end. She had cured herself of questioning him, rebuking him and sulking at him. To suit his time-table, she would cancel at the shortest notice any prior engagement. She had set herself the task of being always decorative, always good-tempered, always punctual; this last was easy, for she was anxious never to lose a second of him; at least he looked grateful when he found her waiting. She had forced upon herself the study of his work, solemnly reading manuals of surgery that sickened her, acquiring medical knowledge from all the sources that she could tap. She had made the decision to stay on at the Rufford Hotel because this was a place where he could come at erratic hours, to sit in the elaborate lounge and eat and drink, still looking respectable and making love only in words. It was when that rendezvous became too public, when the snatched private hours failed to satisfy him, that she began to go regularly to the house in Manchester Square.

Looking back, she could see other assets than the sweetness of his company. From him she had learned wisdom; she respected him even when her mind was at its most detached, seeing them both for what they were. She could sneer at the list of losses on the other side of the balance-sheet; final estrangement from her mother; debts (never revealed to Michael); the collapse of her career and the thinning-out of her friends; Dennis' implacable judgment; a life constantly threatened by time and public opinion and Mercedes. She felt that she had travelled a long way.

"And to-morrow?" she said aloud, pulling the heavy stuff of the dressing-gown more closely about her body. "Will to-morrow present me with that dear old problem on a plate, all freshly-cooked and hot from the oven? Leopold Rokov or Michael? Leopold Rokov or America?"

She was cold. She went back across the landing to hover at the bedroom door. His voice came out of the dark; he sounded very much awake:

"Caroline, why are you prowling?"

"I got hungry. I didn't mean to wake you."

"Waking in the middle of the night is a thing that I can do without assistance; as you should know by now." He turned on the lamp. "How enchanting you look in my dressing-gown."

She stood gazing at him.

"But you will be warmer," Michael suggested, "if you come back to bed."

"What have you just decided to say to me about Rokov?" He smiled at her and shook his head: "You always see it coming, don't you?"

"I was the seventh child of a seventh child of a seventh child of a seventh—the hell with it. Tell me, Michael; let us have the dreary thing."

"It isn't ultimately dreary; I am almost as much divided in my mind as you are."

"But I am not divided at all; my mind is in one solid, unbreakable piece."

"No, it isn't, Caro."

"Very well, it isn't. But I am praying that Dennis has made it all up and that Rokov really wants to ask me whether I can get you to reconstruct his profile at a reduced fee."

"I would, too," said Michael. He moved restlessly: "I have shut so many doors for you. I had hoped that this time I could open one. America isn't such a great adventure, but it is fun. It enlarges the horizons." He said, "However, this isn't by any means our last opportunity. I shall have to go again next year, unless there's war."

"We may be dead next year; even if there isn't war."

"Yes, my love, and you might be run over on your way back to the Rufford, but that is not a basis for argument."

"I think it is."

"It isn't. If Rokov is serious, here comes your second chance. I robbed you of the first one; no, Caroline, you needn't use coarse oaths; if it hadn't been for me, you wouldn't have quarrelled with Jay. I refuse to rob you of this; you must see that."

"Of course I see that, damn it. But can't I do something I want to do, for a change?"

"I could blackmail you there by saying, 'Not if you love me'."

"Yes," she said, "I give you all the right cues."

"But I don't take them. What I want to say to you now is: promise to be good and swallow it down. If he offers you the part to-morrow, you must accept. It is the only honest and intelligent thing to do. Am I sounding like a Spoiler-of-the-Fun?"

"Yes." She was, as always, a little mollified by his use of her phrase.

"Well, there it is," said Michael, "I want you to promise. Don't promise me; promise you. The final importance isn't to us, but to you as an artist. And that's the last pompous thing I'll say."

She said, "Oh, hell," and felt the tears come, suddenly and blindingly; though she had made rules against weeping in Michael's presence. He cradled her and talked over the top of her head. "It seems worse because you're tired; truly, darling. Everything always does. 'When our spirits meet old Weariness, with his rust-eaten knife.' Can you finish the quotation for me? not sure that I can finish it myself. Something like, 'there is no corner of our house kept sweet that is not trampled bloody'. I was always grateful to that poet.

Early in life he taught me to say, 'This is only overwhelming because I am tired.' My love, be quiet and close to me."

His hands caressing her made her quiet. She did not mean to sleep and sleep came. Usually, in this bed, she struggled against it, because to sleep was a waste of Michael. Now she sank down into it without a fight.

When she woke, the light in the room was the dusty light of morning. She sat up, shocked.

"Hell's teeth," said Caroline. "It's almost six."

She flung herself out of bed, scooped up her clothes from the chair and carried them into the bathroom; she splashed through a shallow bath, dressed with a fury of speed and launched herself at Michael's looking-glass to streak lipstick on her mouth. Michael moved and sighed and did not wake. She knew from this that he had slept little before dawn. She bent over him, touched his forehead and ran.

The staircase with the blinds drawn at the windows, the palpable daylight in the hall, made the house stiff, correct and inimical; a housemaid's property. It was almost a housemaid's hour; she thought that she heard a clang and a rattle down in the basement. The childish terror of being caught made her heart race and her hands tremble; she unlatched the door and let it slip behind her so that it banged. She ran down the steps and across the square; beginning to walk only when she was on the south side of it.

She felt dizzy and incompetent; her knees shook. She blinked at the unfamiliar landscape of early morning. "Many dustbins and no people," she thought; Wigmore Street lay empty, like a shiny solid river all the way to Cavendish Square. A policeman, appearing out of an alleyway, looked her up and down with a meditative expression. She found a taxi, a slow taxi with a door that rattled, and an old, stooped driver. She sat on the edge of the seat, limp with tiredness and dizziness, her elbows on her knees and her forehead in her hands. "Coming home with the milk," Caroline said aloud, "A quaint conceit; as though you brought the milk with you."

63

She saw the neat width of St. James's, with the palace-clock accusing her. She had to tell the driver which turning was St. James's Place. As they came round the corner into the cul-de-sac, she saw that the night-porter had opened the doors and was sluicing the front steps. His shrunken nut of a face looked nipped with cold.

"Hullo, John," said Caroline.

"Oh, good morning, Miss Seward," said John, friendly and unperturbed. He paid the taxi for her.

"John, will you please leave a message in writing for who-ever comes on at eight. I don't want anybody put through to me unless Mr. Knowle rings; and I must be called at eleven-fifteen sharp."

"Very good, Miss. I'll leave a note on the pad here, for the day-porter. No telephone calls except Mr. Knowle—called-at-eleven-fifteen——"

"Wait a minute——" An idea had come into her mind; a light-headed, intricate rendering of the words that haunted her. "If he offers you the part to-morrow, you must promise to accept. *If he offers you the part to-morrow. . . .*"

"Look," she said. "Cross out the bit about calling me. I don't want to be called. I'll sleep as long as I can."

CHAPTER THREE

"MR. BROOKFIELD has gone out to lunch, I'm afraid," said Vera Haydon and added reproachfully, "He waited a long time. He was expecting you to get in touch with him."

"I know he was." The voice sounded heavy and sad. "All right; I'll call him later on."

"Can we ring you, Miss Seward? I don't quite know what time he'll be back."

"No, that wouldn't be any good. I may come into the Gallery this afternoon on the chance of finding him."

Replacing the telephone, Dennis Brookfield's secretary

thought, "I wonder if she knows how much I hate her." As soon as she had thought that, she felt awed and guilty. Hatred was a strong word; to hate was unbalanced and Vera had a profound respect for Balance. But her code was no protection against the emotion that she felt for Caroline; it bubbled up like a geyser.

Before the appearance of Miss Seward, she had taken a lively and possessive interest in Dennis's young women. (Her disapproval admitted to doubts of his relationship with them, but this was filed under the convenient headings, None of My Business, and Anyway I've No Proof.) She had treated them as gently, when their ascendancy demanded that he should be brought to the telephone at once, as when their powers waned and she had to tell them lies. There had been an Honourable, whom she had hoped that he would marry, a dancer who was surprisingly Nice, and one actress with a name so well-known that it always seemed to announce itself through the receiver in lights. Those were the days; now there was only Caroline.

"Miss Seward called," she wrote neatly and rose to place the message on Dennis's blotter. She returned to her own desk, took from the drawer a piece of chamois leather and began to polish the silver pen-tray, the paper-knife, and the inkpot with the silver top. These things were her pride; they were a symbol of the first importance. They were the gift of Mrs. Michael Knowle.

The gift had been made when that halcyon term of employment came to an end, seven years ago, at the time when Mr. and Mrs. Knowle had decided to lead separate lives. It was a blow to Vera. She had loved Mrs. Knowle devotedly, disapproving as she loved. Mrs. Knowle came under the heading of Impossible Person, but she had the saving grace, the only saving grace ; she was well-born. This had made Vera's love appear reasonable to her in all the trying moments; they were trying because of the unorthodox nature of her duties. Sometimes she had been drafted to take over Mr. Knowle's appointment-book and shepherd his patients from the waiting-room. Sometimes she had been whisked off to Sussex to regulate the

farm-accounts at Cold Ash. Sometimes she had arranged the
flowers for dinner-parties. Sometimes she had run errands of
an incomprehensible character. Once she had posed with her
bare foot on a block of wood because Mrs. Knowle, indulging
a painting-spell, had wished to paint a foot. (And this was a
tribute to Vera's high insteps; it was consoling to have high
insteps; they were a sign of Breeding and she always mentioned
them when she was buying a pair of shoes.)

The telephone rang again; it was the sad, fussy Mr. Kenrick
from Orange Street, where the Brookfield Galleries owned an
off-shoot, a small picture-gallery dedicated to modern exhibits.
Of all Dennis's preoccupations, this gallery was Vera's main
interest and Mr. Kenrick's needs were of high priority. Mrs.
Knowle had encouraged her enthusiasm for modern art.

"I'm expecting him any minute," she said. Her intimation
to Miss Seward that he might not be back for some time was
based on nothing but the desire to irritate Miss Seward. Dennis
never took more than half an hour to eat his lunch alone.
Which made it all the more exasperating that when he took
Caroline to lunch, he might remain absent for over two hours.

"How he can make such a fool of himself; a girl who's in
love with another man. . . ."

She had become aware only gradually that the "Michael"
to whom Dennis was obliged to refer so often in making
rendezvous with Caroline was the villainous Mr. Knowle.
After the suspicion became strong, Mr. Knowle had dissolved
her doubts by bringing Miss Seward to an exhibition at the
Orange Street Gallery. From that moment Caroline stood
finally damned.

Vera rose from her desk and leaned discreetly on the window-
sill, looking down into King Street. She saw it, as she saw everything, tinted by her dark spectacles. Dennis was standing on
the pavement, looking thoughtfully at the collection behind
each of the plate-glass windows. There were four large windows
and his inspection was always thorough. Vera could not rid
herself of the view that it was a little common to do this; he
made her think of a greengrocer standing beside his stall. She

was fond of Dennis and she was fond of the Brookfield Galleries, but the position of the one looking at the other embarrassed her. It embarrassed her twice a day; on his arrival in the morning and on his return from lunch.

He was obviously in a mood of gloom when he sat down at his desk; he was obviously cheered by the sight of Caroline's name on the message.

"And Mr. Kenrick would like you to call him at once," Vera said.

"What does Kenrick want? I don't think I want Kenrick," said Dennis sleepily. She told him what it was that Kenrick wanted, but he continued to pay no attention, to look through catalogues and make notes on his blotter. She stared at him with affectionate irritation. Her spectacles darkened his skin and his hair to more than their natural darkness. In these tones, the strain of Jewish blood was emphasised; with the hawk-profile and the expensive, unnoticeable clothes.

Vera could not feel happy about the fact that Dennis's grandfather had been called Brückfeldt, and that he had made and mended picture-frames in Charing Cross Road. She was not anti-Semitic; that would have been shameful at this moment in the world's history; she simply thought that it was A Pity about Jews. They ran to unsuitable activities such as growing side-whiskers, charging interest and spending week-ends at Brighton. Of course, she reminded herself, Dennis had cleverly mitigated the taint with two generations of mixed ancestry; and he had a public-school education.

Caroline Seward opened the door of the sanctum without knocking. Vera was forced to admit that she looked more than usually elegant; she was wearing a beautifully-cut black cloth coat and a black turban that ended in a long scarf. The elegance included her gloves, her handbag and her shoes (the details, Vera knew, that could prove or disprove a woman of Breeding).

"Don't you look lovely?" Dennis was saying, while Vera was wondering what had made Miss Seward so palpably unhappy. She looked pale and she did not smile at all.

"Please—Dennis—if you're not busy——"

There he was, snatching his hat, saying that he had nothing whatever to do. "Mr. Kenrick wanted to speak to you," Vera reminded him.

"Well, why don't you go round to Orange Street and put him out of his misery? Ask the switchboard to take messages while you're gone."

"What time shall I expect you back?"

"Oh . . . not to-day," said Dennis, and they went out. Leaning on the window-sill, Vera watched them emerging. Caroline put one hand on Dennis's arm and they walked away together, disappearing round the corner of St. James's Square.

Vera went to collect her hat and coat from the little cloak-room at the back of the building. It was amiable to walk among the foreign persons who did not spend their days in offices. She took the longer way to Orange Street.

She wished that she could stop thinking about Caroline, the last companion whom she would have wished to go with her along Pall Mall. "She is not pretty," Vera reminded herself strenuously as she came past the Carlton Hotel. How could the high head of curly hair, the large greenish-brown eyes, the prominent cheek-bones, that blunt nose and square mouth, add up to a semblance of beauty? Yet it was so; they did; and now she was remembering also the warmth of the deep voice and the movements of the body with its long bones.

"Large bones," Vera corrected herself as she turned up the Haymarket; "She has Large Bones. Like me." There was no other resemblance. Vera knew that her own aspect was somehow heavy and muddy, though she would sometimes think of it as Distinguished because that adjective had been used once by Mrs. Knowle. Mrs. Knowle had said, "You look very distinguished," when Vera had changed into black velvet to eat supper alone with her at Cold Ash. It had been a lovely, intimate evening, with Mrs. Knowle at her most peaceful. Cold Ash was a beautiful house; Vera hoped that they would never sell it; she knew that it was let and she knew the names of the tenants. A surprising amount of information came to her indirectly through Dennis; sometimes she thought that her affection for Dennis rested only upon the foundation of his link with the Knowles; she had no other link. Mrs. Knowle was always abroad now.

Damn Caroline Seward; blissful to understand that Mrs. Knowle refused to divorce her husband. "Not that he would marry her anyway; that sort of girl never does get herself married," Vera repeated as she came to the door of the gallery. "And as for him. . . ."

At first acquaintance, Vera had been susceptible to Mr. Knowle's good looks and placid charm of manner. Gradually, as the tension between husband and wife became apparent, she had learned to see him for what he was; the charm was only the professional stuff that his female patients were happy to pay for; the placidity was only evidence of his obstinate self-will. Mr. Knowle was a bully and Vera could see that Mrs. Knowle, for all her assets of wealth and breeding, was a little afraid of him. He had the morals and the arrogance of a Turk. "What that man ought to have is a harem. The impertinence of it; he was a nobody; just a nobody." She would have liked him to have a common voice. She would have liked Caroline Seward to have a common voice.

Vera entered the gallery and for a moment she was newly aware of it; empty of visitors, with its soft tawny walls and the pictures imposing their queer silence, the glistening black marble leopard lunging across his stone pedestal. She liked it better this way than when it was full of people appraising the latest exhibition. Except that on those days she would sometimes watch the door, playing a game wherein Mrs. Knowle walked suddenly in among the crowd and saw her and called to her and presently, over a cup of tea, told Vera that she was living alone now and would like her to come back; "You always understood me better than anybody else," Mrs. Knowle said in this dream, "And I am lonely; I do need a companion as well as a secretary. . . ."

Now Vera saw Mr. Kenrick coming towards her through the alcove from the inner room, and prepared to hear his troubles.

ii

Dennis said, "Is that all?"

Caroline said, "Yes. I thought I'd better tell you at once."

"And you're off to New York on Thursday?"

"Yes. I told Rokov that in my note."

"I see. Well, there it is, dear. And now there's something I want to say to you."

She said, "I don't think I want to go on driving round and round."

"We are not. We're going to sit beside the Serpentine."

"Why?"

"Because that is the place where people with illicit relationships go."

Though she smiled obligingly, he thought that he had perhaps chosen a bad moment; despite her new elegance, she was looking wretchedly unhappy; he wished again that she were more successful in hiding her distress. But there was beginning to be something adult and remote about her grief. In older days she had talked her sorrows out; now she kept quiet and still wore the mask of sadness for anyone to see. She had not adorned her decision in the telling; there had been only the words and this miserable face. "She knows what an idiotic mistake she is making; she can see how hopelessly she is torturing herself, wrecking her life. That is a thing that she cannot explain to herself, any more than she can explain it to me. Yes, it is a bad moment. Even so," he thought, "the time has come; a plague on both their houses; I can stand no more of it."

He nosed his car into the line that faced the water. It was a showery afternoon and now the rain began to fall again; the water turned grey and mottled; a rising wind lashed the trees, with their light frosting of green, on the other side.

"We'll go on sitting here," he said, "though I rather wanted to walk."

He turned and looked at her; she was withdrawn as far from him as she might be, leaning back against the door, with her hands in the long, soft black gloves clasped round one knee; she looked as vulnerable as a child.

"Do you know what I'm going to say?" he asked heavily.

"I think so."

"Before I do say it, I have to make my hopeless point once again; a mere formality, of course."

She nodded and half-shut her eyes; some of her suffering seemed to be for him.

"There is no need to be sorry for me," he said sharply. "That I do not want and will not have. But I still love you and I still want you to marry me. Is that clear?"

She nodded again.

"All right." In spite of himself, he said, "You needn't sit such a long way away; you should know by now that I do not pounce."

She shook her head vaguely and did not move.

"Well, darling," he said, "This is it. I have had about as much as I can take. And I'm not seeing you any more, except by accident, after to-day."

"Because of Rokov?"

"That has helped to make up my mind for me. But it was on my mind before."

"I see. Look——" she paused.

"What am I to look at, Caroline?"

"How much is it because of Mercedes? I still have the feeling that you are really fond of her and think that she's a holy martyr and that I'm the whore of Babylon."

That, he thought, was a queer piece of mind-reading; "She gets the fact of Mercedes, and misses the truth; the truth that I refuse to tell her."

He said, "How childish you are; I don't feel like that about either of you. It is simply that there comes an accumulation of being unable to bear the whole set-up. Perhaps," he said, trying to be fair, "Rokov is only an excuse. But Mercedes isn't the reason. The reason is you. If I didn't see you suffering so much and so determined to suffer, I might be able to hang on a little longer."

"Suffering?" she said, as though the word were foreign. "I am only sad because I have to be ungrateful to you; and you took so much trouble."

"Are you sure?" he asked, peering at the sad, stiffened mask; the cigarette-smoke and the mist on the windows made a gloom here.

"Oh, Dennis, sure of what?"

"Never mind," he said. "To-day I resign my right to ask anything at all."

She moved restlessly, pressing the palm of her hand against her forehead. "Yes," she said, "I see there's nothing in it for you."

"And nothing in it for you, either, my pretty."

"Don't you see? I have no choice. 'I might go on; naught else remained to do'," she said and suddenly there was a tear spilling over the lower curve of her lashes, dropping off her cheek, dissolving into a small dark splash on the patterned *crêpe de Chine* shirt ; he watched its progress attentively. She sat still, not sobbing nor making any sound, with scarcely a quiver of her lips and the tears following one another.

"My dear fool—No," he thought. "Suddenly she has dignity; I cannot upbraid this. . . ." He put his hand on hers. "All right," he said, "you needn't explain."

"That sounds as though you were still on our side."

He scowled at the windscreen in front of him that was now obscured with the drifting streaks and smudges of rain. "In a sense, of course, I shall always be on your side. But from a distance; from as great a distance as I can manufacture. You see, my beloved, there is a sort of man who can hang around forever, grateful for whatever crumbs he may get. I'm not that sort of man. You nearly turned me into him, but not quite. I refuse, reluctantly, to make me a willow cabin at your gate."

" 'And call upon your soul within the house'."

"Precisely."

She bent her head and took a handkerchief from the black

suède envelope that she carried; he could not help noticing that it was a small, fine handkerchief embroidered with a square initial; and remembering a day when she had cried and borrowed his handkerchief and forgotten to give it back.

All these new things, he thought—clothes bought on credit; for the foolish journey, for Michael's pleasure; like a *poule de luxe*; you, who are a genius in your own right.

"As it's my last day for questions," he said, "here's one more. Have you told Michael?"

"No; and you musn't, please."

"You are putting a considerable responsibility on him, you know."

Her eyes were reproachfully wide. "But Dennis, that is what you always say you want me to do."

"It's no good," he said, "I don't know why we go on talking."

"Do you despise me now more than you did before?"

Angrily, he snapped open his cigarette-case, lighted two cigarettes, and placed one between her lips. "I'm sorry, Caroline, but I cannot make mathematical calculations of that sort. It amazes me sometimes that you can be so common."

"What is common about the word 'despise'?"

"The thought, not the word. I don't despise you; I never did. I think that you are making a crazy nonsense of your life, but that's incidental. Let's leave the whole thing."

"Yes, please," she said faintly. She was so pale and shivering so much that he put his arm round her shoulders, forgetting his rôle.

"Just how ill have you made yourself feel with all this?"

"Pretty ill; but pay no attention."

"Now, damn you," he said, "you rouse my paternal instincts. Why do you always work yourself up into such a state of nerves? Would you like to come back to Albany and lie down?"

She laughed and said, "No; it isn't really that sort."

"It doesn't look a very good sort to me."

73

"I have jitters; take no notice."

"You must remember this," he said, starting the engine, "that I'm only going because you don't want me. If you ever do—and I don't mean as a lover, I mean if there is any way that I can help you, then you must send for me. And I'll be there. That's a cliché, isn't it? I expect they all say that."

"They? Who are they?"

"Other gentlemen in similar situations. *Ein Jüngling*; you should read Heine."

She said, "Yes, well. . . ." That familiar laziness of rejoinder made him chuckle. "You have given me a great deal of pleasure, darling," he said, "and I will not have you being sorry."

"At least I never lied to you."

"And you'd better not. Where shall I take you now?"

"Would the Rufford be out of your way?"

"I haven't got a way."

He drove across the bridge, past Knightsbridge Barracks, to Hyde Park Corner and down Constitution Hill. She said nothing until he spoke and it was small conversation all the way. As they drove up St. James's, he wondered how long this corner would remain haunted ground, how soon it would lose the dimensions imposed on it by Caroline and let him pass by, thoughtless and comfortable. There would be a time; that was all he knew.

She paused for a moment before she climbed out of the car; he sat there, staring ahead of him, not wanting to look at her. She said flatly, "Well, good-bye; take care of you."

"Have fun in America," he said, feeling as fatuous as he sounded. He did not look back; after he had left the car in Albany court-yard and was going up the Rope-walk, he found his mind repeating, "Have fun . . . have fun. . . ." He saw her having fun. Remembering things about her now as though she were dead, he reflected upon her talents as a traveller and as a guest; the ease with which he had seen her move on the background of hotels, restaurants and houses not her own; always amiable, graceful in acceptance;

74

adapting herself without effort; it was his sister Kate who had said that Caroline was her favourite week-end guest, because she never needed to be entertained. She was equipped, he thought, with an endless and spontaneous joy of living. How long would it take Michael to kill that thing?

He shut the oak door and stood in his room; that was a little misty and cold, like all the ground-floor rooms in Albany, a room furnished to his own taste, having about it the solid haunt of the past, when Byron and Macaulay and the rest had made these apartments their homes in another version of London.

Dennis looked at the large, accommodating sofa and saw Caroline sitting there, with her long legs curled under her, saying, "Yes, I think I would——" and holding out her hand with the empty glass to be refilled. He saw her lounging gracefully against the mantelpiece, where the French clock and the miniatures were; lighting another cigarette and murmuring, "If Michael hasn't rung by eleven-thirty." He remembered the evening when he lost his temper with her, cut off her monologue, and said, "I'll take you home"; after which, he had slammed the door and left his keys inside. She had helped him climb through the window and the quarrel had blown away in giggles, and she had won again.

He could hear newsboys shouting in Vigo Street; there could be no news that was not ominous. "And that's the answer," Dennis thought. He could see nothing ahead for any of them, the tight little circle of temporarily-favoured persons to whom all this was important. "It is the last spring; the guillotine is coming down. And after that it won't matter who loves and who is unloved; we are for the dark." How foolish not to be able to be happy now, when there was so little time left.

CHAPTER FOUR

"Oh, dear,——" said Dorothy Knowle. "There's the post-man." She could see him over the top of the hedge, beyond the small strip of garden; he was stopping outside the gate. The second post always arrived just after lunch. Old Dr. Knowle was upstairs taking his sleep. Dorothy's cry of apprehension had no audience except the dog on the hearthrug.

She opened the front door and hurried down the path beside the laurels to meet the vexation half-way. She took the letters; there was a copy of the *British Medical Journal* for her father, a postcard from a friend in Switzerland, a seed-catalogue, and two letters from Michael; one addressed to her father, one to herself. Why, Dorothy wondered, did Michael write so often? It was a passion that mystified her. Letters were a burden to write, an intrusion to receive; and the telephone was, on the whole, worse because it made a noise as well. Dorothy's phobia on the subject of communications from the outside world had once inspired Michael to suggest that her proper place was a nunnery. Anyway, here she was again, feeling fussed and anxious, hurrying to open the nasty thing, with an assurance that something was wrong.

She sat down by the fire in the drawing-room whose main features were chintz and dark mahogany; the room was as it had been in her mother's lifetime, without the natural disorder created by that sweetly inefficient person. The two things that Dorothy liked best in life were order and continuity.

She opened the thick, expensive envelope with the Manchester Square address on the flap, and out came two sheets of Michael's handwriting, with the margin that kept magically straight all down the page.

"Dearest Dorothy,

"I look forward to seeing you on Wednesday, for lunch here. The car will meet your train and take you back in time to catch the 4.10. I do appreciate your break with routine for the purpose of saying good-bye to me."

("He's laughing at me again.")

"As you know, I would have come down for the day if it had been possible to spare the time. I am writing the old man a letter by this post, as I thought he would like it. In any case, as it turns out, I shall be away only six weeks; the idea of going on to the West Coast was too difficult to work out.

"Please do something for me. I fear that it involves visiting Cold Ash, but I can't ask anybody else to do it. On the mantelpiece, in the library, there is a small carved cat, a stone cat, sitting up; a modern thing. You may remember it. Could you collect it and bring it to London with you? I'd like to have it now.

"I may as well break to you the imminence of another battle over Cold Ash; it looks like the last. Mercedes writes me that she has finally decided to make her permanent home in France and that, in her view, the time has come to get rid of the house. That is all right with me. What is *not* all right with me is her idea of putting it at the disposal of a refugee-committee here, who will take it over, including the farms, for use as an agricultural training institution. It would come under a scheme that is operating already in this country and it appears to be one of M's fancies to assist the project.

"I want that house off my mind forever. These people cannot afford to buy it; any idea of holding on, with the place as our joint property, Mercedes acting absentee-land-lord, and a gaggle of impoverished voluntary-workers as tenants, is too wearisome to contemplate. I would rather give the house away. At least our domestic problem seems to have reached a climax and, if there were ever a likelihood of divorce, the time is now. I think that this prospect may cheer you, despite the tangle of obstacles that must inevitably precede it.

"There is, I still believe (though I know that you don't), a basis of goodwill on either side which may make the solution possible."

Dorothy said, "*There!*" to the dog, and was not sure what she meant by There, except that her afternoon's programme of gardening was dislocated and that Mercedes was behaving badly again.

"And he's still frightened of her; after all these years.

77

She won't get a letter like this; oh dear, no; she'll get one of his polite, deferential invitations to discuss the whole thing next time she comes to England. Do you think I'm a fool?" she launched at Michael's photograph. "Yes; you do; everybody does; I'm just your dull old sister with a face like a hatchet, who hates Mercedes and Doesn't Understand. Well, you're wrong. I do understand. I understand why you are making your ultimatum to me instead of to her; bolstering up your courage by putting your refusal down on paper. You'll agree to her scheme; just you see if you don't. This letter is bluff; and she'll call it, as usual."

When Dr. Knowle came into the room, hesitantly shuffling, with his bent knees and his round shoulders and his newspaper folded open at the chess-problem, Dorothy said, "Father dear, I have to go over to Cold Ash. I think I'll go now, before tea. Michael wants an ornament out of the library."

"Michael always wants something, doesn't he?"

The mild resentment of the old man for his distinguished son often expressed itself in similar grumbles. Dorothy said, "This is nothing difficult; it's a stone cat off the mantelpiece. I can slip it into my pocket and take it up to him to-morrow; he's sailing Thursday, remember?"

"What's the point of taking a stone cat to America, I should like to know?"

"He didn't say he wanted to take it to America."

"Stone cats," Dr. Knowle muttered, as though he had been subject to a plague of these all his life. He settled himself in his chair.

"Here are your letters. If you want an early cup of tea, just ring and ask Mrs. Chandler to get it for you. She'll be here till five and I shall be back before then."

"Thank you, dear. Good girl——" he said, absently; she went out, put on her hat and coat in the hall, and pushed her bicycle down the path.

It was an afternoon of still air and spring sunshine, soothing to the ruffled sensations brought by the postman, by the image of Mercedes. Dorothy gave herself up to the sentimental journey, knowing that it was sentimental and hugging it while she shook a wise head at her own weakness.

The road turned off to the left, before the main road reached Telham, and wound inland. It was one of the roads that she had known all her life. Her childhood and Michael's had been spent in the small Sussex town on the spine of the haunted ridge where Harold had died in battle. It was important to her.

Cold Ash had been primarily important. She and Michael had ridden their bicycles this way. In those days the house had stood empty; it was the secret, cherished place where they could play their games and explore. They had planned to buy it and live in it when they were grown-up. She wished not to recall that it was Mercedes who had made that plan work out for Michael. She saw the stone chimneys rising beyond the hump of the ploughed field and thought, "Forbidden ground; for me it has been forbidden ground always."

She came to the gate. It was not an imposing entrance. The road had been cut across the original grounds of the house and this had made the front garden a mere oblong of lawn behind the yew-hedge. The hedge did not grow high. You could see from here that the house was of Queen Anne architecture, with a narrow stone terrace dividing it from the lawn.

Dorothy pushed her bicycle up the short drive. She came to the main door, with the chipped urns on either side of it, the shallow, mossy steps. The side of the house faced the lawn; the front faced only this baffling courtyard, with a high wall running round it and a circular fountain in the middle. She felt the beauty and the melancholy of the place possess her again. As children they had said to each other that Cold Ash was like crying in your sleep. It was only when they pushed open the door in the wall and waded through the ragged garden to look out over the weald that they had ceased to feel mysterious and sad.

The servant who opened the door said that the tenants were out for the afternoon; of course Miss Knowle could go up to the library to fetch the ornament. Dorothy crossed the hall and mounted the graceful, curving stairway; she opened the library door. She looked quickly about her, spying for any changes that the tenants might have made. The library still looked much as it had looked seven years ago, when she had assisted with the inventory. The bookcases went almost up to the carved ceiling. On either side of the fireplace, that was perfectly of the period, there stood the embroidered screens. The bronze Demeter was there, and the long table with its milky polish and claw feet. The globe stood in its corner, touched by a rounded splash of sunlight.

Dorothy went to the mantelpiece and picked up the cat. She remembered it now; it was the work of a celebrated modern sculptor who was a friend of Mercedes. It was a neat slender cat, with its front paws close together, the triangular mask of its face wise and supercilious. It fitted comfortably into her hand and she played with it for a moment, thinking that the fawn-colour of the stone was the colour of an actual Siamese cat. She put it in her pocket and went over to the far window.

This was the view that she loved. Below the north lawn and the thin rose trees, the garden petered out, the fields began. She saw the roofs of the farm buildings, the waves of land solid on the clear, washed-looking sky. They were Michael's roofs; it was Michael's land. How easily, she thought, he might have found peace here.

It was no inaccuracy of her devotion that invested him with this desire for peace, always unfulfilled. She knew what he wanted because he was a man and unmysterious. Poor Michael. In manner and behaviour, he was still a rock; more of a rock now, perhaps, than ever before; his outward calm persisted. But she saw the truth; that he was a person who had suffered inner torment ever since he met Mercedes. With admirable foolish loyalty, he kept silence, never admitting how often he cursed himself for the mistake of his marriage. He did not need to admit it. Dorothy knew.

Mercedes was a woman, and Mercedes was therefore to be blamed. Dorothy believed the sage who had first said, "If

there were no bad women there would be no bad men."
Michael's sins she saw always in proportion. They were male,
with his virtues. As a young woman she had thought that his
cardinal virtue was his love of hard work; he was always a
simple person inspired with a dæmon of energy. Their parents
had been proud of this; they had denied themselves much for
Michael. It was Mercedes who had torn the pattern across;
Mercedes who had turned Michael against his family, married
him half-way through his training and squashed the idea of
his taking over his father's practice. From that hour she had
dominated and terrorised him; but she had made the mistake
of trying to fit him into her own rich and restless world.

"At least she'll never come here again," Dorothy said,
staring at the sunlit hill and the sky. Perhaps the worst years
of all had been the years wherein Cold Ash had become a
playground for Mercedes; a centre for week-end parties. With
quiet horror she recalled their ingredients; artists, actors,
stupid people whose faces were photographed on society-pages.
She had seen Michael enduring them politely, as he endured
all Mercedes' persecutions, being quiet because he was afraid.
She did not blame him for this; men were frequently afraid of
their wives, and the cold, flashy quality that she found in
Mercedes was peculiarly discomforting.

At least Michael had scored a revenge by becoming famous
on his own account, by falling out of love with her. Herself
an immaculately virtuous woman, Dorothy knew that she
should not be consoled by this last thought, but there it was;
quietly consoling. Still Mercedes had the whip-hand; she
could withhold from Kim the chance of a second marriage,
of a peaceful home, a wife who would love him, a family.

"If only I could believe that he would *ever* stand up to her.
But it's too late now, no matter what he says. It's always the
same. Three years ago, she wanted to keep the house and
Michael didn't; so they kept it. Now she wants to turn it into
some horrible institution; so that will happen."

She turned from the window; it was time to be going; time
for her father's tea.

ii

"You sit there," said Joan Bridges, indicating the one comfortable chair in the small boarding-house bedroom.

"Can't I help you?"

"Not in those clothes; you should just sit and be decorative; there's nothing much to do, anyway." Joan had escaped early from the typewriting-agency off the Strand that employed her services. Before Caroline's arrival, she had arranged the flowers in the black pottery vase, pulled the screen round the fitted basin in the corner, spread the large yellow cloth over the card-table and set upon it the bright blue china, the Woolworth knives and forks. Now she arranged the slices of cold ham and liver-sausage on the blue dish; she cut the French bread that squeaked under the knife; she uncorked the bottle of sherry. "You can pour it out. Oh, and better lock the door in case Miss G. is prowling." To eat upstairs was against the boarding-house rules; but with Caroline here, it was unthinkable to sit in the public dining-room eating the dull food and surrounded by other people at the small table that shivered on its uneven legs.

"Tell . . ." said Joan. She opened the tin of soup and poured it into the saucepan; she knelt by the fire, stirring the soup above the gas-ring; she drank her sherry and followed the story as devotedly as though she were reading an instalment of a serial.

"Do *you* think I am crazy?"

"No," said Joan, "I couldn't imagine your giving up America anyway. What is Michael's view?"

"I haven't told him yet. And blow me," said Caroline, "it's the first time I've ever been frightened of telling him anything."

"I don't think you need be."

There was nothing that Joan did not know about Michael Knowle; she had met him once, for a period of three minutes and she knew him better than she knew any man living. His character and customs fitted all her preconceived ideas of romantic heroes; he went in with Byron, Shelley, Sydney

Carton and other forgivably immoral persons of genius. Even his looks admitted him to that gallery. He shed a lustre upon his smallest idiosyncracy, making it important that he smoked fifty cigarettes a day, that his favourite foods were curry and caviar; that he found the Richard Bennett murder-case more fascinating than the case of Crippen or Bywaters; that he suffered from insomnia; that when his mind was at peace he whistled *Loch Lomond* and that when he was harassed, he sang one line of a song dating from the Boer war; "Oh, why did I leave my little back-room in Bloomsburee?"

She liked him especially for never losing his temper and for worshipping cats, with a preference towards tabbies.

Joan tasted the soup, sat back on her heels and looked thoughtfully at Caroline, whose face in the firelight was pale and fated, the way that lovers could be expected to look.

"You know," said Joan, "I don't really see the point of telling him at all. There's nothing he can do about it anyway. You've dished yourself with Rokov; Rokov isn't a friend of his like Jay; he couldn't put those pieces together again if he tried. You've split with Dennis; Michael can't retrieve that. What is the point of worrying him? Go off to America and have a lovely time without spoiling the start."

"And tell him—what?"

"Oh . . . tell him that Rokov cancelled the appointment," said Joan limpidly.

"Just lie . . . ?"

"Just lie. For once."

Caroline rose from the chair and began to pace; as usual, to watch her walk made Joan feel dumpy and fat. From the days of their childhood, Caroline had seemed a spectacular and unlikely companion. She had been the long-legged, queer little girl whose aunt lived in the Georgian house at the end of the High Street. She was invited to tea with Joan's large, noisy family at the vicarage; on one of their escapes to the greenhouse she had explained with pride that she was born out of wedlock; she had been the one who went away to boarding-school while Joan attended day-school at home, involving the exchange of long, facetious letters. Joan never learned to take her affection for granted; when they grew up it seemed likely that they would drift out of each other's orbit, particularly when Caroline went to live with her mother and Joan began her secretarial training. She saw looming, between the R.A.D.A. and the Polytechnic, a gulf that had not divided the Georgian house from the vicarage. She was prepared then for Caroline to shoot off into fame, to achieve glittering friends, and, in due course, to send her dress-circle seats for a major triumph.

"And she is still my best friend," Joan said to herself, carrying the saucepan to the table.

It was odd, she thought, pouring the soup, to compare their two careers and to see that Caroline was a failure while she herself advanced steadily. Merritt's Typewriting Agency chose its employees carefully; it specialised in literary work. As head-typist, Joan read and checked manuscripts signed with august names; she got a preview of popular novels, plays that ran, short stories that sold. The work satisfied her because it was a contribution to literature. She prized her telephone-contacts with the creators and found their occasional appearances in the office rewarding. She made enough money to save regularly, and here again it was odd to think that she was so often in a position to lend Caroline sums varying between five shillings and five pounds. Sometimes she waited long for the repayment, but it always came.

"Anyway," said Joan, "eat first and decide afterwards. Everything gets out of proportion on an empty stomach, or a lack of sleep."

" 'Old weariness with his rust-eaten knife'," said Caroline, seating herself at the table.

"Yes . . . Cameron-Wilson, isn't it?"

"I don't know who wrote it; Michael quoted it last night. Do you know every poem that has ever been written?"

"Not quite," said Joan complacently. "But I think you'll find that one in *Magpies In Picardy*; poem to An Old Boot In A Ditch; we'll look it up afterwards."

Caroline glanced round the cheap wooden shelves that held Joan's library. "If I never act again, I can at least complete my reading. I could set myself a course, and include all those old numbers that one always pretends to have read: *Paradise Lost* and *Tristram Shandy* and *Crime and Punishment*. By God, I'm hungry; may I have some more liver-sausage?"

Joan said pensively, "You aren't really a neurotic, because you can always eat and always sleep."

"Well, is Michael a neurotic? He doesn't sleep."

"I don't know."

"Anybody *less*. . . . Look, if I do tell him the lie, he's bound to find it out. That play will go into production with some daisy or other in the lead."

"Rokov could have engaged her for the part before he saw you; then had a temptation; then developed a conscience this morning."

"Y-yes. Possibly."

"In any case, whatever you say to Michael, he'll forgive you."

She knew this because Michael was too gentle ever to be angry; too charming a person to rank among the Spoilers-of-the-Fun. He had the soft heart of all the romantic lovers; that was why his wife could put it across him. Joan's picture of Mercedes fitted neatly into the frame occupied by the implacable wives of fiction.

She rose and put the eclairs on the two glass plates. Caroline said, "What a nice life, if there were only food in it; one could be a single-hearted gourmet."

"You couldn't. You were born to trouble. And I was born a pudding. And I shal marry a nice dull man, and go on having adventures inside my head and between the covers of books."

She did not add, "And share your love-affairs at second-hand," because this would embarrass Caroline; Caroline might, also, be perplexed by the suggestion that she was akin to the novelists and dramatists who patronised the typewriting agency where Joan made her practical, necessary contribution. Caroline would stare and say, "Blow me," if Joan told her that she thought of her as an artist, not only in her career but in her life; that the love-affair itself seemed to Joan to rank as a work of art. It was immoral; it was altogether outside the canons of the vicarage; but it was like the best art; it was there and it obeyed its own rules.

The contribution that Joan made to it was also there; whether she served as confidante, knowing that to be in love was to be lonely, or whether she fed the situation with the varied supplies that it needed; filling the gaps in Caroline's knowledge of poetry; borrowing manuals of surgery from the cousin who was a medical student; agreeing on a dozen occasions to the request, "May I say that I was with you?"; typing the notes for Michael's lecture to the B.M.A. when his secretary failed him. She had helped Caroline towards a perception, if not a toleration, of Mercedes. Joan had never seen Mercedes, but she was better qualified than Caroline to understand a wife's point of view. She had been brought up in a Christian family that belonged to the accepted social pattern; she could see why a marriage was different from a love-affair.

And she was content with her rôle, not only because she loved Caroline but because, at secondhand, she was in love with Michael, who gave her no more trouble than Byron or Shelley gave her, but who, being alive, was more fun.

"And don't think," she said, "that I wouldn't change places with you any time. Most respectable women would. Going to America for a month, with a chap and a lot of new clothes——"

"And a sense of guilt," said Caroline, "that would make my mother very happy to contemplate."

CHAPTER FIVE

IN the Adams family there was a rule that nobody should come to Wynstay's study while he was working. This rule was broken systematically by his wife, by their three children and by any one of the domestic staff who might be passing the door. It was Daniel Adams who opened the door now; he said, "Hey," doubtfully, remaining half-in and half-out, the family compromise adopted by all apparently in the belief that it absolved them from the sin of interruption. Wynstay, cut off behind his desk and sitting in the white glare from the daylight lamp, saw the walls of the room in shadow and a shadowy boy hovering on the semi-darkness of the hall.

Dan said, "There's a woman for you."

"Gee, thanks. Where?" Wynstay asked with heavy sarcasm.

"On the telephone. I said——" his speech was obstructed by bubble-gum. Wynstay picked up the extension-telephone beside him and the boy dashed away; he could be heard sliding to and fro outside.

"Hullo. Is that you, Wyn?" He remembered the cool voice with the British accent, but he could not place it.

"This is Mercedes Knowle speaking."

"I'll be darned," he said. "Where are you calling from?"

"About half a mile away."

She was never forthcoming; always you had to ask her questions.

"What are you doing in Boston?"

She said that she had designed the sets for a play that was opening here and added that it was destined to close shortly in New York.

"You confuse me," said Wynstay, "I thought you were in Europe."

"I'm on my way. But I was snared into doing this thing first."

"Nobody ever snared you into doing anything that you didn't want to do, my friend," he thought. He said, "Well, come and dine with us. Lee's out; I don't know what the programme is."

"I can't dine to-night, Wyn. But I do very much want to see you both. I'm here till Sunday."

He scribbled her number in the middle of his manuscript-page; she said that she was staying with the Newells on Commonwealth Avenue, and he could not remember who the Newells were. "Is it true," he asked, "that you're going to Europe for good?"

"Yes."

"Is it the best moment to pick?" And that, he knew, was a silly question; if there were going to be a war, the place to look for Mercedes would be in the middle of it. Restless people liked wars.

Perhaps it was her influence that made him restless now. After she had hung up, he sat idle, looking out through his windows to the Charles River, steel-grey in the sunless afternoon. He could still hear Dan sliding and his younger daughter yelling somewhere in the house. His study was suddenly a bore; the exact study where a best-selling author might be expected to work; it was ponderous with his legend. Even the bookshelves that held the cherished classics now looked self-conscious and contrived, as though the books were all dummies, painted backs. There was the rich soft carpet; the table where the signed photographs of other successful persons were assembled. He glanced upward at his own portrait above the mantelpiece; a presentation portrait in a thick gold frame. Wynstay knew that he looked like a happy monkey; that his small dark head and small dark face had not the impressive melancholy given to them by the artist; that was the way that the public preferred writers to look. He thought, as he had thought before: "I'm too successful; too rich; too happy. I'll never do a first-rate piece of work again," and grinned at himself.

His wife put her head round the door. Lee was like Vermeer's Portrait of a Young Girl; with a high round forehead, pale blue eyes and a fair skin. She was still wrapped in her mink coat; she wore a silly hat. It was the year of the beginning of silly hats and this was a cock-eyed velvet chimney.

"Hi. Do I interrupt you?"

88

"Why no," said Wynstay. "They all come here; stick around; you'll meet everybody sooner or later; this is Grand Central Station."

"Have the children been bothering you?"

"I wouldn't say that. Jean was in for an hour or so, dragging a fire-engine across the part of the floor where the rug leaves off. Marilyn came to borrow three dollars and got away with five. Dan's trying out his skates in the hall. The telephone rang fourteen times. Won't you sit down?"

Lee said, "I thought you might like to know we're dining with Michael Knowle. He wants us to meet him at the Ritz Bar for cocktails first. Isn't that something? I'd no idea he was in this country; I met him on the street."

"After which," said Wynstay, "I suppose it would sound pretty silly to say that Mercedes just called."

Lee stared at him. "Do you mean that?"

"Sure. She just hung up."

"Oh, *honestly*," said Lee in exasperated bewilderment. "Did she mention Michael?"

"No. Did he mention her?"

"No. I invited him to dine and he said he was giving a friend a drink at the Ritz and would we join them and go to dinner."

"A friend. Couldn't be Mercedes, could it?"

Lee said that was too corny a line for Michael to take and that in any case the description of Mercedes as his friend would be an outrageous mis-statement.

"Well, I've given up having theories about those two. I can't even remember when we last saw Mercedes."

"When she came to the ranch," Lee said, "and that'll be three years in May; before she went back to Europe."

Wynstay thought about it. He remembered that he had found Mercedes easy company that time; she had fitted into the background and liked the simple things. His memories of her, from an earlier summer in England, when they had visited Cold Ash, were less happy. He saw the uneasy marriage; the beautiful house; Mercedes with all the manners

of a hostess and all the detachment of a cat walking alone.
She was like a cat anyway, he thought; a dark, neat cat.
A striking and troublous creature. His sympathies were with
Michael; Lee's, he thought, went the other way, though she
professed to like Michael well enough.

"Going to call her?" he asked.

"No, I guess not; not now."

"If you're hoping for a line on it from Michael, you'll get
no place. Tell him Mercedes is in town and he'll say, 'Yes, I
know' and change the subject."

"I'm not in need of a line," said Lee, "and as you know I
refuse to take sides. I figure that they are two people quite
hopelessly unsuited, anyway."

"But she wants him back; it's she who's holding out on the
divorce, isn't it?"

"Maybe they're joining up again," said Lee.

"That," said Wynstay, "is the least probable of the
solutions."

ii

After she came out of the beauty-shop, Caroline decided
that she was hungry. Michael had said that he would not
be back before half-past five. She walked down Newbury
Street, looking in the shop-windows. She was still furiously
impressed with the fact of being here. She repeated, "I am
in Boston; this is Boston." It was a city with a confusing
layout. After twenty-four hours she had acquired a small
island in it; the elegant island round the Ritz Hotel. Its
coastlines were the green Common sloping up towards the
State House, the shop-windows of Boylston Street and the
Georgian façades on Beacon Hill.

She ventured off the island; she dodged through a line of
traffic and turned left. Elegance ended here; the city became
practical; crowds were pouring down into subway entrances;
the dusk was blue and noisy; the lighted windows flared.
She went into a large drug-store on a corner, wandered

round the counters for a while, appraising the unfamiliar things, then sat on a high stool and ordered a banana-split.

She saw herself reflected in the glass behind the counter, the new-looking hair curled high, the face that was shiny-smooth from the heat of the drier. "I think I look American now; perhaps it is the hair; perhaps it is having lipstick on and no powder. I wish I knew why their faces look different." She listened devotedly to the voices on either side; it was still odd to hear people talking with this accent; they were fun to imitate. "And I said to Mabel, 'My, this wash looks dingy'," remarked the woman on her right. "My, this wash looks dingy," Caroline murmured rapturously.

She felt cosy in this place and the Ritz felt like home. Nothing in New York had felt like home; nor, she thought, did New York feel like a city at all; it was a sharp and persuasive corridor, full of impossible *luxe* that tapered unexpectedly into squalor. It went vertical when you expected it to be horizontal, and vice versa. After ten days in New York she felt that she had been for ten days in a cocktail-shaker. Here was something that stayed still. And here was a leisured interval; they had stolen Boston for these two nights between New York and Washington; here they could share a suite undisturbed. At the hospital Michael would tell his medical acquaintances that he was going back to New York to-night. "And we have this evening; and to-night, and half to-morrow; and all the time on the train. And then Washington."

She grinned at the woman next to her, who was feeding ice-cream to a small boy girt with a large toy revolver. He was one of those strong lumpy children, who threshed and folded up like jack-knives and slid off things and had to be hauled. On the woman's face there was content and pride, then exasperation, then the loving smile again, then a harassed frown. It was like watching a signal in Morse-code.

Caroline made a face at the child and encouraged him to naughtiness; she played for him the game that consisted of pretending to pull the top-joint off her thumb. Having flexible joints, she could do it convincingly and the child went on saying, "Again," and spilling his ice-cream. When she paid her check and climbed off the stool, he roared. She heard shouts of "I don' wanner" echoing after her.

She came out into the dusk. "It has hints of London and hints of Paris," she thought. It was good to be striding through the unfamiliar streets to find Michael. All the way, on this journey, she had liked the hours of being alone because there was so rich a reward waiting at the end of them. Their subterfuges were smaller and easier than the ways that they took in London. The distance between two bedroom-doors in an hotel was a simpler journey than the taxi-ride from the Rufford to Manchester Square. This was a new continent; a lucky place. Here were no bills, no obligations, no Spoilers-of-the-Fun. The only shadows fell when thinking, "This is how it might be, always," in seeing the days speed off the calendar and in recalling, "this time two weeks ago." "*Past the half-way mark*," said the executioner at her ear; she looked away from his axe toward now.

She entered the side-door of the Ritz. At the reception-desk, the clerk handed her a note from Michael.

"My love, I am in the bar, giving a drink to Wynstay Adams and his wife. You needn't pretend to have read his books. I've acquired them both for dinner because Lee Adams caught me unawares on my way back from the Mass. General; she asked me to dine at their house, so I had to get out of that one.

"In any case you'll like them. I shan't say anything about us; I simply told her that I was giving a friend drinks and dinner. They are quite easy and won't need explanations. Blessings. M."

Caroline cocked her head on one side; she thought it over as she went up in the lift. "There had better be a reason for me," she thought, "Michael always sails over details, but I do not like to be caught unawares." As always, when there was a game of this character to be played, she set to work elaborately; talking to herself while she changed her clothes.

"I am staying at the Copley-Plaza. I am a highly successful English actress—makes a change, as you might say. I may as well be rich, too. Why am I rich? Result of a dead aunt. I am here on holiday, but idly running my eye over some of the New York hits, with the idea of taking one over to London. How well do I know Michael? Christian-name terms, but a casual acquaintance; I met him through Jay Brookfield. And he means nothing to me because I am devouringly in love with a Paris banker; called Raoul."

As at all rehearsals, she began to fit herself inside the skin of this person. It was a refreshing game. When she stood before the long looking-glass she saw a stranger's expression on her face; she looked detached and social, as though the imaginary character were chasing Caroline Seward out. "*Cheri*," she murmured in the direction of Raoul, "*tu m'enivres*."

It seemed a waste of the suite not to walk through the sitting-room; it was the first suite that Caroline had occupied. It was respectably achieved, without false signatures; they had given Michael the bedroom and sitting-room; Caroline the bedroom that adjoined these. As she went through the sitting-room, she saw that Michael had moved the little stone cat. She had put it in the middle of the mantelpiece and it was gone. She had found the cat in his cabin-trunk on the voyage, while she was hunting a book; at once she had felt an illogical affection for it. Michael had seemed shy about the cat. He had put it back in the trunk, saying, "That's the original; you've probably seen copies." It was the work of a Rumanian sculptor called Alencz, and it used to be at Cold Ash; anything from Cold Ash was inimical, but not this cat. "Where has it gone?" Caroline wondered, looking at the space on the mantelpiece. She saw that the time was six o'clock and went downstairs.

Standing at the top of the steps that led down into the bar, she saw the three of them. Michael had not yet seen her; she could spy upon him for a moment, using the eyes and the mind of the other Miss Seward. "There is Michael Knowle; I think he is rather beautiful in profile; difficult to see why that head should be romantic on those well-shaped, formal shoulders. They say he is married to a woman who won't divorce him. If it weren't for Raoul, I might enjoy a flirtation with Mr. Knowle."

He was leaning forward, telling something, about to laugh. Adams was a little dark monkey of a man, with a bulgy forehead and a wide grin; his wife was just a tall velvet hat, bright lips, and long red-nailed fingers laced beside her cheek. Now she came near the table; the two men rose and they all looked quite different. She greeted Michael as coolly as the pretence demanded. "He isn't," she thought, "a good actor. If I were the Adams', I should guess from his eyes."

"And you're British, so I love you," said Adams.

"Why you didn't marry a British girl, I'll never know," said Lee.

"Because no British girl ever asked me. Here, waiter, we'll do this again; and what for you, Miss Seward?" Lee was taking Michael on from an earlier conversation. "But the Nazis want the hell scared out of them; that's all they need; why doesn't somebody do it?"

Michael smiled patiently. "Not for want of sage transatlantic advice, I assure you."

"Break it up, Lee," said Wynstay. Caroline saw the darting glance that she gave him, out of those light, hard eyes. She was an expensive-looking person, Caroline thought, appraising the gloves, handbag and jewellery. "She is tough but kind; probably a very good mother; and probably with money of her own." The eyes met hers now; it was a sympathetic smile.

"Are you having fun?" Lee asked.

" Oh yes."

Michael said, "Caroline is rapidly qualifying for the-most-appreciative-British-visitor-of-the-month award."

"Then don't stay too long in Boston."

"Alas, I cannot stay too long anywhere. But *why* don't you like Boston?"

"Lee's a Californian," said Adams, "She suffers New England under the terms of her marriage vows."

"And, my God, I suffer. But only till May. Any hope of

your visiting the ranch this summer?" she said to Michael; he shook his head.

"What do they do with you in a war, anyway? Leave you in Harley Street mending bomb casualties?"

"No," said Michael, "I go into the R.A.M.C."

If only, Caroline thought, they would leave it unsaid; they brought the black fear of last September out of hiding. While they went on talking, the memories returned; newspaper-placards saying, "Keep Calm—And Dig"; the queue for candles and matches; the hall where she had fitted her face into a rubber gas-mask; the realisation that her sense of right and wrong was finally blotted out; her only reaction to war was that it must take Michael away and kill him; until the shamed relief cut short the nightmare, and the candles, the matches, the gas-mask and first-aid case, all in their cardboard boxes, were stacked at the bottom of the wardrobe. She supposed that they were still there.

Oh, to be an American; to live beyond the range of the shadow; and that was a thought not to be spoken to Michael, who looked calmly at war.

"Well, I'll be there too, if anybody can use me," said Adams. "Nuts," said Lee, "He's nuts," and blew him a kiss. "He'll go to war for Shakespeare and Runnymede and Windsor Castle and Charles Dickens." That mercifully ended it, because Adams began to talk to her about Dickens and it was a relief to find that he liked *A Tale of Two Cities*. "According to tradition," said Caroline pompously, "no Dickensian likes the *Tale of Two Cities* at all." This she had learned from Michael and from Joan Bridges. Adams appeared to know the book by heart; at the end of the third round of Martinis they were still in the wine-shop with the Defarges.

"And it is the only thing that has ever persuaded me that I could die a martyr's death."

" 'The murmuring of many voices.' "

" 'Twenty-three.' "

" 'Buried how long?' "

"For half an hour; both of you," Michael fired at them

from across the table. She was careful to look at him with the eyes of the other Miss Seward. "And," he said, "if you're prepared to come up for air, I booked a table at Locke-Ober's for seven-forty-five; it's that now."

"Have you eaten at Locke-Ober's yet?" Adams asked her. "No; and strictly speaking I oughtn't to come out to dinner at all. I'd vowed to shut myself in my room at the Copley-Plaza"—Michael's eyebrows flickered—"and read a play."

"Which play is it?"

"Oh, one an agent sent to me my first day in New York. I haven't even opened the envelope. It's a study of schizophrenia," she added, aiming the remark at Michael, who nipped in the corners of his mouth, as always when trying not to laugh, and avoided her eye.

There was an argument about the bill, with Adams saying, "This is mine; it always *was* mine:" and Lee rising neatly, gathering up a dark mink coat from the chair beside her.

They stood in the foyer, waiting for the taxi. She saw Lee glance at her now with the same appraisal that she herself had given Lee an hour ago. "You'll freeze without a coat, won't you?" Lee said.

"Perhaps I will; I'll get it." She turned to Michael, "Have you got the key or have I?"

iii

"Everything," Caroline reminded herself, "is always worse in the morning. And the moral is that no lie is proof against three Martinis." She felt sad and stupid waiting for her breakfast in the elegant sitting-room of the suite. Michael had said imperturbably that it did not matter, that Lee and Wynstay were under no illusions about him anyway. The evening had not suffered; if possible, it had gone more easily afterwards, to end with Lee saying, "Oh come to the ranch this summer, you two. Europe can fold quite nicely without your assistance."

"But *oh dear*," Caroline thought, rising to let in the waiter with the breakfast. She signed the check, gave him a quarter and stared at the table as appreciatively as though it were a masterpiece in the Tate Gallery. She admired the cracked ice surrounding the grapefruit, the table-napkin swaddling the toast and hot rolls, the two jugs of cream and the silver dishes. But melancholy stood just behind her back; when Michael came from the bedroom, he said:

"Caroline, I cannot believe that your appetite has failed you at the second egg."

"Well, it has," she said flatly. "Must you really go to that hospital again?"

"Yes; and at all speed." He kissed the top of her head. "You're not still being sad about the key, are you?"

"It is like hot wool and wires in my soul."

"It didn't matter; and it was really superbly funny."

"Bah," she said, giving him his coffee. "Why couldn't I leave well alone, instead of doing all that embroidery?"

"Stop it, darling. I've told you, Lee and Wyn are not precisely the Archbishop of Canterbury."

"It will continue to be a curse and a reproach. What time will you get back, do you think?"

"God knows." He looked vague and placid, reading the headlines of the *New York Times*.

"May I pack for you?"

"As a penance?"

"Well, I should like to. And that would save your coming back here. I can meet you at the train. Leave me enough money for the bill and I could even pay that."

Michael said, "What about your lunch?"

"I'll eat it."

He looked at her meditatively.

"What horrible thing are they doing this morning?" she asked.

"Removal of a spleen," said Michael. "To cure what would otherwise be a fatal jaundice in a baby. It is new."

"I couldn't eat an egg and think about that at the same time."

"Nor can I," said Michael. "But only because I'm so

97

late. Bless you, darling. Here's the money; and here's your ticket."

Nobody, she reflected, could leave a room as rapidly as Michael could. She saw a succession of doors and Michael slipping through them, away from parties where other people hesitated on their farewells; away from the last moments of parting. "It is a gift; I am a loiterer." She poured herself some more coffee and picked up the newspaper. After the foreign news, she turned first to the theatrical pages.

She read the paragraph two or three times; at first the impact of the name, in conjunction with the word "Boston" and the date, spun a nonsensical pattern. At the third reading she believed it. The sets and costumes for *Weather Variable*, to be seen this week in its try-out at the Colonial Theatre, Boston, prior to a New York opening, were designed by Mercedes Barry. "Absent from stage-work for almost five years," said the paragraph; "one of the most interesting of scenic artists"; "she will be remembered for the masterpiece——"

Caroline, with the sensation that her stomach had shut like a box, laid the *New York Times* on the floor.

Presently she said aloud, "funny, if you were here; if I had travelled three thousand miles for the privilege of meeting you. If you were staying in this hotel. . . . 'Struth, I thought you were in France. Why can't you use your married name, anyway? After the fuss you make about hanging on to Michael, one would think. . . ." She got up and began to pace the floor. "Supposing Michael meets Ќer face to face. It would be like coming face to face with Medusa. Oh, really . . . wouldn't you know she'd get into this journey somehow?"

It was absurd to feel thus despairing and thus endangered. She had no proof that Mercedes was anywhere in the vicinity; but it looked like a third unlucky thing. "*Jamais deux sans trois*; and the first was the key and the second was Michael having to spend the morning at the Mass. General, and the third is our chum with the scenic talent." She sat

98

down at the writing-table and began a letter to Joan Bridges.

"Darling,

"I am sorry I haven't written again, but oh dear oh dear oh bloody dear, what a thing New York is. Wildly exciting and at moments unexpectedly beautiful, but a bit much. Now, as you see, we are cooling off in a Puritan atmosphere. (There really *is* an hotel called the Puritan, and I thought it would be fun to stay there and write to all my friends on the note-paper.) This is the nicest Ritz; and we have a suite. But Mercedes is with us. At least I have just read that a play with sets designed by her is being tried out round the corner. And my hunch is that she's round the corner too, but I can't warn Michael who has gone to the local hospital to see about a spleen; not Mercedes' spleen, which I feel I am about to experience at first hand. I have to pack while Michael is away and as I descend to the hall surrounded by pieces of luggage stamped Michael C. Knowle, a hand will fall on my shoulder and a voice like a buzz-saw will emerge from a mouth like a steel trap. Perhaps it would be more intelligent to call down to the reception-desk first and inquire how many women there are standing about with mouths like steel traps.

"I have, of course, the haziest impression of her from the few photographs I've seen in the papers; but my mental picture is hideously clear. Opening gambit. . . .'How do you do, Mrs. Knowle; I've heard so much about you. In fact, not to put too fine a point upon it, I've heard so bloody much that if I saw a two-ton lorry going over your person, I should jump on top to add to the weight. . . .'"

"One is not jealous of her, because, in her context and Michael's, she is like a point, having position but no magnitude. But the sight of her name immediately after breakfast makes me feel very queer."

The telephone rang. "That," said Caroline aloud, "will be Mercedes." She did not know whether the expansion below her ribs, the watery dizziness inside her skull, were pleasant or unpleasant; she recognised only her reaction to any moment of drama. She began to talk vivaciously as she picked up the telephone, saying to an invisible companion, "Oh, but I call that absolutely ridiculous; hullo."

"Hello, there; this is Lee Adams."

"Good morning. Did you want Michael? I'm afraid he's out."

"Never mind; I just called to say what fun we had last night. We wondered if by any chance you'd both have time for a drink with us before you get on the train?"

"Oh, dear, I doubt it. I'm meeting Michael at the train at three. I shan't see him before."

There was a pause; then Lee said, "Are you alone? Then why not come and lunch here? For heaven's sake say no if you've any interesting prospects. There'll only be me and the children."

"But I would like to; very much." She scribbled, "6, Charles River Square" on the pad beside the telephone. She took a leisured bath and reviewed her clothes, that were beginning to exhibit the strain of being on show for three weeks. The valet took away a suit to be pressed, a pair of shoes to be polished; "and I must try to wear a hat because Boston is a hat place. I can take it off when I get there." She held up a stocking to the light. "I wish I were one of those women with a maid. Like Mercedes; hers of course is a devoted character who has been with her for years, and travelled with her from Sark to Stamboul. I will *not* let her spoil my morning. I will pack for Michael."

This was the kind of task that she liked, thinking always that it must be good to share his practical existence in addition to his bed and his leisure. It would be satisfying to work with him, to be his anæsthetist, or even the fluting secretary at the appointment desk in Manchester Square. Most of all, she would have liked to look after him when he was ill, but Michael was seldom ill and when he was he retired into solitude and welcomed nobody.

Presently she remembered the stone cat and looked for it in vain. He must, she concluded, have packed it already; and there was no time for a thorough search because she must pack her own things. She shook out sheaves of tissue-paper, whirled dresses from the wardrobe, uncovered the sediment of the journey, the improbable souvenirs; there was a carved rabbit from Chinatown, a feathered bird from a night-club gala, a propelling pencil bought on the ship; a folder of postcards from the top of the Empire State. She looked ahead suddenly and saw herself playing with these things in a London room.

Across the future there fell the warning shadows. Worst and heaviest, the lie that she had told to Michael, the first lie. She had bought this glorious adventure with it, and there was no reason why it should ever be revealed. And yet it must. "I must tell him, before we get home; that it was I who cancelled the interview with Rokov——" She heard Joan's voice saying, "Why? Why tell him? What good will that do?"

"Because," she argued, shutting down the lid of the trunk, "I'll have to. There is something that goes wrong with me if I don't tell things. It has been there always; it was the trouble when I lived with mother and Leonard; I couldn't tell; I had to conceal and not talk. And when I can't, something happens; a sort of tangling-up of my spiritual machinery. People who are naturally dignified and reserved can keep things back without suffering this sort of poisoning. Michael can, I know. Not me. Everything must be known, and exposed. . . ."

Absent-mindedly, she opened the door to the valet without putting on a dressing-gown over her under-clothes; this diverted her. "As though I were making a practical illustration of the credo," she said, and giggled. She was gay by the time that she had dressed and painted her face with all the new equipment bought in New York. She gave up the idea of the hat. She paid the bill, told the porter to have the luggage brought down to the hall and strolled through the foyer, looking for Mercedes. "Two possibles and one probable," Caroline decided, as she left the Ritz. "I'm willing to bet on the one with the silver fox and the snarl."

It was early enough to go on strolling; to loiter and admire the buds on the dwarf magnolias; to explore a mews called

Beaver Place and to saunter down Charles Street, thinking
that it might have been a street in Chelsea. She saw a florist's
window on her left and went in to buy flowers for Lee. She
spent most of the change remaining from Michael's fifty-dollar
bills on a bunch of freesia and jonquil, with sprays of mimosa.
"If I were a man," Caroline thought, "I should never stop
sending flowers to women. Probably I would send them even
to the women I didn't like much, purely for the pleasure of it.
But the trouble with me is that I always want to buy the whole
shop; just as in a restaurant I always want to order everything
on the menu."

There were good antique-shops in this street. She looked at
them and thought of the Brookfield Galleries, of Dennis. It
was impossible to realise that he had walked away forever,
that it was in her power to hurt another person so much.

She turned down into Charles River Square; at the foot of
the three-sided square there was the river, flashing nearly white
in the sun, beyond the width of green lawn. She stood before
a façade of rose-red brick. The door-knocker was a brass fish.

Waiting for Lee in the drawing-room, she had the sensation
of ease that came with the impact of somebody else's house;
the feeling that there was time to burn; that it was amiable
to wait here alone, looking at the pictures on the walls, the
book-titles on the shelves; lightly curious and not responsible
for any of it, a placid stranger who might find fun here. She
liked the room; its tone was golden-brown; the door opened
and a boy came in; he was a ten-year-old replica of Wynstay;
he said "Hello" and shook hands with her.

"My mother is still out. My name's Dan. Will you have a
drink?"

He was alarmingly grown-up. He poured her a glass of
sherry and lit her cigarette. He explained at length about their
dog which had been taken to the vet after a fight; he told her
about his older sister Marilyn and the younger sister Jean.
"She's four; she's cute," he said in an offhand way. Lee shot
round the door. Seen in daylight she was a little more highly-
coloured; the elder daughter was with her, a long slim blonde

102

banana of a girl, beautifully dressed and so assured in manner that Caroline was reminded of the dramatic critic who wrote, "If Miss X. acquires any more poise she will fall over on her back."

"I brought you these," Caroline said, giving Lee the flowers.

"Aren't you sweet?"

"Gosh, they're pretty——" said Dan.

Marilyn said, "Here, Mummy; I'll put them in water."

The moment crystallised suddenly; Marilyn holding out her hands for the bunch; Dan with the sunlight on his stiff black hair; Lee standing between them, and the tawny curtains at the window behind their three heads. Caroline thought, "But we have done this before; I know these people well. Or is it that one day they will be important to me?" Time shivered; then everything went ordinary again and she was here with three strangers in a strange house.

CHAPTER SIX

When Jay Brookfield saw Caroline coming towards him down the promenade-deck, he knew that she would smile at him and go by. He was aware of their two figures coming closer, two solitary people, slanted and walking with difficulty. The ship was rolling out of a storm. Through the glass now, he watched the ruffled surface of grey and green begin to disappear, the unstuck horizon sliding down. He leaned on the rail, pretending to be absorbed, fighting the battle between his prudence and his curiosity.

Curiosity dated from the moment that he had seen their two names on the passenger-list and cocked his harlequin's head on one side, thinking, " All three of them in New York together . . . what went on? "

Impossible to discover, since he was no longer on intimate terms with Caroline or Michael. "Complicated," he thought, "our slightly chilled relationship of the last three years; a quarrel, as it were, in aspic; the only kind of quarrel possible between people who live our lives." They met at the times and places inevitable in their small world, but they did not talk. "And I should have had more sense than to talk to Michael last night," thought Jay, with his nose touching the glass.

He had found Michael alone, after midnight, in the Main Lounge, that was behaving like the lounge of an hotel in an earthquake, with the sliding furniture, the stewards walking at an angle of ninety degrees, the wet cloth spread on the table to prevent the drinks from going over. Michael was reading a battered poetry-book. Wearing a checked tweed jacket, a green shirt and flannels, he had looked oddly sporting and youthful. But when Jay had stopped beside him, Michael had gazed at him with that air of authoritative and intimidating calm, palpable as a wall.

"Don't you sleep on boats, either?" had been Michael's greeting.

"Not in this weather; may I join you?"

"Do," Michael had said, languidly. He had waited for Jay to begin the talk; the lines of dialogue were hard and clear in Jay's memory; he had been a fool to begin:

"I saw Mercedes in New York."

"Oh?"

"She spoke most affectionately of you."

"Yes?"

"That was a shocking production for her to waste her talents on."

"Was it? I didn't see it."

"She tells me that she'll be in England in June."

"So I understand."

"Are you being severe with me, Michael?"

"If you mean, Do I object to your talking about Mercedes, the answer is No. If you mean, Do I incline towards thinking that you're minding my business instead of your own, the answer's Yes." His face had set in its granite lines and Jay had seen how dull his eyes were; whether from sleeplessness, or drinks or anger, he could not guess.

He was aware now that Caroline had reached the place where he stood. As he turned and saw her, he thought that she had for him still the magic that he would like to deny; a fragile, pacing animal, with hair blown back and the look now of belonging to the weather; a creature lovely and alone. He wondered why, since he seldom saw her alone, she impressed him always as a solitary person. The watery sunlight through the glass made her pale; she gave him a triumphant grin and hesitated, with her hands in the pockets of the coat that was obviously Michael's, a soft camel-hair coat much too big for her.

"Oh dear," thought Jay, with the old affection coming up to hit him. "Hullo, Caroline," he said defeatedly.

"Do you want to talk, or not?" she asked, adding, "I have no views."

"Oh, come and play with me; I am bored. Are you better? Michael said that you were making a choice of attitudes of mind towards sea-sickness."

"How prettily he does put things, to be sure." She leaned on the rail beside him; he looked at her profile.

"Did you have fun in New York, dear?"

"Yes, thank you. And in Boston. And in Washington."

"Work or pleasure?"

"What does that mean?"

"No need to be so wary with me. It means what it says. Were you there on work or pleasure?"

"Does it matter?"

"Not in the least."

"You know," said Caroline, "I cannot understand why a boat rolling as far as this doesn't turn right over; and I am not in the least consoled when people tell me that the reason they don't is that they never do. Jay, I would rather walk than watch this horizon."

"What you need is a drink," he said, taking her arm.

"Well I was going to have one, but Michael and that Harley Street stuffed-shirt, Billy Lloyd, were being so technical about endocrinology that I got tired of waiting."

"You did? I should have thought that you would sit there enjoying a feast of glandular education."

"Let's walk all the way round once."

"Well, I had a very pleasant time in New York, thank you for asking," said Jay.

She pulled her arm away from him suddenly. "Wow . . . there's a rainbow," she said and stood still.

"Two, to be exact," said Jay; he stared at her. "How extraordinary; you really do derive pleasure from it. Two silly, coloured hoops projecting from a peculiarly beastly-looking sea. And if watching the horizon makes you feel ill, dear, I suggest that we move on."

"Don't you like rainbows?"

"I like nothing about Nature. It bores me to catalepsy. I can calculate the exact hour when I came of age; the moment when I first realised that it was not necessary to like sunsets. I cannot describe to you the sensation of release."

She looked at him and laughed. He said in Cockney, "S'orl right, duck. Don't mind me," and added "Go on being moonstruck and at one with the great mysteries of the universe." He rocked on his heels, swaying to the movement of the deck.

"Mysteries. Well, I do like them."

"There are none," said Jay.

"There's God," said Caroline.

"He has no part in my programme."

"Why is that so unattractive?" she said, apparently more to herself than to him.

"Unattractive to you, my chuck, because your whole dreary little gospel is Acceptance. Of the rightness of the people who hurt you and trample you; when you ought to be walking on their necks."

"Miss Seward in her breathless Neck-Walking Act. After the interval she is fired out of a cannon into the Upper Circle," said Caroline. She turned from contemplation of the rainbows. "Look, Jay; all that is the matter with you, if I may be crude, is that you are still cross because I didn't think that acting in your plays was in a bracket with the Beatific Vision. And if it will make things any clearer to you, I still don't. And now may we stop talking about me?"

"Caroline, I hate to admit it, but you are growing up."

She said, "Yes, well . . ." They turned for the last length of the deck.

"Did you meet Mercedes?" he asked.

"Did *I* meet Mercedes?"

"In New York, I mean. . . ."

"No," said Caroline after a pause. "Nor in Boston; nor in Washington."

"You knew she was there?"

She was silent; he thought that she was less composed now, pulling Michael's old silver cigarette-case out of her pocket, lighting her cigarette and saying gruffly, "But of course I knew." She puffed at the cigarette. When she spoke again her voice was taut and shaky:

"It isn't very likely that we should meet, is it, Jay? Oh, in a comedy written by you, I suppose we might; and the whole situation would teem with honest fun; but that's not the way it goes."

"No?" said Jay, "I thought perhaps it did. Pity it doesn't."

"What is the precise threat behind that remark?"

"No threat, dear."

"Oh yes, there is. It appears to be the mission of the Brookfield family to drop me hints about Mercedes."

"That's Dennis; Dennis likes her. In my view she is just a *tiny* bit insane. I'm dropping you a hint about Michael and doubtless, from your defensive attitude, I'm wasting my breath."

They came to the door that led to the top of the companion-way; they went in and she stood still.

Was she, he wondered, waiting for him to say it? He thought that she was; he imagined saying it. In the abominable tradition, it should be introduced by the phrase, "I wouldn't say this if I weren't fond of you"—the outrageous lie. Oh no; the words were safe with him. But he could hear them:

"You know, of course, that Michael could get his divorce any time that he wanted it ; that his martyred attitude is a superb piece of bluff. That, being Michael, he is completely devoted to his career and completely set in the pattern that he has made. He has, at the moment, just enough freedom to suit him. You protect him from Mercedes and Mercedes protects him from you. A nice balance. Neither can encroach too far.

"You see, my pet, Michael for all his sophistication of manner, his careful façade, is really an ordinary little man with a tremendous sense of his own importance because he happens to have reached the front rank in his profession. He is hidebound; and the Olympian quality of his job has gone to his head. It is the same with all of them; there is the doctor-*mystique* accorded to them by the layman. Laymen treat a doctor as God; he can understand their mysterious physical machinery; so they assume that he is endowed with every other type of higher education and human knowledge; and he supports their illusion. Who wouldn't? It is a rôle that anyone would be glad to accept.

"Michael accepts it; Michael is no giver. Michael is a taker. He climbed very cleverly on Mercedes' shoulders to a position of social eminence that he would never have reached alone. She had her uses; and you, in your time, have yours. You worship at his shrine, which he likes; you purport to learn from him as though he were the fount of all wisdom; you are an enchanting companion and you make no demands whatever. Which would matter to nobody if you weren't a person of considerable talent in your own right."

("But why do I want to say these things aloud? I am, *au fond*, quite attached to Michael; and I find magic in you. What is this impulse to go in and stab and end your dream? Dear heaven, it is a thick ear to my arrogance to realise that I am possessed, after all, by normal human jealousy, the desire to destroy; do I hate your happiness?")

"Could you help me off with my coat?" Caroline was saying, "I get tangled in the lining; it is a double lining."

He peeled Michael's coat from her; she emerged in a dark blue sweater and trousers. "How curious," he said, "to assume that because you are in a ship, it is necessary to dress as one of the crew."

"Do I look awful?" she asked humbly.

"You look quite lovely. But the ladies in the Garden Room wear hats."

"That is the last line of a ballade," said Caroline.

"So it is. How clever of you. Wait a minute; ah yes:

"Prince! We can hear the war-drums on the way,
    sounding obituary rat-tat-tats.
But England's safe for just another day.
The ladies in the Garden Room wear hats."

She said, "Oh, Jay, I love you," and seized his hand. They were still holding hands when they came to the table where Michael was sitting with Billy Lloyd. It was early yet and there were few people in the bar. Jay saw Michael staring at them as they approached. Michael wore the same clothes that he had worn at midnight; he might not have moved from this deck since then; the same volume of poetry lay on the table with the drinks. He looked several hours more weary and wakeful; Jay met the stare of the heavy-lidded eyes, then saw their expression change and soften as he greeted Caroline.

"All right?" he asked her, as though they were alone, with the intimate, confident air of ownership. She said, "Yes; we were talking about God and rainbows." She slid into the chair beside him; she picked up his book and began to glance through it.

"God and rainbows," said the dark, correct young man Lloyd. "That would make a wonderful title for a novel, wouldn't it?"

Jay said, "Anyone completely devoid of literary pretensions would obviously think so," and saw Caroline being embarrassed for Lloyd, unnecessarily because he had a devotion to the Brookfield family. She bent her head over the book. This bar was forward in the ship and the rolling was palpable; Lloyd said something about war and the way that the floor tilted became for Jay a diverting illustration of their insecurity; "I have a cheap mind," he thought without shame. Caroline was murmuring aloud, from the book :

> " 'He has taken Rowll of Aberdeen;
> and gentill Rowll of Corstorphine.'

(oh so sad; what a melancholy word 'Corstorphine' is.) 'The flesh is bruckle; the fiend is slee. *Timor mortis conturbat me.*' And so it jolly does." She shut the book with a slam and emptied her glass.

Jay said, "Oh my dear, it can't. Think how restful not to be there."

"*Ce n'est pas peur de la mort; c'est peur de confronter la mort,*" she said over the glass, with her green eyes looking very large.

"Cheer up, Miss Seward," Lloyd said. "You can't confront a bomb. It will hit you before you know anything about it."

"But why should that be all right?" she asked.

"Why, indeed?" said Michael.

"For me," said Lloyd, "I'm afraid the thought of death has always been exciting; I'm so damn' curious about it."

"I'm not," said Jay, "being positive that there's nothing there to be curious about. I resent it mildly, but only on the grounds that I shan't be able to read my notices."

Michael said, "Perhaps you can subscribe to a celestial press-cutting agency."

"And your views on annihilation, Mr. K.?"

"I have none," said Michael, yawning.

"I rather like thinking about reincarnation," said Lloyd.

"Foolish," said Jay. " But comforting."

"On the contrary, tiring," said Michael. "The only point in favour of reincarnation is that it appears to skip the middle-classes, have you noticed? All those who recall their former existences remember that they were either slaves or royalty."

Jay said, "Imagine somebody at a cocktail-party five

hundred years hence recalling that she was Princess Helena Victoria."

"Or a charwoman at the Cumberland," said Michael.

Caroline said despairingly, "You are all so grown-up about being dead. I can't be."

Because, Jay thought, you've no guarantee that you can go on staring at your chap throughout eternity.

ii

Caroline said, "That was fun. It is nice to have Jay back in a good temper."

When Michael did not answer, she said, " Does he irritate you?"

"I wasn't thinking about him; I was thinking about you."

They had reached the door of her stateroom; his own was further aft on the same deck. When she saw him halt and frown, she thought, "Jay has told him about Rokov; it would be like Jay to pick that up from somewhere." She opened the door and he followed her in; for a moment they stood looking at each other; she said vaguely, "Sit on something. Would you like a drink here before you go to change?"

He shook his head. She thought that he looked ravaged for want of sleep; the lines in his face were heavy and all the light was out of his eyes. He sat down in the chair that faced the dressing-table. Caroline threw herself on the berth, rose on one elbow and waited for him to speak; he was looking at her with a steady smile.

"What?" she said to the thought that hesitated behind the smile.

"I was thinking that you were the only person of importance in that foolish conversation."

"I?"

"Because you were the only one who was telling the truth. You always are."

That hurt. She said, "I don't remember saying anything except that I was frightened of death."

"You were the only one who said it."

"But you aren't frightened; Jay isn't; Lloyd thinks that it will be exciting."

"Whistling in the dark," said Michael; his tired eyes were set, as though he would never stop looking at her. "Your gift for truth is extraordinary," he said. Then the corners of his mouth twitched. "That is why you made such an abysmally poor shot at your hotel-story in Boston."

"Oh, Michael."

"Ungentlemanly of me to mention it? I love that thing in you so much."

Caroline shut her eyes; she thought, "Here it comes; I must say it; and not because confession is good for the soul; that philosophy doesn't take into account the other person's feelings. But because I cannot, after that, go on lying. And I have rehearsed the words too often; they are frozen." She found that she had said, "Sorry, Michael; I can't last any longer."

He got up quickly and came to her. "Idiot, why didn't you tell me you were feeling ill?"

"Ill? Don't I wish I were?" And that was true. It was ridiculous to wish for the sudden misery of yesterday, here, with Michael's hand supporting her humiliated forehead. "But that was better than this," she said.

"What is the matter, Caro?"

"Michael. None of it was true about Rokov."

He stared; he had not understood; she had to take the fence again. "Damn," she said. "Look . . . I told you a lie; so as to come to America. Rokov didn't cancel the interview. I did."

"You cancelled it?"

"Yes. I had to. I couldn't keep the promise. I couldn't let you go without me."

She did not know now what she had expected; not this face of granite, nor this silence. She had to go on talking.

"I made all that up. About his having a production in Paris and postponing the London play. There wasn't a word of truth in it. All that happened was that I overslept; on purpose. I told them not to call me. I wanted to make him so cross that there wouldn't be a chance. Then when I woke up I wrote him a letter saying that I was going to America and sent it round to his office by hand."

He was still silent.

"Please say something."

He said slowly, "I can't believe it."

"Are you so angry?"

Again there was the silence; then he said, "You promised."

"I know."

Though he frowned, there was the beginning of a smile on his mouth, the smile of somebody who was confronted with a baffling absurdity; it went. He said, "But how could you do that?"

"It didn't occur to you that I would. Did you trust me absolutely?"

"Yes."

"And now you won't. Ever again."

He did not answer. She lay looking at the wall. She muttered feebly. "I didn't think you'd be so shocked. I thought you'd know it was too difficult," and held back her tears; to weep was the obvious and the unfair way of pleading. After a moment she turned to look at him. She seemed to have stripped him of assurance; he was strange in this defeat. He looked wearier than ever, sitting with his arms folded, staring at the floor.

"I do see now that it wasn't worth it," she said.

He got up.

"Please, Michael, say the things. It is worse if you don't."

He smiled a little, still staring at the floor. "I'm sorry, Caro. I don't think I can say anything now. Except——" he paced the floor and turned back to her, "Do you remember the last thing I told you that night? That it wasn't to us, but to you as an artist, that it mattered?"

She nodded, struggling with her tears.

"You didn't think about that?"

She shook her head.

"It didn't count at all?"

"Oh it counted, I suppose." She was too exhausted to choose her words; there was the painful ridge in her throat, the blood drumming in her ears and Michael had gone; he was only a voice somewhere outside the torment in her head, the torment of trying not to cry. She thought that the voice was saying, "There are sins that you can place on another person's soul," but this might have been in her own mind. She heard his footsteps. The door shut behind him.

iv

After she had stopped crying, she turned off the lamp beside her and lay there in the dark, with the porthole becoming a large pale coin on the wall, the curtains swinging their dark shapes, the ornate room losing its colours. She could hear all the sounds of the ship, the creaking, the queer sighs, the feet that echoed; the rattle of trays carried from the steward's pantry; the engine's throbbing far down.

She thought, "Why did he go? That is the first time that he has gone away and said nothing. I am so frightened of it."

She stretched her hand towards the telephone and drew it back. "I can't. In those few minutes he became a stranger. What is he thinking now that he is alone? What do I know of him when he is alone? That is frightening too. When we are together, he is my authority; the person whose bed I share, the person I laugh with; but there is another Michael. One? There are dozens. I do not know the surgeon on the job, the masked man in the white coat, with those hands in rubber gloves, cutting and tying and sewing. Nor the oracle in the consulting-room, who welcomes them in and says reassuring words as he examines their poor bodies.

"And there is the person alone in the nightmare at two o'clock in the morning; the nightmare where he is operating and his hand trembles. There he is in a place where I can't follow him."

There; and where else? In his past, most certainly in his past. She wanted it all. She wanted his childhood and his youth. She had the photographs; the boy beside the gate; the young man in an ill-fitting suit. She had been to the town with him. She knew the shop-windows that the child had looked into with longing; she had seen the towers of the Abbey, the bridge with the brown water running through the weeds; the Downs that sloped to the sea. She had desired with passion to share the small, bright adventures of that childhood.

There was the house in the Bloomsbury street; the house where the medical student had lived in a room on the top floor. This, like the Sussex town, mattered very much. Sometimes she had taken walks to it alone.

But alas, she thought, you could collect only as much evidence as he would give you. And what evidence could she have of the stranger whose marriage was a façade maintained?

"That, Michael, is your private territory; of that you do not speak. Who is that man? Oh, but I think that he came back to-day. There must have been times when you looked at Mercedes as you looked at me after I told you. And that I cannot bear. Dear God, why did I tell you? My sixth sense must have lost its cunning, to gamble on the belief that you would forgive me."

She got up and began to undress in the dark. She put on her pyjamas and climbed into bed. It was eight o'clock and now she expected the telephone to ring, Michael to ask if she were ready to come down to dinner. It did not ring.

She lay there, smoking cigarettes and waiting for him to knock at her door. Presently the corridor grew quiet. She thought her way about the ship; from the chattering crowd in the forward bar, down to the chattering crowd in the restaurant; up to the dance-floor and the smoking-room where they auctioned the ship's pool; over another crowd playing its silly gambling games in the Main Lounge. She saw all the lighted rooms and the dark sky, the dark water outside. She tried to see where he was.

She felt as though she were sinking down through layers of loneliness. She played the afternoon back in her mind, refitting the last scene of it, so that she did not tell him, but let him go on talking of her truthfulness and after that all was as it had been before she spoke. She remembered saying proudly to Dennis, "At least I never lied to you," and thought it cruel that she could say to Dennis what could never now be said to Michael. She went through a stage of cursing Joan who had prompted the lie, who had said that he would not be angry. Then she tried to change the way that it had gone, so that it was Michael who had deceived her, and asked her forgiveness. "If you had done it to me, I would have understood. But of course you would not. You are much too well-balanced to let your heart choose what your head disapproves."

Slowly she began to see herself with a sane and hideous objectivity; as a young woman whose only possessions were debts and failure; who must cease to be attractive to Michael; or perhaps, she thought, had ceased already. It was obvious now that he would have loved her more if she had held on to her career and made a success. She wondered how, for three years, she had fooled herself otherwise.

"I see—— I see. Of course he has wished that for me ; he has wished that I could get around to my own life, instead of dragging along on the outskirts of his. He has been enduring me patiently, regretting the moment when he first took me on.

"Yes. If I faced the truth, I should see that he took me on because I threw myself at him; because I had left my home and made him responsible for me. He hasn't loved me all this time; he has been loyal to the responsibility and no more. I became a necessary burden. So the others are right; and I am wrong. My credo is punched on the nose. The Spoilers-of-the-Fun have the last word: 'Isn't it a pity about Caroline?' "

She thought, "But this is like looking through the wrong end of a telescope. It makes me feel ill." She felt so ill and cold that she wondered whether she were going to be sick again;

she turned restlessly, to lie as still as she could, watching the curtains. "It is hopeless. When one gets to this stage, one has nothing at all; only limbo. The house has gone; the floor is hollow and the walls are down."

She thought, "Perhaps he is sitting writing to me. That is how he would sign off; by letter. And I shall see the letter coming under the door."

Now it was quite dark. The movement of the ship was less. The bed had ceased to perform its curious, rough-weather function of swelling up suddenly below her body. It was good to be still; perhaps she would sleep; she thought of the ship moving through the dark, the sad voyage home.

> "Well, ah fare you well, we can stay no
>   more with you, my love.
> Down, set down your liquor and the girl
>   from off your knee. . . .
> For we're off to Mother Carey. . . ."

"It is lovely; to drift, to lose hold of your thoughts, to be too tired to care." This, then, would be the moment of dying, when nothing mattered. There were other words for it, words coming past as gently as smoke:

> "Swing dark, swing death! You need no longer fear
>   the agonising day: the night is here."

She muttered, "Please let me remember always that it can be like this," and was still.

v

She came out of it slowly, knowing that there was a reason why she did not want to wake. Michael had turned on the lamp beside the berth; he was sitting in the same chair, reading. She saw that he had changed his clothes; he was wearing a dinner-jacket. She was too vulnerable now to recapture the mood of disbelief; she could only look at him sorrowfully and say, "Hullo; have you had your dinner?"

He shut the book and came over to her. "I have. It is nearly twelve o'clock."

"How long have you been here?"

"Oh, about two hours."

"Why didn't you wake me up?"

"You looked peaceful." He sat down on the side of the berth, "I am sorry I went away," he said.

"It's all right."

"I wasn't sulking. I wanted to think."

"It's all right."

"I brought you a brandy. Is it too late for drink, or would you like it?"

"I think I would."

He gave her the glass. "There are some sandwiches here too, if you're hungry."

She said weakly, "At a crisis in my life, there always seem to be sandwiches."

"You needn't eat them." He was watching her steadily. She drank some of the brandy and sighed and said, "Well, there isn't anything to say. Except I'm sorry. And I do understand your being angry."

"I wasn't angry."

"Unhappy, then. That is worse."

"I have made you unhappy, in my time."

"Yes, well . . . Not like that."

He went on watching her. She said, "I never used to hurt people."

"Hush. That is not to be talked about." He laid his hand on hers.

"What are you adding up in your head, Michael?"

"Nothing. I am waiting for you to be quite awake."

She drained the glass and sat up, hugging her knees. "Come on," she said, "Get it over. You always say that one shouldn't try to break bad news gently."

"Bad news?" He raised one eyebrow.

"You are going to tell me that we can't go on any more."

"No, I'm not."

She said, "Well, say it; whatever it is."

"I will." He paused. "Caro, darling, this isn't easy to phrase; because, being you, you will rush to a conclusion. And for once it will be the wrong conclusion." He said, "Will you please listen to me carefully?"

She nodded; she was now very frightened and she tried not to shiver.

"For a month I have been turning over in my mind the problem of how soon we should talk about ourselves. I suffer, as you know, from an impediment in my speech when I am obliged to discuss my marriage. It is extremely childish, but I have got into that habit and nothing will change me."

("Like waiting for the guillotine.")

"It is over," he said. "The divorce is going to happen. The proceedings look endless, but I imagine that a year will see it through. When it is through, I want us to be married. And I want you to be quite sure of that now; quite sure that I love you before you say 'Yes' or 'No' to it. Do you see?"

She said, in a whisper, "Is it possible?"

"I love you. And I want you to marry me. And that's all," said Michael.

For a moment, incredibly, she had the feeling that here she hauled down her flag; she would not again be the person who had fought out these years alone. That faded. She saw the beckoning image of peace, the straight road where the crooked path had been; the fact that a miracle could happen.

CHAPTER SEVEN

As Vera Haydon lifted the receiver, saying "Mr. Brookfield's office," Dennis snapped "If that is Kenrick again, he knows exactly what he can do with himself." Dennis was like a cross baby to-day. Vera was forced to admit that life had been more difficult since the voice of Miss Seward ceased to come through the telephone. For more than two months Dennis had continued ruffled and unpredictable.

"Hullo. May I speak to Mr. Brookfield, please?"

She recognised the cool voice at once; she said in a daze of pleasure, "Yes, of course. That is Mrs. Michael Knowle, isn't it?"

"Vera. You're still there. It is remarkable how many more people are still there than one would have supposed. How are you?"

"Oh, I'm wonderfully well, Mrs. Knowle. And you? It's a long time since you were in England, isn't it? How are you finding it?"

"Not altogether disagreeable." Mrs. Knowle put an emphasis on the word "altogether."

"Well, it's lovely to hear your voice" Vera said, "I'll put you through to Mr. Brookfield."

"Thank you so much."

Vera stared at the inkpot with the silver top, listening to every word spoken by Dennis.

"How did it go? . . . Yes, dear, one can count on them to take three hours over what you and I can say in five minutes; that's how solicitors make their money. . . . I see. Well, then as far as you're concerned, there's nothing more that need be done. . . . You're off Saturday? That's to-morrow. Rather sudden, isn't it? . . . Well, why not dine with me to-night?" He laughed: "You don't; I'm perfectly willing to talk about her, if you want to. . . . My dear, aren't you distressing yourself rather unnecessarily with all this? . . . I'll pick you up . . . Half-past seven? Good-bye——"

He tilted his chair and looked at Vera. "I'm sorry I cut her off; did you want to talk to her again?"

"Gracious, no," said Vera. "It was pleasant to be able to say hullo, that's all." She put a sheet of paper in the typewriter. She was disturbed by the one-sided conversation and she wanted Dennis to say something more. When he did not, she asked if Mrs. Knowle were going to France.

"Yes," Dennis said. "She's going to make her home there now."

"It's a beautiful place, isn't it, that house of hers?" Vera had her own picture of the house; it was white and it stood in a grove of pines above a postcard-blue sea.

"Depends on your idea of beauty. I should call it a rather dilapidated farmhouse; above the Route des Alpes; very lonely," he said.

"What's happening to Cold Ash these days?"

"They're selling it."

"Oh. How sad. Is that why she came to England?"

"That and to get her divorce proceedings under way," said Dennis.

Vera was silent.

"I'm due somewhere in a minute, aren't I?" Dennis was asking.

"I beg your pardon? Oh, yes, I'm sorry, Mr. Brookfield. You're due at Christie's at twelve."

She thought, "It is stupid to feel like this about it; quite possibly she wishes to marry somebody else. Of course; she must, or she wouldn't decide to divorce him after all this time . . ." Dennis was standing by her desk, giving her some instructions that she noted on her writing pad; her hand appeared to be listening attentively, her voice was making the necessary remarks. He went; she sat there beating a tattoo with the silver paper-knife. She thought "I could have asked him where she was staying. Last time she stayed at Claridge's. I could ring them and find out."

Divorce was among the activities of which Vera disapproved; though persons of Breeding were sadly addicted to it. She thought that it could not make her love Mrs. Knowle the less; the core of her discomfort was in the fear that Mr. Knowle had got his own way again; that he wanted to marry Caroline Seward. It was ridiculous to care so much what happened to these people; they were no concern of hers.

She picked up the telephone; the reception-clerk at Claridge's said that Mrs. Knowle was staying there. "No; no message," Vera said. She thought "I'll take her some flowers; leave them at the desk for her on my way home;

just as a hint that I am on her side. Probably she will understand that; oh, but of course she won't want flowers if she's
going away to-morrow; it will have to be a small bunch;
something that she could pin on her travelling-coat.
Gardenias."

ii

The men worked so quickly that Dorothy Knowle saw the
library disintegrating before her eyes. The men had huge
hands and boots and they all seemed to be called Joe. Two
of them had begun to lift the sofas and chairs; making even
the most valuable pieces look silly and embarrassed, with
flat canvas bottoms exposed and their feet in the air; then
these things were carried out like helpless invalids. There
was a rhythm and a method in the carrying; the men called
Joe steered capably round corners, pausing and shifting the
weight as they negotiated the staircase, making the process
appear perilous but manageable, as the exercises of a
tight-rope walker.

The two men who stripped the bookcases worked with
another kind of artistry, their hands gliding along the shelves,
fitting the books, without apparent effort or calculation of
their size, into the gaping crates. The best things were
gone. That was last week's memory; the crating of sculpture,
pictures, china and glass; with Mercedes coolly supervising
the work.

"That woman is *not* normal," Dorothy thought, backing
out of Joe's way, remembering that she had said, "It is sad to
uproot all these beautiful things and put them into storage."
Michael's wife had looked at her thoughtfully across the
head of the bronze Demeter, replying at last, "I have been
saying good-bye to things since I was three years old."
There had been no sadness in the remark; it was like most
of Mercedes' remarks, chilly and matter-of-fact.

"I have disliked her so much that I've tired myself out,"
thought Dorothy; "and now I have indigestion and the
feeling of imminent collapse that this sort of disturbance

always gives me." She took a bottle of soda-mints from her bag and sucked two tablets, standing by the window, looking, for comfort, at her favourite view. In the hot sunshine the fields lay green; the trees were large and rounded with their summer leaves; she could see the straight backs of the cattle in the pasture, the colours of the old roofs shimmering a little. She turned back into the stripped room. It was really most inconsiderate of Michael to have arranged this meeting for to-day; and in this place.

On the telephone he had sounded gay and placid. He had said "I am staying with Kate Forrest," and had not explained Kate Forrest, beyond adding that she had a house near Rye, and that he would drive over this afternoon. "I shall bring Caroline with me, so perhaps it would be more comfortable for us to meet at Cold Ash. She wants to see it, anyway."

Why should she want to see its corpse? Was Michael merely making this an excuse for not presenting her to their father? "I suppose I should be grateful for that." Dorothy grumbled. The foreman tramped in from the landing. He said, "Lady and gentleman looking for you, Miss." She straightened her hat, saw in the glass that she looked as forbidding as she felt and went out to meet the woman who had, at least, the virtue of not being Mercedes.

Coming down the stairs, Dorothy was startled by the frivolity of Michael's appearance. She saw him most often in London clothes and he was unfamiliar in this blue, sleeveless shirt, these trousers that were a sort of orange-colour. His face was tanned, he looked remarkably well and happy. The young woman wore trousers, too, a suit of dark green linen. She did not cut the deplorable figure that so often affronted Dorothy's eyes on the parade at Hastings, when the August influx of young women bulged in similar clothes; she looked neat, square-shouldered and comfortable. It was an oddly beautiful face. The least reassuring thing about her was her youth; Dorothy had expected her to be at least thirty-five.

All the aspects of the meeting made her shy. Michael remained calm and formal. He said, "This is Caroline Seward;

my sister Dorothy," and stood looking at them peaceably while they shook hands. This was a generous face; and a sympathetic smile; Caroline Seward might have guessed how much discomfort she and Michael were causing, with their funny clothes, their invidious relationship and their presence in this hall. "She's nice," Dorothy decided. "Michael calls that a stupid adjective, but it is what I mean. It can't be what I mean; this young woman is Michael's mistress."

"I hope you don't mind my coming to see the house," Caroline said, as though she knew and admitted the queer part-ownership that Dorothy felt for Cold Ash.

"It doesn't look like anything now, I'm afraid."

"Oh, it always will," Michael contradicted her. "Even if they turned it into a lunatic asylum it would still keep its head and go on being itself."

"But you don't want it any more," she said accusingly, almost forgetting Caroline Seward's presence.

"My dear, I never really owned it, after all. I think," he said, "that it was more truly ours when we used to trespass in the garden than it has ever been since."

It was an unusually soft remark for him to make and he smiled at her with the loving look that could always turn her heart.

"You two go where you like," she said abruptly, "I've had enough tramping about for to-day. I'll wait for you in the garden."

She saw that Michael's new car was parked in the lee of the removal-van; a long green car with a white hood rakish and sporting. She frowned upon it, thinking that it was a young man's car, that Caroline Seward must have chosen this model. She went round the front of the house to the place where the copper-beech tree grew at the angle of the stone balustrade; she lowered herself stiffly on to the grass. She felt all the more on the defensive for being attracted to Caroline. "I hope they won't be too long; Father will want his tea." She conducted a dialogue with the rational Dorothy Knowle, the second uncompromising version of herself.

"He oughtn't to ask me to meet her until they are married."

"Well, you needn't have agreed to it."

"Is it possible that he wants to tie himself up with this girl?"

"Why not? She's nice."

"The divorce won't be through for a long time. Perhaps he'll change his mind."

"Why should you want him to change his mind? You've always said that you would like him to marry again and be happy."

"But she's so young; this looks like a sudden infatuation."

"An infatuation is only the name given to somebody else's love."

She took another soda-mint and watched the corner of the terrace for them. When they came, they looked tranquil and amused, talking together. At the corner of the terrace they paused for a moment; then the girl turned and went back. Michael came on alone, walking slowly; when he was within earshot he said, "We are running short of cigarettes. Caroline is going into the village to buy some."

"I don't know where she'll find any, I'm sure; Saturday's early closing."

"Well," he said, "as good an excuse as any other." He sat down on the grass, facing her.

"What does that mean?"

"She thought that you and I might have things to say to each other alone."

"Oh . . . I see. That was nice of her." She looked at him sombrely. "Well, perhaps we have. What do you want me to tell Father?"

"Nothing at all, please, until the time comes."

She said, "I do want you to be happy; are you?"

"Yes. What are your reservations?"

She saw the look of compassion in his face, not knowing whether it might be for her, for himself, or for Caroline Seward.

"They're hard to express; without appearing offensive." She looked past him, at the urn on the stone balustrade; in this clear light every blot of lichen and mottling of the stone was visible. The shadow of the tree fell just short of the balustrade, a dark wavy margin upon the grass. "I mean, when I say that I wish you could lead an ordinary life, I suppose it sounds silly. Perhaps you sneer at people who lead ordinary lives." (No, said the rational Miss Knowle that is unfair; Michael sneers at nobody.) "Well, I've always felt that you needed a home; family-life; the sort of life our Father had with Mother. Your wife, I've thought—does this sound impertinent?"

"Not yet," said Michael.

"Well, I have tried to imagine the sort of person. Somebody as different from Mercedes as possible. Not a young girl, an actress; but a simple person who would want to look after you and give you children."

"I think that if you asked Caroline what she wanted, that would be the answer you'd get."

"But—oh, well; I'm not prejudiced against actresses, I hope," she said, staring at her large, sensible feet.

"You'll discover that Caroline is a simple person; apart from her antennæ."

"Her antennæ?"

"She picks up other people's moods as though she used a magic mirror."

"Does that mean that you think she picked up mine, just now?"

"Didn't you think so? I hadn't briefed her."

"H'm. Why did she want to see the house?"

"Because she knew that it used to matter to me. I brought her down once, to look at the town and all our places. . . . We came here; but of course we couldn't go in."

She said sharply, "When was that?"

"About two years ago."

(Yes, you said in your letter that you had known her a long time.) She said heavily, "How much harm will the divorce do you?"

"I've no idea. That is something that has to be faced when it comes."

"What made Mercedes agree to it at last?"

Michael was silent. Then he said, "I think the basis of goodwill."

"Goodwill. There wasn't much goodwill about her last week." She brooded; the words of the marriage-service were ominous in her head. "*I, Michael, take you, Mercedes, to my wedded wife; as long as we both shall live. To have and to hold, from this day forward, for better, for worse, for richer, for poorer; in sickness and in health; till death do us part.*"

Those words, she thought, those tremendous words. . . . "Whom God hath joined together . . . Is that why I feel this to be wrong? Is that why I feel sad? Can one, should one, be sorry for God?" She said, "It's funny. All these years I've longed for her to give you your freedom and leave you in peace. Now it has come, I have only the feeling that you're making another mistake."

"I may be," said Michael quietly.

"Do you mean—you aren't sure that this is a right marriage for you?"

He said, "I'm not thinking about me," and turned over on his stomach, propping his chin with his hands so that the words when they came sounded chewed and muffled. "In the matter of making mistakes," said Michael, "as I grow older I can look back upon a lengthening perspective of mistakes; each of which has appeared at the time to be the only intelligent action."

The humility was perplexing to her; she said sharply, "You made one mistake in your life and that's all; your marriage with the wrong woman."

"Oh, my dear, what nonsense; if they had stopped there. . . ."

"Well, don't make another," she snapped.

"I tell you, it is right for me—it could be wrong for Caroline."

"How could it be, when she loves you?"

He frowned. " If we have children, it will go perfectly. I think that anybody who is single-minded about me, as Caroline is, takes on too much."

"In my view," said Dorothy briskly, "She is a very fortunate girl. At least; that is; does she—must she—will she be cited by name in the case?"

He shook his head; his vizor-down look warned her against more questions. Caroline came round the house, walking smoothly, a slender dark green shape against the bright green lawn. Dorothy was relieved that they did not show their affection by an embrace. Caroline sat down beside her and threw a packet of cigarettes into Michael's lap, saying "All the shops were shut. I got these from a man in a garage. He said he knew what it was like to want something you couldn't have because he was waiting for the pub to open. We agreed," she added, "that when you got the thing it was never as good as it seemed when you couldn't have it."

"Thank you, darling," said Michael drily, "I shall bear that in mind." Dorothy thought, "What an extraordinary conversation to have with a man in a garage." She gazed in bewilderment at the curled head, the slanted, faunlike eye; the profile was turned to Michael.

"I just remembered the cat; what happened to it?" Caroline asked him.

"Whose cat?"

"The Alencz cat. I haven't seen it since Boston."

(Boston; so he took her to America. Really. . . .)

Michael sat up and stared at her. After a moment he said, "That cat seems to have disappeared. What made you think of it now?" There was a challenge in his voice.

"I was trying to imagine the house when all the things were in it."

"Was that the stone cat you asked me to come over and fetch?" Dorothy asked severely.

"Yes, it was."

"But Michael," Caroline said, "you loved it; do you mean that it is lost?"

"I mean that I don't know where it has got to; which would amount to the same thing."

Looking at Caroline, Dorothy thought that this represented a tragedy, that she would bewail the loss. She appeared to

change her mind, frowning suddenly and saying, "Yes, well
. . . " Michael said, "Cats will be cats." There was a feeling
of tension in the air. Dorothy murmured, "Wouldn't you both
like to have a cup of tea somewhere? I'm sure the workmen
must have finished by now."

iii

The boarding-house dinner was served at seven-fifteen;
brown soup, cold boiled beef with a limp salad, prunes and
custard. By eight-o-clock, Joan Bridges was back in her top-
floor room; it was warm here; she pulled the armchair close to
the open window. She could see the dusty tops of the plane
trees, beyond them the stucco façades, the chimneys and
metallic sky. Joan began to read and check the typescript that
she had brought home from the office. From time to time she
looked up, feeling restless; this summer evening in London
could be exciting. It belonged to young women in love and
young men in silk hats, who would drive and dance and
afterwards remember this year's tunes.

Presently she made herself some coffee; she put the cup on
the window-sill and leaned there; the long twilight was ending;
she saw a car cruise up the terrace; a car that must belong to
a young man in a silk hat; she appraised its long torpedo-shape,
its white hood. She went back to the typescript.

When a knock sounded on her door, she called, "Come in,"
sulkily, expecting her talkative neighbour from the floor
below. The last person whom she expected was Caroline; who
stood now in the doorway saying, "Do you mind?" and
looking as though trouble had chased her here.

"Mind? I couldn't be more pleased. That's a new dress; I
like it." The dress had a pattern of black and white leaves; a
cloud of scent had come into the room with Caroline.

"Why are you roaming Paddington at night?"

"I don't know where Michael is."

"Well," said Joan placidly, "I haven't got him. Where's he
supposed to be?"

"Crimes Club Dinner," said Caroline. "He was due there at seven-forty-five. And he's never turned up. Banning just telephoned me from Manchester Square, being thoroughly Jeeves and apologetic but Did I By Any Chance Know ——? Billy Lloyd wants to talk to Michael urgently about a case."

"Well, have some coffee; there must be some mistake; are you sure he was going to the dinner?"

"Certain. So was Banning. Michael left that number for emergencies *and* he didn't leave the house till after seven-thirty, so he couldn't have stopped anywhere on the way. The last thing he said to me was that he'd telephone me at the Rufford between eleven and half-past, which was the time when the dinner ought to end. I said to Banning that he might have been called out of the dinner already for some dire cause; but oh dear me no; he had been expected and his chair was still empty at nine o'clock."

Joan said, " I think it's odd; but not alarming; was he driving his car?"

"No; he let me have it for the evening."

"Well, then, he took a taxi. Nothing serious can have happened."

"But where is he ?"

Joan tried to think of an intelligent solution. "Perhaps he got bored with the idea of the dinner and went off somewhere else."

"He wouldn't; you know how he loves those old crimes." She turned restlessly and stared out of the window. "And if he had decided not to go, he'd certainly have let Banning know where he could be reached. He has such a conscience about that."

Joan said, "I cannot imagine his getting into any sort of trouble; and I don't know what trouble he could get into at half-past seven in broad daylight. Unless he was drunk, which isn't his form. He's never ill and he is the last person to fall into the clutches of a raging harlot or a confidence-man."

"People lose their memories suddenly."

"Not Michael's sort; what put that into your mind?"

Caroline said, "Well, naturally, there isn't a single hideous likelihood that I haven't explored in the last forty minutes. And I wondered if it were possible to do that; to lose one's memory or go completely silly for want of sleep."

"Is he sleeping worse than usual?"

"Yes; he's had five bad nights in a row." She said abruptly, "You know, I haven't felt all right since Mercedes was here."

"But why? She left you both alone."

"She leaves a shadow; and she is a bird of ill-omen. Remember all the things that happened last time she came over."

"You," said Joan, "are painting devils on walls."

Caroline got up and began to pace the floor; she halted to say, "I've still got the feeling that she'll win."

"That is only because you've had peace for such a little while. You'll get used to it. Damn it, Caroline, she's out of it; forever; she's gone."

"Has she though?" Caroline's face looked shadowy and watchful. " Supposing that she were still here. . . . "

"That's absurd. Are you suggesting that Michael is with her?"

Caroline was silent.

"He can't meet her now they're divorcing. And he wouldn't meet her without telling you."

" I don't know. Other people's private territories are always surprising."

"In that case, we'll go down to the hall and I'll telephone Claridge's and ask if she's still staying there."

"No, don't."

"I certainly shall; you needn't come——"

She had just pressed Button A on the telephone-box when Caroline ran down the stairs. "Look—don't; this is spying."

"Sorry," said Joan firmly. "Hullo; is Mrs. Michael Knowle there, please? When did she leave? I see; thank you. You have a forwarding address? I will. There; now are you satisfied? Left for the Continent on Saturday."

Caroline said, "Yes, well——" and embraced the banister-rail.

"Look here, nothing's happened to him. Possibly he met a dear old chum in the street and they went off and got plastered. Would you like me to come back to the Rufford with you and wait till he telephones?"

"No," said Caroline. "Get in the car and I'll drive you around for half an hour. It's better than sitting still."

"All right. I've got an idea," she said as Caroline turned the wheel. "Perhaps Mercedes *didn't* go away after all. Perhaps Michael murdered her and is returning to the scene of the crime."

To her relief Caroline took it up. "Where would you say the scene was? Hyde Park?"

"Somewhere less central and more squalid. Streatham Common."

"And there," said Caroline, "she waxes and whitens peaceably."

"Surely not yet; she can only just have begun to decompose."

iv

It was a quarter to eleven when Caroline drove into St. James's Place. The night-porter was standing on the steps, taking the air; she saw him off-guard, letting himself droop as though he were very tired, a small, lonely figure under the lamplight. He turned. He came briskly to open the door of the car for her.

"Hello, John. Any message for me?"

"Mr. Knowle is waiting for you, Miss."

"*Where?*"

"In the lounge." He was looking at her doubtfully, and she had time to see this, saying, "Is he all right?" as she ran up the steps. John said, "Oh, yes," still looking doubtful, and added, "He's been here about half-an-hour."

Michael was standing in front of the marble mantelpiece at the far end of the room. He looked at her thoughtfully and vaguely, without a smile. He said, "I have endless patience."

"But you are early. Where have you been?"

He did not answer; he stared with hooded eyes and smiled faintly. There was a bottle of whisky and a syphon and two glasses on one of the small tables. He moved towards it, ignoring her.

"Michael, what is the matter? What has happened?"

He said, "I waited for you."

"Why didn't you go to the dinner? Look, you aren't drunk are you?" she said, and added, seeing him frown, "I don't mind at all if you are."

"Drunk? No." He picked up the bottle of whisky. It was always a pleasure to watch the neat movements of his hands; now he let the bottle strike the edge of the glass and some of the whisky spilled on to the marble-topped table. He looked at this in a puzzled, peevish way. "I call that very untidy," he said, as though somebody else had done it.

Caroline tried hard to think that it was funny. She had seen him a little drunk before, over-elaborate and doing things with a Regency flourish; that was as far as it ever went with Michael. This was the drowned, fumbling stage that other people reached; it made for hearty jokes. But it was not funny. Laboriously he filled the second glass and held it out to her.

"I don't want a drink, darling."

"Nonsense," he said.

"Really, I don't. I just had some beer with Joan."

He raised the glass to his own lips.

"Look, Michael; I don't want to pry, which as you know is wholly foreign to my nature, but where the hell have you been and how did you get so plastered?"

He stroked his chin. "The two clauses of that sentence," he said, "might have been spoken by two different people . . . which is quite fair because I think that I do see two of you." He placed the palm of his right hand over his right eye. "Still two," he said, "I appear to have vicarious schizophrenia."

That made her laugh; she said, "Idiot" and made a movement towards him; he held her away; the gesture of his arm was stiff and sudden. This hurt her more than anything he could have done.

"Oh Michael," she said miserably, "what is it all about?"

"You know nothing?"

"Well, apparently I do not."

"That," Michael said, after another pause, "is as it should be. Nothing about the room; you have never been there. And one sits and waits; and looks at the yellow lamp-shades on the tables; there are circles going round the yellow lamp-shades; circular patterns in black. And one waits; and the iron enters one's soul. I see that always like rust forming, do you?" He put the drink down unfinished.

She could not answer; nor think why these confused, sing-song words should horrify her; she heard the overtones of other words unsaid; the story of something dark and hateful that had happened to him. He retreated to the mantelpiece, stared at her as though she had just dawned on him and said sharply, "Why were you such a long time coming? You know how much I dislike waiting."

She said, "That isn't fair. You're not making sense. I didn't keep you waiting. I can't understand what you're talking about and I think I had better drive you home."

For a moment she saw in the clouded face a hint of recognition that none of this was as it should be; a reassuring glimpse of the familiar Michael. He said, "No, you mustn't do that. John will get me a taxi," and walked past her; she went after him.

"I'll drive you home."

He said nothing; he moved as rapidly as usual. John came out of the porter's box.

"Did I have a coat?" said Michael, addressing nobody in particular.

"I shouldn't think so," said Caroline placatingly. "It is a very warm night." She saw John looking at him.

"Well then, all I need is a taxi."

"No," said Caroline—"It's all right, John. We've got the car."

She took Michael's arm; he did not stumble. He said, "If you insist," and then stood beside the car, hesitating to climb into the driver's seat. "I don't think that's a very good idea" he said, still speaking to nobody in particular.

"Other side," said Caroline, "I'm driving."

"All right, Miss?" John asked at her elbow.

"Yes; perfectly." She could not bear to meet John's eyes with the understanding glance of one sober person to another; she opened the door for Michael, who climbed in and said, "Thanks very much," in his normal voice.

After a time he asked, "Where are we going?"

"Home. Manchester Square."

"Not my idea of home." He sang in a quiet, awed tenor,

"Oh why did I leave my little back room in Bloomsburee?
  Where I could live on a pound a week in luxuree?"

"I can't imagine," said Caroline.

"But really it is all very foolish," he continued, "based on nothing; a false creation. I don't know why you want to know about it."

She said, "Put your mind at rest on that point; I don't."

He was silent; then he whistled his melancholy tune. Crossing Wigmore Street, she said, "I'll put the car away afterwards. If you can find your latch-key, it would help."

"In my pocket," he said. He walked up the steps and when she had opened the door, he was oddly competent, turning on the light in the hall and mounting the stairs with no difficulty; he seemed to have forgotten her again. He went into the study, turned up the lights there and stood looking at his own portrait. She held out the message that she had picked off the hall-table.

"Michael, this says will you ring Lloyd. Urgently. Any time before midnight."

He turned and smiled at her. "Nothing is ever as urgent as all that; I've told you so before."

"Well, shall I ring him for you?"

"Certainly not."

He wavered for a moment, then shut his eyes; with an enormous effort, he appeared to steady himself. "Caro, I am very sorry, but I must go to bed. If I can sleep, it will be all right; do you see?"

"Yes, of course. I'll help you."

She followed him into the bedroom; he stood by the

dressing-table, taking things out of his pockets; she saw him turning something over in his hand; it was the Alencz cat.

"Hullo," she said. "You found it."

He was silent.

"Put it away now, darling. You must go to bed." It was like talking to a child. Still he stood, turning the cat, tracing its shape with one forefinger, not looking at it.

"Give it to me," she said patiently.

He began to hold it out to her, then he drew back his hand as if to throw it. She muttered, "Oh, don't; please don't," and pulled at his wrist. The cat fell on to the carpet; she picked it up.

"It isn't the real one," he said. "Just a plaster model. I saw it to-day in a shop-window and thought I had to have it. I was wrong."

Now he put both hands up to his forehead—"Please, Caroline, go away and leave me; that's all I ask. I oughtn't to be doing this to you."

"If I leave you, will you undress and get into bed?"

"Yes."

"Promise?"

"Promise."

"All right."

She went back into the study; she shut the door quietly behind her and went to the telephone. The voice at the other end was Lloyd's, sharp and impatient.

"Dr. Lloyd? This is Caroline Seward. I'm calling from Michael's house."

"Is he there? I've been waiting for him to call me."

"I know you have. Look, Michael isn't able to talk to you to-night. He's ill."

"What's wrong?"

"I don't know. I'm worried about him; and I don't want him to know that I've told you that. Only——" she stopped, trying to find words.

"Want me to come round and take a look at him?" The voice was amiable now.

"I think you'll just say he's drunk."

"Well, perhaps he is," said Lloyd, "though that's unusual for Michael. He's been sleeping badly, hasn't he?"

"Yes."

"And what's he up to now?"

"He's going to bed."

"Well, if he's tight he'll probably sleep. Call me again if you're worried."

"Could you come and look at him in the morning? And not say I suggested it? There is something odd here," she said.

"All right, Miss Seward; I'll try and catch him early; you've got my number haven't you? . . . Not at all. Good night."

She waited a while and then crossed the landing, listening, outside the bedroom door. She could hear him now. She opened the door and went in; he was sitting on the side of the bed with his face in his hands; he was crying. He did not move when she sat down beside him and held him.

"I can't go on," he said.

"Don't worry, Michael. What you want is some sleep."

"I can't go on.   I can't go on."

He groped with his hand, feeling for hers; there was in that gesture the comfort that had been denied her in the stiff movement of the arm that held her away from him.

"I can't sleep. I'm so tired. I can't go on."

"All right. Just cry; don't try to stop. I'm here; I'm holding you."

She was astonished by the strength of her pity; it was as sharp as the beginning of passion; as though her body rejoiced in this.   She did not know why she should take pleasure in his weakness. She went on holding him; it was a curious moment, illogically satisfying.

He sobbed himself to silence. He swept his arm upward across his face and rose, leaning on her shoulder. He said, "Please forgive me." He seemed to be sober now. She watched him pouring water into a glass, shaking four tablets from the small bottle that stood on the table beside the bed.

"Will you please take this away," he said, putting the bottle into her hand. "Out of this room and out of the house." She said, "Yes, Michael, of course." This was more frightening than anything that had happened to-night, but it was not unexpected.

"And take the car home, won't you?" It was a whisper; it scraped exhaustedly. He lay down and shut his eyes.

When she saw that he slept, she turned off the lamp beside him and went back to the study. It was odd to see by her watch that the time was only ten minutes past twelve. She felt suddenly placid, strong and wide awake.

She lit a cigarette and stood by the fireplace, examining the portrait. Its half-finished quality was not irritating to-night. It suggested to her that Mercedes had known just so much of Michael and no more, that she had left her own bewilderment here on the canvas.

"You, too?" Caroline said aloud. "I wonder."

CHAPTER EIGHT

DENNIS was sitting on the high crest of the rocks, wondering whether he would swim again or continue the necessary work of tanning his skin. Kate had promised him that nobody was coming to lunch, that there were no plans for the afternoon, that he could lie around all day without his clothes and without interruption. He had spent a charmed and lonely morning between the rocks and the dazzling water.

He looked towards the villa and saw that a woman was walking across the gravel terrace, towards the flight of steps that led down to the rock-pool. Then he thought "How all occasions do inform against me," and retreated down the rock-face to find his swimming-trunks. Michael would follow; for three weeks now Dennis had been a martyr to snapshot views of Michael and Caroline; Michael's car had passed him on the road below Aix-en-Provence, travelling at an insane speed; the green car with the white hood folded back, the glimpse of the two brown profiles and their wind-ruffled hair; over at Eden Roc he had strolled out on to the parapet in time to see Michael dive from the high board, the effortless, graceful dive made by the well co-ordinated animal, with Caroline watching devotedly, almost naked, as they all were, long-legged and statuesque, silhouetted against the sun. Up at St. Paul he had found them eating their lunch among the white doves and the trellised vines. He had suffered them in the Palm Beach Casino on a gala night; and the sight of their dancing was an irritation, because together they had the smooth skill of a couple who made dancing their profession. Each time, he had felt that he was called upon to watch Michael making love to Caroline; and wondered why he had let himself come here, to the patterned holiday that his circle of friends took every summer; this was the mere shifting of the small population from their usual London haunts to their usual French playground. Jay would have none of it; Jay ran away from the crowd whom he biliously referred to as The Boys and Girls and conducted his indiscretions on the Baltic coast. "But this, for some reason, I love—and I will not be hustled by Caroline," Dennis told himself, pulling on his trunks.

She came into view, climbing slowly down the last of the natural steps to the flattened saucer of rock at the edge of the pool. She stopped and looked at him. She said, "Oh, wouldn't you know?" and appeared to await instructions.

"It's all right," he said. "It wouldn't have been all right a moment ago, but it is now." He exaggerated his attentions to the buckle of his belt.

"I am sorry, Dennis. I didn't know you were here. An extraordinary little Provençal dwarf who answered the door said that everybody was out. So Michael decided to take a shower in Alaric's bathroom. We were bathing at Agay," she said, "and there is too much seaweed on that beach."

She remained where she was, steadying herself with one hand against the rocks. The sun had bleached the one loose lock of hair; the dark colour of her skin made her eyes look more than usually green. She wore a white beach-robe over a white bathing-suit; she was shod with sandals of thick white string. On this background she was a poster, advertising a holiday on the Riviera, and the result in his mind was the usual mixture of pleasure and exasperation.

"Would you prefer us to get the hell out?" she asked, "We can quite easily, if you don't want to talk to us."

"What a suburban solution; I should never have thought of that."

"Well, make up your mind," she said, "I can fold my tent as well as the next Arab."

He said, "Oh, come on down and stop being arch. I told you I didn't mind our meeting by accident."

"So gracious an invitation could leave nobody unmoved," said Caroline. She came down the last of the steps. Inconsiderately, she was still using the same scent that he associated with her. "Damnation to scents and tunes," he thought. "The way they sneak up. . . ." She sat down beside him on one of the yellow mattresses.

"Well, dear, you've had a nice long holiday, haven't you?"

"We have been away six weeks," she said primly, "We go back on Thursday; too sad."

"Is Michael well now?"

"Oh yes; is that a porpoise, would you say, or a point of rock?"

He knew that she would answer casually. Kate had met the same blank wall. Kate, with her sharp-nosed passion for detail, had given him the available data; he despised himself for wanting to know more. But the breakdown was not the only mystery about Michael; to Dennis the divorce was the real mystery. Now he thought of Mercedes, living less than a hundred miles away, yet as far from this playground as though she were in Siberia. Michael's breakdown, he guessed, was perhaps an intelligent move in the game; an appeal for sympathy before the dubious publicity began to take the lustre off his reputation. "But if so, he has timed it very badly. It will be months before the case comes on."

Kate had extracted some of her material from Billy Lloyd. According to Billy, Michael had combined overwork and insomnia to a degree at which he cracked. Billy had put him to bed for a fortnight and ordered him three months rest. It was a formidable and unexpected programme. Dennis could not imagine Michael's accepting it; nor, from his series of

Riviera snapshots, could he believe that it was necessary. In all the years of their acquaintance he had never known Michael to be ill, nor to give evidence of owning a nervous-system. He had assessed Michael's insomnia as something of an affectation, with his habit of saying "Lud" and wearing bow ties.

Caroline, Kate said, refused to talk; and that was an unexpected programme for Caroline. "Well, we can but try," said Dennis to himself. "Is Michael going straight back to work?" he asked.

She said, "Of course." She took the bottle of suntan-oil from beside him and began to rub her shoulders. She turned to look at him over her shiny shoulder; her expression was gentle and candid, as though they were still friends.

He felt at ease, drunk with the sun and the sea and the colours; she added to the colours. As she spoke, it seemed to him that she had gone far away; for all her old tricks, there was a change in her.

"You see," she said, "Michael isn't a person who can rest for long."

"And you?" said Dennis. "But in any case I don't suppose you need worry. Soon you'll be a nice little girl in an overall, making munitions."

"Yes, well. . . ."

"Or if you preferred, I imagine that you could put on silver spangles and sing cheerful songs to the troops, sending them off to be killed with all the best tunes in their heads and a memory of how you look from the chin downwards. That is called building-up morale."

He saw that she had stopped listening to him. Michael was coming down the steps; he moved like a cat, Dennis thought, watching the brown body and the shadow that it cast. Michael showed none of Caroline's hesitation at the meeting. He said, "Hullo; good to see you" and threw himself down on the yellow mattress.

"How are you, Michael?"

"I couldn't be better, thanks."

"We are discussing whether Caroline should make munitions or sing patriotic songs in transit-camps."

Michael said, "One of the first things that happens in war is that all, with one accord and without premeditation, stop doing the things they can do and begin doing the things they can't do."

"All very well for you," Dennis thought. "Your work will go on; it is ready-made for war. But I shall go to my silly soldiering because I must, and nobody will find a use for my talents in appraising tapestry, my eye to the genuine article in jade or china, my civilised approach to love or my skill in ordering a dinner."

He said some of this aloud. Caroline said, "To be in it is the only thing that counts"; and since he had heard her say last year that to be out of it was her only ambition, he wondered if she were talking to please Michael. Michael said, "The water looks too good to waste; are you coming in, Caro?"

So that he would not be forced to watch them, Dennis too went into the water; but his eyes again took snapshots of their effortless animal pleasure. They played with the scarlet canoe and raced each other between the two curving rock horns that enclosed the pool. When he hauled himself out they were still at the far point, Michael demonstrating a dive and inviting Caroline to follow. Perhaps the hardest thing to bear was always the sight of two other people having fun.

He saw them again on their last evening, when he was walking past the Malmaison garden in Cannes. The brilliance of the early evening dressed the scene as though for a ballet, with the coloured clothes and the brown skins, the long, expensive cars, the dazzle of water on whose silken floor there still flashed a few speed-boats with surf-riders strung out behind them. The backdrop was made by the palm trees and the pinkish terraces, the two-dimensional blue frieze of the Esterel mountains.

Looking up into the garden Dennis saw Caroline and Michael at a table under a palm, among those of the corps-de-ballet who were drinking their aperitifs. They waved and invited him up to join them, but he shook his head and walked on, pretending an objective.

ii

Caroline followed Dennis with her eyes, until she lost him among the runnel of people walking on the Croisette. She said, " Anybody looks sad, walking alone."

Michael said lazily, "Anybody includes you."

"Yes, well . . . I never see me."

"I do. Caro, you really are a pig. Do you realise that you have eaten all but one of those cheese hors d'œuvres and that is the third plate we have had?"

"I'm hungry. Ask for some more."

"I haven't the face to ask for some more."

"Well I have." She beckoned the waiter. She leaned back, looking at the sea that began now to be paler than the sky; it was luminously white; on the white sails coming into harbour the shadows were blue, with the same tint as that of the mountain frieze. It was, in sane prophecy, the last time she would see these things; the last evening when they would dine here, with the dusk coming into the garden and the Aladdin's cave of the Casino waiting. She said to herself, "If I have to fight for all that matters to me, that will include the Casino." It was magic; its spell came to meet you every night; a fever; a most enjoyable plague of superstition; a bout of shadow-boxing with Chance as the shadow. There were few better things than the moment when the wheel slowed, and the ball lay there below the number that you had chosen. The stature of the triumph was absurd; and it was not because you had won money but because you had won. She remembered, having played roulette for the first time, saying to Michael, "But look —it has nothing to do with money," and Michael replying, "There you have made a highly expensive discovery."

Standing by the table, with all her energies pointed in mystic focus upon the number Eleven, she was as much alone as though Michael had never existed. This was pure concentration; nothing else mattered. (He had said, "The only time that you are ever unfaithful to me is with roulette.") As the wheel began to move, she narrowed her eyes, looking down at the numbers on the cloth, trying to see whether any of them shimmered, in the way that Twenty-Four had once appeared to shimmer at the last minute, with a profitable result. Sometimes it was fatal to do this, because in her eager imagination six numbers would shimmer and she would scramble her stakes on to them all.

"Control yourself," Caroline said, "it is early yet. Plenty of time. *Il ne faut pas insister*," she added, quoting the barman who took a fraternal interest in her play.

It was just eleven o'clock; the crowd was beginning to drift in through the glass doors. She stood away from the game, watching it in perspective, from the ceiling that was open to the stars, down to the lights above the tables; hearing the click and the sing-song voices calling the numbers, the sweeping rattle of the counters that were raked away; this noise was like the breaking of short waves on a pebble beach. She looked at the serious faces, the motley clothes; evening-dresses and jewels; coloured shirts and white trousers; dinner jackets and variations upon the pyjama-suit. A balloon of sound seemed to swell and float above the heads. The croupiers looked as the assistants round an operating-table might look. She thought of all the supplications going up to the gamblers, assorted gods; all the conflicting hunches, all the talisman-thoughts. Perhaps it was a very silly game. At least you could think so for a moment, keeping away.

She walked to the long windows and went out on to the terrace; she stood by the water, with her back to Aladdin's cave, watching the lights pricking out the contour of the coast. There were many lights. There were the electric letters spelling the names of bars and hotels; the masthead lights in the harbour; the flashing headlamps coming along the cape from the town. The phosphorescence on the sea, and the stars overhead might have been another purer element. Or perhaps the earthbound lights should be called by a different name.

She thought of the people who did not know this scene; Joan Bridges; Dennis's sullen secretary; her hairdresser who said that Felixstowe was always nice; John, the night-porter at the Rufford, who went to a cousin at Gravesend.

She looked at her watch and saw that the time was eight

minutes past eleven. At eleven minutes past, she would back
Number Eleven. She looked up at Orion, who was a talisman,
and returned to the tables.

She chose the table near the windows; it was crowded and
she had to press into the mob to attract the croupier's attention. She gave him all her counters, grateful that Michael was
not watching; he was playing chemin-de-fer. Michael would
not be angry, but she had been losing for three weeks; he
had suggested a regime of caution. She would have to cash a
cheque at the *caisse* if this hunch failed.

Passing the head of the table, she saw the woman who
looked like a lizard; the hoodoo-woman; one whom Caroline,
in her vein of Casino-mysticism, had written down as a
bringer of bad luck. The woman paused, looking at the wheel.
"If she plays here, I'm sunk. No, don't think that; think the
lucky things. Stand in the trench, Achilles, flame-capp'd,
and shout for me. . . . But once atop of Lambourne, down
towards the hill of Clere. . . . Rats, rats, we've got to get rid of
the rats. . . . Come, Almighty, to deliver. . . . Oh, it couldn't
not be Eleven. Quite placidly, and with the utmost certainty,
I know that it will be Eleven."

"Numéro Cinq; Rouge; Impair et Manque; Transversale,
Carré, Cheval et Plein."

Caroline turned away with the noise of the breaking wave
in her ears. "It was that woman," she said without rancour,
accepting the doom. Michael said that she was a good loser.
"Well, so I should be; I get enough practice. Now, have I
anything left?"

Michael said at her back, "Trouble?"

"Hullo, darling. Yes. Trouble."

"Perhaps," he said, "it would be intelligent to take some air."

"It is lovely outside." They went towards the long
windows. "Did you lose?" she asked.

"No, I won. But my mind wasn't on it."

"That is why you won. Where was your mind?"

He said, "Over the hills and far away."

They stood looking up at the night. He put his arm gently
round her waist and kissed her hair.

"You've liked it, haven't you?"

"So much that I cannot bear to think that it is the last time."

"It might not be."

"Oh, Michael."

She could not explain to him that she did not need false consolations any more. There was the huge door, creaking on its iron hinges to shut out the sun, the war that would be the end of all that she knew. But this insecurity was small beside the one that had endured for nearly two months.

She thought, "If he would only speak of it, only remember. He has blacked out that night. For him it didn't happen." She went back to the afternoon in his bedroom, hearing the sound of his voice, sleepy and good-humoured.

"You see, I don't remember anything. I do know that I was very tired after I finished work; I thought that it was foolish to try and sit out the Crimes Club dinner. I drank whisky while I was changing. And vaguely, I remember walking down Wigmore Street, looking for a taxi. After that it is entirely blank; the next thing was waking up feeling awfully ill and full of headache, with Billy asking me questions."

He remembered buying the cat; he had seen it in a shop-window early in the afternoon; he did not remember putting it in his pocket before he went out. The restaurant with the black and yellow lamp-shades was in Soho; it was called the French Horn. He had not dined there for years and he could not imagine why he had chosen it. "The regrettable fact is," said Michael, "that I got myself as near paralytic as I have ever been in my life, and proceeded, in an unforgivable manner, to take it out on you. I am so very sorry."

"Where have you gone?" he was asking; she looked away from the sea to the shape of him beside her. She said, "I don't go; I stay." She, who had once found it so miserably hard to dissemble, must hide this fear from him always, without knowing why.

("Why can't I tell you that the memory of that night goes on haunting me? Why can't I ever ask you about it again? What is it I am afraid to know?")

146

BOOK TWO

(1943–1944)

THE CALENDAR OF LONG HOURS

"I never hurt you.
  You drew your sword upon me without cause."
                                   Twelfth Night, Act V, Scene I

BOOK TWO

FRIDAY, JUNE 25th, 1943

WHEN the newly-appointed officer from the Public Relations Division came into Vera Haydon's room, he made a creaking sound as he walked. The sound came from his artificial leg; he had the habit of mentioning his leg frequently in conversation, and this embarrassed Vera, who could never make herself reply naturally.

He creaked across the carpetless floor, grinning at her, holding a fat file in his hands. Vera's table was in the corner farthest from the door, which gave him a long way to walk. The room was strikingly bare; the more strikingly because it had once been the drawing-room in a luxury flat and still wore melancholy traces of that function. There were rose-coloured tiles round the empty fireplace, stippled walls, and dirty pink paint on cornice and wainscot. The only furniture besides Vera's chair and table was a large bookcase on whose lowest shelf a few Ministry publications leaned together. Half the windows lacked glass and had the emergency-fillings, talc and wire-mesh.

"Here's trouble," said the newly-appointed P.R. officer, putting down the file in front of her. She moved the silver paper-knife and pen-tray to give it room. The creaking of his leg was audible as he bent over the table.

"The Minister has come back from leave in a mood. Doesn't care for the way we've handled any of this; says the note's all wrong. I did point out that the note was precisely the one he'd suggested before he went away. But it's no good. It's got to be done again. Here are some lines that he thinks you'll find helpful." The Minister always wrote his helpful lines in red chalk. Vera studied the large hieroglyphs.

149

"Very well," she said aggrievedly, "I'll see what I can do. How much hurry is there, Mr. Bessingham? I'm on a rush job for the Commodities Division."

"It ought to go out this afternoon; or to-morrow morning latest," said Bessingham, swaying and creaking. He offered her a cigarette, then said, "Oh, I forgot; you don't," and grinned at her. He was a curly-haired young man with blue eyes and he would have been personable were it not for the scars that riddled and puckered the left side of his face. He was, Vera regretted, Common. He had held a commission, he was something of a hero, but the vowel-sounds in his voice betrayed him.

"Gosh, I'm squeaky this morning, aren't I?" he said, patting his thigh. "Believe it's the weather, you know. Always seems to squeak more in wet weather."

She had resolved that next time he mentioned the leg, she would have to say something about it, something casual and gay, duplicating his easy manner. She set her face and pitched her voice determinedly, asking, "Is it comfortable now? Are you getting used to it?"

"Oh, yes. Takes a bit of time, of course. They warned me it would. I remember Knowle making a frightfully funny crack the day after he operated. He said——"

She lost the joke and while she stared she saw that he was looking disappointed because she did not laugh.

"I'm sorry, did you say *Knowle*?" she asked.

"Yes. Colonel Knowle; surgeon out there, wizard man," said Bessingham. "Friend of yours?"

"I used to know him."

"Wonderful chap, isn't he?"

"I—I never knew him very well."

"Ought to see him on the job," said Bessingham, "Wouldn't be in that racket for a million on a plate. Don't know how they do it when there's a show on. Working by hurricane-lamps with all that stuff coming down; taking chaps to pieces; putting 'em together again. Cool as bloody cucumbers. He got his about ten days after me. I gather he's okay now."

He glanced at his watch. "I say, it's ten to eleven. Must whistle up the girls. Suppose you can't be persuaded?" He was creaking away to the door, taking her refusal for granted.

Ever since the circulation of the memorandum requesting the officers of the Division not to go out for morning coffee, Vera had been scrupulous in obedience. She was now the only abstainer. The arrival of Mr. Bessingham, who committed other enormities besides reading the memorandum and saying "What bloody rot," had stimulated opposition. He was, Vera thought, the kind of person who could Get Away with Things.

As the door shut behind him, she took off her dark glasses and rubbed her eyes. Her private kingdom was now brought near. She glanced apologetically at the urgent file; it was powerless; the thoughts had begun, the reverie that was so much brighter in colour, blacker in shadow, than all the drab realities. It was like a physical symptom; she could think: "It is being worse than usual to-day" or "It let up a little this afternoon."

Suddenly she picked up her handbag from the table and hurried to the door. Mr. Bessingham, with the two young women whom he called "the girls", was just stepping into the lift.

"*Don't* say *you're* coming out for coffee? Well, well."

"The last incorruptible citadel has fallen."

Mr. Bessingham said "Good show."

The lift descended slowly. "But it is so curious," Vera thought, her mind now making the accustomed comments, "that the years between have folded up. When I think 'before the war', I go straight back to Manchester Square and Cold Ash. I never think about the Galleries at all. I was with Dennis Brookfield for seven years. Seven years; and none of those years are real; any more than Now is real."

The lift reached the ground-floor. "Got your passes, girls?" Bessingham was asking. "There's a flap on about passes to-day." They walked out into the greyish weather;

past the shattered, hollow building on the corner and across the street that went down towards the Thames Embankment; the coffee-shop was a little way up the street on the left-hand side.

She saw bright pictures of the garden at Cold Ash; Mercedes planting out a flower-bed and the Siamese cat stalking a butterfly.

"Two whites; one black. How do you like it, Miss Haydon?"

"White, please."

She saw the studio room; Mercedes in a blue overall, screwing up her eyes and stretching out her arm, measuring proportions with the paint-brush.

"Any buns this morning?"

The young women were telling Mr. Bessingham a story in unison; one of the blissfully enjoyable Ministry stories about a stupid mistake; the kind of story that made everyone happy.

She thought, "I should know if she were dead; I am certain of that. It is silly to go on believing it, after all this time; but I should know."

"Penny for them, Miss Haydon," said Bessingham.

It should be easy to say, "I was thinking about the Knowles;" to add, "She was more my friend than he was;" even to tell the story, here, to the three at the table.

"She was caught in France when the Germans went in. I have just a little information about her. In the summer of '40, she was working with one of those polyglot ambulance-units; they went on doing relief work after the Armistice. She left them and went South. She had some property there and I suppose she wanted to see to that. She hasn't been heard of since. Except that last year there was the name of an Englishwoman, spelled 'Noel,' in a record of the deaths at one internment camp. The Red Cross got it. It may have been Mrs. Knowle."

She could not say any of it. One of the alarming symptoms of the reverie was its way of shutting the gates on its private kingdom. Just as the thoughts came up into words, she would find that she had said something quite different.

"Oh, I was thinking about that dreary file you brought me. How long do you suppose the Minister's mood is likely to be with us?"

Then they were off on that; she could be quiet again.

She saw the bedroom-door standing open; the shiny white luggage with the initials on the lids; the expensive clothes laid out across the bed; Mercedes turning from the looking-glass to call, "Vera! Could you locate my passport, do you think? Somewhere in my desk."

It was bad to-day. Bessingham had compelled it; and now he was flavoured with a new importance; he had known Michael Knowle. With a damnable lack of discrimination, the reverie insisted on chasing after Michael, after Caroline Seward, counting them only as links with Mercedes; making an importance of the day when Michael's name appeared among the wounded in the first casualty-lists after El Alamein; scoring the fact that a Caroline Seward had been attached for a short while to the same A.T.S. unit as Vera's cousin. Astounding to think of Miss Seward in khaki, but the description was unmistakable.

She stared at Bessingham, who was now picking up the bill and saying, "This is on me." There were the usual protests. "No idea how rich I am," he said sunnily.

They pushed back their chairs and went out. Mr. Bessingham paused to look at the hollow building, with the space beside it, the emergency water-tank and the wooden fence. "Must have been a smacker," he said; "If they start anything like that again, girls, I warn you I'm getting myself transferred to Rhyl with the Admin. blokes."

The two young women began to reassure him, and to swop their gay reminiscences. "That was the Saturday; not the Saturday after the Wednesday, but the Saturday." "Funny, the only blitz I minded was last February"; "Suppose we'd got out of practice, sort of." "Sometimes it's rather fun, actually."

She thought, "I don't mind how I hear the news of her death provided that it isn't just picking up *The Times* one day and seeing that Mr. Knowle has married that girl; that would be the worst way of all."

The lift was crowded; they packed in and the closing doors pressed against their backs. Beside her Bessingham's leg was creaking.

"D'you know if Knowle's wife ever got back to England?"

For a moment she thought that she had imagined the question; then he repeated it. Her lips seemed to stiffen, letting out the confused words reluctantly. Then the doors of the lift opened and she was beside him in the corridor, saying, "But that's all I know. Did he talk about her? What did he say?"

"Oh, Knowle never mentioned her. I got the story from one of the chaps in his unit, an R.A.M.C. type. Then I ran into somebody who'd seen her."

She heard a queer, moaning voice that gasped, "Oh, who? where? Please——" and Bessingham, creaking to a halt at the door of his room, looked a little embarrassed.

"He was a chap in the American Red Cross, actually. Chap called Wynstay Adams. Apparently he was a friend of hers; saw her in France."

Vera said, "And she is well? She's safe?"

"Oh, yes. I think so. Can't remember all the details but he talked about her."

"Could you—could you possibly put me in touch with him?"

Bessingham's telephone began to ring. He said, "Oh, hell, excuse me—Yes, sir; sorry, sir. I had to step along to one of the other departments. Right away, sir—— That's his nibs, Miss Haydon. I'll have to run." He creaked more than ever as he darted round his desk, collecting papers.

"Could you put me in touch with this Mr. Adams?"

"Well, he gets about, you know; like all those boys; don't quite know where he's based." He looked at her perplexedly as she hurried beside him. "It's all right," she said, "I was

154

going up to the Secretary's room anyway. Did you meet this Mr. Adams here or overseas?"

"I met him here; over a few drinks with some of the M. of I. types. Daresay one of them could tell me." He grinned at her, waved and disappeared round the Minister's door.

Back at her table, Vera opened the file and began to write the draft for the Commodities Division. She kept looking up from it, feeling that her eyes were dazzled with sunshine. She would always now feel affection for this particular memorandum; she would turn back to it in future months and recapture the glow of to-day. Perhaps this was truly the end of the lonely search; the end of hurrying down the column of death-notices on *The Times*' front page; the end of composing and discarding letters that began "Dear Colonel Knowle"; the end of collecting information about French internment camps. "He mustn't forget" she thought. She took a sheet of paper from the wire basket on her desk and wrote, under the printed heading, MEMO TO:

Mr. Bessingham.

I shall be so grateful if you can note here the name of any of your friends at the M. of I. who can put me in touch with Mr. Wynstay Adams.

FRIDAY, JULY 16th, 1943

The sergeant said, "Want your tea in here, ma'am?"

"Sure," said Joan Bridges, without looking up. On her writing-pad she was making spasmodic figures in answer to the Paymaster's query:

"Tradeswoman Clerk, Class III; Trade Pay; Credits." The dull little details about the dull little woman whose destiny, with the destiny of two hundred others, was Joan's affair. The sergeant hesitated in the doorway of the Company Office.

"Yes, what?" Joan said, still adding.

"Wouldn't you rather have it up in the ante-room? Give you a bit of a breather."

"I can't; I'm a long way behind myself as it is. How are those Returns getting on?"

"All be ready for you to sign in about ten minutes," said the sergeant.

When the tea came, Joan lit a cigarette and blew her nose violently; she was suffering from hay-fever. She looked round the room in a catarrhal daze, thinking that because she had sat here since nine o'clock, it began to have the effect of a railway carriage in which she had travelled all day.

It was an uninspired room. The present headquarters of " A " Company, 2nd Sussex Group, had been a girls' school ; this room on the ground floor was one of the smaller class-rooms. All that Joan saw was drab and brown; the wallpaper, the cupboards, desks and chairs. Her own greatcoat, respirator and cap, hanging on their hooks, carried on the dingy tones. The only colour was in some Canterbury bells, hopefully squashed into a brown jug on the top of the filing-cabinet. Outside the windows there was the erratic light of a stormy summer afternoon; a wet tree shining; a purple cloud hanging low.

Joan drank the tea; it was good to her dry throat. The telephone rang.

"Group to speak to you, ma'am," said the sergeant; by her dryness, Joan thought, she conveyed her dislike for the Group Commander as emphatically as though she had called her the old cow.

"Good-afternoon, ma'am."

"Oh, Bridges." The brittle, authoritative voice had some favour to ask. "I wonder if you could give the P.T. officer a bed on Wednesday night? She'll be in the district and she'd like a chance to see your people."

"Damn," said Joan, with her hand over the mouthpiece; the voice went on—"It isn't an official visit; she's going to look at a course that some of the ack-ack people are laying on."

"Look, ma'am; if she wants to inspect their P.T., she couldn't have chosen a worse day. Wednesday night the

Security officer's giving them a lecture. They have their P.T. on Saturday mornings."

"You couldn't lay it on for Thursday morning?"

"Not without going on my knees to Records, ma'am. They've altered the hours so many times that they're nearly crazy. The colonel will have kittens."

"Oh, dear, Bridges. Well, I'm afraid we can't refuse. D.D.A.T.S. is so anxious for us to co-operate."

"*All* right, ma'am."

Joan put back the receiver, drank the cooling tea and scowled. The sergeant came in with the Returns.

"You heard all that."

"What, ma'am?"

"Come off it, Warne; you were listening. You always do."

"Something about P.T. on Wednesday was all I caught," said the sergeant.

"Well, that's your story and you stick to it. But you'll have to put up a camp bed in my room for Miss Seward. The spare-room will be occupied by the P.T. daisy and there's our whole evening spoiled."

The sergeant made a clicking noise.

"Why didn't you tell Group you couldn't manage it?"

"What, and have her asking why I make so bold as to entertain my friends on W.D. property?"

The sergeant said that it wasn't as if Miss Seward wasn't an officer.

"No, and it isn't as though she had any business in this Command either. O.K., give me those Returns." She signed her name on each; J. M. Bridges, J.-Cmdr. " A " Coy., she wondered how many times she had signed her name since the war began. There was a knock on the door and the clerk came in with the afternoon post.

"Thank you, Simmons. Did you get my evening paper?"

"Last one was sold, ma'am, just as I got there. Terribly sorry."

"You're a hoodoo; they're always sold when you get near them. How am I to know what's happening to the war?"

There was the bump of an explosion towards the coast and the windows rattled. The siren sounded and the sergeant, leaning at the window, said, "There go Gert and Daisy," as the two fighters skimmed overhead.

"That's what's happening to the war, ma'am," said the clerk facetiously.

"Well, keep away from that glass. He may be coming inland." She glanced through the post; it was the usual bunch of long buff envelopes, limp at the edges, re-addressed over Economy Labels. "Group, Group, Command, Pay, Records—Hell, I know what that is. Here you are, Warne; all for you." The last letter in the pile was a fat, square envelope, postmarked from Edinburgh, its label at an angle, addressed in Caroline's small, savage handwriting. A second bomb fell, nearer now, and Joan glanced at the clock. The girls in her Company worked at the Records Office a mile away. "They won't have started home yet, ma'am," the sergeant said.

"Ooh, there he goes; look; with the flak about five miles off target and Gert and Daisy nowhere."

"*Will* you two take yourselves away from those windows?"

"It's all right, ma'am; he's over the sea and far away. What a sauce."

Joan opened Caroline's letter.

"No 1. A.T.S. O.C.T.U.
                                          "Wednesday.

"Dear God,—I don't mean you, darling, but what an afternoon I've had. The latest experiment among the keener and cleaner girls on the staff (led, needless to say by the adjutant) is a ceremonial parade, a surprise for the chief's birthday. So we rehearsed it for two solid hours. Not one of us had the smallest idea of the drill. The facetious little cadets were rolling about like barrels in their vulgar mirth, while the poor officers marched monotonously in a dozen different directions. The lines curved so much that I asked Lockwood if we were meant to spell 'Happy Birthday To

You' when seen from the air. In my view it will give the chief less of a surprise than a Nasty Turn.

"Look, the whole Wednesday-Thursday programme has been given something of a jolt. Michael has a Board on Thursday so he won't be able to leave for Sister Dorothy's till after it's over. He has found me a billet within a yard of the hospital gates. There I shall sit while the Board sits and we'll probably travel down on Thursday evening, fetching up in your ante-room for drinks. He insists, in his last letter, that Dorothy is ready and anxious to put me up at the house.

"So I shan't, if that's true, need your spare room for my hols. (You know I really think that this school stuff is getting into my blood and that another six months in this institution will finally establish me as a case of arrested development. Recreations, Ragging at Meals, Lavatory-Jokes, and Pranks Played On The Big Ones.)

"The Board. I shut my mind to it, but I think Michael and I both know the answer before it happens. He is entirely fit now thank God, and they'll have no alternative but to pass him for Active Service. (Again the torture and again the road.) But I know he's getting bored with Branley, and impatient to rejoin his chums as they proceed against what is so prettily called The Soft Under-Belly. Extraordinary how one's prayers adapt. My only prayer now is that his embarkation leave will be postponed long enough to coincide with our long-leave week-end in the middle of the next course. Too much to hope that he'll be kept hanging around any longer than that. Well, we shall all get some fun next week, at least. I'm *fascinated*, by the way, that you now have troops working at Cold Ash. And wonder how the old mausoleum looks in its military guise.

"The course is going quite well, I suppose; it's routine-stuff now and I feel as though I never had been anything but an instructor. To my horror, they have at last wished on me the tedious rôle of Drama-Adviser. I've been dodging it for months, but the chief got wind of my previous preoccupations. All it adds up to is keeping an eye on the cadets' end-of-course entertainment. I'm supposed to give helpful theatrical hints and cut out any coarse jokes. (Yes, me. I have a creeping fear that between my standard of coarseness and the O.C.T.U.'s there is a great gulf fixed.)

"Oh, cocky, I was looking forward to our Wednesday night gossip and gin. But you do see . . . ? The stocks here, by the way, remain fairly adequate though Lockwood (Queen Spoiler-Of-The-Fun) has twice suggested to me that three before dinner are not the distinguishing mark of an officer and temporary gentlewoman.

"Now the candles which, in defiance of regulations, I have stuck upright on my mantelpiece (each in its tiny pool of grease) are burning low and I'll stop. See you Thursday. You really did exhibit brilliance in getting yourself posted within ten miles of the Knowle family seat.

<blockquote>
"I have the honour to be,
   "Madam,
    "Your obedient servant,
     "CAROLINE SEWARD, Sub."
</blockquote>

Joan threw the remaining papers into the basket marked "PENDING." When Warne came back, she said, "Oh, Miss Seward can't make it, so I can devote myself whole-heartedly to P.T. on Wednesday night."

Warne looked desolate; Warne had the rare quality of wanting other people to have a good time. "What, not coming at all, ma'am? Has she had her seven days cancelled?"

"No; she'll be here Thursday, with Colonel Knowle; they're staying over at his sister's. He's got a Board."

"Thought that would be coming up," said Warne. "Well, why don't you call it a day now, and have a drink upstairs?"

"You couldn't be more right."

As she mounted the stairs to the ante-room the troops came pouring into the hall; with the loudest clumping that army boots could make and a shrill skirl of voices. "Little less noise there, please——" Joan called over the stairs. The hush was instant. She thought, "What does it matter? I'm mean to take it out on them because I am sad."

She thought, "And not only because I shan't have Caroline to myself on Thursday. That damn Board. And he'll go back."

She opened the door on the landing; the door was labelled "Officers Only". In a different hierarchy, the headmistress of the school had once occupied this self-contained flat. There were two small bedrooms, the slightly larger ante-room and a bathroom.

Joan went into the ante-room; it was furnished to the usual pattern by the Army Welfare Branch; there were four moderately comfortable chairs, a table that held A.B.C.A. pamphlets, old copies of literary magazines and a wireless set. In the cheap bookcases she had stored the nucleus of her library. She had put up her Van Gogh reproductions on the yellow wallpaper. The carpet was brown and the curtains were brown. Each bedroom opened off this room.

Joan took the bottle of gin from the cupboard and filled one of the Woolworth glasses, adding some ersatz orange juice. She stood in front of the fireplace, solemnly toasting Michael and Caroline. She thought, "Here's luck; but they never had any luck. No, that is absurd. Compared with many people they have been lucky enough. Why do I think that? Just because there was a moment when it looked as though they would be married? Curious how long ago and far away the prospect of that marriage seems."

Almost, now, it looked like a mere illusion of that last care-free summer; gone down with the other illusions. "I don't think I ever believed in it, even then. And somehow I don't think Caroline did." She remembered when Caroline had paced the flat, in the top room at the boarding-house, saying restlessly, "I still feel as though she'd win." "And, by God, she was right. If Mercedes wanted to play them a mean trick, she couldn't have played it better than by vanishing in France."

Caroline had developed an odd reluctance to mention Mercedes. It was the eccentric, abrupt Miss Knowle, pillar of the local W.V.S., who talked of her. Since her father's death, Miss Knowle had lived alone. She came here some-times to spend an evening and she hated Mercedes more than she hated Hitler.

MONDAY, JULY 19*th,* 1943

It was warm in the platoon-hut. Caroline sat at the table just inside the door, facing the short rows of tables and benches that were ranked down the narrow space. The twenty-three women in khaki were engaged on one of their last assignments here, the completion of their personal documents for the War Office.

At the beginning of the course there had been twenty-four women in the platoon; while she watched the majority busily recording their status as officers, Caroline looked at the blank space in the second row. She remembered the one who had failed. In the blank space, next to the virtuous Sellars, whom she distrusted, she now conjured the dim, puzzled features, birds'-nest hair and tortured tie belonging to Groom; Groom whose epitaph was written in bewilder-ment. "She never had a clue," Caroline thought. "I wish she hadn't cried; but they always cry."

On the walls of the hut, various decorations surrounded the names and achievements of past platoons. One smug enclosure of illuminated names, set within a laurel wreath, surmounted by the A.T.S. badge, announced "None Faltered." It was always an irritation to Caroline. Vale, the brightest member of the present community, had drawn a panel of caricatures. "She is a talented child," Caroline thought, looking at the new addition on the wall. "I like all this lot with the exception of Sellars. I'll be sorry to part with them. But that is how it goes every time. Nine days from now I shall be meeting a bunch of cowed, unpalatable strangers who will take less than two weeks to become my dear old platoon, my favourite girls. *What* are you saying,—Nine days from now? There's no such thing. There's only Wednes-day, and leave, and Michael."

"Ma'am?"

"Yes, Palmer."

"When it says 'Any other information', would it be relevant to put that I used to breed Kerry Blues?"

"No, I don't think so."

"Breed Kerry Blues? I thought only Kerry Blues could do that," said Vale.

Caroline said, "Look; I've nothing against your laughing but could you make less noise about it?"

At least they were now at the showing-off stage; which she found more bearable than the white-faced, conscientious hysteria of the first weeks.

"Please, ma'am, Sellars and I have finished ours," said Vale. When she placed her papers on the table in front of Caroline, she said, "The rehearsal's immediately after supper, if that's all right with you."

"I'll be there," said Caroline brusquely. It was impossible not to feel instincts of favouritism towards Vale, who had a lively mind and a dark boyish beauty; she was the most vivid person in the platoon; she talked Caroline's language; like the potential favourites on other courses, she received carefully anonymous treatment.

"Lucky there's the rehearsal," said Vale, "I feel drawn towards going to the Aperitif and getting tight. Could they fail us now, ma'am? After we've passed? For getting tight?"

"Sure," said Caroline, irritated because she was thinking, "It would be fun to go to the Aperitif with you." Again she saw the danger-line of this incarceration among women; the school-atmosphere breeding emotion where none should exist. She was still thinking about it when she walked out of the hut. All the cadets exploded into conversation as she left pausing at the door to light their cigarettes.

She walked on in the sunlight, up the gravel path to the green quadrangle that was set about with four grey stone buildings. Caroline took the officer's privilege of walking across the grass. She saw Hadow just ahead. Hadow was a long thin blonde with a silly laugh and no respect for the

163

O.C.T.U. *mystique*. She appeared to be divided into two halves, like a wasp; her wriggling walk was accentuated by the tightness of her leather belt. She turned to wait for Caroline and this Caroline did not want, valuing in these days the moments of solitude.

"My splendid women," said Hadow, who never referred to her platoon in any other way, "have all lost their reason. You never saw anything like the mess they made of their documents. What is it about filling in forms that turns adults into cretins?"

"It's end-of-term. Spiffing hols," said Caroline. "And I love them all."

("And I love this evening; and the look of the mountain over the roofs; and I love your company and I love time because he must have a stop.")

"More than I do," Hadow said. They went into the staff building and took off their belts in the hall. In the ante-room Caroline thought, "And I even love Lockwood; with her 'Here comes That Girl' face."

"What are you having?" Hadow asked.

"Whisky, please; a large one. I'll sign. Please, Hadow; let me sign while the mood is on me. Isn't it soothing to reflect that at this moment, throughout the length and breadth of the country, persons dressed hideously, in depressing surroundings called ante-rooms, are all doing the same thing?" She saw Lockwood's delicate, pettish face turned towards her. She grinned and the grin drew a faint, downward-curving smile. She sat down with Hadow on a leather sofa.

"I've finished your Marshall Hall book," Hadow said; "kept me awake all night."

"Did you read the Bennett case? Isn't that a thing?"

"I think he was guilty," said Hadow.

"You don't? I'd go bail for him any time."

Hadow began to natter. "No, no, *no*, Seward. All the evidence was there. The railway-ticket; the journey. The alibi with what's-his-name——"

"Sholto Douglas——"

164

"Well, that was completely ruled out."

Caroline said, "Listen. If you were separated from your wife; on the worst possible terms with her, and in love with somebody else, would you kill her that way? I ask you. You might shoot her, but you certainly wouldn't rape her."

Lockwood put down her newspaper. "Seward, please——"

"Ma'am?"

"Must we always have these squalid details of crime just before supper?"

Caroline said, "Last time you objected to them, it was because they were just after supper." Hadow gave her loud foolish whinny. Lockwood was flushing, in a steady glow of scarlet. "Have you no other subject of conversation?"

"Certainly, ma'am; a very wide selection. What would you like?"

"Oh, don't be silly, Seward," said Lockwood wearily, "There are times when you behave as though you were twelve years old." It was the stock A.T.S. gibe; they all used it in time of quarrel; monotonously accusing one another of not being grown-up.

"Well, if you don't like rape," said Caroline, "I suggest, in all humility that you should pay no attention. This place is alleged to be my home and in my home I can discuss what I like without restriction." ("What a thundering lie; the only home I ever had was much like this, and my mother much like you.") She stood up with the rest of them watching her, the differently shaped and coloured women in their sameness of khaki. She went to the sideboard and helped herself to a second drink. "These are the moments when one wants to pack the whole issue up and get the hell out. Don't think about her. Think about Wednesday." She heard the bells clanging from the other houses for the cadet's supper. Lockwood was saying, "There is such a thing as consideration for other people's feelings."

"Oh, God bless us, everyone, said Tiny Tim."

Hadow whinnied again. Caroline swallowed the second

drink rapidly; the cadets were capable of eating their supper in fifteen minutes, with a rehearsal pending. She said to Lockwood, "As the Eminence Grise of the establishment, ma'am, can you reveal to me whether the Chief Commander will be dining in mess to-night?"

"No; she's gone out" said Lockwood heavily.

"That relieves my feelings. If you'll excuse me, I'll go in now."

"The orderlies may not be ready for you."

"That would be just too bad."

She went into the long room, cursing herself for playing this childish game of insolence; the large bowls of salad were already set out on the tables. She cut some bread and gobbled the salad and went.

Now this is mine, she thought, walking out into the silence of the quadrangle; this square of green with the early evening light fallen upon it; the colours in the sky; the solemn shadows; this place now has an immemorial, college look; it isn't attuned to war. I can be quiet here.

She was ahead of the cadets; she could see a line of khaki backs seated against the long windows in the building on her right. She walked across the grass; pausing to light a cigarette. "Absurd to let that woman get under my skin. My trouble is that I'm tired; and when I look forward now, I see that I am almost done with the pleasures of anticipation. They are not enough to feed on any more. I have reached the stage when I stumble, and kick time out of the way and dread that something will stop it at the last minute."

She went in under the archway; into the long lecture hall with the stage at its far end. It had the especial hush of any room built for a crowd and deserted by the crowd. It had, almost, the dramatic haunt of empty theatres long ago; and in a past life this was the hour when she had felt the strong excitement, waiting in costume and make-up for the rise of the curtain. She was suddenly homesick for that. The lost magic beat its wings about her head. She was aware that she had been an actress of promise and quality, that it was all betrayed and deserted too soon.

She walked up to the stage. First she had the impulse to mount the boards. Then she began to repeat, softly and scornfully, where she stood:

"A blank, my lord. She never told her love,
    But let concealment like a worm i' the bud
Feed on her damask cheek. She pined in thought——"

—"And with a green and yellow melancholy," said the voice of Vale in her ear. She did not know for how long Vale had been watching her. There was something important about the two of them here, looking at each other.

"You played Viola in '39 didn't you, ma'am?"

"I understudied the part," Caroline said.

"My father saw you play it; he was crazy for it. When he got my letter saying you were my platoon officer, he wrote back saying that if you were the same Caroline Seward he'd seen as Viola, the Army was entertaining a genius unawares."

"Thank you kindly."

"I shouldn't think," said Vale, extracting a cigarette-case from her breast pocket and offering it to Caroline, "that facetious performances by cadets were much fun for you." She flicked industriously at the wheel of a brass utility-lighter; Caroline murmured, "They ought to sell utility thumbs to go with them."

The dark boyish face was turned to her now with a look of sparkling curiosity. "Go on," Caroline said, "what's on your mind?"

"The usual question," said Vale, "wondering what made you come into this racket."

And here, Caroline thought, I should like to be able to answer you honestly; to say, "I love a man who was sent overseas with his regiment in December of '40. This was the nearest that I could get to him." But for so long one has lost the luxurious habit of saying the thing that one means; it will come back, perhaps, some day, that habit, with oranges and eggs and petrol. She said, "It seemed to me a satisfactory and obvious way of fighting a war."

"Does it still?"

"Why do you ask?"

The other cadets were coming into the hall, carrying bundles of miscellaneous property-clothes; shouting and only lowering their voices a little when they saw the officer; the caste-mark was almost rubbed off now; in another twenty-four hours they would be wearing officers' uniform. Vale said, "It's too permanent for me. I can imagine going crazy with it and wanting to get out and banging my head against its walls." She put a sheaf of paper into Caroline's hands. "Those are the final versions of the song-numbers. You said you'd like to look them over. Do you think the orderlies will object to that?"

Caroline read the opening chorus; the Instructors' Lament:

"We're officers and gentlewomen, pillars of the O.C.T.U.,
By the time the evening's over, we hope we shan't have shocked you.
In June of 1941, we came across the border,
To civilise the Scottish race and keep cadets in order."

Vale's finger was pointing on the fourth line, "They're all Scots, aren't they?"

"Yes, but I shouldn't let that worry you."

At the back of the hall, Caroline found herself wondering how good it was; how much she was beguiled by two whiskies, by the imminence of her leave, by Vale, who flashed through all the scenes, directing, acting, criticising; leaping from the lights to the piano-stool, where she corrected Palmer's rendering of the Sullivan score to which they had adapted their lyrics.

"It is the mixture as before," Caroline thought. "Not so much better than the Company Concert that Corporal Seward produced at Woolwich. And Lockwood will loathe it; too smart-alec for her. Who cares?"

It was almost dark when she left the hall. Behind her she could hear their voices singing the end of the opening chorus.

"Our brains are blank. Our thoughts aren't worth a penny;
Our trouble is—we've had one Course too many."

"Me too," thought Caroline. She passed along the dimly lighted hall and went up the stairs to her room. There was much noise of running bath-water, scuffling of slippers along bare corridors; somebody's wireless playing. She opened the door; her room-mate was not here. She turned up the light; the one electric-bulb, shadeless, with its lower half painted blue, completed the effect of a garret. There were two army beds, two small, box-type dressing-tables and two chairs. Each dressing-table was a minute patch of private possessions. She said to Michael's photograph, "Less than forty-eight hours, now."

The room felt cold. She took off her uniform and pulled on over her shirt a pair of battle-dress trousers. She set up the forbidden candles. From the brief-case that lived under the bed, she began to take out Michael's letters. They were all in bundles of twelve, fastened with rubber bands. There were eighteen months, she thought, when letters had been the only truth and the fact of him a sweet, imagined lie. "These were you," she thought, looking at the grey envelopes, "this series of affirmative punctuations that I dreaded not to find. You weren't a man in those days. You were this accumulating pile of treasure in the brief-case." (She had reminded him before he went, "You said once that you ought to be cured of writing letters; don't let it happen now.")

She strewed them across the surface of the grey army blanket; lifting one at random, she unfolded it.

"In my view, the alleged comradeship and team-spirit of which so much is made, consists solely of suffering, without undue savagery, the company of people whom one would find intolerable in peace. It would be stupid to add that here there is only the illusion of company; it always was an illusion. More intelligent to look at one's lonely soul and to say to it, without wishing otherwise, 'There is only God and you'."

"Only God and you," Caroline repeated, familiar with the disturbing echo of this phrase. "No, Michael. I couldn't take it then and I can't take it now. It denies the validity of you and me." She put away the letters. She thought, "You are going from me again; you will turn back into these thin grey envelopes. In a few weeks now, that will happen. But I don't believe it. This is the odd curse, or mercy of the war; the belief that each stage will last forever. There was a time, six months ago, when I thought that you would be always a person on sick-leave; a child whom I could not cherish enough because the damned Army called me from your side. But your wound was more my friend than you are; it kept you safe."

This was too lonely. It could be thought and said in his arms, forty-eight hours from now; not here in the sad little room with the dripping candles. She got off the bed, lit a cigarette and went down the corridor to Hadow's room.

Hadow was lying in bed, balancing a cup and saucer on her knees. At the dressing-table, Lockwood sat, braiding her hair. The looking-glass in this room had a light over it; at bed-time people wandered in to do their hair under the light and Hadow entertained them with cocoa. Lockwood did not look round.

"Did you bring a mug? Well, use the tooth-glass," Hadow said.

"Thanks. Good evening, ma'am." Lockwood answered cloudily, as though from a long way off.

"How did the rehearsal go?" Hadow asked.

"I thought very well. That child Vale is extremely talented."

"Vale?" Lockwood's voice sharpened. "Isn't she the very masculine-looking girl with the cropped hair? The one who was acting Company Commander on the parade?"

"Yes; that's Vale."

Lockwood gave a little laugh. "She did badly in her interview with the chief."

Hadow winked. Caroline sat down on the bed, wrapping her handkerchief round the hot glass. "I know about that," she said. "Apparently the chief was a little drowsier than usual. She didn't drive up to Vale's idea."

"My dear Seward, I happened to be there. That young

woman rushed in and said she wanted a staff job; the chief very reasonably told her, as she tells all these A.O.E.R.'s, that she ought to have some experience in platoon work first."

Caroline yawned. "Yes, she missed the point. Vale came into this game ear-marked for a P.R. job."

"Nobody," said Lockwood, "comes in *ear-marked* for a job. That is what these people, these A.O.E.R.'s, imagine; just because they're whipped in through a back-door by a War Office Board. The chief——"

Caroline said, "——feels very strongly about it." Hadow whinnied loudly. In the mirror Lockwood's face was turning scarlet.

"Poor Vale," said Caroline, "wanted to know whether, in view of her possible appointment, she had an opportunity of applying for platoon work first. The chief smacked her down before she got to the end of her sentence."

"That, no doubt, is her version, Seward."

"Well, of course, it's her version, ma'am. Whose else should I hear? And I believe it; seeing I've never got beyond my first semi-colon with the chief myself."

Lockwood turned from the glass; the tightly braided hair, straining up from the forehead, exaggerated the lift of her eyebrows.

"I'm not talking sedition," said Caroline. "She doesn't mean to snap. She is so extraordinarily nervous at interviews that she jumps in too soon. One has seen similar cases."

Lockwood's attention appeared to be diverted. She said, "Seward, *what* have you got on?"

"These, ma'am? Trousers. Battle-dress trousers."

"With your shirt and collar and tie?"

"That is correct, ma'am, yes."

Lockwood fluttered her eyelashes and said, "I don't think I understand."

"It's quite simple, really," said Caroline, " a pair of trousers. Not complicated."

"Did you attend the rehearsal dressed like that?"

"No. I didn't get on a tram and ride into Newington like this, either."

"You mean that you have just put them on?"

"By God——" said Caroline, "you're on the right track. I put them on when I went into my bedroom."

"Oh, I see. . . . But, Seward, I don't think you should."

Caroline put down the tooth-glass on the floor. "If you're serious," she said, "I think I may be rude, and that would be a pity. Are you suggesting that I'm not entitled to walk along the landing dressed like this?"

"It isn't a question of being entitled. It is a question of the example. One of the orderlies might see you and think that she could wear them."

"Wear my trousers? Like hell she could."

Hadow began to scream like a horse in pain. Lockwood said, "You're impossible. But I must ask you not to wear them again."

Caroline said, "And I must ask you, ma'am, to remember that we're at war, not at Roedean."

Lockwood rose from the stool, picking up her hairbrush and drawing the cord of her dressing-gown tightly about her waist. "Good night," she said formally and departed.

Hadow snorted happily. "You know the next thing, don't you? She'll get a ruling from the chief."

"Dear God, I couldn't care less if she got a ruling from Queen Mary."

"She's not a bad old twerp," said Hadow.

"Who? Queen Mary?"

"No; the Adj. You just get in her hair because you won't conform."

"The awful part is that she reminds me of my mother."

"She's everybody's mother," said Hadow, "Go to bed."

Caroline walked back down the dim corridor; she said moodily and aloud,

> "I have been studying how I may compare
> This prison where I live, unto the world."

TUESDAY, JULY 20*th*, 1943

When assisting Colonel Knowle in the operating-theatre, Lieutenant Purvis, R.A.M.C., was liable to forget that he was Lieutenant Purvis, R.A.M.C. He went back into the frame of the medical student watching miracles. It had been so now for nearly three hours and these were the last performances of the inspired, meticulous hands.

Purvis thought that the man on the table would live; from time to time he caught himself urging the man to live, so that this astonishing work would not be wasted. It was the craftsman in Purvis, not the humanitarian, who saw what Knowle had done with the smashed and ruined face; smashed by the explosion of a hand-grenade under the jaw, with the half-inch thickness of metal cap embedded deeply in the mess of splintered bone; a most unnecessary accident; a Home Guard casualty.

For three hours he had been neither a casualty nor a person, but a job to be done; a complicated and untidy puzzle, set below the white lights that poured on the table, subject to the solution devised by those hands; all identity lost to the figures moving above him; a problem divided between Knowle, Purvis, the nurses and the anæsthetist. The problem had no recognisable shape. There was the interrupted head and the motionless arm linked by the tube to the red bottle. The heart, with the anæsthetist keeping watch over it, seemed to be a separate person, an enemy who was against this work and eager to drag it all down. "God, I'm tired," Purvis thought, feeling the sweat begin to chill upon him, "And if I'm tired, what is Knowle? We'd had a brisk day before this."

Knowle had not called it a brisk day; it was made up of hæmorrhoids, a Collis fracture, a straightforward appendix and the interesting cervical rib that had been giving its owner acute neuritis for years. Just before they brought the Home Guard in, Knowle had remarked that this was a light and pleasing programme. Knowle did not talk about his experi-

173

ences in the Western Desert. But he had sometimes the look in his eyes, the look to be observed in other eyes that had seen action, the look saying gently but plainly, "You have yet to learn what trouble really is." Purvis, raw from the Depot at Leeds, was sensitive to this look.

"*All* right," said Knowle; in his short experience of assisting Knowle, Purvis had noticed that this was his inevitable epitaph on a job completed. While he removed his mask and gloves and gave his final instructions there was an elegant weariness about him, as about a star actor taking a last curtain-call. Purvis went out behind him. All the time that they were washing, Knowle was silent. Purvis saw that his hands trembled violently and thought that the three-hour addition to the "light and pleasing" programme had left its mark. There was no colour on Knowle's skin at all; it looked transparent, and his wet forehead was creased into three vertical lines above his nose. The charity of his eyes and mouth struggled against the frown. Knowle could frown and smile at the same time, like a cat purring and twitching its tail.

Reassembled in the likeness of two officers wearing service dress, they walked out into daylight. It was a fine evening; between the scattered, modern brick buildings that made up the large encampment of Branley Hospital, there were flowering shrubs, neat lawns and well-tended earth. Along the paths, they met and passed the hurrying shapes; V.A.D.s in dark blue cloaks; an orderly pushing a man in a wheel-chair back from the X-ray department; two small A.T.S. girls strolling in tight, rounded uniforms; they had impudent faces and untidy hair, forage-caps set at exaggerated angles. Three patients from the officers' ward came past in noisy argument, not looking at the girls. Two Q.A. sisters in scarlet and grey said, "Good evening" to Knowle and Purvis.

As always when he was tired, Purvis found his mind awake and prying after the meaning of things. He knew that he was one of the earnest Scots, and that his enforced companions found him funny; he could not help saying, "Hrrmph; the institution that ought to be the first in war-time to stage a strike; against the treatment of our finished products."

Knowle said, "Certainly. If you are going to be logical about it. I understand that we hung up logic on September the third.

"The sun on the left, the balloons on the right.
My courage, good morning. My reason, good night."

"What?" said Purvis.

"A transposition of Belloc's couplet; composed by Mr. Michael Knowle of Manchester Square; while looking out of his window at the barrage-balloons and listening to our late Prime Minister telling him that his world lay in ashes; the Prime Minister's world, not Mr. Knowle's."

"I see," said Purvis.

Knowle halted in the path.

"Care for a drink? I don't mean in the ante-room."

Purvis had noticed that Knowle avoided the ante-room; he himself was new enough to enjoy its set pattern of shop-talk; to join heartily in the curses, whether they pilloried O.C.'s weekly inspections, unnecessary paper-work or the hardness of beds. It was as much routine as the work itself, the hour of drinks and grousing; the professional jealousies; the cynical criticisms and speculations; all the little groups of numbers and letters embroidering the words: A.F.B. 256, G. 1098, I. 1220. He found it fascinating; he supposed that it would bore somebody like Knowle.

"I usually go to The Bear," Knowle was saying. "The old boy keeps a little whisky under the counter. Coming?"

"Thank you, sir."

They went out of the main gates. The Bear stood on the opposite side of the road. The tiny saloon bar was decorated with the usual posters: Careless Talk, Save Food, Dig For Victory. Two patients from the officers' ward were leaning on the bar, steadily ignoring the rule that put The Bear out of bounds. Knowle in turn ignored them; he carried two small glasses of whisky to the table under the window.

"Get the ether out of your nose," he said.

Something fatherly in his manner made Purvis wonder how old he was. His hair was entirely white, but the face was younger than the hair. Knowle was a gift to the ante-room gossip, a never-failing target for debate. He was alleged to have wangled himself a longer stay in Category C than his health warranted; and equally to be a dying man who would never see active service again. He was rumoured to have deserted a wife, to be impotent, to keep two mistresses. As O.C. of his surgical division in the desert, he was described as a Nazi-type martinet or alternatively as an ineffectual drunkard. There was a story about his shooting a French soldier with his revolver at Rouen during the retreat in '40; a story about his fathering a child by a Q.A. sister; a story about his having refused a knighthood in '38. Purvis prudently disbelieved them all.

"If we get many more elderly gentlemen decapitating themselves with firearms" said Knowle, "I shall find Italy comparatively peaceful."

"You've got a Board coming up, haven't you, sir?"

"That ignominy is for Thursday."

"Ignominy?"

Knowle said, "I'm getting thin-skinned in my middle years. Tell you what I hate—you will too: the moment when your body begins to give warning that one day, not too far ahead, it will have its own way again."

Purvis thought this over.

"Somebody put it like this," Knowle said, "As a child, you know quite certainly that your body is you; you've no existence without it. As an adult, you know that that is absurd; that you are a separate controlling entity; your body is just a useful vehicle. In old age, it becomes more powerful than you can ever be, a bandit who will destroy you. I was thinking about that, dealing with our friend just now. No way to die; aged sixty odd and blowing your face off in a Boy Scout exercise. But certainly better than creaking on towards cancer, or a stroke."

"And yet I'm rather looking forward to growing old," said Purvis.

"The nearer you get to the prospect, the less you'll like it."

"It is possible," said Purvis, "that I shan't get very near, things being as they are."

Knowle looked at him ruefully. "We were the lucky ones," he said, "those of us who reached the thirties and forties before it broke; we did at least get a run for our money."

"But going back to your statement," said Purvis hurriedly, disapproving in himself the aspect of an appeal for sympathy, "Surely, we in our trade have an advantage; we become quite brutally familiar with the behaviour of bodies."

"Other people's bodies; not our own," said Knowle. "When they start playing their humiliating tricks——" he laughed and shook his head. By which Purvis understood that he was expecting an unfavourable decision from the Board.

WEDNESDAY, JULY 21st, 1943

Caroline's taxi cruised uncertainly along the short length of Branley village. The hospital gates came in sight on the left side of the road; immediately opposite the gates, she saw the public house, The Bear. Mrs. Heron's cottage, Michael had said, was the last but one on the right, before you came to The Bear. This cottage, then, with the slate roof, the small patch of garden, the hollyhocks. She climbed out of the taxi, dragging her suitcase after her. There was an old woman opening the front door and looking round it. She began to talk as Caroline came up the path.

"There you are. The colonel just came along to see if you'd arrived. He said he'd come back for you; had to go over to one of the wards for a few minutes. Gracious, you must be tired. Bin travelling all day?"

She went on talking, leading Caroline through the front room and the kitchen; up the stairs into a room with a monstrous bed, a small margin of floor-space and a slanted ceiling. There was a candlestick on a table by the bed; heavy

177

red curtains at the windows. Mrs. Heron was saying that she would bring some hot water, that the what's-its-name was downstairs, out through the scullery. " And I'll bring you up a key. The colonel said he'd be taking you out to dinner. Don't worry about waking us when you come in. That's a feather-bed; feel it."

Caroline splashed in the hot water, pulled on a clean shirt and collar, peered at herself in the looking-glass. It was cracked but it gave her enough of the flawed reflection to see that her face was now greenish-white; and this was not the result of tiredness, of the long day's journey; this was the old, childish reaction to excitement. She amended it with make-up heavier than that prescribed in A.T.S. regulations. From the little window she would be able to see Michael coming up the path; she stood, watching for him, repolishing the buttons on her jacket with the buttonstick and the soiled yellow duster; these things had become as necessary as a powder-puff used to be. She rubbed a second duster across her shoes and her belt. She went down the stairs that led into the kitchen. Mrs. Heron, at the stove, said, "Like a nice cup of tea while you're waiting?" A large old man in shirt-sleeves was sitting by the table.

Gently, Caroline refused the tea; Mrs. Heron went on chattering; "There's been goings-on with some of your girls at the hospital. I had to laugh. The Bear's out of bounds, see? I had to laugh."

When she had listened to the story, she said, "I think I'll walk up the road and meet my boy friend half-way."

"Boy-friends, ah," said the old man, looking at Caroline's legs. " Know who she reminds me of, mum? Marjorie. That's who she reminds me of. Ta-ta now; don't you be too late."

"You be as late as you like" said Mrs. Heron, "though I expect you'll be glad to get to bed."

Caroline walked slowly; the trains seemed to have been going on for ever; her knees wobbled. There were birds singing; a smell of dust and pollen; after Northern evenings, the air was surprisingly warm. She sat down on the bench outside the public-house, keeping her eyes faithfully upon the hospital

178

gates. First there were three small A.T.S. girls coming out in a hurry, giggling, looking across the road at her and looking away; one making a sketch of a salute, more loud giggles rising as they hurried towards the bus-stop at the crown of the hill. She stared after them rancorously and when she looked back Michael was coming through the gates.

She stood up and saluted him; making a punctilious gesture of it, so that he replied with decorum before he seized her arm.

"You are earlier than I'd hoped for. Let me look at you. As I expected——"

"I couldn't be less tired."

"Come into the squalid Bear and have a drink. I wish to God I could have got away to meet you at King's Cross."

"If you had," said Caroline, "the train would have been two hours late. Whereas it was on time and I was moving equably out of St. Pancras within ten minutes of arrival. So convenient of St. Pancras to be there. Now" she said, watching the old man behind the bar pour the drinks, "I shall get very drunk, very quickly, because of having shared my sandwiches with a cadet who'd lost hers."

They sat at the table under the window; before she drank at all, she rested her elbows on the table and stared at him. He was saying "I've got a car coming to take us over to Harpenden for dinner, and bring us back. It was the most peaceful thing I could think of. We can sit in the garden afterwards." She thought that these first moments did not vary. It was as incredible to see his face and his hands as when he had returned from Rouen, from the Desert. Always their old pattern was slow in weaving itself again across the tear that time had made.

She waited for the shock of his presence to subside. It was delicious to sit still, with the drink in her hand, having kicked time out of the way, having got here.

They drove through the tired sunshine to Harpenden; the street, with the village green and the Georgian houses, looked the same. It was a symptom of the precarious years, she thought, that made you score in credit-balance the things that stayed. Here was the driveway with the chestnut-tree and the ragged border; the bar with its red leather stools; the dining-room where they sat at their old table, looking out on to the lawn. They were so late that there was nobody else in the dining-room. The proprietor, who was a friend of Michael's, had saved for them cold ham and salad and baked potatoes.

"Shall I take away your appetite if I ask you about anaphylaxis?" she said. " Because the woman I share a room with, suddenly blew up and looked like Boris Karloff and was covered with lumps."

"Yes, darling. Who had been giving her serum? That can be very disagreeable," he said. "What did you do about her?"

"Well, I didn't. Fortunately they got the M.O. and some adrenalin. But I was thinking all the time I was waiting with her that I would have to perform a tracheotomy with the rather rusty knife that we keep in our room for spreading potted meat on rolls. Would that have been correct?"

Michael shut his eyes and said, "In theory. How on earth did you know about the tracheotomy?"

"I read it in one of your books, ages ago. Funny," she said, "how one's sense of drama predominates at those moments. My mind went on a long way ahead. I was being decorated by D.A.T.S. for having saved her life, and equally being court-martialled for having killed her. And there she lay, groaning and retching, quite ignorant of my thoughts."

Michael said, "Your life at O.C.T.U. is full of quiet charm."

She catalogued the sins of the Medical Officer. It was fun to have this meeting-place of jargon and routine; they were doing the same job, as she had wished always that they might be able to do. They talked the same absurd language, sprinkled with numbers and initials.

"And to-morrow? Is the Board at Branley or Millbank?"

"Branley, by a gentlemanly dispensation" said Michael. "Eleven o'clock. Then we'll have lunch and get going."

"D'you hate it?"

"Oh, it irks me slightly. Only because I know the answers

so much better than they do. Your friend Billy Lloyd will probably be one of them." He narrowed his eyes, staring at her. "How you can look so enchanting in those clothes remains a mystery."

They went out into the garden, down past the rose trees, to find the bank, which in spring had been a ripple of daffodils and narcissus. Now the grass was long; some of the yellowed leaves from the bulbs were still visible.

"Funny to think we saw those flowers," she said.

Michael lay back with his arms behind his head ; he quoted softly.

> "and among the grass shall find
>   the golden dice wherewith we played of yore."

"Oh lovely—but sad."

"Nothing's sad now you're here." He grinned at her and began to fill a pipe.

"Who polishes your shoes?"

"A batman," said Michael indifferently.

"They are much better than mine. Ours are done by little Scots girls who don't care."

"Women can't polish shoes." He held her hand. "Lord, how I want to make love."

"Oh, me too; but where?"

He said, "If I hadn't to be on call to-night, we could have had rooms here, like last time."

"The army," said Caroline, "is a Spoiler-of-the-Fun."

They lay holding hands, not daring to be too close to each other, playing the game that they called the Quotation-Battle and talking shop until the light faded. They had a last drink before the car came to fetch them. When they came out into the drive she looked back at the hotel and thought, "I wonder if we'll come here again." They climbed in and she said loudly, "Seven whole days; and it is still only the first evening; they don't even begin till to-morrow." This was a moment when you could sneer at your destiny that was spelled in terms of hullo and good-bye.

They stood outside the gates of the Herons' cottage. Michael said, "You might take a discreet look inside. If they are still about we'll walk up and down here for a bit, then I'll take you into the mess and give you a night-cap."

Caroline opened the door with the large key. The rooms were dark; an oil-lamp with the wick turned low, stood on a table just inside the front door. She turned up the wick and saw that a piece of paper with a stubby pencil had been placed beside the lamp. Its legend was WRITE TIME YOU WANT BREAKFAST, with the "S" the wrong way round, and in a frivolous scrawl "Nighty-night." She crept through the kitchen and listened at the foot of the stairs; she could hear one long rattling snore and a counterpoint theme of slow puffs.

Now it was almost impossible not to shout with laughter, moving together in the comic conspiracy, appalled by the creaking noises that shot through the silence. She set down the lamp beside the bed; she was conscious of the low ceiling, the heavy shadows, the stuffy smell in the room; suddenly hysterical because of the simultaneous gesture with which they removed their ties and collars.

At first it was spoiled and made too greedy by the sense of guilt; the over-anxious army guilt, nagging at you to remember the frame in which the service ordered you to live, sending you back to the panic of childhood, the fear of being found out; it was doubled by the thought of the two old people on the other side of the wall.

But presently nothing could endure against their familiar delight; they ceased to be the hurried travesties of themselves and became the people they were.

"And you still love me?" he said, when they were quiet.

"Love you. I am you; and you are me."

"You must think that when I go," he said. "Promise? And whatever happens, to either of us, I haven't the smallest doubt that somewhere we'll go on as two. We have shared so much."

"Yes." Curious, she thought drowsily, how far, how impotent, the shadow of Mercedes had become in these years; dead or living, she was now only a pitiable ghost.

THURSDAY, JULY 22nd, 1943

She was seated again on the bench under the swinging sign with the bear painted on it. She kept her eyes on the gates. She had no idea how long the Board would take, and Michael came sooner than she had expected. He was walking with another officer and she rose and walked tactfully to a distance while they exchanged farewells. Then he came across the road; he looked relieved and gay.

"All over," said Michael. And now they were back in the tiny saloon-bar, at the table by the window, under the Dig For Victory poster. He said, "Did you sleep?"

"Forever. I had an egg, too. Tell me, Michael."

He went on looking at her compassionately. "Nobody can turn as pale as you can. Want a drink?"

"Not really. Beer might be nice—— Tell me."

"Just what we expected."

"Category A?"

"Category A."

"Clever chap. Congratulations. And?"

He said, "That one can't know; but it doesn't look too hurried. Depends whether I go back under the pompous title of Individual Reinforcements, or with another unit."

"No chance of the old unit?"

"No; that would be too much to hope for." He sat down beside her and called to the old man behind the bar, "George, be kind and bring us two pints of bitter over here, would you?"

She smiled, thinking, "Such a short distance to walk and fetch them, but, being you, you won't turn your back on me and leave me alone that long, just at this moment. But you needn't worry, Michael. I have learned to ration my thoughts;

I allow them the fact that we've had the Board, and that's all." She said gaily, "Was it very boring and hideous?"

"Not really," said Michael. "And now, God be praised, we can get out of here and out of these clothes."

She took his cigarette from between his fingers to light her own. "I know you hate my doing that but it does save matches," she said. The old man brought the beer.

"You are a good girl," said Michael.

"Shut up."

TUESDAY, JULY 27th, 1943

On the last morning she woke early and went to the window, looking down into Dorothy Knowle's garden; at the neat rows of vegetables; they shone with dew in the misty sunshine; they were important, were glistening, smug. They grew, Michael said, where the herbaceous border used to be.

She heard the thin, hurried sound of Dorothy's alarm-clock. It would be kind to go down and help Dorothy with the breakfast. She lingered, looking at the elm tree whose leaves shook and rustled ; at the lawn, the patch of jungle-garden at the end of the lawn, and beyond it the sky dipping to the sea.

For six days she had belonged to his family; living in the house where he had lived as a child; she had been made free of the memories that he shared with his queer, undemonstrative sister; privileged to share old snapshots and hold battered toys in her hands; admitted to the streets of his town and the pathways on his cliffs. She thought that she had seen another Michael here, Michael as he might have been if he had never met Mercedes ; a person who liked to mess about with boats, to dig the garden and play darts in the pub where the old men remembered him.

All the week, she thought, the war pushed impotently with its giant fingers against the peace that they had built here. The tip-and-run raiders came over to drop their single bombs before they fled out to sea. Dorothy, hatchet-faced and wearing her green linen uniform, bicycled furiously to W.V.S. activities. They had driven past Cold Ash and seen the Nissen huts in the garden, the notice "W.D. Quarters" on each stone gate-post. They had grumbled at the forbidden beaches, made hideous with barbed wire and concrete emplacements, with rusty iron stakes. When Joan Bridges, wearing khaki, came over to dine with them, she was like an invader, and her A.T.S. shop-talk was a bore. Caroline knew that she had treated Joan carelessly on this leave. But she was part of their enemy that threatened this citadel and could not make it fall.

It would fall to-day.

She saw Michael coming out of the jungle-garden, stopping to tie back a straggling plant at the corner of the overgrown flower-bed. He wore the same grey flannels that he had worn all the week, grey flannels and a faded blue shirt. He walked slowly across the lawn; she could hear him whistling *Loch Lomond*. "After six years I still feel the same excitement and pleasure at the sight of that person coming towards me, at the look of that head and shoulders." He did not see her leaning there, she called and he looked up. "You're very early, Michael. Didn't you sleep?"

"I slept magnificently. Look at you, idling your time away."

All the morning they lay on the cliff, sunning their shoulders. They strolled back into the town at noon, and drank beer; they ate the cold luncheon that Dorothy had left for them, and wandered into the garden with their books. It was the same as the other days, she thought, but you could hear the clock ticking. She let her eyes slide off the book to take a snapshot of Michael sprawled on the moth-eaten brown rug, with a cushion behind his shoulders. His hair was ruffled; he was holding his empty pipe in his teeth; his shirt was wide open and she could see the ends of the red scars that came up across the right side of his chest as far as his collarbone.

He looked up and met her eyes. He took the pipe out of his mouth. "This I like," he said.

> "Cease your wooing: you should know
> Warm Daphne cannot be remade
> Out of the dark laurel shade."

He put the white book on the rug, leaned over to her and held her face between his hands. The elm tree was shivering above them in the wind that came from the sea.

"Take care of you," he said. "Please take care of you."

"What harm could befall me in Edinburgh, I ask myself? Other than apoplexy from exasperation?"

"When you were at Woolwich," said Michael, "I had a very precise nightmare about your death in a blitz. It always began with Dennis arriving at the door of my tent to tell me; breaking it gently in his most careful terms of under-statement."

"Dennis," she said. "I dream about Dennis. He comes back all the time and he's got something to tell me, but I don't hear it. He never writes, the old cad."

"I shall catch up with him somewhere en route."

She said, "But why do we both dream that thing about Dennis?"

"Why shouldn't we?"

"I don't know." There had been the beginning of a thought in her mind and it was gone. She lay with her head on Michael's shoulder, thinking, "Our words run on. You, like me, hear the clock ticking; you look ahead past the train to London, the expensive dinner, to the station and the two trains going different ways. And I want to ask factual questions and be reassured. How long will they keep you attached to Branley? Is it a ridiculous hope that you'll still be there four weeks from now when I get my forty-eight hours? Supposing that they push you off on embarkation leave as soon as I get back? Supposing that I have to say good-bye to you on the telephone outside the ante-room; in that dingy brown hall, with a bad line so that your voice is faint, and the radio is playing inside the ante-room door. . . ." She said brightly, "That last layer of sunburn on your neck is going to hurt like hell when you put on your collar."

He looked at his watch. "Time," he said.

"Yes, well. . . ."

He rose from the rug, leaving the white book fallen beside her, open at the first page. She read it.

> "I think Odysseus, as he dies, forgets
> Which was Calypso, which Penelope,
> Only remembering the wind that sets
> Off Mimas, and how endlessly
> His eyes were stung with brine;
> Argos a puppy, leaping happily;
> And his old Father digging round a vine."

Above her, his voice said, "Coming, Caro?"

"In a minute." She read it through a second time. She thought, "It echoes. It is a queer thing. It was unlucky to read it just then." She followed him into the house. She stood in the sitting-room, with the chintz and the oak furniture, blinking at the darkness after the sun. Dorothy pushed open the door and came in, carrying a tray with half a bottle of whisky and two glasses.

"Hullo. Oughtn't you to think about changing?"

"Yes." She blinked at the bony face that suggested Michael in a tantalising way.

"Well, have a drink first," Dorothy said unexpectedly.

"That would be lovely. Not for you?"

"Heavens, no," said Dorothy, grimacing. Like many tee-totallers, she poured enormous drinks and would be affronted at a protest.

"Here's to you. And thank you," said Caroline. "Thank you very, very much."

"Whatever for?"

"Letting me come here. Giving me such a heavenly leave."

"Oh . . . well. I liked having you. Come any time you like. Only I don't suppose you will like Hamlet without Hamlet."

187

"I would love to come."

"You'll be bored. Don't know what you'll find to do all day." She took two soda-mints out of the bottle that she carried in her pocket.

"Wish you didn't both have to go," she said, "I hate people to go. Gives me indigestion."

SUNDAY, AUGUST 15th, 1943

It seemed to Vera Haydon a remarkable coincidence that Mr. Wynstay Adams should be staying at Claridges, because Claridges was the last place where she had seen Mercedes Knowle, in the early summer of '39. The hotel façade looked different now, protected, like all the glass doors, with a bastion-wall of brick. Claridges was somehow less intimidating than it had been on that showery afternoon when she took the flowers to Mrs. Knowle.

She was remembering every detail as she walked up the shallow steps into the foyer; the flowers themselves, gardenias from the shop in Piccadilly, their petals smooth as white kid, with shiny dark green leaves; a pin like a dagger to attach the heavy spray; swathes of cotton wool and waxed paper; a white, oblong box.

Vera remembered standing at the desk, with her dark glasses dimming the colours of the crowd; Mercedes had come past her while she was still waiting to catch the attention of the man behind the desk; Mercedes who was moving so rapidly that Vera had to run to catch her before she went out through the glass doors. Mercedes had come back up the shallow steps. They had met just here; jostled by lavish-looking women in an atmosphere of mixed French perfumes.

"Mrs. Knowle . . . I brought these for you."

"Yes, madam?" said the same man at the same desk.

"I have an appointment with Mr. Wynstay Adams."

She crossed the foyer. It was full of uniforms and such lavish-looking women as accompanied the uniforms were different from the '39 vintage, though it was difficult to say how. She had not entered this gilded lift with Mercedes; they had talked for a few minutes only, standing at the top of the steps.

The man who opened the door of the suite was a small dark person, with the face of an amiable monkey. He wore American Red Cross uniform. His luxurious traces were all about the room; cartons of cigarettes; a plate of oranges; bottles ranked along the dressing-table.

He offered her a drink and apologised for the disorder of the room. "I'm leaving again to-night," he explained. He took some clean shirts off a chair, "Do sit down. I'm afraid I'm not quite clear what this visit is about. You're at the Ministry with Bessingham, aren't you?"

"Yes, I am; and he told me that you had been in touch with Mrs. Michael Knowle in France—I hoped you'd be able to tell me a little about her. She was such a friend of mine."

Adams said, "Oh, sure, delighted. Michael a friend of yours, too?"

"I used to work for them both; a long time ago."

Adams sat down in the opposite chair; crossed his legs and wrinkled his forehead. "It was in 1940," he said. "Just before the French signed the Armistice; when we were evacuating the front line villages. I wasn't in the same unit as Mercedes; she'd hooked on to the Comité de Secours Civile and I was with the Quakers."

Feeling suddenly cold, she interrupted him. "But that wasn't the *last* time you saw her?"

"Yes. We all got separated after that. I never heard anything of Mercedes again."

"But——" Oh no, she thought, this cannot be true; this cannot be the news that I have built on in these weeks. "But Mr. Bessingham said your work brought you in touch with the camps; the internment camps; that you had news of her there."

He looked more monkey-like than ever, his face folding into puzzled creases. "Why, no. Bessingham must have got me wrong. That is part of my work, now, of course; the International Red Cross. But it was back in '40 that I saw Mercedes."

She sat still, hidden behind her glasses, aware of nothing but the downward plunge in her mind. He was talking, but she missed the opening phrases.

"Doesn't necessarily mean she's dead. There's a lot we don't know. Civilian internees aren't anywhere near as easy to trace as military prisoners."

"But the Englishwoman who died; the name that came through as Noel. Do you think——?"

"There I'm afraid I know nothing, Miss Haydon. Maybe somebody in the British section could tell you."

She shook her head: "Oh, no. I've done all that. It's Mr. Bessingham's mistake, that's all." She thought, "Why does this sort of thing always happen, since the war? People getting messages wrong; mistakes in names and times; nothing anywhere that you can rely on any more?" She said, "Oh, well, I'm sorry to have taken up your time."

"Please . . . I'm sorry to disappoint you," said Adams. He gave her one of the strong cigarettes and she smoked it clumsily; it was years since she had smoked a cigarette. "Michael will be the first person to hear, if there's any news. Do you keep in touch with him?"

"He is overseas," said Vera dully.

"He's in England now. Going out again quite soon, though. I saw him last week."

"And he hadn't heard anything?"

"No. I could see he didn't want to talk about it. They were getting a divorce, as you may know. Though I guess that's all held up till they find Mercedes."

"Mr. Adams, tell me something; about the civilian internees; do they treat them well?"

"I wouldn't like to be too definite. The whole picture's kind of fuzzy. There are people, elderly people, living quite comfortably still in their own homes." He wriggled his shoulders. "If you're over sixty and have no politics, you'd get by. But Mercedes doesn't come into either category. She hates the Germans like poison, the way a lot of these Francophiles hate them; she doesn't know how to keep quiet and she's perfectly capable of shooting her mouth off in four languages. I don't see her acting wise and lying low."

Now she wanted to ask him about the time in 1940, when they were evacuating the French villages, but it seemed as though the moment had passed. He was saying that information was always coming in from odd sources; that it would be wrong to give up hope. "And leave me your address; if I do get news of her on one of these trips, of course I'll let you know."

Then there was the handshake and his apparent bright relief at the end of the interview; and going down in the ornate lift, and looking at the place where she had stood with Mercedes in the foyer.

FRIDAY, AUGUST 20th, 1943
16.45 hours

In the early afternoon it had been comfortable to sit on the lawn in front of the house. Sergeant Warne had carried out two deck-chairs. The wire-baskets, full of their dull, necessary chores on paper, had lain in the grass, with Warne reducing them at Joan's dictation until both baskets were almost empty. Now a wind had come up from the sea. They could no longer find the place in the sky where the air-battle had written itself in frozen trails; the shadows of low clouds came over. The papers began to flutter and blow; the leaves of Warne's notebook flapped. The branches of the pine tree overhead shook and wrestled with the wind.

"Do you want your tea out here, ma'am?"

"No; I think this is getting too wild." Joan stood up, rolled down her shirt-sleeves and picked her jacket off the chair. "Here's Simmons now, with the post," the sergeant said.

"Damn its eyes. Ask her to bring it into the office. I'm jumpy to-day," Joan thought, "I've been sitting too long in the sun." When she walked into Company Office, there were bright circles in the darkness and she blinked them away.

The brown room felt stuffy and hot. She sat down at her table and at once the telephone rang. She was still debating with the Group Commander the business of requisitioning the house down the hill for the new intake, when Simmons brought the post and the tea.

"Thank you. You don't mean to tell me you got an evening paper?"

"Last one going, ma'am; I nipped in ahead of an R.A.F. boy, ooh, he was wild."

"And I observe," said Joan, looking through the envelopes, "that you have brought me a lot of unwelcome bumph from the Paymaster. My 01771 back; that's very jolly. Give it to Warne with my love and ask her why the N.C.O.s' school didn't teach her how to make out a claim."

She drank her tea and lit a cigarette; she unfolded the *Evening Standard*. She saw the headline and the photograph in the right-hand column.

WELL-KNOWN SURGEON FOUND DEAD
COLONEL MICHAEL KNOWLE, R.A.M.C.

Absurdly, she saw that her first gesture was to slap her hand down across the paragraph and cover it, as though by doing this she could make it not be there. She heard herself saying aloud, "No—No—No. . . ." She drew her hand away and read the rest of it.

"Lieutenant-Colonel Michael Congreve Knowle, D.S.O., R.A.M.C., was found early this morning dead in his bedroom at the Strand Hotel, London. A bottle of sleeping-tablets was by his side. An inquest has been ordered by the coroner."

The next paragraph gave details of Michael's pre-war career and Army record. The last line read, "Colonel Knowle was shortly to rejoin his unit overseas."

She stared at the picture; a flat, unconvincing version of Michael, a postcard grin and an old-fashioned tie.

Simmons knocked at the door and came in. "Please, ma'am, Sergeant says . . . ooh, ma'am, is something the matter."

"No—Yes. I've got to think. Don't talk to me, there's a good child."

She was angry with herself for wanting so urgently to weep. She drew hard on the cigarette; she said aloud, in a voice that scraped, "Caroline can't have heard yet." Sergeant Warne came in without knocking.

"Something I can do? Simmons says——"

Joan held out the paper.

"Colonel Knowle. . . ."

"Look, Warne, help me to make sense. Get through to the O.C.T.U. and see if she's there; official call and make it priority if they'll play."

"You wouldn't ring Miss Knowle first?"

"No. If they found him this morning she's probably in London by now."

"Perhaps she's rung Miss Seward."

"I don't know. Get on, Warne."

She walked about the room. "Better for her to hear it from me. Five o'clock. If she's in the ante-room, she can get hold of a drink." She looked down at the paper and the column seemed to detach itself from the rest of the page; reading the words again, she felt that she had heard them spoken aloud in a solemn tone whose echo would go on.

The telephone rang.

"Coming through now, ma'am," said the sergeant.

The voice at the other end said that it would put her through to the staff ante-room. She waited, drumming with her fingers on the table.

"Hullo" said somebody young and breathless, "Is that my call to Chester?"

"No, ma'am; this is an incoming call; priority."

"Oh . . . hullo?" came disappointedly.

"Is Subaltern Seward there? I've an urgent message for her."

"Seward? I don't think she is, actually. I think I just saw her go out. Hang on."

There was another long wait and then Caroline's voice.

"Caro . . . this is Joan."

"Oh, hullo." It was a disquieted voice. "Why are you calling? Is something wrong? I've been feeling like hell all day."

"You've heard nothing?"

"What is there to hear?"

Joan said, "This is going to be tough."

"All right; get on; never break bad news gently."

Joan found that her upper lip had begun to twitch in a stupid way. "It's Michael."

"Yes; go on." The voice was toneless and steady.

"He died in his sleep this morning."

There was a pause and Caroline said flatly, "Who told you?"

"I've just seen it in the evening paper."

"Is he at Branley?"

"No; in London. Would you like me to read the column to you?"

"If you would be so kind." The voice that spoke the formal words was thinner now.

"Are you within reach of a drink?" Joan asked.

"A drink. . . . Oh, yes, I expect so, Joan. Read it to me, will you?"

She rubbed the back of her hand across her eyes and began to read slowly and clearly.

"Colonel Michael Congreve Knowle. . . ."

17.30 *hours*

Caroline put back the receiver. The telephone stood on a ledge in a corner of the hall. She saw the door of the ante-room standing half-open; the light coming through. She stood looking at it with her eyes; in her mind there seemed to be another door that slammed, a huge iron thing on which she hurled herself, beating with both fists. She heard one sob come from her, and then she was silent. She shut her eyes; there was the door, and a small impotent shape battering itself to pieces, crying, "No!" and failing and becoming weaker.

Inside the ante-room somebody had turned on the radio

and there was a violin-solo playing, the notes long and high and sweet, like golden wires. She was not aware of having moved; she saw that she was beside the radio, turning it off. An aggrieved voice reached her: "Oh, don't. It's lovely I'd only just got it."

She said, "Look——" and then nothing at all.

"What's the matter? Turn that up again, Seward, there's an angel."

"Could you give me a light for this cigarette?"

"Yes; coming over. What's the matter with you?" The box of matches went past her on to the floor. She stooped down to pick it up. She stood holding it in her hand, looking at it thoughtfully. And at once there was Mitchell standing beside her, fat Mitchell who was the officer commanding the Headquarters Company.

"Seward; what is it? You'd better come and sit down."

"Please don't touch me or make me do anything."

"Have you had bad news?"

Oddly, it was impossible to say "Yes." She said, "If you would be so kind as to ask the orderly to bring me some cigarettes. They've got some extra packets in there with the liquor, and I particularly don't want to run out of cigarettes." She began to walk up and down the floor, staring at the pattern on the carpet. The sob came again once. She thought, "What was I just going to do, when it happened?" Here was Mitchell with the cigarettes and a cup of tea.

"I thought you might like this."

"Thanks very much. Very kind of you." ("There, you see; you can still say ordinary things; you're all right. Doesn't she know I don't take sugar; or is this perhaps hot sweet tea for shock, as prescribed in the First Aid Manual?")

"My chap's dead," she said looking at Mitchell; the word "chap" displeased her and she frowned at it. She thought, "Can't think what else I could have said." Mitchell's rounded voice was saying, "Oh, Seward, how bloody awful. Have you got anything to do now that somebody else can do for you?"

"Well, that's the point. I was on my way to something;

what was it? Oh yes, the rehearsal; the first rehearsal for the entertainment."

"You needn't do *that*."

"I think I'd better." She finished the tea. "They're waiting."

"Let 'em wait."

"No. Look, you could do a thing for me, if you would be so kind. (And why do I keep saying that idiotic phrase?) I don't know where Lockwood is; but I'll have to go to London to-night. She can't stop me."

"Of course not. I'll find her. Seward, can't you stay here and get drunk or something?"

She said, "No. I'll go now. If you could find Lockwood."

Here was the sunlight on the green quadrangle, and walking quickly, directed as though you were an automaton, watching yourself for another sob; they came unexpectedly, singly, like hiccoughs. Two-dimensional figures met you, on the way, flat laughing faces, white shoulder-flashes, voices that you did not hear.

She went into the hall with the stage at the far end; she stood in the doorway, thinking.

"Oh, yes. Vale . . . and 'We're officers and gentlewomen.' Seems a long time ago and it was only the last course." She saw that the cadets were waiting for her, scattered in groups on the stage and about the front rows. The leader of the committee was a plump, red-haired girl with a pretty complexion and dimples; an Edwardian face, Caroline thought; it sat incongruously on top of the uniform.

"Sorry to keep you waiting." (Now that is a perfectly reasonable remark, spoken in a normal voice; she looks a little startled. Am I very green, I wonder? "Nobody can turn as pale as you can.") "Oh, yes; I'd like to hear about it; is it a sketch? Sorry, no, I see; the framework for the whole concert. A good cadet and a bad cadet, yes? The Fairy Queen and the Demon King? That sounds rather fun, Merriman." (The way that their faces blur and then come clear; the way that I cannot stand still.) She took the scribbled sheets of paper and began to look through the list of items, being careful to light one cigarette from the stump of the other. ("Your least favourite trick, Michael. Sorry, darling, but I have to. . . . How these words slide away. And now it is time to make my little speech, the little speech that I always make. Plenty of room to walk on this stage; up and down, up and down.")

"The first thing I want to say is that this is all your own production. I'm here to give you advice if you need it; but the chief doesn't like the staff to interfere, or to give ideas. We can, within reason, lend you props; and there are two acting-boxes full of junk that you can examine at your leisure. There are always three things that I tell the entertainment-committee at our first meeting. Three things. . . .

("And what the devil are they? I can only think of 'We're officers and gentlewomen, pillars of the O.C.T.U.')

"Yes. Do bear in mind that the entertainment is primarily for the fun of the orderlies, the household staff.

"Then—Don't break your hearts if you find that some of your ideas have been used before. There is a limit to the number of jokes that can be made about the set-up here.

"Something else—Yes. You can make as much fun of the chief and the rest of us as you like; provided that you go gently with our physical disadvantages—if any."

They were laughing. She walked down the steps from the stage. Merriman was saying that they had a violinist, a trained soprano and two tap-dancers. ("Tap-dancers; really. On the day that you die, I am called upon to judge the merits of two tap-dancers.") I must tell him that, she thought, because it was impossible to think that Michael was not waiting somewhere to hear about all this. She said, "There's an awful lot of dust here, isn't there?" ("She looks surprised; perhaps there isn't; but I think there is; dust and sun.") "Yes, what's worrying you?"

"This is Slater's idea, ma'am. In the third scene the demon king is making love to the adjutant in the hopes that he can get her to tell him the postings before they're officially announced. And he's disguised as a War Office Inspector, so he talks in War Office phraseology all the time. And he says, 'Exquisite creature: I should like to explore your every avenue.' "

"I think that's funny." ("I do, too and I laughed without any difficulty at all. Things can still be funny and nothing's any trouble, provided that you go ploughing along, using your voice and the top of your mind, and keep on pushing the knot down to the end of the piece of string. I don't quite know what I mean by that, but it is what I am doing; and it gets harder to do.")

The soprano was standing on the stage, a square parcel of a girl with big legs. Another cadet had gone to the piano.

"By yon bonny banks, and by yon bonny braes,
      Where the sun shines down on Loch Lomond——"

"Here——" said Caroline to the invisible executives who seemed to be stage-managing the afternoon, "Aren't you overdoing it a little?" She got up and stood with her arms folded; but it was quite all right; there seemed to be a thick, opaque wall round her mind.

"Lovely. Usually I suggest to the singers that they wear something that isn't uniform. If you haven't a dress with you, can you send for one? A long dress, to hide those legs." ("I hope I didn't say that; no, I couldn't have said it; she still looks pleased.")

"Yes, I'd like to see the tap-dance."

("But now I have smiled too long; I can feel that my skin will split across the bones of my face, and my eyes hurt; and these little people jigging and capering on the stage go up and down; up and down. *Les petites marionettes font—font—font leur petit tour et puis s'en vont—vont—vont.* And Merriman I am sure is asking me something that I should answer, but they are all turning into those frightening, two-dimensional ones like the people I met on the path outside ; and why in the name of God am I sitting here listening to this nonsense when you are dead?")

She looked at her watch; she saw a tear fall, splashing on

the glass. "Can't cry here," she thought. "Can't cry anywhere, really. Silly to begin; never stop if you begin. Now
did I say good-night to them? I thought it, but did I say it?"

She was walking across the green quadrangle saying to
him; "Look—it's all right. I'm not making a fuss, truly I am
not. You couldn't help it. But you see I don't know anything
about it, Michael; it will be all right when I know. And it's
only a week to go till the long-leave week-end; oh, of course,
we shan't have that now. And here is Lockwood, hurrying
across the grass, with those two crimson blotches on her face.
Good evening, ma'am."

"Seward, I've only just seen Mitchell. I was coming to
fetch you out of the rehearsal."

"It's finished." ("Now there is no need to bark at her like
that, is there? She will be good at this; she thrives on these
things.")

She stood still, lighting another cigarette. Lockwood was
full of words—"Take the train to-night; your platoon can
amalgamate with Hadow's for to-morrow morning's lectures.
. . . Railway-warrant. . . . One of your leave-warrants."
("Really, she couldn't be more gentlemanly.")

"Did I get a telegram? No, ma'am; was there one for
me?" ("From Michael, I suppose. No. That's queer to think
of—All those empty spaces left; where the important things
used to be; telegrams, telephone-messages, letters; they won't
matter any more. How does one get used to that, I ask myself?")

"Oh sorry; I see what you mean about the telegram. No,
he wasn't killed; he wasn't overseas."

("And here we sit, Lockwood and I; on my bed; with a
half-bottle of whisky and the syphon from the ante-room
tray. And I can have an early supper; here in my room, if
I like; and they'll get me a taxi and cash me a cheque. . . .
It's an atmosphere somehow like a wet Bank Holiday; a
time of cursed privilege.")

She got up and stood by the dressing-table with the glass
in her hand, looking at Michael's portrait. "What rubbish,"
she said.

MONDAY, AUGUST 23rd, 1943
11.30 *hours*

While giving his evidence, Lieutenant Purvis was haunted by the conviction that, somewhere, Knowle was laughing at him; Knowle in his mood of detachment, finding the earnest Scots manner, the respect for detail, thoroughly amusing.

"I had been assisting Colonel Knowle in the operating-theatre all day Thursday. We had a heavy afternoon because at 14.00 hours three casualties were brought in; the result of an accident on a Home Guard exercise. The men were all seriously injured and none of us left the theatre until 18.15 hours.

"I was going on leave and before I left I had a drink in the ante-room. Colonel Knowle was present. When he heard me say that I was catching a train to London at 19.25 hours he asked if I could give him a lift to the station. He said that he would dine in London and catch a later train back to Branley. It was obviously a spur-of-the-moment decision. He went out of the ante-room and when he came back he was carrying a suitcase; he said that since he was off-duty until the morning he would stay the night at his club, the Travellers'. This seemed to me more reasonable, as he was looking very tired and he had remarked to me earlier in the day that he was sleeping badly. No, sir; he did not seem worried about that, nor about anything. He struck me always as a very calm, well-balanced person, as the Brigadier has also said.

"We arrived at St. Pancras at 20.15 hours. We shared a taxi. Colonel Knowle had said that he would like to be dropped at his club, which was on my way. But when we reached the top of Shaftesbury Avenue, he said, 'Oh, this'll do. Let me off here.' I did ask him then if he had reserved a room at his club, knowing how difficult accommodation in London is just now. He said he would chance it, and he got out of the taxi and walked away, in the direction of Piccadilly

Circus. My taxi passed him; he was walking slowly, looking as though he hadn't quite made up his mind where to go; and that was the last I saw of him or heard of him until the police called upon me at my leave-address on Saturday.

"No, sir, nothing about his behaviour struck me as in any way abnormal; I admired Colonel Knowle professionally and I admired him as a man. The news came as a very severe shock to me."

Quite clearly now, against the panelled wall just above the jury's heads, he saw Knowle's face; the face that was too young for the white hair; the calm grey eyes and the deeply curved mouth. Almost he heard the voice say, "*All right*," and add with affection, "Pompous young ass."

He sat down and glanced automatically at the people sitting on the benches. He saw that Colonel Knowle's sister, the hatchet-faced woman in W.V.S. uniform, who had spoken to him before the inquest began, was now red-eyed and used a handkerchief. Next to her, staring straight at the coroner's desk, was the A.T.S. officer, the girl with the cropped curly hair and slanted eyes whom he thought he had seen with Knowle outside the main gate of the hospital a few weeks ago. She was motionless, uncomfortably still. Next to her sat Brigadier Lloyd, who had given brief evidence of the proceedings of Knowle's Medical Board. Purvis approved the painstaking detail that the inquest demanded. But the little Gothic court-room with its aqueous light seemed a curiously trivial and sordid place in which to be saying good-bye to Knowle. He listened to the old man with stiff grey hair, who had just kissed the book ; M. Georges Parron, who owned the restaurant, the French Horn, situated on the corner of Dean Street and Soho Square.

Parron said that as soon as he read in the paper that Colonel Knowle was dead and that an inquest would be held, he had communicated with Scotland Yard. The foreman of the jury immediately asked why he had done this. Parron said that he thought the police would like to know where Colonel Knowle had been dining on the night of his death. The coroner made a facetious reference to a possible allegation of food-poisoning. Purvis scowled.

Parron said that he had known Colonel Knowle for many years, that Knowle was one of his oldest patrons. He was a medical student when he first came to the French Horn; then he had dined there regularly until the year 1932 or 33; after that he came less often; and Parron did not think that he had seen him since war began.

"So I was surprised and glad to see him on Thursday. He came in very late; it was half-past nine. I thought that he had had a few drinks. He was in very good spirits, but I was shocked by his appearance; he had aged so much; the white hair.

"I gave him his old table. I let him alone. He was a person who did not like to be fussed over, and I never talk to my clients too much. He ordered wine with his dinner, and while he was drinking his coffee he did what I have often seen him do when he is alone; he had some notepaper with him and he began to write."

The jury wanted to know what he was writing. "Did it look like a letter?"

"I did not look at it; it would not be my affair. He sat there writing for a little while; he ordered a second cup of coffee and a liqueur brandy and by then he was the last person left in the restaurant. I close my doors at half-past ten these days; the waiters go off duty then, but I am never disturbed if there are clients who want to stay on a little later. My wife and I do the kitchen-work. By now it is after eleven o'clock; three minutes past eleven."

Another person, thought Purvis, with a respect for detail. But the coroner was going to cut him short. No; the foreman of the jury again; he managed to make every question imply an unpleasant thing.

"No, he didn't strike me as in the least drunk; he had eaten a good dinner. But when I gave him his bill, I did think that he was looking terribly tired. That is why I asked him if he were staying in London. Then he laughed and said that he had forgotten about reserving a room. He used my telephone to call his club; they were full up. So I telephoned to the night-porter at the Strand, who is a friend of mine. And very luckily they had had a cancellation; Colonel Knowle was grateful to me. He shook hands and he told me that he was going overseas again soon."

Glancing to his right, Purvis wondered whether the A.T.S. officer were going to faint. The pallor of her face made it a sharp mask, between the bent head of Knowle's sister and the dark face of Brigadier Lloyd. "If I were Lloyd," he thought, "I should get the young lady out of here."

Now the night-porter, the friend of M. Parron.

He had admitted Colonel Knowle at half-past eleven. He had thought at the time that the Colonel had been drinking, but since listening to the evidence he assumed that he might merely have been very tired. In answer to the foreman, asking why he thought that Knowle was drunk, the night-porter said that his eyes looked funny and that he was kind of slow in the uptake. Knowle had signed the register, asked to be called at seven and gone to his room. The night-porter said that he was still on duty at seven when the chambermaid on Knowle's floor came down in a state because she couldn't wake him. Then there was the chambermaid, in a chatter of Cockney, adding nothing except that he had looked queer and she had shaken his shoulder.

The foreman of the jury was now, Purvis thought, going after that letter again; the fact that Knowle had been writing what might have been a farewell letter seemed to be on his mind. Was any letter found among Knowle's possessions? No. The police sergeant said that in the room was a small leather wallet with writing-paper and envelopes in it. Much of the writing-paper was scribbled with notes of surgical cases; it was obvious that Knowle had been making these notes at the French Horn.

"But how they press the point," Purvis thought, "even calling attention to the fact that he could have posted a letter on his way from the restaurant to the hotel. They want drama; they are fascinated with the idea of suicide; when the evidence is so clearly otherwise that the idea is laughable. But they would like it so."

And apart from Knowle's personal character, the evidence and the post-mortem findings proved this to be a simple affair. According to Lloyd, Knowle had been a victim of insomnia for years. The barbiturate made up regularly to his own prescription by the dispenser at Branley was in two-grain tablets. Knowle, off-guard because he was tired out, had taken an overdose. Purvis particularly disliked the implications that Knowle had been drunk. But with the most excitable will in the world, the court could find no evidence of suicide.

Purvis thought that the tiresome foreman sounded disappointed when the jury returned, after fifteen minutes' absence, to give the only possible verdict of "Death by Misadventure."

As he went out into Horseferry Road Purvis thought, "What a waste it is; that is the most shocking thing about it; the waste." And Knowle's voice answered him ironically, "Better than creaking on towards cancer, or a stroke."

14.30 *hours*

Brigadier Lloyd, in his large room that looked out on to Hyde Park Gate, said, " Yes, certainly; ask her to come up," and to the clerk in the corner, "Would you mind going somewhere else?" Billy Lloyd was miserable and he could not stop thinking about Michael and he said "——" when the clerk reminded him that he was due at Millbank in twenty-five minutes.

He had expected Caroline Seward to come; he thought that he knew what she wanted to ask him. He had seen her asking it with her eyes all the time that they were having their drinks in the dingy bar off Horseferry Road; while the flinty Miss Knowle refused a drink and swallowed little white pills for indigestion. He found Miss Knowle alarming and thought it odd that she and Caroline should be friends.

The messenger opened the door and admitted Caroline. She still looked ugly with grief; the face was white and shiny, the high cheekbones looked too prominent, the eyes narrowed; there was still the hard glitter in those eyes, the thrusting toughness in the manner. Her uniform was neat; the buttons, belt and shoes highly polished so that they seemed to carry on the dreadful glitter. She saluted him at the door.

"Come in; sit down; take off your cap and be comfortable."

"Thank you. You don't mind my coming? I couldn't talk to you in front of Dorothy and it seemed rude to her to ask if I might see you alone."

"I was hoping you'd come. This is a bloody business," he said staring away at the trees outside the window; the atmosphere of violent sorrow that came in with Caroline was uncomfortably moving; it hurt him in the throat.

"Look, sir, first of all——"

"For God's sake don't call me sir."

"Could you do me a favour? A military favour?"

"Surely."

"I want to go to Michael's funeral to-morrow; and I was due back at the Edinburgh O.C.T.U. this morning. I've sent a telegram, but that ain't good enough. I don't want to go back there at all," she said.

Lloyd grinned at her, trying to get through the barrier. "You'd like some sick-leave?"

"I despise it, but it seems to be the only way."

He said, "Well, I can write a note; saying that I recommend you for a week's sick-leave. Which is probably a good idea for you anyway. But that won't keep you out of trouble; particularly if they're a stuffy lot. You're A.W.L. at the minute, I suppose."

"Couldn't matter less. If you'll just give me a thing I can send."

He scribbled rapidly on a headed half-sheet of paper and signed his name. He gave it to her. She said, "I suppose I am a rat; but my view at the moment is Stink and Drains to them.

Thank you. Look——" She leaned forward with her elbows
on her knees, clasping her hands and staring at the floor:
"When you said, in your evidence, that you'd never known
Michael to have any sort of trouble, apart from his insomnia."

Lloyd said, "That was true."

"Please—I'm not implying that you were being unpro-
fessional or telling lies—But I must know."

She raised her head and looked him in the eyes: "You
didn't attach any importance to the thing that happened in
the summer of '39; when you put him off work?"

"No," said Lloyd, " I thought that was on your mind. Why
does it bother you?"

She looked wary and he thought that she was not a person
used to choosing her words. "He had been overworking—
that was all?"

"Overworking; getting less sleep even than usual; and had
a black-out after too many drinks. There was no need to
mention it this morning. There's been nothing like it in his
medical history since he joined the Army."

She said, "Don't think I'm trying to dig professional secrets
out of you."

"Of course not." ("How conscious she is of that; Michael's
training.")

"But do you remember what he said to you? When you
came round to see him in the morning. Did he say where he
had been—or why he thought it happened?"

Lloyd said, "No; he didn't feel like talking; he wasn't in a
good way at all and on top of everything else he naturally
had a thundering hangover. All I got from him was that he
had blacked out on his way to dinner and ended up somewhere
else."

"You know it was the same restaurant; the French Horn?"

"Ah, that I didn't remember." He thought about it;
"Well, I don't see anything odd there. You heard the old
man say he'd been going there for years."

She was silent; then she muttered, "The things that one
carries around inside one's head and doesn't talk about."

"Meaning Michael? Was there something else that happened that night? Something that you know about and I don't?"

She frowned; she said, "No, not really."

"Because if there was, and it worries you, tell me."

She said, "No." She was obviously lying.

"You're sure?"

She said heavily, "Quite sure."

Lloyd gave it up. He said, "I can't tell what you're thinking; but if that '39 incident was a sudden amnesia—which the drink-factor made it hard to establish—there's nothing to suggest that Michael had a similar crack-up on Thursday."

"No," she said. "No."

"And there can be no question of suicide. It was a pure accident; just one of those damned unlucky things. Curious how it's always the good ones who go. I can give you a dozen chairborne Harley Street boys—like me—who wouldn't be missed. But it is the Michael Knowles who get taken."

She looked at him and laughed. She said,

> "He has taken Rowll of Aberdeen
> and gentill Rowll of Corstorphine.

Remember? In the ship coming home."

He did not remember ; he did not like the laugh; it was hard as a wooden clapper, and her whole toughness seemed to him likely to crumble. Dimly while he watched her, he recalled hearing her name spoken with a precarious overtone in the Brookfield family; something about her not being a stayer, having let her career go for Knowle.

He said, "This may be heavy-handed of me, but I think you owe it to Michael to take pretty good care of yourself at the moment. He wouldn't want you to feel too much alone."

She said—"I thought about that when I was looking at him in the chapel. He looked very calm and wise and lonely. How do they manage to do a post-mortem on a person and still leave him tidy?" She spoke with detached interest.

"It isn't difficult," Lloyd said, hurrying his next point. "Now, if they do grant your leave, where will you go? Have you got family, or friends who'll be right for you?"

She stared past him. She said, "The illusion of company," and presently looked back at him. "Sorry. Yes, of course. I'm staying with Kate Forrest." She got up. "Look; you're busy and it was damn good of you to see me." She pulled on her cap; the peak dropped a shadow like a highwayman's mask across her eyes and nose. He said, "I'll sign that pass for you," and she took it and saluted him. He walked with her to the door: "Just one point, if I may go on being a bore, Miss Seward. A shock like this does in some ways resemble a severe motor-accident. Keep in touch with me and let me know how you are."

He turned back into the room; the atmosphere was still troubled; he shouted at the clerk. "See if you can get hold of a location-list that has the number of that Edinburgh Attery; it's an O.C.T.U. And try to get me through quickly."

While he waited, he thought that he was doing this for Michael, believing half-consciously that some day Michael would thank him. It was not yet possible to accept the fact that he would never see Michael again.

Presently he was saying to the unseen female adjutant, "I know this young woman quite well; and I'd like her to be where I can keep an eye on her for at least a week. Hope you'll overlook the slight irregularity." As he convinced the matronly presence at the other end of the line, he decided that he would not care to give a prognosis upon Caroline Seward. The short wooden laugh still sounded here.

WEDNESDAY, SEPTEMBER 8th, 1943
16.30 hours

Mrs. Roberts, who kept a lodging house in Taviton Street, was listening to the wireless; she thought that the door-bell must have rung several times before she heard it. As she hurried up the stairs from the basement it was pealing again;

whoever stood outside was keeping his thumb on the bell. The stairs were hard on her and she panted. She opened the door. On the background of the rain there stood a young woman whose bare head was dripping wet. She wore what looked like an army coat, with its collar turned up; the buttons were not fastened and it hung loosely, showing the front of a plain black dress. The young woman's stockings were splashed with mud and her shoes were soaked. She looked ill; she had the kind of face that Mrs. Roberts called Onusual.

"If it's about a room," said Mrs. Roberts, "I'm afraid we're full up; and likely to be so for some time."

"In a sense, it is about a room; and in another sense it is not," said the young woman. "May I come in? I don't want a room; I want to look at one."

Mrs. Roberts thought that this sounded extremely queer, but she could not keep the young woman standing in the rain. She said, "Er, would it be for later on?" The visitor peeled off her coat, hung it on the hatstand and put up her hands to smooth back her dripping hair.

"Do you remember a medical student called Knowle, who used to lodge with you?" she asked.

"Knowle . . . Let me see; we've had such a lot of medical students. Did he recommend you to come here?"

"He is dead."

Mrs. Roberts clicked her tongue, as proper to the news of a death.

"It was the top room," said the young woman, "And he was here in 1920."

"All that time ago. I believe I do remember; yes, of course. Mr. Knowle; such a nice boy," said Mrs. Roberts, dutifully trying to disentangle him from the other nice boys who had come and gone, "Dear, dear."

"Might I see the top rooms?"

Mrs. Roberts was confirmed in her opinion that this person was a little queer: "I suppose you can. They're all out. It's Civil Servants mostly these days. I'm afraid I don't recall which was Mr. Knowle's. But there are only two."

She hauled herself up by the narrow banister-rail; she would have liked to let the young woman go up alone, but queer people were not to be trusted. "Terrible house to keep clean," she said. The young woman was polite enough to go slowly, despite Mrs. Roberts' injunctions to go ahead. "Now, this is a nice room; the first floor front; nice big windows. Perhaps you'd like to see it." She opened the door, "The students always had the smaller ones, of course."

"It is a nice room." She looked about her in a kindly daze. "Gives you the feeling she's been hit on the head," Mrs. Roberts thought: "Only half there, as you might say." She puffed up the further flights. "Getting a bit old for these stairs," she said.

"I'm sorry; I know I'm being a nuisance."

They came up on to the top landing; Mrs. Roberts waited a moment to get her breath; she looked at the dark paint, the linoleum, the pile of old trunks in the corner and suddenly it came back to her. "There" she said, "Funny how you remember. Mr. Knowle had the back room. This one was Ginger's room; we always called him Ginger. Mr. Knowle and Ginger; that's right." She opened the door. The young woman walked ahead of her and stood with her hands on her hips. The room was neat; Mr. Fisher was a tidy person. "Only a small one of course; but it's quite cosy," said Mrs. Roberts, as though she were contemplating a let. "Gas-ring and all."

The young woman had to bend her head at the place where the ceiling sloped; she stared out of the rain-smeared window. She said nothing.

"Not much of a view, of course. Just roofs and chimneys." There was no reply.

"That cupboard's new," said Mrs. Roberts, "Used to be out on the landing. But Mr. Fisher, he wanted a cupboard."

The young woman turned from the window. "Thank you," she said, "That was kind of you."

"No trouble, I'm sure. I used to do breakfasts for them; and supper too if they wanted it. It's only tea and toast these days. Still, the news is good, isn't it? Can't be long now."

When they were in the hall, she said, "Excuse me asking, Miss, but have you been ill? You look as if you ought to take care of yourself."

"Bless you, I'm all right." She smiled and for the first time Mrs. Roberts saw that, in less dishevelment, she might be nice-looking. She held out her hand with a pound note in it. "Would you have this? As a present?"

"Good gracious, no; wouldn't dream of it." ("She *is* queer; but a lady, with it; as you might say.") She opened the front door.

When she came downstairs again to the basement, Mrs. Roberts opened the back-door quietly and looked up the area-steps. She did not know what made her do this, but, as she had expected, the visitor was standing on the wet pavement, staring at the house. It worried Mrs. Roberts and she could not settle to her mending and the wireless programme until she had peeped out for a second time and seen that the young woman was gone.

17.40 *hours*

The rain had stopped when Caroline walked into Manchester Square; there were greenish rifts between the clouds, a stormy night. She had expected to be tired by now, but her body still seemed eagerly energetic, carrying her along. The only hint of trouble came from the throb at the side of her head; signalling that the neuralgia, which had held off all day, was on its way back.

She stood still at the foot of the steps. The smart-alec of a house no longer deserved her gibe; it was dingy and in need of paint. The brass plate with Michael's name on it was gone from the door and a wooden notice-board reading "Y.M.C.A. Hostel; Please Ring" was nailed in its place. She looked at the wrought-iron lamp that had been buckled and now tilted absurdly; perhaps that was done by the blast from the bomb that had fallen on the other side. She peered over the railing into the wet area; it was full of empty crates.

There were no memories, and this was odd. Perhaps

somewhere in her mind a censor, whose presence she had not guessed, kept them banked down and hidden. But they might have made for company. In this mad, staring loneliness, she wished for them and they would not come. There was only the half-world here; the half-world of your own mind. It was a room without a wall; it had a floor whose little space broke off and showed a black cellar down below. Outside, there was a road, and the knowledge that, no matter how far you walked, no matter whom you met on the way, the lights were out forever; you would not be you again.

Wearily, she turned away from the house. She raised her hand in farewell to it; as she had waved to the house in Taviton Street; as she had waved to the black and yellow facade of the French Horn. Looking at her watch, she saw that already she had kept Lieutenant Purvis waiting for ten minutes. It did not matter. That was the curse of these days, that nothing mattered; there was nothing that you wanted to do or wanted not to do.

You tried, she thought, being tricked for a little while into the belief that you did want something. For two weeks, these illusions had persisted. After the funeral, it had been a necessity to get away from the haunted Sussex town; back in London she had wanted to be at the graveside again. There had been an illusion that when once she was granted leave officially, she would feel free; and when this was granted, there was a sense of disappointment as though she had hoped to be recalled. Then there was another small hope; it would be comforting to meet Purvis and talk to him; and now that was done and Purvis was unmagicked for her. He was a solemn Scots bore who wanted to see her again. And although this morning it had seemed that there was something to look forward to in spending a few days with Joan Bridges, in visiting the grave and seeing Dorothy, now that the time had come, she dreaded the place. But the journey was waiting; so was Purvis; faithfully sitting in the Grosvenor Hotel at Victoria Station, because she had said weakly that it would be nice to have a drink before the train went.

"If the salt has lost its savour. . . ." That, Michael had said, was the phase wherein the suicide took his life, not in the time of pain; but in the dull timelessness of despair. When you thought, "Nothing will ever change," you did it.

"All right, then; this bus coming now. It couldn't possibly pull up in time. Why don't you? God knows." She joined the bus-queue south of Portman Square. Inside the bus, swaying against the knees of the people who were sitting down, she saw an A.T.S. officer eyeing her thoughtfully: "Because I'm wearing my British warm over plain-clothes. All right, chief-commander, drains to you. If you want the full facts of the case, I oughtn't to have a British warm at all, because I'm only a subaltern and it was bought in bravado."

She had to stand all the way to Victoria. That was all right; it was still useful to be uncomfortable.

She hurried across Grosvenor Place; the rain had returned. She walked up the steps, through the glass doors and saw the clock at the end of the foyer pointing ten minutes past six. She turned to the right and there was Purvis, sitting in an arm-chair at one of the little tables, in the corridor that led to the bar.

When she saw his look, she said, "Just how untidy am I?"

"It's the first time I've seen you in civvies," he said carefully.

"It is more what one might describe as a blend than civvies." She swung off the wet coat and sat down in the empty chair. There was a glass awaiting her. "I'm sorry they're out of whisky; I ordered you a large gin," he said. His young, heavy face wore a frown and he looked as though he were just about to make the same clicking noise with his tongue that the old landlady had made with hers upon hearing that the student called Knowle was dead.

"You're terribly wet, Miss Seward."

"I've been walking."

"You know, I'm worried about you."

"Please don't be."

"Has the Brigadier extended your sick-leave?"

"Not yet. He will when I ask him."

"You don't think," he paused, "that you would feel better

213

if you went back fairly soon? That some work would be a help?"

"I do not. I've had the Army."

"You mean, you'll be getting your discharge?"

She nodded.

"How will you do that?"

"I don't know. Somehow."

"But you would be called up for National Service of some kind, at your age."

"Oh, sure" (leave it, for God's sake. I do not want it examined in detail and discussed. I do, however, want another gin. It won't help the neuralgia, but it will at least seal off the higher cortical centres, the bloody little busybodies. No, Mr. Purvis, I cannot say with any truth that I have ever thought about the Land Army. I have better things to do with my time than think about the Land Army. That is a lie, too; I have nothing whatever to do with my time). She said, "Once there was never enough time and never enough money. Now, by the recent ingenious dispensation, there is more than enough of both; and I don't need either."

"I wish I could help you."

("You always look pursed-up and embarrassed when you say that sort; as though the fact of my not having been married to Michael got in your hair; or do I mean in your porridge?")

"Look," she said, "I'm being a nuisance. There's no reason why you should feel you have to trail along in my dark. It isn't fair to anybody to engage him in all this, as a kind of crutch. You must please realise that and not go on wanting to see me."

He said, "As you wish, of course," and, "Would you care for another drink?"

"No, thank you. I have to go slow because of my headache. I don't mean," she said, "that I'm not grateful to you and that *I* don't want to see you any more." ("Why do I tell him a lie? I never used to tell lies just to be kind.")

"No, no; I quite understand that." He checked the bill carefully, took out his wallet and put down a very clean pound note.

"Have you got your ticket?" he asked. "And what about your luggage?"

"As well that you reminded me. It is in the left-luggage place. I should have gone without it."

He was shocked; he was shocked again when she forgot to pick up her change at the booking-office. He stood at the door of her carriage saying, "Well, perhaps you'll write me a note to Branley, telling me what you've decided."

"Yes, of course I will." The whistle blew; just as she was pulling up the window, he said, "You know I think Colonel Knowle would be sorry to think that you wanted to get out of the Army now." The window moved past his face and she sat down in her corner, lighting one cigarette from the stump of the other.

22.30 *hours*

In the small ante-room that was once the headmistress's study, Joan Bridges looked at her visitor and wondered about him as a change from wondering about Caroline. He was a quiet young man. He had been attached only a few weeks to the unit at Cold Ash; he was long-limbed and he had a thoughtful, monkish face. He came from the Welsh border; his name was Hellyar. They were discovering that they liked the same books, the same country places, the same music. These things led her to ask herself the question that phrased itself always thus absurdly: "Could you ever be Michael for me?"

There was a reassurance in having him here while she waited for Caroline.

She looked at her watch. "You know, I'm beginning to be worried. She must have missed the seven-forty-five, too."

Captain Hellyar knocked out his pipe in the ash-tray; he said placidly. "A lot of people miss a lot of trains. If she isn't here by eleven, we'll take the truck and go down to the station."

"Caroline isn't making sense at the moment."

"And you are very fond of her."

"Yes. I've known her all my life."

"Did you know the man?"

"I did; very well."

Beyond the fact that the man was dead, she had told him nothing of the story. It was still a shock to realise that the story was over. Try as she might, she could not see Caroline going on alone.

Hellyar said, "You would say if you wanted me to leave you?"

"Of course. I like to have you here."

He smiled at her and refilled his pipe. "One wastes too much energy in wishing that things might go better for the person one loves."

"But one can't not," said Joan.

"There are prayers."

"Do you pray?"

"Sometimes."

Joan said, "I can't help wondering if God has time to cope with all the prayers in this war. Blasphemous it may be, but I see them in wire baskets and pending-trays, getting lost. "Distribution: the Holy Trinity; copies to St. Anthony, St. Christopher and St. Jude.""

Hellyar laughed softly. "They might conceivably have a better filing-system." He lifted his head. "Something happening downstairs now," he said.

"Yes; I thought so." As they went out of the door that shut away the officers' quarters from the rest of the house they heard voices coming up from the hall. A man's voice, grumbling, "Well, it seemed queer to me," and Sergeant Warne's voice replying, "I know this officer, Mr. Baynes. Everything's quite all right." Joan and Hellyar came down the stairs.

"You are a well-meaning, but an exceptionally stupid man," said Caroline. Joan thought that she looked like Bacchante, with wet horns of hair twisting up from her forehead; an ill-dressed Bacchante, wearing a British warm over dark civilian

216

clothes. The coat was stained with mud all down one side and as she turned to look up the staircase, Joan saw that she was hurt; there was blood on her cheek and temple. Baynes the special constable was being brisk and ineffectual, saying, "Now, now." From the door of the orderly-room a head was peering out; it dodged back as Joan and Hellyar came down the last steps.

"Hullo," said Caroline. "Charming local customs you have. I can't take a walk without being run in by the police."

"I was only trying to help you," said Baynes aggrievedly.

"So you pull me in for lurking on W.D. property. I can't do more than show you my identity-card, can I? Do take your ridiculous hands off me."

Captain Hellyar with gentle nonchalance, removed Baynes' hand, said, "Thank you very much. Good-night," and turned with him towards the door. As she took Caroline's arm Joan heard the retreating grumble. "Face all bleeding like that; couldn't give any account of herself. Thought she'd been run over. Abused me like I was a pick-pocket."

Caroline said dreamily, "Have no fear. I couldn't be less drunk." She was greenish-white.

"But your head——"

"Nothing unbecoming to an officer and gentlewoman. I walked into a parked car in the black-out. Being slightly dazed, it took me some time to find your gate. When that aimless bobby took me in charge."

She put up her hand to the side of her face, looked at the blood on her palm and said, "What a thing."

"Come upstairs and we'll fix it."

"Who's your chum with the brooding eye?" Caroline asked. "He's nice."

"Suppose you stop talking." In the ante-room she pushed Caroline into the softest of the chairs. "I'll get you into your pyjamas and dressing-gown and we'll wash that wound. Where's your luggage?"

"God knows," said Caroline, sprawling. "It must just take its chance with the rest, that's what I say. Have you got

217

any liquor? I had two gins with a Scotsman at six and I haven't seen a bottle since."

"A drink won't help that head. Stay where you are and be quiet. I can lend you things." She came back with a pair of red pyjamas and her Jaeger dressing-gown. Caroline stood on the hearthrug, undressing in a docile manner.

"Where have you been?"

Caroline frowned, buttoning the red jacket. "I don't quite know. I thought I'd go and say hullo to Dorothy; then it seemed rather late; I couldn't find any signs of life. So I went to the cemetery and of course it was shut; which was presumably what the taxi-driver was trying to tell me, before I sent him away."

"You mean you walked back here from the cemetery?"

"Oh, yes. No trouble; till I hit the car," said Caroline. She sat down, fingering the cuts and bruises carefully. Warne came in with hot water and bandages. Warne was like a nanny, Joan thought; Caroline helped her, holding the lint and the end of the bandage.

"There," said Warne. "Now I'm going to bring you a hot drink and some aspirin."

"Thank you kindly; no hurry," said Caroline. She looked piratical, with the bandage round her head and the scarlet pyjamas. She grinned at Joan. "Fine thing," she said. "Now I know what my father felt like when they hauled him into Vine Street. They say that these hereditary traits will out. Give me a cigarette."

"Caro, can't you really remember what happened to your luggage?"

"No; the hell with it. There's nothing in it but uniform and I shan't need that any more."

"You'd better go to bed."

"I've no views about bed. And don't give me any of that 'there-there' stuff. I mean what I say. I've had the Army." She got up and began to pace. "The Army can't use lunatics —and I'm as good as crazy. There is a borderline and I've put one foot over." She threw her cigarette into the fireplace and at once began to look for another. "On the table," said Joan. Caroline halted by the table.

"Funny day," she said inconsequently. "Looking at all the places. Only place I can't make up my mind to go into is the French Horn. Private territory." She came back to the chair.

"I'll tell you the way this goes; it's interesting. Might happen to you some time, who knows? First you're playing the drama, and you're safe inside; anæsthetised; slap-happy. Easy. Then you thaw. And you cry. And after that you get to limbo and limbo is the worst. Care for me to tell you about limbo? It's half a house and a broken floor and flat grey thoughts drift round in it. And the salt has lost its savour and nothing changes."

Joan said gently, "I might go on: naught else remained to do."

Caroline's mouth twisted. "Our old favourite. But with one difference. I can't go on. The gentleman in the poem was looking for a Dark Tower. I've had mine."

Joan was silent.

"And another thing. When you know that they didn't think about you at all; just went away alone and forgot you. No letter; no message; no good-bye. Remember how he used to go out of a room? Quickly, before you knew it."

"If he had died in battle, you would have had the same feeling; that he wasn't concerned with you."

"What's that got to do with anything? You can stop thinking up nice comfortable words. I'm through. 'Isn't it a pity about Caroline?' "

"You'll get out of the Army?"

"Faster than light, I will. It's composed of Spoilers-of-the-Fun. It's a bloody cage. It behaves like my mother. That child Vale was right, she said she could imagine banging her head against its walls. But I'll kick them down. The only point of being in the Army was Michael."

Warne came back with the hot drinks on a tray; she said, "Now, don't sit up talking all night, will you?"

"Okay, nanny," said Caroline, "we'll be good." She kept

up a pretence of amiability until Warne had shut the door; then the look of furious doubt returned. She put down the glass without drinking from it.

"God damn them all to hell——" she whispered. "*Why*?"

"It was you," said Joan, "who taught me that one mustn't ask why."

"*I* taught you? You're crazy."

"You did. You taught me a lot of things. It hurts me to see them all spat on and thrown away."

Caroline swore.

"Your relationship with Michael meant more to me than you know. I shall miss it dreadfully. I don't want to lose you both."

"Oh shut up," Caroline muttered. "Don't say those things."

"I must, darling. All my life I've looked up to you and admired you and, though I wouldn't admit it, envied you."

Caroline was silent, staring at the fire.

"I saw you through your devotion to Michael from the beginning. I was like somebody outside a gate looking into a garden where I could never go."

"Shut up; please shut up."

"No. This sort of love, your sort, isn't a thing that happens often. It is the stuff that art is made of. That's why I loved it. You know my passion for books; this was the same passion. It may sound silly, but I loved your love."

Caroline put out her hand as though to push the words away.

"This stage, even limbo, is part of it. It must be part of it, don't you see? It is yours; it belongs to you. You're still making something. You can't curse it and run away."

She thought that she had said too much; but Caroline raised her head and stared at her questioningly; she did not seem angry now, nor tortured.

"That's all," said Joan.

"Is that really all?"

"Yes."

She bowed forward, resting her bandaged head in her hands. "That's what you care about? An unfinished work of art."

"I do."

Caroline said dreamily, looking at the floor. "And no little sermons about duty and service, the needs of the Army, and discipline; insignificance of private grief on a background of total war."

"I'm not your friend Lockwood."

Caroline looked up and smiled at her; she looked utterly exhausted now.

"You don't know it all," she said.

"Of course I don't know it all. You're the only person who knows that."

Caroline shut her eyes. She said, "The things one doesn't tell; and I, who like to tell."

THURSDAY, SEPTEMBER 9th, 1943
05.00 hours

Caroline woke and saw it waiting. The morning did not vary. By night, she thought, you could sometimes work up a little courage, but the morning found you stripped of it.

She rose in the dark and fumbled with the black-out board at the window. When she had dislodged it, there was still darkness, a cold air blowing. She stayed there, trying to find the tops of the trees.

"Nobody here," she thought dully, "there never was. The illusion of company. He was right."

No talisman nor magic out of the past could help her. They were all enemies with knives. There was one certainty, come with the dark and the silence, a stony truth suited to the hopeless hour. "Only God and you." She had spent the rest of her inheritance; there was that single coin of wisdom left.

Only God and you. And since God, despite your belief, was unknowable, there was only you. And for that reason, you would go on; alone, as you began. You could not run away.

TUESDAY, JANUARY 25th, 1944

As he moved with the group of passengers down the slippery pier in the dark, Wynstay Adams found himself performing

221

the usual gesture, a shrug of the shoulders, that implied "What-the-Hell?" It was the equipment that he put on for the journey; the flight from Cabo Ruivo to Poole Harbour was now a routine affair. He had endured these preliminaries often enough; the take-off at three a.m.; the pretence of mystery surrounding the hour of the flight; the taxi-driver who brought him out from Lisbon to the seaplane-base, playing the game obligingly. They all knew; and the Germans in the city knew. There was no risk; only an occasional misjudgement.

"How many have I done? At least six. Too much trouble to count," Wynstay thought, "Maybe when I get nearer thirteen I'll begin counting." The launch moved away across the lit river; the group standing in the launch was quiet; cigarette-ends glowed in the dark. You could see the wing-tip lights of the Short-Sunderland. The Portuguese boys who were loading the machine were yelling at the man who steered the launch. "One time I came this way," Adams said to his neighbour, "the launch rammed the fuselage and half of us went into the water. Nice cold start for a nice cold trip."

"How long is the flight?"

"It varies. Around ten hours. We go way out over the Atlantic once we leave the coast."

He climbed through the narrow doorway. He remembered grumbling, in '41, at the sparse comforts here. Then he was still the spoilt child of many flights in his own country, missing the trays of food and drink, the adequate heating-system, the pretty manners. Now, after years of air-travel in bucket-seats or lying on mail-bags, he found his adjustable chair luxurious. And the cold was nothing in these machines that flew below a thousand feet all the way. He had spent some unforgettable hours at fourteen thousand with no oxygen.

He sat in the front chair; the single chair on the left of the aisle; facing the clock, the altimeter and the entrance to the cockpit. He lowered his chair until it slanted comfortably, huddling down in a cocoon made of his two coats and his rug. Presently, below the wing, he saw the Tagus river sliding back, the tiered lights circling and dropping away into the dark. Always now he thought of Lisbon as the last lighted city in the world.

He began to doze at once, and in his half-dream to continue a dialogue set in motion by his memories of Mr. Lorry in the Dover coach; the speech with the unburied man.

"Buried how long?"

"Almost eighteen years."

"You had abandoned all hope of being dug out?"

"Long ago."

"I hope you care to live. . . ."

Only in Wynstay's dream the question phrased itself otherwise. It was, "I hope you care to die." And the face that haunted him was not the face of an old man, but the face of a woman; a thin yellowish face below a cropped forelock of colourless hair; a face on a hospital pillow.

He had found Mercedes Knowle, and Mercedes was dying. "I hope you care to die," his roving mind repeated anxiously, because it seemed important that she should. If her escape into Portugal, via Marseille, had been made with the object of living, then this end was particularly wasteful and unfair. To get that far, he thought, and then to die, in a Lisbon hospital without seeing familiar things again. But many of those who escaped did not, paradoxically, escape that they might live; they fled, lest, when captured, they should betray others to death. It might be so with Mercedes.

His head nodded forward:

"Buried how long?"

"Almost four years."

"What happened to you?"

"*J'étais dans la montagne*." She had said this, they told him, before she became unconscious. He had heard the phrase before, from those who fought the Resistance campaign.

"You were captured?"

"Almost."

"How did you escape?"

The pale mouth did not move and the sunken eyelids were still. There would never be an answer to that question until the end of the war. He knew about the people who

223

came through from Marseille and across the frontiers. They did not talk. Soldiers or pilots, men or women, they did not talk.

He muttered, "Cold; you must have been cold," and the words snapped him awake to realise that he was cold. He saw the light on the wing-tip moving along beside him in the dark.

It was a curious ending for Mercedes Knowle, the restless, favoured person, with the wreck of a marriage on her hands and little else. She had no roots; always she had had money, but never roots; her only preoccupation the queer, half-finished duel that she fought with Michael. The logic of that duel remained mysterious. But she was always a little mysterious, never belonging entirely to the circle of café-society that she sometimes frequented and sometimes left; not wholly a creative artist, not wholly an idler, neither a wife nor a divorcee; a figure without context. Of all her strange and short-lived passions, perhaps the most fitting was the cause of France, the last passion and the last fight. It would kill her before she knew of Michael's death. "They've both killed themselves," he thought; his head nodded forward again. This time the face on the pillow drifted away; the dreams drifted away and left the dark.

He woke and saw the sunrise on the coast; he blinked upwards at the altimeter; the needle was steady at seven hundred feet, the precaution in case they were shot down.

The coast tapered off below the right wing; they were out in the Atlantic under a gold sky. He tried to think himself on through the stages of this flight, the nothingness of sea and sky that would endure until their escort came to meet them at the place in the air called Rendezvous Corner. First they were two black dots against the sun; then they grew wings as you watched and soon after that the opaque shades were fastened across the windows. Only when the air bumped differently could you at last tell that you were flying over land. England was below you then.

That made him think of the cigarette; he would step out into the launch, gratefully lighting the first cigarette for ten hours. He could see Poole in his mind; a misty stretch of water; a tall camouflage-painted chimney to the left; the little street of stone houses above the landing-stage on the right. Somewhere, a line of sandbags piled along a bank. He could not place the sandbags precisely where they should be. He tried to remember them and then he was bored and let them go. There was the face on the pillow, drifting back to haunt him.

Lee would be sorry. Lee had admired Mercedes for the very toughness that he himself found inimical. Lee was a long time ago and a long way off. He had written to her from the Aviz last night; rather a drunken letter.

The gold sky faded. "We're flying into weather," he thought, as the aircraft lurched and quivered. There was a stream of rain at the windows.

He could not remember much of the letter to Lee; nor the few lines that he had sent to the queer Miss Haydon with the black glasses, who waited for news. He thought that he was a skunk to write the news to her; in London he could see her and tell her. But she was a bore.

In this game, he thought, one dodged the avoidable bores even more energetically than one avoided them in time of peace, because there was now so much that was boring and unavoidable. This flight, for example. Now the air was rough and they must not fly above the storm. Adams shut his eyes and felt giddy. "I guess I ought to see Miss Haydon, just because I don't want to. My New England conscience," he grumbled, trying to relax and sleep again.

"My New England conscience. Look where it's got me. For nearly four years now I've been bumming around Europe, dressed like a doorman, just because I wanted to be in this damn thing. Me, that was the toast of the Book-of-the-Month Club. Tell you what I'd like if you could fix it," he said to God, "I'd like to be sitting in front of the fire, looking out at Charles River Square under snow; with a highball in my hand and a story in my head; and I'd like it to be damn cold outside too, so as to make it more fun to be warm.

"Or the ranch on a summer afternoon; that's an idea. The afternoon that they all tell you is too hot for California.

225

I'd settle for it." He could see the corner of the guest-house with the magnolia tree beside it, the pattern of shadow that the tree made upon the lawn; the sprinklers playing. Sudden twilight and Lee grilling steaks on the broiler.

It made more sense, really, to think about uncomfortable things; flying high in real cold; bucket-seats in Dakotas.

The aircraft was rolling and sliding in the storm; at moments it felt as though it thudded down a flight of steps, then hung and quivered and shook itself all over.

Adams was used to the motion now; he thought that he liked it; he began to be drowsy again, to take up in his mind the adventures of Mr. Lorry, the halt on the Dover Road. "*He's hoarser than suits me, is Jerry*"; "*Pull off the gentleman's boots in Concord*"; and then he was in the wine-shop with Defarge. Now the movement of the aircraft became the lumbering of the coach in flight—"*The wind is rushing after us, and the clouds are flying after us, and the moon is plunging after us, the whole wild night is in pursuit of us, but so far we are pursued by nothing else.*"

He opened his eyes. Beside him his suitcase, with the label "W" for Westbound, its only admissible destination, was sliding across the floor. He got up to pull it back and as he rose he saw the shape of other wings on the mist outside.

The floor beneath his feet tilted upwards, throwing him down across his chair. Above his head, just for a second, he saw the altimeter-needle revolving wildly; then something came that was like a thunder of darkness. The last thing that he knew was a phrase repeated; "*The murmuring of many voices; the murmuring of many voices. The murmuring. . .*"

THURSDAY, FEBRUARY 3rd, 1944
14.45 *hours*

Captain Hellyar reflected that, against the disadvantages of his being orderly officer, of the rain and the cold and the fact that the mess had run out of beer, he could set one credit item: to-day was Thursday and Caroline Seward would come over to Cold Ash to pay the A.T.S. "Unless that toothy Junior Commander foxes me by coming herself. But I suspect," said

Hellyar, "that Miss Teeth has gone on leave. She was talking about it last week."

He looked out of the blurred window, down across the wet slopes that were clustered with Nissen huts, wire fences and temporary wooden buildings. The skeleton of good farmland lay under this atrocious plantation.

He was restless to-day. He had been increasingly restless for three months; ever since Joan Bridges was promoted and posted to the A.T.S. Group Headquarters, while the toothy Junior Commander took her place. It was the last development that he had expected to trouble his mind; Group H.Q. was no further from Cold Ash than the former school-house on the hill.

Leaning against the window, he recalled the moment that Joan had told him. Joan had said, "You'll like Doyle. She's bright and schoolmistress-y but she knows her job. And Caroline's coming as her subaltern." His picture of Caroline at that time was a wild-eyed person with a cut head, and Baynes' large hand upon her shoulder. He had asked, "Is that a good idea?" Joan had said that it was a good idea, that the Edinburgh O.C.T.U. was closing and that Caroline, when a corporal, had worked in a company office and knew the drill. Joan had been a little on the defensive when she said this; speaking from behind the closed door that he began to recognise. She shut that door upon the importance of her friendship with Caroline, upon the tragic story that she would not tell.

Three months ago, it had teased him that there should be a place in Joan's mind where he could not follow her. He had been in love with her then. His pace of decision was leisured; he had not asked her to marry him; but he had known that he would. Joan, like himself, was a person with a quiet façade and an adventurous mind. She was not beautiful; but he had no doubts that she was the one. He had walked back from the first evening in the ante-room, thinking "that is my woman," and the weeks of September and October had been spent in voyages of discovery with her; in planning, alone, the future that they could make. Hellyar had told her his peace-terms, a farm in South Shropshire and a family; she had liked them.

"Why didn't I ask her to marry me the night before she went to Group, the night we dined at the country club? I meant to; she knew it; it was floating about in the air all the evening. And I thought, 'Plenty of time'. Which is a damn silly thing to think in a war anyway," Hellyar sulked, looking at his watch.

"Well, suppose I had? Would it have made any difference? Wouldn't this have happened anyway?" Perhaps it was foolish to think that the statement of his love would have made a protector, a bulwark against the extraordinary invasion of Caroline Seward.

It was the aura of tragedy that had made him curious; that had kept him going to the Company Headquarters on the hill. Walking back from his first evening with Caroline, he had not thought "This is my woman". He had thought with equal certainty, "This will never be for me," and at once he had begun to wish that it might.

He had told himself eagerly that she was important because she was Joan's friend. He had seen certain likenesses between them; likenesses of speech; the same direct manner; the careless devotion to the job that made them swear at it and do it well. It had been fun to discover Caroline's authority for an opinion held by Joan; to recognise the origin of a phrase or a thought that he had found sympathetic.

There had been a period when he and Joan agreed that Caroline made an ideal and undemanding third. The shifting of the pattern had come gradually; now he seldom saw them together. Now Joan would ask, "Seen Caroline?" and he would feel the effort behind the casual question. He spoke of her less and less.

Joan, he reflected, had probably recognised the difference in him before he did. They met regularly in their hours off duty, and when they met, the sad perplexity behind her gay manner seemed to match the sad perplexity in his own mind.

It was futile that his fortunes should be twisted by a woman who was far away from him in her own grief. It was painful to be persistently aware of her beauty, to have her dark-toned voice in his ears all day. There was nothing tangible here but the beauty and the voice, the controlled friendliness and the over-tone of sorrow. She was a haunt, he thought, not a woman at all.

> ("No mortal woman ever was
> so swiftly still, so unaware
> that anyone is watching her.")

He wished that they would send her away.

Now it was almost three o'clock; she would be here at three. Perhaps, after all, it would be better if the toothy Junior Commander dashed his hopes. Oh, but they weren't hopes; he had no hopes; these were only the emotions of a drinker, warned that whisky would kill him, putting out his hand for the glass.

The approaching hour made Hellyar look restlessly about his mind for something that belonged to him. The only thing that belonged to him at the moment was his owl; he thought that he would risk leaving the office empty and go to see how the owl was getting on. He looked through the partition into the outer office. The telephone-clerk was there, a chubby A.T.S. girl with a striving manner.

"I'll be back in about ten minutes," he said, tramping through the room that must have been beautiful in its original shape, before the partitions were erected; it had been a library. As he set foot on the staircase that led to the upper floors, he heard the voice down in the hall; Caroline Seward's voice greeting the private on duty by the door. She was saying, "I'm a few minutes early."

"If you are a few minutes early," said Hellyar, leaning over the banisters, "I've got something I'd like to show you."

She came up the stairs, pulling off her cap; here it was, the baffling face, with the green eyes and the hollow cheeks, the delicate line of jaw and throat; he wanted to see the whole of that line; it should end at the base of her neck and not be interrupted by the forbidding collar and tie.

"What is your thing?" she asked, eyeing him with her look of absent-minded charity.

"Come and see."

At the end of the top-floor corridor there was a small high

window; he stooped and opened the cupboard door in the wall; a place where dustpans and brushes might have been kept. Hellyar groped in the dark of it, saw the two eyes shine and lifted the bird out of the box of soft shavings. One or two shavings clung to its feathers; it was dumpy and soft like a kitten; the banded markings on its wings and breast were beginning to show through the babyish down. It kept its eyes tightly shut and rolled a little on its feet inside the cup of his hands.

Caroline stroked its head with the tip of her finger and tweeked the incipient tufts above its ears. "Where did you find him?"

"Flapping about in the cinders outside Naffy. He's hurt a wing. Do you see? It isn't bad; those long feathers are a bit bent but they'll straighten out again." He began to show off his countryman's knowledge to her, naming the feathers and using technical terms. He said, "By to-morrow he'll be twice the owl he was before. Of course he's young yet. And I've put him on the evil path by feeding him bread soaked in beer."

"Why in the cupboard? Can he breathe?"

"He likes the dark. Those two holes in the door give the old boy enough air. He won't die now," said Hellyar, pretending to be wholly absorbed with the owl. "Yesterday I was afraid he would." He touched the soft head with his lips, stooped and put the owl back, hearing it rustle among the shavings. He shut the door.

When he rose he saw that Caroline was staring at the corner pane of the high window. He said, " I only saw that when I brought the owl up here. They must have used a diamond."

She was silent; she seemed to have departed into a dream of her own. She put up her hand, running her finger across the surface where the two names were scratched; one above the other :

Michael
Mercedes

The uneven lettering was frosty and transparent, letting the light through.

He thought of the message that Leicester wrote with a diamond: *"Fain would I climb, but that I fear to fall"*; of the words inscribed by the recusant, Walmesley, at Whittington: *"Terrena despice; eterna suspice."*

"Something fatal about writing on glass," he said, "I don't know why." Still she was silent. He said, "Tell you a funny thing. One sees names and initials carved in all sorts of places; on monuments and trees and bridges; but one never catches anybody in the act of carving them. Or I never have; have you?"

Slowly she drew her finger again across the first name on the glass and let her hand fall at her side. She stared past him; she was looking at somebody who was not there. On her face there was an expression that he knew; the loving look that accepted and forgave all hurt; the look that did not ask "Why have you done this to me?" He had seen it on Joan's face, looking at him.

Suddenly his thoughts made a positive shape. He knew that now, if ever, was the time to learn his lesson, to see that all desire for her was futile; if he could acknowledge this and turn away, he would defeat her, exorcize her, as though she had the powers of a witch.

She said, "I shall be leaving here."

"Oh, no," his vehemence was absurd.

"It was only a temporary posting; it wasn't likely to last long." She went on talking, but he did not listen; he was thinking that Joan and he would be left in peace. He heard her say something about a Board, a possible job at the War Office. Their military likenesses were now a little dim, he thought, dim but convenient; "each of us dressed up as something that we are not; both of us now making jokes about the War Office, tramping down the corridor in our thick shoes." She paused at the head of the stairs. Now she was saying, "How is Joan? I haven't seen her this week," and there was no resemblance to Joan asking, "Have you seen Caroline?" He smiled at her.

"I think you know," he said abruptly.

"I've tried not to know."

231

"But it is all right. You couldn't help its happening."

Her lips quivered. She said, "Have I spoiled things, for you both?"

"No," said Hellyar. "I thought you had, but you haven't." He began fishing in a pocket for his pipe. "Perhaps the reason why I fell in love with her was that I fell in love with a bit of you. Does that sound like nonsense?"

"No."

"But it is all right. I knew that just now; when you were looking at somebody who wasn't there." He did not add, "That look on Joan's face is for me; as yours never could be. And still I think that she learned it from you." He said clumsily, "Anyway; don't give it another thought. Nothing has been spoiled, I promise."

She smiled at him, saying hurriedly, "I must pay these troops."

When he went back into the library, he picked up the telephone and asked for the A.T.S. Group Headquarters. He said, "It seems such an awfully long time since we talked," and he thought that Joan's voice sounded differently as though she too knew that their danger had passed.

THURSDAY, FEBRUARY 3rd, 1944
16.00 hours

Dorothy Knowle was driving a car that belonged to the W.V.S. pool of cars; a battered Morris whose engine objected to the steep succession of hills leading up from the town. Poor town, she thought. Built up in crescents from the sea, it had been a thriving holiday place. Now it was a shabby amphitheatre; its terraces showed the scars left by the tip-and-run raiders; its shops were martyrs to boarded windows; its streets were interrupted by road-blocks and barbed wire. All the hotels except one were requisitioned. Most of the boarding-houses on the front had long ago lost their look of modest welcome and seemed to have been always these drab warrens where soldiers lived.

She was relieved to reach the crest of the last hill, to take the road that led home. It was a grey afternoon; once she had liked the winter here, but now winter had become a long tunnel of anxiety and inconvenience, from the cold dark morning to the hour when you must pull the black-out curtains into place, shutting out the last of the light before it left the sky. Even the bare trees and the low hills, the winter fields, seemed to wear a look of ruined difference. It had been so since Michael died.

Caroline was waiting for her in the drawing-room. The tea was laid and the kettle boiling, the fire lit. "That's nice," said Dorothy, "First nice thing to-day. Sorry to keep you waiting."

She was still not used to the presence of Caroline, who wandered in on the afternoons when she paid the girls at Cold Ash, sprawled by the fire, ate her tea, helped with the washing-up and disappeared again in the direction of her army duties. She was, Dorothy had decided, an unexpectedly adaptable young woman. Now she poured the tea and said, "I scrounged you some more sugar. They've killed another nice one."

"Oh, don't." Dorothy said sharply. "Who?"

"I didn't know him well, but I liked him. Wynstay Adams, the American novelist. Shot down in that Lisbon plane."

"I read about it."

"He was a friend of Michael's. We had drinks with them in Boston. Nice little man with a passion for Dickens. What-the-hell? Silly to be surprised at people being killed." She sat down and drank her tea; adding softly, " 'Threadbare Death commands, hardly observance at our busier hands.' But that isn't how it feels. Should it?"

"I don't know."

"I'll be leaving here soon," Caroline said.

"You'll be posted?"

"So it would seem."

"Damn!" said Dorothy; she saw Caroline's eyebrow lift in a look of startled amusement; she thought that it was not only the firelight and the shadow that made the face so thin. Caroline was a fragile, shrunken version of her last summer's self; more boyish in appearance, more abstracted in manner.

"But why must you go?"

233

Caroline hesitated. "There's a memorandum from the War Office; inviting applications from officers with my sort of experience. I put my name in. It's up to Joan to recommend me; I think she will."

"You mean you needn't go? It isn't an order?"

"Oh, no."

"I thought you were happy here," Dorothy said.

"Last autumn it seemed the only place to be."

"And now you want to move on?"

"M'm," said Caroline; but she did not sound convinced.

Dorothy said exasperatedly, "Another change; how I hate them."

"Sorry." She still looked bewildered, Dorothy thought, as though it were a shock to realise that Dorothy liked her and wanted her to stay.

"I suppose I never say nice things; I don't take trouble; she has warmth and she has pretty manners, she always thanks me; I'm no good at those details." She stirred her tea vigorously and tried. "It's been awfully nice, having you here. Wish you'd come before. With Michael, I mean; all that time he was on sick-leave; you could have come; don't know why you didn't."

"I thought you wouldn't want me. You see," Caroline said, running her hand through her hair: "I knew how much you disliked Mercedes, and I, well—I was just another one."

"You were not," said Dorothy. "You aren't in the least like Mercedes." She laughed abruptly. "Mercedes was——I *am* bad at expressing these things; possessive, nine-points-of-the-law on her side; she grabbed Michael, swallowed him whole. Typical wife."

She was discomfited by Caroline's mischievous grin. "And I am a typical——?"

"Don't think you're a typical anything, and I mean that as a compliment. You see, in my view, it's a narrow view, I suppose, most women are greedy. If they are wives they are greedy for their rights; if they're the other sort they're greedy for what they can get out of men."

She had not voiced these thoughts before; she saw the

two categories plainly enough; the wife, holding jealously to her prestige and position behind the silver tea-pot; the tart making sure of her mink coat and her bank-balance. Each had a background. The young woman in uniform, now smoking a cigarette and sprawling comfortably in Dorothy's mother's favourite chair, had none. And Caroline was the first woman for whom Dorothy had ever felt this tenderness. Absurdly, she found herself saying, "You'll have a home of your own when all this is over, won't you? Now that you've a little money." Michael's will had been a simple one; his capital divided between Dorothy and Caroline; his pictures, books and furniture to Caroline. That there was no mention of Mercedes would have pleased Dorothy had she not known that Mercedes' impatience with property would make any legacy a bore.

Caroline said, "A home? Yes, well . . ." and was silent until she asked uncertainly, "Would you have called Mercedes a greedy person?"

"Greedy and spoilt," said Dorothy; "cold and flashy; that is if one can be cold and flashy at the same time."

"I should think one could. Fish are," said Caroline, staring at the fire. "Isn't it curious to think that if Mercedes is alive, she knows nothing of Michael's death?"

"None of her business," Dorothy snapped. She could not see why this made Caroline laugh so much. Coming to the end of the paroxysm, Caroline said, "And I think she's alive. I've thought so much more positively since he died."

"I feel exactly the opposite way," said Dorothy. "It would be so like her to get there ahead of all of us and have him to herself."

Caroline laughed again.

"Perhaps you're right. She goes on winning, doesn't she? She always did."

"Winning? She lost Michael to you," Dorothy snapped.

Caroline cocked her head on one side.

"What's on your mind?"

"This afternoon—Cold Ash in its dreary disguise. Remember how Mercedes wanted to turn the house into an institution, in '39? And Michael fought her. Well, it's an institution now, by all that's holy. She got her way."

Dorothy frowned; she did not want to think so. "Mercedes wanted refugees in it," she said.

Caroline shrugged her shoulders. "Anyway it's ruined. A wreck with her signature still on it; and his. Did you know that? Their names scratched on the top-floor window?"

"I believe I did. I'd forgotten."

"I saw them to-day," said Caroline.

"Shouldn't let it worry you."

Caroline was silent.

"He never talked about her, did he?" Dorothy mused.

"Not to me. Nor to you, either?" She was sharply attentive now; sitting up straight in the chair.

Dorothy shook her head.

"One learns to bury things deep," Caroline said; and after a moment added as though to herself, "I thought I never could." She looked troubled; then she glanced at her watch. "Let me help you wash this stuff; that bus goes in about twelve minutes."

"Run you back," said Dorothy; "I've got the car till six. Nonsense. Perfectly legitimate piece of official transport."

When she had left Caroline at the gates of the school-house and seen the cone of light from Caroline's torch go up the steps, she drove home in the dark, thinking that life would be emptier still without this unorthodox companion.

MONDAY, FEBRUARY 21st, 1944
16.30 hours

"Has anybody any more questions to ask this officer?"

The faces round the table said no. Caroline had been interested in the faces. There was a narrow, curved one, a flat, pink one, a withered-old-lady one and one like a horse. The stars and crowns upon the shoulders added up to a formidable total of rank. The women all wrote rapidly on the paper in front of them as soon as she opened her mouth. This was the intimidating circumstance, a War Office Board and it was difficult, Caroline thought, to go on being you;

partly because there was no assurance that they wanted you to be you. There was the temptation to try to please teacher by assuming a virtue.

"Thank you very much, Seward. You'll hear the result of the Board within three weeks," said the narrow, curved face. Caroline stood up, clicked her heels and went to the door. Outside the door, a corporal handed her her cap and gloves. She went down in the lift, with two wearers of red tabs, and gave the man by the door the signed pass that admitted her to these mysteries.

"Shouldn't wonder if I've got that job," Caroline thought. "The operative reason being that I don't really want it." But she knew that it was the answer to the problem of Joan and Hellyar. His queer monkish face came before her eyes, and she heard the soft voice saying steadily, "I think I fell in love with a bit of you."

She came out into Eaton Square; she looked at her watch. She felt childishly at liberty because she was alone in London until to-morrow morning. You did not, she thought, realise how cramped your current existence was until you left it. But there was a hurdle ahead; the appointment with Miss Haydon, whose odd, prim letter defied all Caroline's speculations. All that she could remember of Miss Haydon was a pair of dark glasses and a hostile manner, obtruding between herself and Dennis at the Brookfield Galleries. If Miss Haydon expected her to have news of Dennis, she would be disappointed. In two years he had written only once, the short letter that sent his love when he heard of Michael's death. "And in any case, she could have asked me to write her that sort. What is the point of 'seeing me personally'? A foolish phrase; how could she see me impersonally? I used to have a hunch that she hated my guts," Caroline thought, looking for a taxi as she came into Sloane Square.

There was one taxi on the rank; she hailed it and as they moved she caught something of the feel of the old London; a taxi on a winter afternoon; time to burn. It was always an astonishment to her now that these moments of illogical liveliness could come back. They came unexpectedly; they were brief and there was the grey plain waiting at the end of them; but they were a signal of hope.

> "As the crocus, insolent under slaty skies,
> Strikes a green sword-blade through the stubborn mould,
> And throws, in the teeth of Winter,
> Its challenge of gold."

she chanted, looking out at the Pimlico streets that were smashed and spoiled. "Eh?" said the taxi-driver, turning his head. "Sorry, I always talk to myself." (But you could welcome the signals of hope too greedily, so that they vanished and the devils came back instead.)

She reached Miss Haydon's Ministry. There was another drab hall with its official traces; another pass on which she signed her name; another lift and another corridor; then a long bare room with incongruous pink tiles round the fireplace; a table at the far end of the room, and Dennis's former secretary rising to greet her.

The sight of Miss Haydon brought back the Brookfield Galleries so vividly that Caroline's current existence vanished and she was somewhere in '38, coming to lunch with Dennis. On Miss Haydon's table now she saw the silver things; the inkpot, pen-tray and paper-knife. (I remember those. How she beams at me; perhaps she didn't hate me at all.)

"Do sit down. It was so good of you to come. Are you on leave? I hope I'm not using up precious time. Do have a cigarette—I've got heaps."

"Thank you. No, I had to come up for a Board, so it couldn't have been easier."

"A Board? Oh, dear; that sounds as though you'd been ill." ("This eager, lunging approach is going to wear me out.")

"It wasn't a Medical Board; it was a Selection Board for a job."

"How do you like the A.T.S.?"

Caroline said, "You know, I find that difficult to answer. It is just the thing I'm doing and I can hardly remember the time when it wasn't. Like being alive; you don't really have a point of view about that. I'm sorry," she apologised to the dark glasses. "The influence of the board is still upon me; all their questions had to be debated and turned over."

"Oh, please."

There was a silence. Caroline said, "What was it that you wanted to see me about?" And now Miss Haydon seemed shy, playing with the silver paper-knife.

"It was about Mrs. Michael Knowle," she said at last.

"Well, what a thing; blow me," said Caroline vulgarly to herself. Miss Haydon added, "I was very fond of her; as you probably know, I was her companion-secretary once; before I worked for Mr. Brookfield."

("Well, strike me pink; Dennis never told me that. No wonder you hated me.")

"Mrs. Knowle is dying; in a hospital in Lisbon. She is perhaps dead by now."

"How do you know that?"

"I got a letter about it," said Miss Haydon with an air of importance. "From the American novelist, Wynstay Adams, actually. He wrote to me after he'd seen her. He was killed flying back from Lisbon last month, you may have read about it."

"Yes, I did. I liked him. ("What a curious friend you are for Wynstay Adams.") I ought to write to Lee; do you know Lee too?"

"Er—no. I only got in touch with Mr. Adams about Mrs. Knowle."

There was another silence. A clerk came in with two cups of tea. Caroline said, "Look, we'd better get this tidy, hadn't we? I never knew Mrs. Knowle. I was, as you may or may not understand, highly unlikely to know her, or to be a friend of hers. In fact, we never met."

Miss Haydon's lips pursed. "Oh, of course. I don't expect *you* to mind about her death."

Caroline said, "Surely there is no need to be truculent. How can I mind or not mind? Of course I am sorry if she suffered; obviously she must have had a hell of a time in France. But what can any of it have to do with me?"

"You seem be my last link," said Miss Haydon solemnly.

239

She had set one elbow on the table and was resting her chin in the palm of her hand. She was disagreeably impressive; she wore her dark hair parted in the middle; the features of the face were heavy and the olive skin very smooth. She wore a dress of purplish red. ("She suggests to my mind a fortune-teller and there should be a portière made of beads hanging behind her, and a lamp and a crystal on the table.")

"As soon as I saw that Wynstay Adams had been killed, I knew I had to get in touch with you. As a matter of fact I thought of writing to you after Colonel Knowle died, to send you my sympathy. But I thought you wouldn't like it."

("And if somebody could suggest to me a graceful reply to *that* one I should be enormously obliged.")

"Anyhow," said Miss Haydon, "this is the point: you're stationed near Cold Ash now, aren't you?"

"I am. I was wondering how you got my address."

"Doris Malling told me; she's my cousin; do you remember a Sergeant Malling? She was in your company when you were at Woolwich."

("Bossy type with a tooth that whistled. This gets curiouser and curiouser.") "Yes; I remember Sergeant Malling."

There was silence again. Then Vera Haydon said, "It has all become very important to me. I don't expect you to understand. But I would so much like to visit Cold Ash again."

"It's a District H.Q. now."

"I know. I thought you would be able to arrange it for me. I could come down on my day off; I can get a pass to visit a restricted area; from the Ministry, you see." Her heavy eagerness was maddening; the instructions were maddening. "I thought, if you said that I was a friend of yours; that I used to know the house; that I only wanted to be there for an hour or two, just to look round."

Caroline thought, "And why didn't you ask me in your letter; why drag me up here to talk about it?" She frowned, trying to choose kind words and not feeling kind at all. She remembered Michael's precept: "If you are going to say No, say No at once; don't lead up to it."

"It would be all right, wouldn't it?" Miss Haydon prompted her.

"I'm sorry, but I don't think it would. It would be an extremely tricky favour for me to ask. First of all, I'm not attached to that military unit; I don't know the Commandant and the only time I go to Cold Ash is when my Company Commander sends me over to pay some of our troops who work there. Secondly, and I don't want to sound officious—that isn't the sort of thing that the army's in the habit of doing."

"Oh, I can imagine *that*," said Miss Haydon scornfully. "They're terribly stuffy and hidebound, aren't they?"

("Now, keep your temper; the woman can't help being an ass.") "Well, they have work to do and their regulations are made with that object."

The silver paper-knife beat a long tattoo on the edge of the table. "Miss Seward, do you mean that you can't arrange this for me, or that you won't?" The voice shook.

"I mean exactly what I have said. That it would be a difficult proposition to suggest and that I'm not the person to suggest it."

The black glasses went on staring at her; the lips pursed again.

Caroline said, "I'm sorry, but there it is. And, look, if you did care for Cold Ash, you honestly wouldn't like to see it now. The grounds are ruined; built all over with huts and cookhouses and storage-dumps. The house itself is a mess; they've partitioned the rooms and turned them into offices; the paint's dirty, the wallpapers are peeling; you can imagine what sort of a job they've done to it. Even if I could get you there, I wouldn't advise you to go. I know that if I had liked it I would rather remember it as it used to be."

"You know nothing about it."

Caroline rose from her chair.

"I never heard such damned, pompous rubbish in my life," said Miss Haydon. "Just because you wear a uniform—"

—"Watch it," Caroline interrupted, "I can be just as rude as you can. And with a rather better choice of words."

Silence. Caroline picked up her cap and gloves. "Goodbye," she said and went to the door.

"Miss Seward——"

"Yes?"

"Your pass. I have to sign you out."

It was irritating to walk back to the table. Miss Haydon signed the pass and handed it over.

"Thank you for coming to see me," she said in a muffled voice, as Caroline reached the door.

"Oh for heaven's sake," said Caroline wearily. She wanted to slam the door; she shut it quietly. She walked fast in the dusk, letting her temper cool. After a time she remembered that Mercedes was dead, or dying, and this now seemed to have no importance whatever. The only point of interest was that Dennis had never told her about Miss Haydon's former employment. She wondered why not.

MONDAY, FEBRUARY 21st, 1944
22.45 hours

The impression in the hotel lounge was reminiscent of a storm at sea. There were the people who went below and the people who stayed on in their groups, all with their ears cocked to the fury of the weather outside. It was appropriate to be sitting here with Jay Brookfield and Billy Lloyd. Their war-time disguises faded, and now, she thought, we are back in the ship, with Michael; "*Timor mortis conturbat me.* Except that it doesn't any more." Jay wore naval uniform; Jay was attached to the Admiralty and had just returned from Washington. She had found him at Kate's house. He and Billy had walked her back here as the warning sounded and the first gunfire began to rumble up the river.

The nearest guns cracked in thunder and the chandelier overhead performed a small, ominous dance.

"Tedious," said Jay, "and typically German. What else can one expect from a nation whose language resembles a sausage with hiccoughs?"

Billy Lloyd said indignantly, "Oh, look here. It's the only language for opera. In what other language would you choose to hear opera?"

"Put your mind at rest on that point," said Jay, "I would never choose to hear opera."

His harlequin face, with the flat peak of black hair dividing the forehead, became agonised: "*What* a language," Jay groaned, "all gargles and retchings."

The rockets went up with their noise of a panting giant; the great breaths tearing the air; there was a patter of shrapnel falling outside; the curtains blew.

"Aren't we a little too near the window?" said Lloyd. They got up, carrying their drinks, and moved to the opposite corner. "Heine; Goethe; Schiller," Lloyd was saying.

"Bah," said Jay. "Somebody always says that at this point and quotes that *heavenly-little-piece* beginning 'Uber Apfelstrudel ist ruh'."

The noise of the guns hurled itself higher; there was the different thunder of a bomb exploding and the floor shook. Jay went on improvising,

> " 'Uber Apfelstrudel ist ruh.
> In Eiernudeln
> Spurest du
> Kaum einen Hauch.' "

Lloyd said, "You ought to be shot." Caroline said, "Oh, Jay, I love you." She stopped on the speech. A woman was coming slowly up the steps of the lounge; she stood between the glass doors, looking anxiously to left and right. Jay said, "I have seen that great Caryatid before somewhere; who is it?"

"It is your brother's former secretary, Miss Haydon."

"Ah yes; I sometimes thought that I would like her to throw me across the saddle of a huge horse and carry me off."

Lloyd said, "What an extraordinary idea; why should she?"

"But why——" said Jay, "are you looking so unhappy, Caroline?"

Vera Haydon saw them and hesitated. She had taken off her dark glasses; she had reddened her lips, and with the high fur collar of her coat held round her face she looked oddly different. Caroline called, "Looking for me?" She came to their table.

"I—I was. It doesn't matter; I just wanted to see you for a minute; I thought you'd be alone. Oh, please don't get up."

The near guns fired again and a voice from the hall shouted, "They're dropping flares right overhead."

Caroline said with an effort, "You know Jay, don't you? and Brigadier Lloyd? Miss Haydon. Do have a drink."

"But I don't want to disturb you."

(Really, Caroline thought, I cannot be bothered with this. Let Jay do it; Jay is doing it, settling her in a chair, being charming and bitter; showing off. Even Billy now has that slightly tautened, preparing-for-action smile that men get when a new woman appears in the party. Fun for Miss Haydon. But why has she come and how did she know I was staying the night here? Did I write this address on the pass that I signed? I did. Miss Lynx-Eyes; our woman-detective. But she's being gay, in her outsize manner; Lord, it's getting noisy now. Any hope of a direct hit, I ask myself? Here comes Jay, having placed her with Billy; Jay determined to have deep thoughts about me and to ask me if I'm still in tune with the gospel of acceptance.)

"You're too thin, my love."

"Yes, well. . . ."

"You are still lovely, but in that uniform you are a sexless frame of bones."

"It sounds like a bicycle," said Caroline.

The guns were in crescendo now. It was the moment when you said to yourself, "There cannot be a louder one than that," and were at once contradicted. Jay said, "How safe we are—You won't die simply because you want to; I won't die simply because I don't care." There was Miss Haydon's face, steadily vivacious; Lloyd saying, "How true that is" and Miss Haydon looking pleased. Her eyes were bright; she turned her head happily and lifted her glass. "She isn't like a fortune-teller now," Caroline thought. "She is like a large black swan."

"But oh, my dearest Caroline, the things they do to you."

"They?"

Jay pointed to the ceiling, "Not the dear Germans; the boys further up."

"Leave it," she said.

"Miss Haydon and I," said Lloyd, "are having a debate on the meaning of kindness."

"Kindness can be a tyranny," said Miss Haydon loudly. She looked pleased with herself. "For example, people giving you what you don't need. I always say that's a tyranny; and those people sort of follow their presents up all the time. For example, I've got an aunt; quite a rich aunt; she likes to give me shoes. Now actually I've got very high insteps," she swung her foot, "and I cannot wear just any kind of shoes. But if ever I go to lunch with my aunt, she comes up to London quite often, she's extraordinarily plucky about bombs, and takes me to Harrod's, well, I see those eyes looking at my feet before she looks at my face. Have you noticed that?" she said to Jay. "But of course your trade is to notice things, *and* yours," she said to Lloyd, "I suppose one might say mine was too, now. Public Relations, Mr. Brookfield. I do dislike that name, don't you? It's genteel, like people saying Serviette. Actually I think all the words that we use in this war are so ill-chosen that what we want is a Ministry of English. Only of course they wouldn't call it that, would they? Nothing so simple. What would it be? Yes Mr. Brookfield, Ministry of Terms and Appellations; of course. But when you *think* of the words, austerity; utility; restricted; short-supply—all so dreadfully dull. Now that would be a perfect job for you, Mr. Brookfield; running a whole Ministry of writers to produce attractive and intelligent slogans." She smiled dazzlingly, finished her drink and said, "A lot quieter now, isn't it?"

"I hadn't noticed it," Jay murmured to Caroline.

"But I ought to be going. Oh, I'm sure it's all over now; besides, they don't worry me a bit. Thank you so much. It's been wonderful." She said to Caroline, "I wonder if I might just have a word with you," and Caroline rose and walked with her across the lounge.

"I didn't expect a treat like that," Vera Haydon said, "Jay Brookfield's wonderful, isn't he? 'Terms and Appellations.' How does he think of those things? And the Brigadier's a perfect charmer."

They came down the steps. In the hall, opposite the reception-desk, there was a sofa under a potted palm. "I won't keep you two minutes," said Miss Haydon. "Might we just sit here? I wanted to say how sorry I am that I behaved so badly this afternoon."

"Oh, please——"

"No, Miss Seward, I did. And I want to explain. I'm not a person who finds it easy to talk about myself. But I feel I can say this to you.

"Actually, I've never had much life of my own; I've always been somebody's secretary or companion and in a funny way I lived more in their lives. I always rather laughed at them for being society sort of people, but now I think I may have been a teeny bit jealous of them.

"And Mrs Knowle was always my favourite. She did lots of things that I couldn't bear, but she had breeding and she could be quite charming and I grew to love her very much. And somehow, after I heard that she was missing in France, nothing seemed quite so important or so exciting to me as those years when I worked for her; and I got into the habit of going back in my mind and living them over and over again. And I let myself get quite desperate about wanting to find out what had happened to her. It was all a sort of dream.

"And then I thought it was over; with her death. And that was foolish too, because there was nothing really there to *be* over; I don't suppose I'd ever have seen her again or worked for her. But it made me want to go down to Cold Ash, to say good-bye to her there, do you see? You look as if you understand; I expect you do.

"But I realise now that it would be all different and probably depressing, as you said. I thought about it after you'd gone. What it means is that one can't live on memories; dead things; one must stop chasing after them. So I'd seen on your pass when I signed it that you were staying here; and I thought I'd screw up my courage to come along and just explain; and say I was sorry; and thank you. Because really, if you hadn't said that—well." She got up quickly, taking something out of her handbag.

"I wanted you to have this; Mrs. Knowle gave it me. Would you have it? Just as a sort of souvenir, to say it's all right now."

Caroline unwrapped the silver paper-knife. At first she thought, "Oh damn this; why should I want it?" and then there was the movement of compassion, like a physical movement beneath her ribs. She said, "Thank you. I'll always value it."

"You ought to give me a penny, really, oughtn't you?" Vera Haydon was brisk and beaming now. Caroline found the penny. There was another rumble of gun-fire.

"Look, hadn't you better stay till the All Clear goes?"

"Oh rather not! It must be almost over. I'll pop down the Underground. Thank you so much. It was wonderful," she said, "I don't know when I've had such a good time."

Caroline stood looking at the black-curtained doors as they closed behind her. She put the paper-knife in her breast-pocket and walked slowly up the steps into the lounge. A group of people wearing coats over their night-clothes were debating whether they should now go to bed. Jay and Billy Lloyd were pouring out a jug of beer. "No more whisky," said Jay. "Too sordid."

She sat down between them. "*Dear*," said Jay, "how pickled Miss H. got—and how quickly." Lloyd said, "Rather a nice woman." Jay said, "I loved the bit about the high insteps and Harrods." The guns opened up again. "She couldn't have enjoyed herself more," said Jay. There was the swish of the rockets; the triple burst from the nearest guns; then a long liquid whistle coming down to meet the echo half-way.

"Get down; that's right on top of us," said Lloyd. Caroline found herself angry because he pushed her, registering the anger and the change of the sound from a whistle to an express-train that roared over the roof; observing that her face was close to the respectable valance of the chintz sofa and that Lloyd's arm was heavy across her back; thinking, "This is it, Michael," and then there was the thunder. The lights went out. Somewhere close there came the whole noise of a house falling, crumble and creak and crash, with the endless tinkle of broken glass pouring on afterwards. The floor beneath her elbows felt like a deck swaying; she was aware of the depth and the hollowness under it. "I thought they'd got us," she said disappointedly, sitting up in the dark.

"Tell you who they have got, I shouldn't wonder," said Jay's voice, sounding more clipped than ever, "and that is our friend Miss Haydon."

The clanging of bells outside and the racing wheels and engines began. Lloyd said, "I'd better go and see if I'm wanted."

SATURDAY, MARCH 18th, 1944

"Don't wait for me," Caroline said to the driver of the Bugatti, inevitably termed the Bug. "I'll walk back into the town and get a bus from there." She had a conscience about using His Majesty's petrol for private purposes and the cemetery lay north of Cold Ash, so that they had already driven four unlawful miles.

It was the new cemetery, where only a few graves were dug; it had as yet the look of a public garden, with green slopes and flower-beds and an illogical cluster of headstones in the centre. It stood higher than the road, behind iron railings. There was a gate in the middle of the railings.

The garden was circled with trees, still graceful and leafless on the hard blue sky. Caroline pushed open the gate and turned left along the path beside the railings, passing the cluster of new headstones on the right. Further ahead there was a slope of rising ground. Low in the grass, a metal tablet recorded that this plot was the property of the Imperial War Graves Commission.

There were only seven crosses; uniform crosses of white wood, with the regimental name and badge painted on each, awaiting the time when the Commission would raise the stones. Sergeant Field, No. 2 Commando; Driver Hawton; L. A. W. Wick; Lt.-Colonel Michael C. Knowle, R.A.M.C., with the badge of the Aesculapian staff and the coiled serpent. Caroline stared at it for a long time. Some of the graves were green mounds; one was an enclosure of white marble chips; on Michael's grave they had made a flower-bed of earth, and the bulbs were pushing through; there were crocuses already in bloom.

Caroline stooped and pulled out weeds, coating her fingers with the clay. "I shall miss it," she thought. "It has become a place that one knows by heart; so many steps to the tap where you get the water for the flowers; so many to the wire basket where you throw the dead flowers in. And the names, Field, Hawton, Wick, Knowle, Roberts, Grace, Turner. (*'William Dewey, Tranter Reuben, Farmer Ledlow late at plough; Robert's kin, and John's, and Ned's, and the Squire, and Lady Susan.'*)" She observed once again that the R.A.M.C. badge was slightly crooked.

"Well, I'll be back, Michael," she said aloud. She saluted the graves and walked away. It was, for the time being, the last of the regular pilgrimages made almost without thought, like the halts of a dumb peasant when he came to a shrine on the road in France.

While she walked, with the high wind in her face, she was aware of him beside her, a palpable ghost. She was conscious of his body, of the hair on his head, the shape of his hands; he was wearing the clothes that he had worn on leave, the grey flannels and the faded blue shirt. The look of him and the sound of his voice were as near as though she could, if she knew the trick, demolish the little wall that thwarted actual vision and hearing.

"Well, here we go," she said. "Something else again. Don't let me feel as though I'm leaving you behind."

"I told you, Caro; we shall always go on as two."

"Easy to say, my boy. It doesn't feel like that when I wake alone after the dreams. Nor when I think of you by yourself in that hotel. Did you weep there? Did you say, 'I can't go on'? Oh Michael, that is my King Charles' Head and you never answer me. That's the devil, that is."

"There are things I cannot tell you."

"Certainly. There always were. But this is the thing that I also cannot tell. Because nobody knows. I saw it; I only.

Did it happen again? Did you depart into that nightmare world of yours? Of sorrow and hopeless anger? I go hunting clues; and I never find them."

"What of it?" he said. " 'I think Odysseus as he dies forgets, which was Calypso, which Penelope.' "

"Oh, but that sounds peaceful; an old man's death; not yours."

"How do you know mine wasn't peaceful?"

"Well, it isn't easy to know."

"Caro, please listen. If, every time that I return, I bring the thought of my death with me, how are you ever going to be happy remembering?"

"Have patience; it will come."

The road sloped up and she could hear him saying,

> "Over the hill the highway marches
> And what's beyond is wide.
> Oh soon enough will pine to nought
> Remembrance and the faithful thought
> That sits the grave beside."

"Yes, Michael. And if this is a quotation-battle, I can continue,

> "The skies, they are not always raining,
> Nor grey the twelvemonth through.
> And I shall meet good days and mirth,
> And range the lovely lands of earth
> With friends no worse than you.

"I shan't, though. That is how people would like it to be. Perhaps I shall. Do you remember saying to me, 'There is no limit to the mistakes that the human animal can make'?"

"I never had your verbal memory, darling."

She said, "There are the towers of your Abbey. It has been fun, living so near. Always I remember the last leave. Do you remember it ? "

"Of course. It is still going on."

"And here we turn. You haven't thought that I am spying upon you? I know I snatch crumbs. Dorothy's stories; and some of the snapshots that we didn't look at together."

250

"They are all yours."

"Even the names on the window at Cold Ash?" she asked him, laughing.

"Oh, those. Well, it is a long time ago. We were young and gay. I am sorry that you had to find them alone."

"I wasn't alone," she said, "I was with Hellyar; Joan's Hellyar; you know about him?"

"Yes. I know everything that happens to you."

The outskirts of the town began; she felt the diminishing quality of his presence. "Michael, swear you'll still be with me in London?"

"Always. Everywhere. Till the end of time."

"And you didn't—die on purpose?"

That was the question that broke the communion between them; she stood still in the road that ran between the little red houses, knowing only that it was cold and that she had come a long way.

WEDNESDAY, APRIL 26th, 1944

Dennis Brookfield walked down the steps from the foyer to the cocktail lounge. He saw that Kate and Alaric were waiting already, that Caroline had not yet arrived. In the Middle East and in Italy, he had thought about the things that he saw now. After five days at home, they made a natural setting; there was nothing remarkable about sitting down at the table with Kate, lifting the cocktail that she had ordered for him. The distance between the other world and this had shrunk; and widened.

There were too many uniforms here; and some of the people who wore them were out of context, like himself. Alaric was one of these. Kate, wearing evening dress, was the same person that he had left behind. Alaric, wearing red tabs, was not. Alaric was a companion in both worlds. He wondered whether Alaric felt as he did, that this interval, with the music sounding from the ballroom, the lights and the luxury and the glasses on the table, belonged less to their current selves, who had become so rapidly accustomed to it, than to the dreams of another Alaric Forrest and another Dennis Brookfield; far-off types better acquainted with trouble.

"Caroline will be late," his sister was saying, "She went home to change."

Dennis grinned to himself. "Caroline in khaki is the one image that I can't picture. I've tried all ways, but it doesn't fit."

"She looks damned smart," said Alaric, "I ran into her yesterday in Sloane Square. Tore me off a smashing salute."

"Oh, really——" Dennis protested, still finding military clichés intolerably silly when they concerned themselves with Caroline. He drained his glass and was glad that Alaric had already ordered the second round; he tried to tell himself that this moment of waiting for her was easy stuff.

"Very remarkable," he said, looking at Kate.

"What is?"

"My pictures of all of you living in rubble and slacks, eating carrots."

("And it feels as though it were over," he thought. "This is insidious. Need we have D-Day? I've had several of those. All I want to do is to stay here and drink this reasonable gin and watch the top of the steps for Caroline. No, you don't, Dennis. You're through with that. It all died a long, long time ago. This is merely a sentimental revisitation.") "Tell me," he said to Kate, "does one mention Michael's name, or not?"

"She talks about him a great deal."

He saw her coming to the top of the steps. He had not expected a repetition of another cliché; the pain as sharp as a needle. For a moment, everything between that time and this was lost; he was back in a third-row stall, watching Viola walk across the stage. This particularly, because the dress that she wore was black and silver, her hair cut short and tightly curled. There was the beautifully smooth walk. Without hesitation she threw her arms about him and hugged him, and stood back holding his hands. "But oh, my love," he thought, "what have they done to you, that your face is now thin and there is a line between your eye-brows and you have no more look of youth, but a dazed and knowledge-able brilliance instead? The old light has gone and there is a

252

light that I do not know. Possibly because I have had two drinks, it suggests to me the light of tapers shining beside a coffin. Hell, I can see that something of you died with Michael, and you will not be jagged and lively and vulgar and a thorn in my flesh any more."

He had held her hands for so long that now he feared her thought-reading trick and let them go. She said, "All those ribbons. And a Major. What a thing," and with the sound of that voice she emerged from the sad disguise.

"You are two drinks behind us," Alaric said, putting the glasses in front of her on the table.

"Yes, well . . . I had to change. I couldn't feel odder in these clothes. I've fallen downstairs because of high heels and I keep patting my bosom in search of matches; and this hand-bag. . . . . Kate, what used one to do with a handbag? Hold it all the time? I left mine in the taxi and the driver came after me with it; an honest type." She set it on the table. "I feel as though it were a dog I was leading."

("When you look at me, you appear vulnerable, but that, I think, is because I remind you of the time when there was Michael. You are much too thin. And I am in love with you again, and I thought I'd had it.")

"You are wider all over," said Caroline, "travel has broadened you."

Alaric began to talk to her about her job at the War Office and once she said, "Oh, lud, yes," faithfully copying Michael. When they went down into the ballroom, Dennis let himself think that this moment was as it ought to be, with love requited. She walked beside him; asking, "How does it feel?" and "Do you hate women in uniform?" and "Does the bomb-damage look very trivial and invisible?" the questions that everybody asked.

As soon as they had ordered their dinner, he said, "Come and dance," and this, for a while, was magic, with no need to talk. Then he said, "I hope—though it's a forlorn hope, knowing you—that you are not hungry. I should like to do this for a long time. I had forgotten, I think, what a lovely dancer you were."

"Thank you kindly. I am being cautious because of these heels."

"You're still using the same scent."

"The last of the Molyneux Cinq. It was practically fossilized. I carved it out of the bottom of the bottle with a nail-file."

"Well, I brought you some scent. I couldn't get Molyneux, though. There are four different sorts; you had better come along early and take first pick."

He remembered buying the scent in Naples and saying to himself, "None of this is for Caroline."

"You're back in Albany?"

"I'm camping there, for my forty-eight hours. It smells of mice."

"I was so worried the night they nearly hit it," she said.

"And you? Kate says you're living in a boarding-house."

"It would be very angry if you called it anything but a private hotel. And it is just as expensive as the Rufford used to be."

"What's happened to the Rufford?"

"Oh, it was shut for ages, and now they have requisitioned it for something or other. But there isn't much left of St. James's Place," she said thoughtfully, "as you may have seen. That was the Wednesday; I watched it burn."

"Were you in London all through that?"

"Well, the Wednesday was in '41. April, I think. I know I was stationed at Woolwich and I'd got forty-eight hours. I took a room at Athenæum Court, and had a bath and drank, and bought myself a delicious dinner. And then it all began. And I was standing outside A-Court, watching all the fires; and suddenly a thing like a plum-pudding bursting with fiery sauce came down; and a soldier lay on me and a lot of glass fell out of the windows on to us. We looked for traces of the pudding afterwards, but we couldn't find them. Some said it was the land-mine in Green Park."

"They must have been quite bloody."

"Sometimes they were."

He kept waiting for a cue to speak of Michael, but it did not come and he wondered how he should begin. Presently she said, "That's finished it, Dennis, I'm sorry. I've seen a woman eating lobster," and he was amused to see that she ate as heartily as ever. Alaric had ordered a magnum. He found the thought of Michael growing dim; now Michael took his place among the other dead. He danced with Kate. "How does it go?" she asked, with her shepherdess head on one side.

"It's a lovely evening; it's a nice war."

"She's all right, isn't she?" Kate asked.

"How do we know? And it is none of our business."

"If you are fond of somebody——" Kate began indignantly.

"Still none of our business. And she doesn't talk to me—I doubt that she'll ever talk to me."

Caroline said that she wanted to concentrate on the sweet, and he sat with her while Kate and Alaric danced. He drank more champagne. He meant to say something about Michael and found that he had said instead, "The Army . . . you can't really like it."

"I have liked some of it. Not sure I like being a War Office stooge. I liked having my own platoon in Sussex."

"Looking after a gaggle of dingy women? Pay? Returns? Imprests? Orderly-rooms? Foot-inspection?"

"It was people," said Caroline. "Whereas Octu was school-girls. And now I just go to a desk in Eaton Square and see on paper all the things that were my problem a month ago; from the other side of the counter. I don't think I shall ever acquire the War Office angle."

"You seem to have acquired a good many angles."

"It hasn't been difficult; it has been acting a series of parts, and that's all. I've simply played the rôles of private, corporal and officer to the best of my capacity."

"That's a funny way of making good in the Army," said Dennis.

"Yes, well. . . ."

He thought about it.

"It isn't dishonest, Dennis, if that's what you're thinking. I always could convince myself that I was the person I was playing, provided that the part was sympathetic enough."

"Having a long run, aren't you, dear?" he said.

255

She looked at him, slant-eyed, over the edge of her glass. "I feel khaki all over; drab; the colour of this war." She pointed to the piece of bread on her plate. "That's the colour. And, have you noticed, we have even got National Wheatmeal toilet paper now? Well, it is, Dennis. Nothing's white any more. And I went to the Orange Street Gallery last week; Kenrick didn't recognise me; and I saw a picture, on a far wall in the second room, which I took to be Cannes, because it looked so dazzling and sunny; a street of houses with striped blinds at the windows. And, blow me, it was Belgrave Square in '38. Houses were painted in '38. That's what London used to be like."

It was during the last dance that he said to her, "Why not come back to Albany and choose your scent? It's still early; we haven't talked."

The four of them waited in the Savoy courtyard for a taxi. Dennis took a walk back in time, to the supper after *Twelfth Night*, to Leopold Rokov and the magic wind. He wondered if their well-dressed ghosts were still sitting around in the empty, unused lobby, with time to burn. The four of them shared the taxi as far as Albany; then she was beside him in the Rope-walk and at once there were the old summer nights. She went ahead of him into the same room, with the ceiling and one wall wearing their emergency repairs after the bomb. She loitered a moment before the mantelpiece where the French clock stood, and then curled into a corner of the sofa. "It is colder than I remember," she said. He lit the gas-fire and poured the drinks.

He sat down in the armchair, conscious of the clock ticking while he stared at her. She was pale. She did not appear interested in her drink; he had seen that she left her second cocktail and abandoned her champagne. The black and silver dress now seemed a tax upon her beauty, accenting the pallor and the shadows where the flesh had shrunk. He threw the old adjectives at her in his mind; Slavic; Byronic; stricken.

"My dear," he said, "I have been wondering all this evening what I should say to you."

"But of course you can say anything, Dennis. I like talking about him."

"Perhaps I am in a slightly different category from the other people to whom you talk."

"Yes, well. . . ."

"I wished very much when I heard of his death that I could have been beside you. Knowing you, I imagine that the hardest thing to take was your not being with him."

"Yes."

"Does it get any easier?" he asked, cradling his glass and staring into it.

"Some things do; and others less easy. At first I read and re-read his letters. Now to look at his handwriting makes me cry. And the dreams get more unkind. But one's grief, I find, takes a regular pattern after a time; one begins to have the same moods in sequence. And one comes back, always, at last, to a raging 'Why'? As though one were angry with him for not being able to tell."

"I can imagine."

"And every now and again it walks up and hits one a wallop, till one says, 'Oh, look; this is nonsense; you can't have gone and left me here. We used to do everything to-gether.'" She frowned, "He taught me so much. That was what all the Disapprovers and the Spoilers-of-the-Fun never understood. Any wisdom that I have I owe to Michael. For so many lessons; like keeping my temper, and loving people even if I didn't like them. And saying No when I meant No; and poetry and the English castles and medicine; and he gave me security; always. Reassurance. It was that rocklike calm and confidence that I warmed my hands at, all those years. That grown-up sanity; the sense of having been there forever and knowing all the answers, do you remember?"

Dennis nodded.

"And when *that* snuffed itself out in a second-rate hotel on an overdose of barbiturate," she said, her voice now as rough as the words.

"At least you know that it was pure accident."

She said, "Yes," quickly and hurried on. "Selfish, I suppose, to go on wishing that he'd thought of me that evening; telephoned or written me a note. Your poor Miss Haydon——"

"What has my poor Miss Haydon got to do with Michael?"

"Oh," Caroline uncurled herself and rose to stand before the fire: "Why, I happened to hear her last speech; I told you in my letter; she said she was happy, and thanked me for something and walked straight out under the bomb. If I could know that Michael was happy——" She shrugged her shoulders. "Dennis," she said in a different voice, "why the devil did you never tell me Vera Haydon used to be Mercedes' secretary?"

He put down his glass. The mild intoxication that had been with him all the evening went in a sudden premonition of nervousness that sent his fingers to fumble with the knot of his tie.

"Oh . . . I don't know, dear. Was it important?"

"It was funny not to," she said, watching him steadily.

"Mercedes wasn't always your favourite topic of conversation, you may recall."

She narrowed her eyes; she was not going to let this alone.

"And you knew her very well, once, didn't you? You liked her. You always kept it pretty quiet, to me."

"Yes."

"And you knew quite a lot about the situation that you kept shut in a box, no?"

"I suppose I did." He thought that it was foolish to feel guilty for a silence that had been painful to keep.

"You knew that he never could belong to me," she said. "Didn't you?"

"What do you want me to say?"

"Say it," she said. ("And if it would have been cruel then, isn't it far more cruel now? But you are walking on the edge of it. Let me take your hand and lead you over the last step.")

"There was only one person to whom Michael belonged entirely of his own freewill," he said, "and that was Mercedes."

On her face he saw, repeated, the look that was on Viola's face before she spoke of the willow cabin; first the rueful sighting of her destiny and then the triumph that seemed to run after that hopeless grief and throttle it. Almost he expected to hear her say the words. Then the flashing look was gone.

"Yes; I think I have known that for a long time." She said it so lightly that he stared, wondering if she had missed the point.

"What you mean is," she was saying, bending to take a cigarette from the box on the table beside the fire, "that he was always in love with her."

02.45 *hours*

Caroline watched him steadily, while he came to the fire and stood before her, with his hands in his pockets. She saw again what she had seen at the first impact with him, in the cocktail-lounge at the Savoy; that his brown hair was dashed with grey and that his skin had hardened and dried. He was not Dennis any more. He was a major who now wore an expression implying that he was thinking out a tricky problem concerned with stores or quartering. It seemed unlikely that he had come from overseas to confirm her private knowledge.

She spoke the words that came to mind. "There needs no ghost, my lord, rise from the grave to tell us this."

"You knew it?"

"Well, let us say that I knew with a question-mark; you have supplied the full stop."

"When did you know? Always? Before he died?"

She said, "Yes. But I can't make it any more definite than that. It was a gradual realisation; that he had his private territory; as everybody has, I think."

"He didn't talk about her?"

"Never."

"He didn't tell you that for years it was Mercedes, not he, who wanted the divorce?"

She found herself grimacing, as though somebody had pricked her flesh with a needle. "Oh, it is funny that it should be all right for me to think these things, but not for you to say them. How do *you* know that?"

"From Mercedes. She wasn't a liar."

"Nor was Michael," she said.

"I think you were fooled a little, though; weren't you?" He said it sombrely, not with malice.

"Never. Michael never deceived me, Dennis. He said from the beginning that he couldn't love me my way. He let me be around in his life because he knew I had to be. He saw that that was my dedication; and where, I suppose, a more *rusé* sort would have been strongly-mindedly cruel and cut it off at the roots, he was too kind. And in due course he did grow to love me. But I don't think I ever thought that he was *in* love with me. If I'd thought that, I shouldn't have been aware all the time that I might lose him."

Dennis looked her in the eyes and grinned. He said, "How you spike my guns."

She said, "Mind you, I'm being grown-up about it now because it's late at night. Don't imagine for an instant that I shan't wake at eight with something heavy sitting on my chest and think 'What is this? Oh yes; Dennis has said that Michael loved Mercedes; as I always suspected'."

"But if you did suspect, didn't you ever talk about it?"

"No." She tried to choose intelligent words. "It became a piece of etiquette; I had my clues, but I was always thinking that it would be ungentlemanly to show that I had them. Even his silence was a clue. Perhaps I merely caught the silence. Once he had asked me to marry him, I thought that something must have changed it; I never knew what that was. Why she suddenly agreed to the divorce—or do I mean he did?" Suddenly she saw a period ahead that would be like a long session of arithmetic, revising values; substituting minus for plus signs; she saw whole columns of figures whose sum had been changed because, in place of a question-mark, there was now a full-stop. She sighed, passing her hands upwards across her temples.

" 'Oh, time, thou must untangle this, not I.' Shakespeare seems to come in useful to-night, doesn't he? Tell me; what made the marriage go wrong?"

"Temperament. She hated to be tied down. And I think he tried to hold on too long. You don't like me to say that."

"No."

Dennis said, "Sorry, darling." He looked at her again and laughed. "Do you remember making me a speech once—I

believe it was while we were having supper, after *Twelfth Night*
—a speech about not wanting things, property, hating to be
tied?"

"I remember." ("And now" she thought, "those two words,
'I remember', seem useless; but they are all that I have left.")

"That was Mercedes' philosophy. At that moment you
might have been Mercedes."

The name sang on in her ears; she shut her eyes and saw
the two names written with the diamond on the window-pane.
She opened her eyes and looked at Dennis; the honest frown
and the half-smile, watching her.

"Wasn't it very good of you to keep quiet about that?" she
asked: "All those years? To me? Wasn't it like having a
winning card and not playing it?"

"Would it have been a winning card, my dear?"

"Perhaps. Perhaps not."

He took her hands. "Of course it wouldn't. You were
always faithful. You always will be. And so will I. Let me say,
just for the pleasure of saying it—and you need not answer—
I love you so much."

"I wish I could love you."

"What are *you* hiding?" he asked her.

She was silent; she had no wish to tell.

"You're the last person I expected to acquire a private
territory."

She thought. "How did he get that? What have I said or
not said? Is it because he loves me that he knows it?"

"And I think," Dennis said, "that it must be very bad for you."

"It is bad. I have had it for months now."

"Couldn't you tell me?"

("I could say 'It was no accident. Michael killed himself.
He went back to the French Horn; that was her place, hers
and his. He went back there before in '39, just after she left
England for good. He went to say good-bye to her; he couldn't
help it. He went like a sleep-walker. He sat there and waited
for her. That night he had enough sense left to give me the
bottle, because he knew what he might do. And on the night
of August the nineteenth, that was the way it went. And after-

wards he sat alone in the hotel-room and wept and said "I can't go on". And if you ask me why he should do this suddenly, I think that he must have heard a rumour of her death. I know this, and only I.' ")

"No," she said. "Bless you, but it isn't our business, it is Michael's."

WEDNESDAY, JUNE 28th, 1944

The snarling noise came nearer. It was not unlike a dentist's drill, Caroline thought, and she could picture it descending in zig-zags, just a noise, boring downward through the sky.

"Into the corridor with you," said the woman sitting by the window; her gay, Irish voice always became gayer and more Irish at the approach. She herself rose in a leisurely manner and Caroline, having the desk nearer to the door, felt absurdly under the obligation to wait and not go out first. This happened every time.

"Jesus, Mary and Joseph," said the Senior Commander, with the utmost placidity. It had cut off directly above the roof. As they dodged round the door together, they saw other doors opening; khaki figures emerging to stand pressed against the walls. From the hall below, just as the flying-bomb fell, there came a clanging noise and the messengers were still chanting "Danger over*head*——" after the echo of the explosion faded.

They went back into the room. "It is wonderful," said Caroline, "how accurately they manage to mis-time that warning."

The pink, untroubled Senior Commander said, "Ah, but it is a very wise precaution, Seward."

"I don't see why." She stared down at the papers in front of her and thought that her fear had taken all the meaning out of the words; they were just black marks on paper. "In fact," she said, lighting a cigarette, with fingers that jumped, "I call it highly unnecessary. It means that the clerks spend half the morning lying under their tables."

"But before we had the Imminent-Danger signal," said the Senior Commander, "they spent the whole morning lying under their tables."

Caroline grinned and rested her damp forehead in the palm of her hand. "I cannot in honesty blame them. And I still don't know why these things appear to have shattered my morale. I never minded the quaint, old-fashioned blitz."

"Perhaps," said the Senior Commander, "you feel like the woman who talked to me in the bus yesterday. She said that what she missed was the personal touch."

The All Clear sounded.

"Nothing to look forward to but the Alert now," said Caroline. She glanced at her watch. "Ma'am, I have to go up to Gower Street."

"Are you sure you want to do it? I'll send Iddisley if you'd rather not."

Caroline thought, "Why can't I take advantage of that kind offer? Amour-propre or sheer imbecility?" She said, "Oh, no, thank you. I'll take my lily-liver into the Underground." She collected her cap and gloves and put the relevant papers into her brief-case.

"God go with you," said the Senior Commander. Nice, Caroline thought, to be a Catholic and to be on such good terms with God. She was envying the Senior Commander as she ran down the stairs. In the hall, the messengers were talking about the one that had just fallen. As usual, they knew its exact location and the number of casualties. The odd factor here was that they were almost sure to be right. "I believe there is a tom-tom system in London now," Caroline said to herself, "or else this development has brought out unsuspected telepathic powers in everybody."

The messengers said Good Morning to her and one came out on to the step and stood looking after her as she hurried along Eaton Square. She had the uncomfortable feeling that he did this because, if a buzz-bomb fell on her, he would not want to miss being first with the news. She took the turning to the left; the small public-house near the corner of Elizabeth Street opened early. She saw that the sky was still grey and overcast; the best sort of sky for letting them through.

The bar was empty; from the back-room she could hear the

radio playing Mozart's "Jupiter" Symphony. For a moment she felt illogically safe and ordinary, standing at this counter, sniffing the smell of beer, listening to the music. A woman came from the back-room.

"Make it a pint of bitter," said Caroline.

"Awful night again, wasn't it?" She filled the large glass tankard, wiped the rim and set it down. "I've got some cigarettes, if you're short."

Fifty yards off, the siren above the Gerald Road police-station began to moan.

"Here they come again."

"Getting warmed-up for the lunch-hour," said Caroline. She lifted her head and poured the beer down her throat as though her throat were a pipe-line; she saw the woman watching her with admiration. "Never can do that, myself. Makes me retch, like."

"It is a gift. Thank you." She took the cigarettes and paid and went out, reassured because in a moment she would feel the effect of the sedative. She heard an explosion, thought. "That one's down," and headed for Sloane Square. She talked to herself. "If there is anything to be thankful for in these days, which I gravely doubt, it is that I am not sitting on the hill above the Sussex coast, trying to support my platoon's morale, with the guns driving me crazy. I wish I could stop worrying about them all; Dorothy; and Joan and Hellyar; and Doyle and Sergeant Warne. And I wonder if they have hit Michael's grave. Idiot, what does it matter about graves?"

Now she felt brave enough to take a taxi.

"Not many people about," the driver called to her, through the glass panel that was pushed back. Perhaps, she thought, he too felt the need for company; she moved over to sit on the small front-seat. The dialogue went the usual way:

"He's got a nasty weapon here, all right"; "If the weather would only change"; and then the talk of the fighting in France. Two weeks ago people had talked only of the invasion; now it came as a poor second to the flying-bombs. And from the flying-bombs they went on to the rockets that would come next. "He's lucky with his weather, as per," said the driver. "Sunday afternoon, when we had a bit of sun, that was nice and quiet." "Yes; they shoot them down on the coast then." These phrases were worn-out already.

"One over now, Miss." She could not hear the dentist's-drill noise because of the traffic. They were caught at the red light below Hyde Park Corner. "What a mess it could make here," she thought, looking out of the window, seeing the people on the pavement dodging undecidedly, looking up, running into doorways. There was a bumping explosion on the Park side. "He's down," said the driver. "Nasty things."

"I always feel better when we're moving," she said.

"So do I," said the driver. He took no trouble to observe the speed regulations on Constitution Hill. Caroline looked out through the back window and saw the watchers on the Palace roof, the perspective of the Mall; it was almost deserted. The All Clear sounded as they reached Admiralty Arch. And now it was a run-the-gauntlet feeling; Trafalgar Square, still safe; Charing Cross Road, still safe; Bedford Square, still safe. They drove between the flat faҫades of Gower Street. The driver grinned at her as she climbed out.

"Good luck."

"Thanks; the same to you."

What a damned nightmare-world, she thought; I wonder how much longer I can last. She prolonged the business at the Transit Camp, drinking a cup of over-sugared tea with the subaltern, who had fair hair and a babyish mouth and said, "I don't mind them a bit, actually, I just feel, well, if it comes, it comes—you know." "I wish," thought Caroline, "that I did know."

"Won't you stay and have some lunch?"

"Thank you kindly, but I must be on my way."

("But it's a nasty, uncovered feeling in the street and I think I heard the siren again while we were talking.") She hurried along, walking close to the houses; when she came into Tottenham Court Road, she saw a man standing on a refuge look up and then begin to run. Overhead the bomb had cut off and was sailing down, in a long diagonal; a small black aeroplane, a toy. ("And it looks gay and conceited, as if it were shouting, 'Here I come.' ")

It struck, a few hundred yards south of where she stood. The explosion was thunderous and a thick bonfire-column of grey smoke billowed up. It was curious to feel more frightened after it had fallen; to be dumb with fear while all around her people were chattering. "I *saw* it," a woman was repeating indignantly, "a *tiny* little thing; *tiny*." She sounded as though she had a genuine grievance against it for its not being larger.

"Come on now," Caroline said to herself. "Get this knotted feeling inside you straight. Stand up and settle for it. Walk with your shoulders back. But, Michael, it is galling to find that I really am a coward. If you were walking beside me, you would be calm and quiet; your voice wouldn't change."

She went through the entrance to the Underground. There were people on the platforms, sitting on the wire bunks; fewer, she decided, than there had been last week at this hour. "Perhaps we're getting used to them; perhaps I shall get used to them." When the train came in, she chose a seat next to a haggard young man with a falling mane of hair; he was reading the Bhagavad-Ghita. He looked up and said to her peevishly, "Didn't one just come down in Tottenham Court Road?"

"Yes, it did. I saw it. It looked disgusting."

"I hate being able to see them," he said, "I never mind things that I can't see. I think morale generally is very bad, don't you?"

"I think mine is," said Caroline, lighting one cigarette from the stump of the other.

"And I think the Government has handled it all disgracefully." He went on reading. Presently he looked at her. "You really are nervous, aren't you? I can feel your aura. That isn't meant to be funny."

"I'm sorry," said Caroline, "I thought it was."

"Of course, being a hopeless neurotic myself," said the young man, "I could be of some use in all this. Here are people developing neurotic symptoms right and left who've never had them before; they simply don't know what to do about it."

"What does one do?"

"Nothing at all; far the best thing. But if we could all learn to breathe. . . . Don't think *I* can breathe, by the way; I'm hopeless at it. I'm simply saying that if we all could——"

"I thought everybody could."

"Not correctly." He continued to peer at her in a melancholy way.

"The situation has a great many advantages," Caroline said. "There is food and liquor in abundance: taxis most unnaturally plying for hire; cigarettes; you can get a table in any restaurant at any moment without standing in a queue; and the waiters outnumber the eaters by a proportion of ten to one."

"*Don't* you despise the people who have left London?"

"Lud, no; I'd go myself if I had the chance."

"Well, I despise them," said the young man, returning to his book.

Caroline said sharply, "I call that a neurotic symptom," but he did not answer.

When she came above ground again at Victoria, the time was half-past one. She could see one of the hideous smoke-columns growing and spreading over the roofs, in the direction of the river.

She was just deciding where to eat her lunch when the afternoon's appointment loomed up in her mind. "Dear God, I've left all the papers on the writing-table in my room. That's what comes of working at night. I'll have to go the whole way back to Queen's Gate to fetch them."

She thought that she was going to cry.

"I must have a drink first; I can't make it without a drink I can't have a drink; there isn't time; the meeting is at two."

She signalled to a taxi and found that she could only croak the address; the driver had to ask her to repeat it twice. As she threw herself into the corner of the seat, she shot one straight grumble at God, saying, "Why don't you stop all this? Or kill me quickly. Let one of those damned things be dropping out of the sky now this minute; and then it will be over, and I'll see Michael again."

But where was God in this and where was Michael? There was only annihilation waiting; utter blackness, and before it, this continual torture, the tightening and slackening of terror, the inevitable return from the lull to the panic; like a hateful dance that must never stop.

Wherever she looked in her mind there was a thought that she did not want to think. There was the ruin of the Brookfield Galleries, as she had seen it yesterday; there were the crowds with frightened, up-turned faces, swaying back and forward across Brompton Road; there was the woman ticket-collector in the Tube, screaming angrily at a white-faced boy, "Be a man and get up them stairs!" There were the packed shapes on the platforms at night; the bunks all filled; beyond the bunks the people lying on mattresses and quilts, the bodies so near the platform's edge that you had to walk carefully to avoid stepping on them as you came off the train. Last night, being a little drunk and brave, she had stared at them with compassion, thinking that it was her desire to be each one of these people, to share it and understand.

There was no wisdom to be learned to-day; only a certainty that she waited for death, that it was long in coming, that it played with her like a cat and she was tired.

She took her last refuge in words:

"Noon strikes on England, noon on Oxford town.
  Beauty she was statue-cold; there's blood upon her gown.
  Noon of my dreams, oh noon!"

Only verse could act as a drug; its solace was small, but it was there. She shut her eyes and went on chanting in her head,

    "I think Odysseus, as he dies, forgets
      Which was Calypso, which Penelope."

She said, "Michael, that is true of me now. It matters so little. I'm too tired to care about Mercedes, about your private world, about the news that Dennis broke. It means nothing, any more."

"Sun's coming out a bit," said the taxi-driver. She stood on the pavement, taking the change out of her pocket. The private hotel was at the north end of Queen's Gate; a corner building with one side that faced Kensington Gardens. She looked down the wide, sloping street and saw the shadows beginning to be sharp; she looked upwards and saw the blue break of sky in the clouds.

She went into the hall. She could hear the talk and the rattling noises from the dining-room; there was a smell of hot food here. She found a letter addressed to her, stuck below the crossed tapes on the green board on the wall. The battered envelope was marked "Opened by Censor". She did not know the handwriting. She carried it upstairs to her room.

The room itself was a little reassuring, the sunlight nearly strong. She looked at Michael's photograph, at the books on the shelf. There were roses in a vase on the writing-table; the man selling them had said, "I've had bad luck to-day, lady," and offered her a dozen for the price of six. At the foot of the vase lay the silver knife and the leather blotter, the papers that she had come to fetch; she picked up the papers, put them in her brief-case and sat down on the bed to read the letter. It was from Lee Adams.

"L.W.A. Ranch,
"Saratoga, California.

"Dear Caroline,

"You were sweet to write; and I remember you so well. Wyn died for what we both thought a damned good reason and that must be my consolation. But the days are long. Yours too, I guess. I'd have written to you about Michael if I'd had an address for you. He was a great person and we loved him.

"I've a job (with the Red Cross in San Francisco) that irks me enough to make me believe I count in the war-effort. But I'm spending a few days here, coping with the raft of refugee-children who are occupying the ranch for the duration. They are of mixed nationality and more harassing than a zoo on wheels.

"I don't know if you heard, or wanted to hear, about Mercedes Knowle. Threads and strands are funny things; you may have a thread of curiosity pulling that way because of Michael. I know I should. Mercedes is alive, and that's something of a miracle, after what she went through. When Wyn saw her, he thought that she couldn't live. I just heard from some friends in Lisbon that she's through the worst.

"It wasn't easy for me to say to you when we met in Boston that she was really quite a friend of ours. It doesn't seem difficult now; I believe that wars plane off the details. And, curiously enough, though we only met just that one time, I should feel disloyal to you if I didn't mention it. (Get me. . . .)"

There was more, and there was no time to read it. Caroline folded the thin paper and put it in her breast-pocket. She went out and down the stairs.

As she walked out on to the steps, the All Clear was sounding. She wondered when the warning had been and why she had not heard it.

She walked into Kensington Road and stood waiting for a taxi, looking across the street to the gates of the park and the green trees. A woman was leading a child in through the gates; they moved at leisure, as though there were no danger, and the child was dragging a yellow wooden toy on wheels.

Watching them, she had a sudden illusion of peace; perambulators; boats on the Round Pond; tulips in the Flower Walk; ordinary people in ordinary clothes, walking there. It was a glimpse of lost time.

She thought, "I shall see it come again. I'm not going to be killed. I shall live past the end of the war." The conviction was sharp and instant, the gambler's hunch.

She crossed the road and began to walk beside the park railings, thinking, "Michael is dead; Mercedes lives. I might meet her some day, when all this is finished. And perhaps, by then, I shall have ceased to wonder." The noise of the warning began to moan its uneven message through the sky.

BOOK THREE
(1948)

TIME HARVESTED

"All the occurrence of my fortune since
Hath been between this lady and this lord."
Twelfth Night, Act V, Scene I

BOOK THREE

CHAPTER ONE

THE lights were going down as Lee Adams and her son reached their places; the theatre was dark when Lee opened her programme; she was wildly trusting that, by some last-minute miracle, Caroline Seward had been prevented from making her appearance; that she had been called back to England, rushed to New York, taken with appendicitis. Lee had had these hopes for a week.

The curtain rose on Caroline Seward and on Jay Brookfield, the two leading performers in Jay's tragi-comedy, *The Grape and The Vine*. Lee had seen it already in New York. It had run there for six months, after a year's run in London. The movie, made in British studios, was due for general release. At the Curran Theatre, San Francisco, *The Grape and The Vine* was coming to the end of its last tour.

Within five minutes, as she had known that she would, Lee forgot her private worry and forgot that Caroline was Caroline. It was a straight story; the young woman of courage, spirit and only one loyalty—to the man who was weak, a noceur and a liar. There was nothing, Lee reflected, that Jay had not done for Caroline in writing this play. It was the part that every actress would like to have; and the man was really no more than a background for the woman. Watching Caroline, you frequently forgot to notice the fine quality of Jay's own performance. And it was difficult not to watch Caroline; even if she were far up-stage, with no more business than a door to shut, you followed her with your eyes. She varied between the effortless detail that the best French acting could sometimes show and a flaming straightforwardness of attack that turned the other members of the company into shadows.

273

She was free from the British comedy-tradition, the affected
naturalness; when Caroline was natural, Lee thought vulgarly,
she was natural from the guts. So was her voice; there were
British accents which, to Lee's Californian ear, always put
an umlaut on the "o" sounds. Some of the company spoke
like this. Caroline did not. The strange voice, with its alternate
effects of roughness and purity, was haunting. Though she
knew that it was Caroline's voice, Lee now could hear it
only as the voice belonging to Jay's creation, to the woman
in the play. You could imagine the woman with no other
voice, with no other looks than these, with no other grace
than this.

Now, catching Jay in his first lie, she rounded upon him;
it was the movement of a duellist; you wanted to applaud the
movement alone. Then he beat her down; slowly the challenge
departed from her; she shrugged her acceptance. It was nicely
timed, because here in an instant you saw that she would
always begin to fight him and always lose.

It was the end of their scene together; not again until the
curtain of the first act would Caroline be alone with Jay.
There was an interval wherein she did not speak; she listened;
she poured out drinks for his friends; she was on the edge of
the action. You knew what she was thinking. Her face, her
gestures, explained her. She was still the central focus of the
scene. This trick of talking in silence, this quality of vividness,
made the mysterious "plus" sign. Any competent actress,
Lee thought, could have done all the rest, but not
this.

"Did you say she was thirty-five?" Dan whispered; he
sounded affronted.

"I'll thank you to recall that I'm forty-four," Lee whispered
back.

"She's so-o beautiful," Dan crooned.

She was skilful in the presentation of very slight drunkenness; drunkenness on the stage could be a bore, could be
amusing, could be unpleasant. This was a mere beginning;
you could tell that she was only half a pace away from the

others who were all sober; there was only the smallest accelera-
tion and emphasis in her speech; her eyes were wide; she
was seeing a vision that the others did not. She was clear in
her mind because she had had one more drink. In a moment
of general tension, she was the only person who was not
tense, who took all the alarming prospects and implications
with a dazzled certainty.

And now the two were alone again. She came downstage
with her exquisite smoothness of movement and stood before
him; she spread her hands a little way.

"You'll have no regrets?" Jay was asking.

She said, sounding hypnotised, "What are those?"

"What are regrets? They are small insects, darling, that
crawl over your soul in the early hours of the morning."

"Pooh," said Caroline, with the effect of using an Anglo-
Saxon word instead. She moved a step nearer to him and stared
at him. You could see her thinking; she put up her hand to
touch his forehead with the tips of her fingers.

"Stop frowning," she said. "You don't need to worry
about me."

(Now in the stalls, Lee thought, you had a genuine sense
of eavesdropping; that this was a private conversation and
that you had no right to be here.)

"I don't worry," said Jay, "I just don't want to make you
unhappy, that's all."

"You couldn't."

"Are you sure?"

"Quite sure."

She put her hands on his shoulders and looked at him
and laughed, a deep chuckle that was uncomfortable to hear
because it detached her from her love completely; she was
laughing alone, at herself as much as at him. She went back
up-stage to the tray with the drinks.

"From this moment onwards," she called to him derisively,

> "I fling my soul and body down,
> for God to plough them under."

ii

After he had changed for the second act, Jay went into Caroline's dressing-room. She was still behind the screen. He called, "If you do that thing again, I'll wring your neck."

"What thing?" called the weary voice.

"You know perfectly well. I suppose you have done it a hundred times. I suppose I have asked you not to do it a hundred times. Will you for God's sake speak the curtain-line that I wrote for you instead of quoting R. L. Stevenson?"

"Oh; ever s'sorry," said the voice in Cockney.

"You swore you'd never do it again."

"It comes over me suddenly; like the desire for certain foods said to obtain in the early months of pregnancy," murmured Caroline, strolling into view. She wore her second-act dress, a long dress that was Florentine green and sealing-wax red. She picked up a cigarette from the box on the dressing-table.

"But I've done it for the last time," she reminded him.

"Good God, so you have," said Jay.

Their team relationship had lasted more than two years; he thought of the play as their joint property, thought it would perhaps be more .correct to assess themselves as the play's property. It was difficult to think that the team was about to break up; this was February; by April Caroline would be playing Shakespeare with the Old Vic Company in England; he would be writing a script in Hollywood. They had cursed *The Grape and The Vine* together; they had talked in parody of it; they had improvised a 1968 edition of it, with the action played throughout in bath-chairs. "But Mr. and Mrs. Frankenstein," Jay said, "will develop a nostalgia for their nice monster."

"We can always see the movie," said Caroline. "We can keep a copy of the movie and run it through on Sunday afternoons."

He saw that her hand trembled violently as she held her cigarette towards the flame of his lighter. They had both been

276

tired for so long that they had forgotten what it was like not to be tired. Their digestions were strained by four months' diet of American food and American liquor; their tempers were worn thin and their nationalism was exaggerated. Alone they quarrelled; in company they stood ranged together, touchy and acid and doomed to talk politics.

Now he looked at her suspiciously. "Why are you darting your head towards me in that slant-eyed way, wreathing and twining?" he asked. "It's a frightful waste of energy."

"Wreathing? Twining? I'm standing as still as a telegraph pole."

"Well, you are giving the impression of wreathing and twining, which must be even more exhausting than doing it in fact," said Jay.

"I was going to ask you if you thought I need go to this party," said Caroline.

"Oh no," said Jay, "Oh dear me, no; there is not the slightest necessity; what made you think there was? It is only being given in our honour—a mere four hundred supper-guests. I don't suppose that they've laid out more than three thousand dollars on the whole thing. Don't dream of going, dear; don't give it a second thought. I'll run you back to the Mark and put you to bed with a hot-water bottle; there, there."

"Gee, thanks," said Caroline in an exaggerated American accent. He went on fluting, "Only a column or so each in the *Chronicle* and the *Examiner* this morning; won't be more than forty press photographers in the place; and a mouldy little orchestra flown up from Honolulu; you couldn't be under less obligation."

Caroline lay down on the sofa and went limp; her blue eyelids shut. She said, "Oh, all right. But I have hysteria, alcoholic and nicotine poisoning, anxiety-neurosis, paroxysmal tachycardia and absolutely no views about anything."

"Yes, dear. What you mean is, you're tired. So am I."

"I think I died in Milwaukee. It is just the tradition that's carrying on."

"We shall sail through this evening," said Jay, "on a tide of Benzedrine and Scotch. To-morrow all will be over; except Pebble Beach and a nice nervous breakdown apiece."

"Jay," she said, still with her eyes shut and sounding as though she were dropping off to sleep. "Would you, if you were me?"

He knew what she meant. "No I wouldn't," he said sharply. "That's another thing I've said a hundred times."

"Lee Adams is in front to-night; she'll be at the party."

With an effort Jay sat up and wagged his finger at her. "Listen to me, Caro. If you go to Lee's ranch for the purpose of meeting Mercedes Knowle, you'll deserve anything you get."

"And what will that be, I ask myself?" the drowned voice murmured.

"I hope, a thick ear," said Jay.

It was no use arguing with her. The question, "Would you, if you were me?" was idle. Caroline was going. Caroline preserved an unbroken record of doing what she wanted to do; of avoiding what she did not want to do. He was relieved to hear that Lee was attending the party; this at least must ensure that Caroline would play no tricks to get out of it. Her credo in these days was that of the coloured man who argued, "I don't *have* to do anything except die."

It was, he supposed, the formula for intelligent living; and that Caroline, of all unpromising beginners, should have arrived at a formula for intelligent living was remarkable.

"I thought I'd come up from Monterey," she was saying, "And spend one night there."

" I'm sure Lee would be charmed," said Jay. " 'Give her a few days to rehearse the introduction. Fool," he said. "Apart from the insane atmosphere that you'll create all round, you will only hurt yourself very much."

But he doubted if this were true; he thought that the most topical aspect of Caroline was that she was immune.

Acting with her, you could forgive her anything, and to-night, she, like himself, drew up from the last unsuspected reserves. It was an evening wherein nothing could go wrong. Jay watched himself and Caroline play out the doomed life-story. It was ham; it was cliché-thinking; it was the Rake's Progress; it was "We are dropping down the ladder rung by rung." There were moments when he realised how much the bright young man Jay Brookfield owed to the heaviest of his predecessors; to Pinero, Sardou and Henry Arthur Jones. This thing was good; it was good because he had laid his own patina upon it, added his own flavour to the ancient mixture; because he and Caroline had belief in the play and in themselves.

So they came to the last scene, where he had accomplished all his acts of vile behaviour and she had damned her soul devotedly for him. Now his fate was left to her; she could kill him or she could hand him over to justice; she could not die for him nor set him free. There was always a moment here when he thought that he could see the thread that bound her to him, a visible thread, stretching from where he sprawled by the gas-fire in the dingy lodging-house room, across to the O.P. side where Caroline paced by the window. He had but to twitch on the thread with his fingers and she would obey him, for the last time. He could not help stretching out his hand, jerking his wrist, performing the gesture of pulling on the thread.

She came round to meet him, with the duelling-movement of the first scene repeated. Watching himself over his own shoulder, Jay saw his weak, weary body slumped in the chair, the head thrown back, the unshaven chin, the cheaply-tailored clothes. He saw the line of Caroline's body in her listless black dress; the lock of hair falling beside the forehead; the scared courage in her face; It was the David-to-Goliath pose that always reminded him, even at this crescendo, of a young, furious Caroline a long time ago.

"Kill me," he said.

"No."

"You have done everything else for me, you can do that. The last favour I'll ever ask of you. If you don't grant it;

listen." On his quietest note he began the speech that described the hanged man; the description made in an obscenely flaccid version of his earlier wit. It was a revolting speech. He doubted that he had ever given it better measure. Beyond the lights, he heard the audience begin to lose control; with a shuddering gasp and a high-pitched giggle and all along the lines down there in the dark the effect of a solid surface breaking up.

But he was not talking to them; he was talking to Caroline, and as he talked he watched her change because the thread was throttling her; it was she whose life he strangled out with these words. Now he could feel the strength leave her and come into his own body, so that when her hand came up holding the gun, he was lifted to his feet, as dominant as ever.

She whispered, "Take it; with my love."

He dropped and huddled on the floor with his face buried in his arm. He would have liked to be able to watch Caroline for the moment when she stooped and made the short pass with her hand above him, the gesture that said, "Ego te absolvo." He knew how after that she straightened herself; and how, as the running footsteps grew loud on the stairs outside, she moved to the door ; not with the slow, tranced walk of Martyrdom, but swiftly. He knew the way that this looked from the front; he never knew if it were a trick or a miracle, the Winged Victory walk, that seemed to be free of the earth, the movement of a soul set free.

Now he heard the curtain sliding down, the frenzied noise coming up. He rose, brushing the dust off his clothes and holding out his hand to take hers.

iii

Here it all was. Another beautiful party, another long room full of noise and lights, food and drink, men and women. There had been a time, Jay thought, when this was international; now it was specifically American. The European had the feeling that, in sporting vocabulary, his eye was out; he saw crookedly.

He saw the women as set pieces. Each, in her carefully thought-out detail suggested the striving skill of a designer who had completed the arduous labour just half-an-hour ago. However exquisite the effect, it was studied; it demanded recognition and forced a compliment that was received with the American woman's cool "Thank you." Always he expected her to add, "A hell of a lot of work went into this."

He heard the noise as a shattering roar; the voices that would have composed a roar anyway, without the music to make them roar a little louder yet and the drinks to take them up another octave.

He saw the food; its effect was Roman in lavishness. There were no peacocks nor whole oxen roasted; the supper conformed to its traditional pattern ; creamed chicken, Virginia ham, cold turkey, glazed tongues ; the salads that created improbable marriages between peach and cottage cheese, aspic and strawberries, sliced avocado and cottage cheese, whipped cream and walnuts, chives and pineapple and cottage cheese. Jay saw a vision of a kitchen ; in the middle of the floor there stood a concrete-mixer churning out cottage cheese.

He saw the drinks; the tray of drinks kept coming; all the glasses standing close together; Bourbon and Scotch; the long cold drinks that would never come to an end; there would be another tray coming round in a minute; and another; and another. There was nothing that you could not order. (Make mine Tokay with equal parts of nectar and ambrosia.) "May I have a Scotch and soda with very little ice?"

He heard the words.

If he were not so tired, they would not sound like this; the words untiringly emitted by the people who could not let words well alone. They were forever stirring the language about.

"Now that's just a difference in value-judgments," said the

critic. Jay could see the sweat standing out on the hyphen. He began to pity the nouns, robbed of their privacy, hitched together by the sweating hyphens, to create a " group-tension" here, a "reality-situation" there, a "behaviour-pattern " somewhere else. The American language was becoming as tiresome as the German. It was clinical; it was complex; it made an idea out of nothing, as French housewives were said to make soup. "I find that the interest-span is about forty minutes," said the College President. (But there was no such thing as an interest-span until he said that. Just as in architecture there was no such term as a "living-area". Somebody looked hard at two rooms and, persisting in finding a deeper meaning here than a bedroom and a sitting-room, created a living-area.)

"I would like a Scotch and soda with very little ice."

(Ice. Do I mean "ize"? They ice their drinks; they ize their nouns and make new verbs; they hospitalize, personalize tenderize.) And now, Jay thought, the faces are over-lapping and the phrases are tangling together and the result is like this:—

"We love the play; she saw you in New York; we're perfectly darling; you're going back to England; Mr. Hoover says the Marshall Plan saw you in London; she knew you in Paris; they saw each other in Detroit; not that I am a Freudian Determinist; my allergy, my analyst, my aunt, my auto-intoxication, my atomic energy, your nuclear-fission in the last scene; my daughter met you in Budapest; Mr. Brookfield may I present Mr. Zweiback Justback from Europe. Ah Europe; since the war I have been literally bleeding to death."

"Literally, madam? You must have been doing it very slowly."

"We are crazy for the play; crazy for the movie; my sister's crazy. May I present Mr. Adam, Mrs. Eve is our chairman, out of this world; and she knows you quite well, her husband was at school with your mother. Of course you've been in San Francisco before the Fire, the Bay, the view from the Top of the Mark, the cable-cars, the Golden Gate Bridge. Cosmopolitan; I remember Lisbon, Athens, giving such a beautiful performance, we all want to thank you. Of course you re-member madame; the ballet is her passion; she wants to talk to us about the British ballet."

"Well, why doesn't she talk about it, then? Who's stopping her? I should like a Scotch and soda with very little ice."

"And are you writing another play, acting another play; writing a movie, having a drink, having enough to eat, having a good time, going home soon? Your Labour Government."

Oh dear, Jay thought; the Labour Government is with us again; it comes to all the parties, bless its little heart.

"A Socialist Government; I felt badly about Churchill; she felt badly about Churchill; we all felt terribly about Churchill, about sending jet-planes to Russia and nationalising the cottage cheese."

Pull yourself together, he said to himself; it is these punctu-ations of flashlight photography that are the trouble; they are like hiccoughs. He stared over the shoulder of the woman who was greeting him to where Caroline stood with a glass in her hand, giving a fevered and flawless interpretation of a star actress having fun. "Come out from behind those orchids, Caro," he thought, "I know it's you."

The orchids showered from her shoulder to her waist and she had put on so much make-up that only Jay knew the colour of her skin underneath. Just why she had decided to behave herself, he could not tell. Perhaps out of compliment to their last public appearance together. "But I would not have put it past her to discount that. She may turn tiresome yet, the dear, dear child."

He said, "A Scotch-and-soda please; with very little ice. How enchanting of you to say so; yes, she is lovely, isn't she?"

("She is not lovely at all. She is the ill-mannered little genius that I spotted in '36 and decided to bring up by hand. All that is happening to her now could have happened twelve years ago if she had let it. She has for me the unmysterious, beloved, exasperating aspect of a younger sister. Heavens, how I am going to miss the little cad.")

Now he saw her greeting Lee Adams, turning out of the

283

crowd to be alone with Lee, and he tried to create a wave-length of furious condemnation that would reach her; he stared stonily at her back; the small, high head whose curls shone, the long neck and the naked shoulders; he could see no more of her than this and she might have been sitting in her bath.

He said, "How sweet of you to say so; we have had enormous fun; we have adored every second of San Francisco. *Isn't* she lovely?"

("I wish I had a basilisk. I have never been quite sure what a basilisk was, but if I had one, I am certain that it would convey to you my implacable and venomous disapproval of what you are discussing with Lee.")

She was shaking hands with Lee, saying good night to Lee and the dark Adams boy who was a faithful replica of Wynstay. She was turning now, coming towards him, crying, "Isn't it a beautiful party?" and whispering, immediately afterwards, "Can we go home now at once, please. I've got a pain."

He said, "I'm adoring every second of it. You've met Mrs. Flashback, haven't you, darling?"

"Lovely to see you again," said Caroline, "*What* a beautiful party. Please, Jay, I have got such a pain."

"You want a drink? Yes, of course; here you are. And this is Mr. Pojarsky who is quite madly in love with you, he wants to hear all about the Old Vic programme for this year. (Caroline, tell the nice gentleman *at once*, before I hit you. All you mean is that you have now achieved your purpose in coming here; you have forced the wretched Lee to invite you to the ranch; so you're ready to go home. Well, you're not going, see? It's only just after one o'clock.")

"That was very, very rude," he said to her as they walked out of the Fairmont courtyard and across the top of the Nob Hill. The wind blew strongly at this peak; the sides of the peak shelved down in lights to the bay. "I am always afraid of blowing away just here," said Caroline, clinging to his arm.

"Your behaviour was quite detestable," said Jay. "Everybody hated you. And quite right too."

"They didn't; they couldn't have been sweeter. Don't the trees sound like brown paper in this wind?"

"I suppose you are pleased with yourself?"

"I am not. I have a pain. You know nothing about it."

"I know all about your pains, dear. I should. They have punctuated our acquaintance. They occur every time that you decide you are not enjoying yourself."

"Yes, well. . . ."

They leaned limply against opposite sides of the elevator. He winked at her; she winked back. They began to giggle stupidly as they walked along the corridor. They halted outside her door.

"I haven't a pain," said Jay. "But I do feel horribly valedictory about this. Which is absurd, seeing that we have at least a week more of each other's company."

"I feel the same," she said. "I think I shall have to go to bed in these orchids. You might put up a few candles on either side of the catafalque."

"Want some Secconal?"

"I think I've got two left."

"Then the decent thing to do would be to go back to the Fairmont and give them to your poor friend Lee."

"Oh," said Caroline, "put your mind at rest on that point. I didn't ask her."

"You're not going?"

She hesitated. "I didn't say I wasn't going. I said I didn't ask her. I could see her eyes being afraid that I would, and I got sorry."

"Well, then you can't go; and I'm delighted."

Caroline went on playing with the orchids. "I must get there somehow," she said.

"But why? Dear Caro, as chap to chap, can't you once and for all give up this witch-hunt after Mercedes?"

"As chap to chap," she said, "No. I've got to get there."

"It is lunacy."

"No, it isn't."

"But *why*?" he repeated.

She looked up at him with her old rueful smile. She quoted,

> "I've got a date with Death;
> Well, isn't that fun for me?"

He did not need this to remind him of the fact that was always there. No matter how far they travelled together, it always would be there. He could feel a sense of ownership in Caroline the artist, in Caroline the exasperating chum. But the ownership ended with the present and her allegiance was to the past. There were two dead men who could laugh at him; his brother Dennis, killed in Normandy, and Michael Knowle.

CHAPTER TWO

PAUL DUFAILLY walked in his garden, smoking the first pipe of the day. It was a quarter to nine and the sky was clear; still no sign of rain in this, the third week of February. The drought that had persisted through the Californian winter was beginning to be serious. Paul, the farmer, was afraid of it. There were forest fires down the valley, recalling to him other fires of summer in the French Alps.

He loitered among his memories, only half-conscious of the present. He should have been up at the chicken-farm hours ago. But it was a two-mile walk and Mercedes had taken his dilapidated car, for the transport of his three grandchildren and the two little Boches to their school in Saratoga. Paul, who at sixty looked more and more like an elderly goat, grinned as his thoughts formed the forbidden words: "les deux petits Boches." Back on the other farm in the Dauphiné, that word had not been forbidden; in those days Mercedes had sworn at the Germans merrily with the rest of them. Life had been good in the years between the wars. Meanwhile, he told himself, it was agreeable to lean here, on his fence, smoking his pipe, looking across to the green mountain. There was another week of this kind of peace; then the Boches would be their neighbours in the new cottage, fifty yards away. Paul, being old, was less troubled than his daughter Renée by the prospect.

The two cottages, the old and the new, stood high on the Adams property. Behind them a dry gold hill sloped up, with a few clumps of elm and eucalyptus straggling across the gold. The farm was out of sight round the curve of the hill. Immediately below Paul's fence there were the vegetable gardens and below these a small orchard planted on terraced earth. From where he leaned now, the near horizon was made by the tops of the fruit trees and some greenhouse roofs; the further horizon was the green mountain wall that hid the Pacific. In the steep dip lying between, out of sight from here, there were the gardens, the Adams house, the guest-houses and the pool.

An amiable place to end my days, Paul thought; and he felt suddenly old and peaceful, pitying Renée, whose emotions were all concerned with the present; with her children and her work and the new cottage. She coveted the new cottage; in Renée's view Mrs. Adams should have allotted it to her and let the Boches move in here.

Paul stared at the white frame house, on its square of brown earth, with the scaffolding still around it. The earth, that would in time become a lawn like the Dufaillys' lawn, was still heaped with odd lengths of timber; tools lay there and some leaden piping of wide circumference, the concrete-mixer stood outside the garage door. He decided to walk over to the garage and see how the painting was getting on. Mrs. Adams had bought some second-hand furniture for the Boches; and, according to Renée, all Mrs. Adams' house-guests were being recruited to paint the furniture. Under the direction of Mrs. Adams' brother Charles, the manager of the ranch, the guests lined up in the garage with their paint-brushes. The Americans were a mysterious race; Paul could not imagine any of the French families whom he had served employing their guests to work for their servants. He stood for a while looking at the piebald collection of furniture and thought that it was beginning to look nice, that the Boches ought to be grateful.

He heard the sound of the car's wheezy engine coming up the hill and turned back to meet Mercedes. She came sauntering through the vegetable-garden; he saw her stop to look over the beds of squash at the edge of the gravel path. She looked like a man in her blue dungarees; she wore her silver hair cut short. "She still has the movements of youth," he thought, "and she still whistles like a boy."

They met at the gate.

"I delivered the brats," she said, speaking in French. When she smiled, Paul thought, you could still see that she had been a beautiful woman. She had a square forehead, large dark eyes, a short nose and a small, square chin. He could remember that face without its lines and its pallor, and the hair when it was black. As the smile faded, it left only a certain weary distinction and the fine shape of the head.

"May I trouble you for a glass of water, Paul?"

"*Je vous en prie*——" He went into the house to fetch it. When he came back he said, "And how does it go this morning?" He knew from Renée that she had been invisible all yesterday. When she had the headache she retired and saw nobody; she was only a cloudy voice speaking from a darkened room. And on the day after the headache, she always looked like this, her eyes large and clear, her skin transparent, some of the lines smoothed away from her forehead; and she was always thirsty.

"Very well, thank you." Of all the voices that he knew, hers was the most impersonal; mellow and of medium pitch, a voice that expressed detachment from herself and the world. It became even more detached when you asked after her health.

He said, "That is good. Another year of this food and this climate and you and I will be tough."

Mercedes tilted the water down her throat, looked at him

ironically and jerked her silver head towards the new cottage. "Almost finished there, what?"

"Yes; did you speak to Mrs. Adams about the possibility of our moving in?"

"I did not. You know that the cottage has been built for the Veits; and if you could hammer the idea into Renée's head, we should all be grateful."

She handed him back the glass. He stood looking at her. "Renée is young," he said, "and very much alone; she has only you and the children."

"She has her work; the panacea," said Mercedes; "and if she would only make up her mind to see the affair reasonably she could begin to be happy. For two years the Veits have lived in that ramshackle place down the hill; Renée was given the first cottage because she has three children, where Georg and Liesel have only two. Simple mathematics; simple justice. We should be going, Paul. And you might remind Renée that it isn't practical for near neighbours to quarrel."

She was right; they were all in the same boat; they were all fortunate to be here, the refugees, the former comrades-in-arms; and that, oddly, must include the Germans, the enemies of the Hitler regime; it must include Mercedes herself, who though half-English and half-American, was in his mind a native of France. As they strolled through the garden, she said, "Above all, it is important that the children should be friends; Renée must see that. I wouldn't care in the least how often she and Liesel threw the saucepans at each other. I only care about the children."

He looked at the quiet profile as she moved beside him. "Do you care?" he asked himself, "Yes, you must care, but one sees no hint of it in you; only in your actions." She would be a puzzle to him always. There was her dossier and there was herself; they did not tally. All her actions were those of a woman with passion. There were the efforts that she had made in bringing him and the remainder of his family here after his son-in-law was killed in France; and what did she owe to them after all? They were only the family who had lived on her property and worked for her; yet she had bankrupted herself in transplanting them. She had found them work and a home. She, who hated the Boches, had performed the same services for Georg and Liesel Veit.

She had loved France enough to stay and fight there, with the men and women of the Resistance. The enemy had burned her house and killed her friends; she had lost everything; almost, she had lost her life. And her charity extended to these curious Americans. If it were true, as Renée said, that the last remnants of Mercedes' money had been put into this ranch to keep it going, that was another gesture. But he could not imagine that it had been necessary. All Americans were rich and he was sure that Mrs. Adams could afford to pay better wages.

Mercedes said, "Have you a cigarette?"

He knew that the doctor had put her on a regime for cigarettes and as he handed her the pack, he could not help asking, *"Ca fait combien déjà d'aujourd'hui?"*

She did not answer; she gave him another ironical look and returned the pack to him. She stood beside the battered car, lighting the cigarette. She climbed in at his side and they began the slow, bumpy journey. She was talking about the children; about the play that the children wanted to act, *L'Oiseau Bleu*; Mercedes did not sound enthusiastic about it; she was merely asking him to acquire certain properties for it. She kept the cigarette at the corner of her mouth while she talked.

She took endless trouble with the children; neither the Boches nor his daughter Renée had the time to organise their leisure; she taught them drawing and poetry; she played games with them; she kept their own language alive for them with French and German books. All five pledged their allegiance daily to the American flag at the local grammar-school, but Paul could never get used to the idea that his grandchildren would be citizens of the United States. He had ceased to argue this point with Mercedes, the contradictory and exasperating woman. (She was devoid of maternal instinct; she treated the children as people; he never saw her kiss them nor heard her talk to them except in adult friendliness. But they were her main preoccupation here.)

"The goats," she said, as they climbed out of the car and crossed the yard. "Are you taking the nanny goats and the kids down to the pasture to-day?"

"I thought of it; but that depends on Monsieur Bush. He may have other ideas."

"I'll talk to him," said Mercedes, "and if he agrees I'll drive them down in the truck."

He watched her, walking away, whistling; stopping for a moment at the newest chicken-houses and looking in.

She went on her way, still whistling. It was like seeing the ghost of the woman who had been his employer all those years ago. Did she sorrow for that time? Surely she must. Surely she must remember with nostalgia the days when she had her health, her money, her mountain home. She had been a wanderer always, but always she had returned to that other farm above the terraced vines. Could anybody as wayward and as solitary be content to live as she lived now? To settle, at fifty, on the outskirts of an American family, doing such chores as came her way; a semi-invalid, placed at some social level half-way between Mrs. Adams herself and his own servant's status? Did she like it, tolerate it, find it unbearable? He thought that he would never know.

ii

Mercedes found Lennox Bush at the far end of the chicken-houses, studying the latest clutch. He was Lee Adams' son-in-law, married to her elder daughter; he had come back from the war without a job and Lee had put him in here to run the farm. He was a fair, chunky young man with a chip on his shoulder; he had, she thought, the worst type of American manners; it had surprised her since childhood that the nation capable of extreme courtesy could produce as easily the extreme of rudeness.

"Hello, there," he said, talking with his pipe in his mouth.

"Good morning. Is it all right with you if I take the two nanny goats and the kids down in the truck?"

"Thought Dufailly was going to do that yesterday. Sure it's all right by me," said Bush. "I don't know why they want to move them but go ahead, move them."

"The point being," said Mercedes "that the two youngest children are to have goat's milk; that is their doctor's order. As you would have heard, if you had been listening, Charles and I decided to move four of the goats down to the pen on the pasture. By next month there'll be too many kids up here."

"Sure; okay, Mercedes. Go ahead."

"Well, I shall want some help getting them into the truck."

"Take Dufailly. About time he did some work. He ought to have been here hours ago."

Mercedes looked him up and down reflectively. "If you will remove that pipe from your mouth and look at me for a moment," she said, "I want to tell you something."

He said, "Sorry" abruptly; his face was beginning to flush.

"Paul Dufailly is not a young man; if you care to send the truck down for him, he can be up here as early as you wish. If he drives up here in his own car, somebody's got to take it down again to get the children to school. I will not have Paul walking two miles uphill before he starts his day's work; do you understand? And I might remind you that he stays on up here until after seven every evening."

"Yeah, sure. I know. Sorry, Mercedes." He was afraid of her and this made it too easy to bully him. She saw him now with the lucidity that came to her on the day after the headache; she had the feeling that her brain had been washed. She saw that Lennox was as much at a disadvantage here as any of them were, a misfit who had been given a job and a home by his mother-in-law; a boy who had known adult life only in the Army, whose responsibilities, from fatherhood to farm-management, fitted him as badly as his deliberately shapeless clothes.

She said, "All right—I'll bring back the truck when I'm through."

"Wait a minute. I'll come and give you a hand."

As she walked down over the field to where the goats were feeding round their covered trough, Mercedes found that she was whistling Michael's hackneyed tune from long ago. She had woken with it in her ears. She was at peace this morning; to-day she would continue to be aware of the clearness in her head, the lightness and comfort of her body; the reward for pain. She valued this aftermath. It was almost a mystic experience; it was only the final effect of the drug; making her see the sky and the gold hills and the green mountain with a completeness of vision, a sense of awe. Curious, when your body had been tough all your life, to know at last the periods of devout gratitude for feeling well.

The large grey billy-goat was advancing towards her, twitching his thin tuft of tail and shaking his head from side to side. She stopped to play with him while Paul and Lennox went on beyond the feeding-troughs to corral the nanny goats and the two skipping kids. The grey goat came close. Mercedes put out her hands and pushed against the hornless head with both palms. He pushed too, until she felt the whole weight of him, solid as a wall. He broke away and pranced on his hind hoofs, pawing the air and curving his neck; he came down on all fours with a thud and stared at her. Despite the barred eyes and cynical lip, the grandee beard, he roused her pity as though he were still a thing cursed; the scape-goat, the friend of Satan. She received the lowered head and held it off, scratching him behind his ears. Slowly he began to drive her against the fence; she had to give ground because he was so heavy.

"Gee, I wish you wouldn't do that!" Lennox shouted. "He's mean as hell."

"He likes to play." She slipped away from the thrusting head and he narrowly missed charging against the fence;

he slithered clumsily on his small hoofs, then reared up
again.

"Capricorn; child of the devil," she said to him. The
smell of goat was now all over her hands; the nostalgic
smell. God be praised that goats from Savoy to Saratoga
smelled alike. She clapped her hands at him; he did not
dance again, but came on with his ominous head lowered
once more.

"He could kill you," Lennox said, with one kid in his
arms and the nanny-goat circling round him on the end of
the tether that he had looped round his wrist. Paul came
after him with the second kid and the second nanny. The
kids' legs hung down and they screamed, one to another,
and the nannies became wild at the end of their tethers; the
grey billy was only momentarily distracted by the procession;
he was, Mercedes knew, determined to ram her once against
the fence before they parted. She dodged him; he reared
up and the descending hooves missed her foot by a few inches.
She reached out and tapped his nose.

"You know, you're crazy," said Lennox.

"My child, I was ordering goats about while you were
in your cradle." She gave him one more chance, letting
him drive her towards the gate; she slipped through ahead
of him. He put up a pleading foreleg, sticking it through
the wire; all his legs looked too thin to support the massive
shaggy body. The pointed, tortoiseshell hoof scraped and
rattled on the wire-netting. She said, "Au revoir, mon vieux."

He looked resigned and sinful, turning his profile away.
After they had loaded the other animals into the truck,
Mercedes looked back and saw that he was still there, staring
after her.

Lennox said, "I'll drive down with you if you like. Then
I can help you unload them and bring the truck back."

"Thank you, but it isn't necessary. Charles will be there."

"Well, but, you'll have to walk all the way down again;
unless you want to spend the morning up here."

"I'll walk down; I like it."

"Okay," said Lennox sulkily. Foiled of a gesture, he walked away with Paul after him. She could not explain to him that this morning was to be treasured; that now, alone, she might not be here, but back on the mountain road between Briançon and Lautaret. She had become expert at the trick of slipping back, or blotting out such features of the landscape as were specifically American, of playing the game with the toys available. It was interrupted when she came to the pasture behind the two cottages and Charles helped her lift the scared goats out of the truck. Charles was Lee's brother; he had an irregular version of Lee's face, the round forehead, the light eyes, a longer neck and the general appearance of a startled, benign bird. He was another person who would have no work if it were not for this place; Lee called him the busted flush. He was the American tragedy, the business-man who had failed. He still had his bouts of drinking; his only other activities were his passion for detail and his capable hands. He liked to be praised and it was now easy to praise him for the work that he had put into the new pen for the goats. She had to let him show her details; hasps and hinges; the dovetailing on corners of wooden troughs. The kids began to dance and frisk; the nannies cropped the dry grass.

"And the next thing," said Mercedes thoughtfully, "will be to impress upon the children that the goats are not here for their amusement. You'll recall that Marie-Thérèse and Lucien dressed one of last year's kids in a red flannel petticoat."

"That's your worry, not mine, thank God," said Charles. She was conscious of his speculative, birdlike stare. "Wouldn't care to handle that bunch of toughs myself," he said. He went on his way to the new cottage and she drove the truck uphill again to the farm.

Still on the long walk down, she whistled Michael's tune and the haunt of it threatened to make the day different.

It was almost eleven o'clock when she came to the house. The house and its lawns were circled by trees; the lawns made a green lake and the two houses stood on its north shore; there was the main house, long and low, built of dark wood, with a covered patio; the small white guest-house along the path, with the magnolia growing in front of it. Mercedes saw the ranch as a place of separate encampments. There were the two cottages up above; there was this territory that belonged to Lee and Dan and Charles; there was her own small house, south of the lawns and now invisible. Lennox and his wife had another little cottage down the hill, near the road.

The sight of the sprinklers playing on the grass made her thirst unbearable. She went across the patio and through the living-room; it was a large room with an open fireplace and a built-in bar. There were fur rugs on the polished hardwood floor; horned heads looked down from the walls. Wynstay Adams left a gap in this room: particularly at night when the fire was lit and his corner chair stayed empty. By day, Wyn was still all over this place. She half-expected to see him now, coming across the patio, hunched and smoking his pipe, greeting her abstractedly on his way to the study.

She went on into the kitchen and found Lee drinking a cup of coffee with the dark, gloomy Liesel and the flashing Renée Dufailly. Towards eleven o'clock they all drifted in here for coffee.

"Hello there," Lee said, "are you better?"

Nobody knew how much she dreaded the little round of kind enquiries that came punctually as the ticking of a clock; it was absurd to go on hating them, to freeze and to hear her voice saying abruptly, "Yes; thank you; I'm fine." She went to the sink and filled a long glass with water; went to the refrigerator and emptied ice-cubes into the glass; refilled the tray; drank off the first glass and the second; came to the table with the third. Lee, freckled and sunburned, was reading the morning paper and the mail.

"See what Santa Claus brought," she said, indicating the two solid packages; "Wyn's memoir and a syrupy letter saying for me to go through the proofs and cut what I don't care for."

"Are you so sure that you won't like any of it?" Mercedes asked.

Lee nodded. "I saw the first chapters, remember. The hell with it; I guess once you're dead you're anybody's property." She went on reading her letters. Mercedes, aware that Liesel Veit was waiting to corner her with some mournful request on behalf of the little Franz, picked up the newspaper. Lee spoke to her twice before she raised her head.

"I'm sorry; what was that?"

"I said I have to go into Saratoga this afternoon, so I can get the children."

"Thank you very much." She glanced down again at the paper, at the photograph of the young woman standing silhouetted beside the pine trees, with the sea behind her. *"Caroline Seward takes a vacation at Pebble Beach."* She was familiar with photographs of Caroline Seward; in this morning's lucid reverie she found the profile as clear and familiar as though it were the face of a friend. Lee brought the coffee-pot from the stove and refilled her cup.

"For you?"

"Not for me," Mercedes said, still looking at the photograph. She lit a cigarette. She avoided Liesel and went on her way. She went down across the lawns and past the high hedge that bordered the swimming-pool.

South of the pool, among the trees, there was a barn; one of Wynstay's haphazard projects from long ago. He had meant it as a study for his own use; Dan and Marilyn had annexed it as a rumpus-room; since then it had done duty as a storage-dump, a gymnasium and, in war-time, as a dormitory for the evacuees. Mercedes herself had annexed it a year ago; it was the place where she gave the children their drawing-lessons, their readings and their games. Nobody else came here. At her request, Charles had built a platform at one end, and they had hung old curtains to make a stage.

She stood still for a moment looking in; aware of the bird-song outside, the dusty sunshine that went ahead of her through the open door. The place was a mad mixture of schoolroom, theatre, nursery and studio. On the walls there were paintings and drawings done by the children; their models in clay were here, their toys and games and books; mixed comfortably with the possessions that Dan and Marilyn had outgrown, the baseball-bats and boxing-gloves.

There were benches drawn up in front of the stage; and on the stage, behind the rickety footlights, the tall white paper screens awaiting decoration. There was a communal collection of working-materials here, palettes that the children were allowed to use, some of her old paints and brushes. She felt too idle to go to her own studio for the better tools; these would do. Still whistling, she selected what she needed and began to improvise on the first screen an outline of cloud and castle that would suggest the Kingdom of the Future.

"It is absurd to wonder about Caroline Seward," thought Mercedes, "to feel any further curiosity. According to Lee, she is now changed and spoiled; merely a successful actress with a hard head. And yet I, who have never met her, cannot believe this; and the fact that she is near, within two hundred miles, nags at me as though I should make some gesture; as though we ought to meet."

She stared in a momentary trance at the outline growing beneath her hand; it was easy this morning, effortless; she had known that it would be. She had not been able to touch it yesterday. She had begun it on the evening before. Old Dufailly had been here then, mending the footlights. She had stood painting inept lines and painting them out; aware of the cold feeling in her head, the pressure behind her eyes, the beginning of nausea; the early stage when she could see the pain coming. Dufailly had known that she was tired; he had argued with her about the trouble that she took with these things; it was not important for the children to have painted scenery; they could act in front of the white screens. It was good enough for them. Because she was feeling ill, she had snapped at him. "I despise 'It is good enough'. I despise the thing that is not done well merely because to do it better involves taking pains."

It seemed to her that she had laid this thought down here to be picked up now and transmuted to the present preoccupation of her mind, to Caroline Seward. "The thing that is not done well." *The work left unfinished.*

"But what is the work? What have I left undone that I could have done for her?" She slashed the outlines across the second screen. *The work left unfinished,* said the whisper in her mind, and now she no longer whistled Michael's tune.

By lunch-time she had finished three of the four screens; she went down the path to her own house, a white-framed cottage like the two on the hill. She had painted the front door and the shutters dark blue; there was a small patio, a flower-bed with daffodils and narcissus, a square of lawn.

The living-room was divided into two separate halves; the front of the room was walled with low bookshelves; there was a brick fireplace on the right of the door, two comfortable arm-chairs; a divan; a small dining-table. The back half was her studio. The kitchen opened out of the studio; her bedroom and bathroom were on the other side.

Mercedes went into the kitchen, made herself a sandwich and coffee, carrying these on to the patio, to eat her lunch in the sun. "Crazy weather for February," she said to herself. She was enough of a farmer to be disquieted by it. She smoked her fourth cigarette devotedly, watching a turkey-buzzard sail up over the trees. She turned on the sprinkler for the lawn and went into her bedroom to rest, reminded now, as often, that once she could lie all afternoon in the sun and the cold at four thousand feet without harm.

It was a plain room, with white walls and yellow curtains. There was a large crucifix above the mantelpiece and on one wall a painting that she had made of the mountains above the Lautaret pass. There were no other decorations. There was no dressing-table; that lived in the bathroom, with the bottles, the lotions, the creams and the rest of the frivolous equipment that she despised and could not live without. This room contained only the large bed, more books in low white shelves, white rugs on the floor and a

299

glass-topped table where there stood a bowl of daffodils and jonquils.

She had to make her afternoon sleep light, because to-day was Thursday and her doctor, Ferris Russell, would probably call. Over at Los Gatos he had a rich patient who gave him luncheon and he liked to look in on Mercedes on his way back. She hated him to take her unawares.

At three o'clock she woke and prepared herself for him, with the painstaking care that was necessary when you lived in a body that had been beautiful once. It was not yet a body to be ashamed of, but she minded very much about the signs that the ruthless eyes of the young woman had once observed on other people's middle-aged bodies.

While she waited for Ferris, she wandered round the bookshelves, choosing the children's reading; she put the small pile of books ready with paper markers in each. Her methods were erratic and this evening's menu included *Cymbeline*, Hilaire Belloc's *Bad Child's Book of Beasts* and the *Dream of the Rood*.

Ferris appeared on the patio, stuck his head round the door and said, "Anybody home?" He was an intelligent, abrupt creature; she had known him years ago in Washington; his base of operations was now the Palo Alto clinic; he had a long, thin head and small blue eyes. He put down his bag on the table.

They were all routine questions; it was a routine examination. His matter-of-fact gentleness made her wonder why she must go through the period of icy resentment before it began. It was no trouble; they were both so impersonal about it that they might have been concerned with a third person's weight, cough, headache and blood-pressure. It was part of the routine that he should give her a cigarette "as a reward for being a good girl," and sit with her for a few minutes, talking of other things. To-day, because she was feeling well, she asked him the question that she had not asked for many weeks. "Ferris, how should I make out if I went to Europe in September?"

He tapped the ash off his cigarette. "You'd probably make out all right, just to spite me. But if you're asking my permission, I have to say no to the idea."

"Still?"

"Mercedes, you're an intelligent woman. You know as well as I know what that trip would do to you; and you can guess what one European winter would do to you."

"Worth it, perhaps."

"Could you afford to travel comfortably? To take somebody along? Who'd look after you when you got there?"

She was silent.

"And if you lyingly gave me satisfactory answers to those three—I still don't know that you'd get the permission," Ferris said. He stabbed out his cigarette in the ash-tray, rose from his chair, smiled at her and added, "But always remember, you don't have to ask it."

"Meaning?"

The small blue eyes narrowed: "Meaning that, since I haven't your religious scruples, I think you've a perfect right to live where you please and for as long as you please. You've earned it, if anybody has."

"I wonder," she said, "if anybody does earn it."

"You," said Ferris, "have created certain obligations for yourself here. I repeat, created them. They needn't bind you; you owe these people nothing. And your future is your own affair. Nobody else's."

"Seeing the amount of work that you've put in on this body since '45——" she began.

"Oh, you did most of it yourself," said Ferris. "If they were all as tough as you, I shouldn't make money." She watched him go and then went into her room to dress.

iii

Franz Veit read slowly; he stood with his feet planted apart; one lock of dark hair falling over his forehead. He and Lucien Dufailly were the two out of the five who liked to stand, to take the centre of the floor.

> "Fear no more the heat o' the sun,
> Nor the furious winter's rages;
> Thou thy wordly task hast done,
> Home art gone and ta'en thy wages.
> Golden girls and lads all must,
> As chimney-sweepers, come to dust."

He made the most of it; for a boy of nine, he had a remarkable ear for poetry; he was her problem-child, the only one who preferred always to be alone, to keep himself aloof from the community; though he adored his mother, he seemed devoid of affection else. He had a cold, furious temper. His younger brother Nikki was a roly-poly tough, subject to demonstrative moods. He was sitting on the floor now with his arms round his fat knees, and his eyes fixed faithfully on the cardboard box, with the holes bored in the top, that held his pet frog. Next to him was Suzanne, the youngest Dufailly; a fair, prim little girl of seven; and she too was looking at the box where the frog was. The Dufailly twins, Lucien and Marie-Thérèse, were listening to Franz; staring at him with identical expressions of unwilling admiration. They were beautiful children; always in repose they looked like young, dignified angels, a façade perennially contradicted by their behaviour. They were, Mercedes thought, among the valid examples of original sin. But for the moment, looking at the quiet heads, hearing Franz's full pure voice, leaning back in her chair with the sixth cigarette lighted, she had the illusion of peace.

"Thank you, Franz." He shut the book, gave it back to her with a small bow and sat down.

"What did it make you think of—Nikki?"

"I don't know."

"Did you like it?"

"Yes."

"You don't have to say 'Yes' if you didn't."

302

"Honestly I did."

"All right. Lucien, what have you got to say about it?"

"It's sad and it sings."

Franz interrupted. "It's like another poem we read."

"Which?"

He said, "I can't remember what it's called. It was the one that began 'Soldier rest'; something about 'sleep the sleep that knows no waking'."

She let them dig at the likeness before she took up the last poem. "Where did we get to, in the Dream of the Rood— anybody remember?"

"Slay the fell fiends," said Franz.

Lucien made a hideous face at him. It was Lucien's turn to read; as usual with twice the drama and half the accuracy, that Franz gave to the task.

> "The young Hero stripped Him there.
>   He that was mighty God,
> Strong and stout-hearted,
>   strode he up to the gallows of shame.
> Steadfast in sight of all;
>   man he would save.
> I trembled as tenderly——"

"Take it a little more slowly, Lucien; they are tricky lines——, and stop at the end of the verse." He looked at her reproachfully; he spoke the last lines in subdued, angelic fashion.

> "A rood I was raised.
>   Aloft I lifted the King of rank,
> Lord of high Heaven,
>   nor dared to bow."

"Marie-Thérèse, will you take it on from there—— No. Lucien, please don't show her where. You haven't the remotest idea, have you, Marie-Thérèse? You weren't listening at all."

"It sort of puts me to sleep; it's a lovely feeling; it's the words."

"If you would tell me the truth and say that you were in fact looking at the castles that I painted this morning and thinking about the *Blue Bird*, I should be more impressed," said Mercedes.

"It is a difficult poem; it isn't like a poem at all. You read it; it sounds swell when you read it."

"I'll read it if you listen. Nikki, do have mercy on that poor frog. The box is its room after all. You wouldn't like somebody to keep tilting this floor." She stared them into solemnity and began,

> "Dark nails they drove through me;
> On me are still the scars,
> Wide wounds of malice;
> Nor revenge durst I one of them.
> Us both they besmeared.
> All with blood I was wet
> From that Man's side shed
> When His spirit forth he sent."

She read for her own pleasure now, forgetting the children:

> "Darkness deepened,
> Covered with clouds
> the corpse of the King."

They were quiet when she stopped. She said, "That is all for now." They scrambled up gladly when she rose. She said, "You can do what you like."

"I'd like to learn my part," said Franz.

She gazed at him ironically. "It isn't your part yet. I've told you that you and Lucien are going to see who makes the better job of it." He shut his lips tightly, went to the bookshelf, detached the copy of the *Blue Bird* and walked to the farthest end of the barn, where he sat on a table, with his fingers in his ears.

Marie-Thérèse said, "Come on, Lucien. Get the book, and we'll hear each other. Is it okay if we go on the stage, Mrs. Knowle?"

"Surely. Be careful of the screens, though. They'll split if you treat them rough."

She sauntered out into the air. She was tired now; behind her the voices gabbled:

"Tyltyl?"

"Yes, Mytyl?"

"Are you asleep?"

"Are you?"

"How can I be asleep if I'm talking to you?"

"Oh, I've got a swell idea; let's go and do this in the cave —can we go to the cave, Mrs. Knowle?"

"Not now," she said, "By the time you're there it'll be time to go up for your supper." The cave was the private place, made by these two in the trees; a kind of wigwam. Mercedes discouraged it because most of their villainies seemed to be plotted there.

"Time," she called, "Off you go. And don't forget what I told you about the goats; I'm talking to you now, Lucien."

"Yes, ma'am."

She watched them go, Lucien and Marie-Thérèse ahead; Nikki and Suzanne quarrelling over the frog; Franz alone, with the copy of the *Blue Bird* under his arm. It was against her rule for them to take books out of the barn; she felt too idle to call him back. She shut the door and turned the key.

She shook her head at the crowding trees. She could laugh gently at her own efforts with the children. It would not be long now before they grew tired of all this. She looked ahead and saw them a year hence, tough and different, finding poetry "sissy," devising fun of their own. *The work unfinished*.

"Foolish," Mercedes said to herself, "Only one person who could ever say 'Consummatum est'."

When she came into the empty room the telephone was ringing. Lee said, "Hello; you'll come up for supper, won't you?"

305

Mercedes hesitated. "I don't believe I will. No, I'm feeling fine; only tired. I think I'll make myself something here."

She stood by the mantelpiece, looking down at the small stone cat that was its only ornament. She looked from the cat to the bookshelves; from the bookshelves to the desk. The clues to the past were here. She tried for a moment to concentrate upon the ordered present, looking back along the day, making it into a book of hours. It was different from the other days because it had begun with Michael's tune.

CHAPTER THREE

1922

At a little after nine o'clock on a September evening, Mercedes Barry parked her car in Soho Square. Having driven two hundred miles and eaten no luncheon, she was hungry. The doorway of the restaurant on the corner had the words "The French Horn" painted over it in looping, elaborate script; there was a small design of musical instruments at either end of the scroll.

It was not an elaborate restaurant; it was cheap; it was shabby, but it was entirely French and anything that was French was to be loved. She went in. The air was warm and odorous with the right smells; onion soup; herbs; coffee and a whiff of caporal tobacco. The musical-instrument motif was repeated on panels round the walls. There were a dozen tables, with cloths of black and yellow check; the lamp-shades on each table were yellow, painted with black circles. Mercedes was met by Parron, the proprietor; the plump man with the stiff hair cut *en brosse* and the swaddling apron tied over his dark clothes.

He remembered her. She was well-used to being remembered by head-waiters on an extensive map throughout two continents; but she was surprised by this because she had been here only once before; a year ago with a young man who had seemed important; he was not important now; nobody was. It was obvious that the young man, whom she recalled as a person of social ambition, had at one or another time given Parron her dossier. He was asking after her father, saying that he had read of her father's re-appointment from Paris to Washington. Parron like everybody else, seemed to think Washington an excellent destination.

"Je n'y tiens pas, beaucoup," said Mercedes. Parron seated her and looked over her shoulder as though he were expecting an escort to arrive for her.

"I am alone," she said.

At once becoming sprightly, Parron invited her to have a drink with him, un petit verre; she accepted, but she hoped that he would leave her in peace. There were few diners to demand his attention; the few all looked her way and she stared tranquilly back at them, one by one, over the edge of the glass of Dubonnet.

"Je m'impose," Mercedes thought; it was impossible not to be aware of this and to know why. She was a vivid person; she was dressed expensively and with the exaggerations of the moment; she was without a hat; she wore her dark hair cut as short as a boy's and she smoked her cigarette in a long green holder. The diner at whom she stared the longest was a young man sitting alone; he did not lower his eyes; they were large grey eyes and it was diverting to see that his head and forehead were like her own; his hair grew the same way as hers, though it was not the same colour; it was light brown, tousled hair. He had an interesting face; good bones; a clear, pale, skin. "Il a quelque chose," she thought and wondered what it was; it might be dignity. When he smiled, she smiled back, absent-mindedly, before she bent her head over the menu.

Parron left her in peace. Mercedes went a long way in her restless thoughts while she ate her dinner. It was perhaps an affectation to think in French. Her thoughts took her over her life from the first memories of childhood as far as now; and informed her, as she had known that they would, that she was a spoilt young woman whose assets were all on the

worldly side of the ledger. This way of thinking owed itself
to her convent upbringing; sometimes she thought that she
would like to free herself from the beliefs; to burn her boats
and watch the flames for fun. But there was the other person,
the natural penitent, aware of the sins; sins of rusting talents,
sins of self, sins of appetite. It was highly inconvenient; as a
pagan she would not have needed to be a rebel.

This was the conclusion that she had reached when she
lifted her coffee-cup and saw that the young man was still
there. He was talking to Parron and she could hear their
conversation.

"I haven't got that much money on me. Will you wait till
next time?"

"Anything you wish," said Parron a little stiffly, the
Frenchman receiving an appeal to his pocket.

"Sorry," said the young man, smiling at him.

"It is perfectly all right, Mr. Knowle."

"I can lend you some money, if you like," said Mercedes.

She expected him to look surprised. He did not. He said,
"Oh, no, thanks very much. I'm always one meal in arrears,
aren't I, Parron?"

"I trust him," said Parron to Mercedes.

Mr. Knowle rose from the table, with the book under his
arm; he said, "That was kind of you," as he came past. He
had a gentle voice.

"No, it wasn't. It was ridiculous and rather offensive.
Have some coffee."

"All right; thank you," he said; he put the book on the
table. It was a chunky book with a dull library binding.

"What is that?"

"That is work," said the young man; he wore a tweed
jacket whose sleeves were rubbed; his cotton shirt was patched
just below the collar. He offered her a cigarette from a packet
of ten Players; she saw that he had interesting hands.

"I usually have my coffee at home," he said. "But it isn't
very good. I make it in a jug."

"Where is home?"

"Taviton Street."

"Where is that?"

"Bloomsbury," said the young man.

"What are you studying?"

"Medicine. I've one more year."

"And then?"

"When I've qualified, I take over my father's practice in the country."

"That sounds rather dull."

"It will be. But he's got a weak heart and he can't keep going much longer. Do you always ask people to tell you the stories of their lives? You'd be a gift to the Ancient Mariner, wouldn't you?"

"If you don't like the questions, you needn't answer them," she said.

"May I ask one?"

"But of course."

"What is your name?"

"Mercedes Barry. And I don't live anywhere; which comes of having a father in the Diplomatic Service and an American mother; that is to say I had an American mother. She died when I was fifteen."

"And what do you do?"

"Do?"

"Lady of leisure?"

"Intermittently. It doesn't feel like leisure, because there are always people to be talked to and entertained. As far as a career goes, I'm an artist *manquée*."

"Aren't you too young to be anything *manquée*?"

"I can only paint in France," she said.

"Good Lord, why?"

"There's nothing that the French don't do better than the English; except poetry and Yorkshire pudding; and I don't care for Yorkshire pudding."

"I still can't see how that affects your painting," said the young man, "but I've never been in France."

"I've left my heart there."

"Is that why you are in a bad temper?"

"Am I in a bad temper?"

"You were when you came in. I thought what a sulky young woman. Then you suddenly grinned at me and looked quite different."

"I was thinking about our heads being the same shape," she said.

"Are they? Yes, perhaps they are." He said, "Are you still cross?"

"Not really. Somebody made the fatal error of trying to shut a door on me, that was all."

"You don't like doors?"

"I don't like anything much at the minute. I have the prospect of spending about seven years on the wrong side of the Atlantic. I've got to get out of that one."

"Can you?"

"Oh yes," she said, "if I fight."

"Then why be cross?"

"Because I am enduring what purports to be an English country-holiday with my father. And at eleven o'clock this morning he suggested to me that I should mend my ways and set about entertaining his week-end guests; with the result that you see."

"You walked out?"

"Oh yes. I always do. He knew I would."

"Have you anywhere to sleep?" the young man asked with concern. She reassured him quickly. "We have a suite at the Carlton; there's nothing dramatic or final about the gesture. Now I've made it, I am very sorry and I shall go back in the morning. But I got bored."

"I don't think I have ever been bored," he said thoughtfully. "And I can't imagine trying to avoid the prospect of going to America. Have you been there before? Where else have you been?" She told him. He said, "Well, you've been pretty well everywhere, haven't you? Everywhere that matters. I think you're awfully lucky."

"So do I," said Mercedes.

"Well, thank you for the coffee. I must be going." He picked up his book.

"Want a lift home? I've a car outside."

"I was going to walk; it helps to clear my head; I work pretty late."

"Very well," she said, "Good night."

He stood beside the table, looking down at her. "It must be nice," he said, "to do as you please."

It was quietly and tragically said; for the first time in their dialogue, she felt wiser than he. She said, "Wait a minute while I pay this bill. I'll walk with you to the corner. You see," she said, as they went up through the Square, "there are some people who should be able to do as they please. I don't think I'm one of them. But you might be. What is the thing that you want to do?"

He did not answer for a moment. Then he said, "I'd like to ask you to come back to Taviton Street and talk. We could have some more coffee. But it isn't much of a room; and Mrs. Roberts has strictures upon lady visitors at this time of night."

"*T'en fais pas.* You have to work."

"Oh, I could work later on. I've trained myself to exist on very little sleep."

"Even so," she said. They stood under the lamp on the corner of Oxford Street.

"I'll leave you here," she said, "Good night. God bless you."

"What an unexpected remark from you."

"Why unexpected?"

He looked her up and down. "I don't know; rather old-fashioned."

"That is the first cheap thing I've heard you say."

"I apologise. In my profession, one gets away from God."

"Are you an atheist?"

"I have leanings that way."

"Could you tread on a crucifix?" Mercedes asked.

"Heavens, no."

311

"All right," she said. "Hope for you yet. Good night."

"Like to dine with me there to-morrow?"

She wanted to ask, "Can you afford it?" but that would have been offensive. She said, "Yes, I would like to; very much." He walked away and she heard him whistling *Loch Lomond* as he went.

ii

There were moments when she was sorry for him, but these came less often. It took her three days to fall in love; it took her four days to discover that the surgeon under whom he was completing his training thought more highly of Michael Knowle than of any other student in his year. The top-floor room in Taviton Street lost its appeal to her pity and assumed the same significance as she might have found on an empty canvas, with a picture taking shape in her mind. She was at first appalled that anybody only a year younger than herself should have had so little fun; and bewildered that he should be so uninstructed and naif in matters that were for her the obvious mechanics of living.

But he had something that she had not. He had his innocence. He was all of a piece; he fought no battles inside himself. When she mixed him with her heterogenous circle of friends, he was neither impressed nor unimpressed; he did not change his manners; he continued to behave as though he were the constant in variable surroundings. He liked best to be alone with her in his small high room, where they looked out at the Bloomsbury chimney-pots and played Quotation Battles, and he made her tell him travellers' tales. The light would fade out of the room and she would lay her hand against his cheek for the pleasure of feeling the smooth skin.

She said, "Arise, my love, and come away with me."

"Where?"

"Anywhere. Over the hills and far away."

"To Egypt?"

"Why do you think of Egypt?"

He said, "Because you look like an Egyptian cat, silhouetted there."

"I think we'll go to Paris and live in a garret and have two Siamese kittens."

He was humble with her. "Why me? Why should you want me?"

The answer might have been " Because this is something new." She sat there, saying softly, "Arise, my love and come away with me."

He showed her his book with the things written in it; as neatly tabulated as his medical notes; her own words; some of them, she thought, the most obvious clichés: "Never break bad news gently"; "Say No at once when you mean No"; "Company is an illusion; there is only God and yourself."

"But why write them down?"

"So that I still have them when you are gone."

"Gone? Without you? Arise, my love."

The fight began; with the two unmatched families ranging up on one side against them. There was the doctor's house in Sussex; the dim bewildered parents, the bony sister in her blue serge dress; saying that it was very sudden, that Michael could not afford to support a wife, that they ought to wait; all the conventional arguments with their overtone of alarm at the thought of the world from which Mercedes came.

There was her father saying wearily, "As I recall, you have been falling in love with clockwork regularity since you were fifteen."

"This isn't the same."

"It never is the same. I grant you that he is a good-looking young man, a highly intelligent young man and probably an admirable young man; too admirable a young man to be content to live on your money."

"That will not be for long."

"And I cannot imagine your being content to settle down."

"But that is the one thing I want to do."

He looked at her ironically.

"For the moment, Mercedes; how long will that moment last?"

How long, she thought, had any of the moments lasted? Impossible to reckon, when you had tasted too many flavours too soon; when you had moved on a background of embassies and hotels half the world over; when you had learned to study all the tricks of human relationship and found them fascinating. You had had a soufflé named after you at Foyot's when you were seven; you had been the care and pride of Dominican nuns when you were twelve, shone as Depuy's brightest pupil when you were seventeen. These things mixed themselves up when you tried to see yourself clearly and all that emerged was that, since adolescence, you had lived half-way between caring nothing and caring very much.

Until the night at the French Horn, she had been convinced that she had no dream any more. She had only her mystic moments; her groping for God that was so persistently interrupted by the diverting manners of the devil. Michael's dream of a career was solidly shareable; as shareable as his other dream of owning the queer house that decayed in its Sussex garden: Cold Ash, the house that had put a spell on him in childhood. With me, she thought, he can grasp the two dreams.

Her father was saying, "You're wise; too wise for your age. Which is why I ask you this; what makes you think that he can hold you?"

She shook her head, as though she, too, found it hard to fathom. She knew that Michael aroused in her two impulses; one the envious admiration of the simple man, *l'homme pur*, with his hardships, his set course, his passion for work; she longed to be one with that, after so many voyages. She tried to explain it. But of the other impulse she was too shy to speak; it was the creator's impulse, the same compelling thrust that made her paint or draw or model in clay with the speed and application of a dement. This was virgin soil; on this simplicity she was already forming a design. Together they would make a world. In the fever, she forgot something that

Depuy had mourned regularly; that her best work was always
left unfinished.

1930

Mercedes walked into the Brookfield Galleries and asked the
oriental-looking young man who advanced along the parquet,
if she might see Mr. Dennis. (To see old Brookfield would mean
spending the entire morning here and buying on a prodigal
scale. His was an artistry of persuasion; he could weave spells
until your head swam and you woke up writing a four-figure
cheque.) Dennis came bouncing down the stairs; he looked
like a dark colt, kicking up his heels.

"Hullo; I can't believe it's you. What do you want? Have
a Rembrandt? A cigarette? A very old commode used by
Oliver Cromwell?" He ran his eyes over her with the approval
of the expert, the look that he could not help giving to anything
that was decorative.

"When I marry," said Dennis, "I shall marry a woman with
your taste in clothes and your ankles."

"Thank you. Meanwhile my advice on marriage would
be not to."

He looked at her ironically. She was not yet used to the
flame of friendship that was burning now between herself
and the middle Brookfield. His sister Kate was not a close
friend; Mercedes had no close woman friend; she explained
this on the grounds that she had no talent for Ladies-Cloak-
room conversation: lovers, illnesses, superstitions, rumours;
all-girls-together and down with the back hair. Jay Brookfield
was intelligent, but she found that his affected impertinence
became a bore. Dennis had a quality that was lacking in
Jay; it might have been sheer good taste.

She had begun to invite him regularly to Cold Ash for
week-ends, and she had begun to see on Michael's face the
expression that was least reassuring to her; the chilly reserve
worn, as it were, inside out, so that you saw the vulnerable
side first.

"I have just bought a house," Mercedes said.

"Why, you've got one already, greedy," said Dennis.

"This is in Manchester Square."

"You and the Wallace Collection. How does Michael like being moved out of Harley Street?"

"*Ciel*, it is his idea, not mine. I was quite happy living in the flat, above the patients. Not so Mr. K. He wants elbow-room."

Dennis now looked a little stricken, as though a house implied another permanence, a barrier. He was not, she had noticed, entirely comfortable at Cold Ash. Perhaps he thought that she was going to have a baby. She could reassure him on that one, she thought sadly; there would be no more babies. As always, the beginning of the thoughts that led from there brought the tears to her eyes; they were automatic; she could do nothing about them but blink them away, and ask quickly, "Will you help me furnish it? Matching, as far as you can, what we've got already in Harley Street—the Queen Anne stuff?"

"Yes; with pleasure. May I come and see the house?"

"Now? Naturally; I've got my car outside."

"I didn't mean now," he said, "but that would be fun. What an adaptable person you are. Any other woman would say, 'I have an appointment with my hairdresser.' "

"As a matter of fact, I have," said Mercedes. "Will your nice gentleman with the almond eyes cancel it for me?"

"He will. Joseph——" Dennis called, "would you telephone Antoine and say that Mrs. Knowle cannot keep her appointment."

"How did you know it was Antoine?"

"You said so."

"When?"

"I think about three months ago."

"And you remembered."

"I remember everything you say," he replied solemnly. She did not like that. He was asking her how long the visit to the house would take. "Half an hour; the car can bring you back here." She respected his working time-table because she respected all working time-tables. They walked across the pavement to the black Rolls-Royce.

Dennis leaned back in his corner, crossing his knees, folding his arms, watching her.

"For a person who doesn't care for property, you seem to acquire a great deal, don't you, Mercedes?"

"A great deal," she said. "Tyranny, that's what it is. Unless one can afford to hire people to take the impact of the tyranny. And then they themselves turn into possessions. Look at my Miss Haydon."

"Must I?" said Dennis, "she alarms me."

"Nothing alarming about her, darling; she is a reincarnated spaniel."

She saw the look in his face when she called him "darling"; it was a careless habit and she disapproved of it; she disapproved of the drive through the sunny London morning, with the young amiable companion whom she had not yet hurt nor changed as she had hurt and changed Michael. Always, in these days, it was a relief to get away from him; but to be alone was not always enough. Still the old war, she thought, "the powers of darkness within us."

They drove through the park. Dennis was talking about the small modern gallery that his father had just acquired. "If you want an exhibition, it is yours."

"My child, I shall never give another exhibition. When will you realise that I am an idler as well as an amateur?"

"And when will you realise that the difference in our ages is exactly five years, and stop talking as though you were my elderly aunt?"

"I feel terribly like your elderly aunt sometimes. Oh dear," she said, as the house on the corner came in sight, "There it is. I wonder why as soon as I've bought something I always wish I'd bought something else." She stood on the pavement, looking up at the notice-board with "SOLD" stuck across it. "Do you know, at this moment I have, for the first time, a clear picture of the house that I want."

"And what house is that, Aunt Mercedes?"

"It is a very old dilapidated *château-ferme* in the Dauphiné."

"Splendid for Michael's practice," Dennis said. He walked with her through the empty rooms. Their feet echoed on the bare boards. Dennis was busy and interested, making notes, listing some of the pieces already in the Harley Street flat, measuring angles, screwing up his eyes to see the rooms as they would be. The mood drained away from him suddenly, leaving a question unspoken. As they went down to the front door, he stopped on the first-floor landing; he stood still, facing her. She was aware of the atmosphere of dust and sunlight; the smell of an empty house.

"You're not being kind to me, are you?" he asked. "I warn you I shouldn't like it much if you were."

"What do you mean by that?"

"Letting me be near you because you know it's important to me. That is the worst kind of charity."

She thought, "Oh, fool——" and shook her head.

"You're generous," he said, "without discrimination. I have a theory that you'd toss your last gold piece without aiming; it might land in the lap of the rich or the poor."

She said, "I don't make friends out of charity."

"Well then, have I the right to ask what is happening between you and Michael?"

"The right . . . I don't know anything about rights."

"You see, I like Michael," said Dennis sombrely; his face aged as he said it. "But I love you."

"Which isn't a very good idea for you."

"Oh, I'll behave. As long as you want me to. But do you want me to? I can never guess what you're thinking. Can anybody?"

"Perhaps I can't be sure myself."

"Are the things they say true?"

" 'They?' "

"About you and—other men; and Michael not minding?"

She was disgusted; not for herself but for Michael. She heard herself replying coldly, "I am happy to think that I have never heard what 'they' say; I don't concern myself with it. May I give you a piece of advice, Dennis?"

He was red; he looked hurt and defensive. He said, "Go on."

"Never ask that sort of question. It is a prospector's question and as such peculiarly unattractive. When you're older, you'll thank me for that one."

He was silent, walking beside her to the door. Outside the door, he said, "I won't take the car, thanks very much. I'll have a taxi," and grinned at her and took off his hat. "Thank you, Mercedes; I deserved it. And I don't think I'll take on the job of furnishing your house."

"Why not?"

"I'd like to go on being friends with you both. You've just shown me how I can do that; and it isn't by this sort of meeting."

She tried to discover whether she were disappointed or relieved. Her impression was that Michael had won again. Dennis was saying, " You see, I would rather have your friendship than nothing at all."

(If only some of the others had said that. Nevertheless, she was still angry with him; in time she ceased to be angry. She saw him with increasing gentleness; one of the occasions of sin that she had avoided; not entirely, said the examination of conscience, by her own will.)

1932

It was the hottest of summer afternoons and Mercedes quoted from Colette; "Jamais je ne me suis si mal trouvée qu'à ce moment."

She was lying in a long chair, under the shade of the copper-beech tree in the garden at Cold Ash. Everything in sight was wrong. Nothing suited her worse than pain or illness. Her ankle, which the local doctor had strapped tightly, was throbbing like a steam-hammer, and it was stupidly humiliating to lie here alone, with one fat leg. The

guests whom she had assembled for the week-end had turned
suddenly from charming and amusing companions to a gang
of privileged Yahoos. At least, for the moment, they were
elsewhere; obeying her commands to leave her, to go away
and have fun. She thought that Alencz had sent himself a
telegram, he had planned to stay over until Monday; he had
been called away immediately after lunch. He had been
exquisitely courteous in his farewell; he had left the cat sitting
on the balustrade for her diversion. It was his gift, he said, to
Cold Ash. She looked sadly at the small stone shape; the
perfect replica of Saki, the Siamese. Exactly like Alencz to
have made this and to have brought it here three days after
Saki's death. The fluid Alencz; she saw him, with his smooth
black hair and his bright blue eyes—"and all the durable
quality, all the solid content, of an empty meringue-case,"
said Mercedes.

She went on mourning Saki. Michael, she thought, would
be sad, though he had always preferred the moon-faced tabby.
Joe the tabby was, in theory, Michael's cat; just as Saki had
been hers, but Joe had gradually deserted the house for the
fields and the farm. Saki and Joe belonged to an easier state
of affairs than the present.

Now Mercedes kept saying in her mind, "We must put an
end to this," and gazing at the cat, and thinking that she
might more sensibly take up the stick beside her, hobble into
the house and let her maid help her to bed. But that was too
much of an effort. It was easier to lie here and be miserable.
By the convent's rules, she should have offered up her pain
and Saki's death and the problem of Michael, in one of those
pathetically silly human parcels that the Lord had infinite
patience in unwrapping. But not now; not here. Now one just
lay, feeling weak and cross and sad by turns.

The copper-beech tree's shadow made a wavy margin upon
the grass; it fell just short of the balustrade; in the sunlight
every blot of lichen and mottling of the stone was visible.
The little cat shone, a wise Egyptian shape. The stone from
which it was carved had a crystalline surface; the famous

double line of Alencz's chisel, his trade-mark, brought out the curve of the haunch and the folded tail; it was the essence of cat. It made her remember:

"Cats, no less liquid than their shadows,
    offer no angles to the wind."

The last person whom she expected to see coming round the corner of the terrace was Michael. He had said that he could not come down this week-end. Work was Michael's life; he was no less diligent now than he had been at twenty-two. Despite the brilliance of his success he still took pains.

He waved to her and walked across the lawn, looking out of place in his London clothes; formal and a stranger on his own property. He was the well-dressed, assured version of the boy in the shabby jacket; the dreamer whose dreams had come true (God help him).

He said, "Hullo. I didn't expect to find you alone." He looked down at her foot. "What have you been doing to yourself?"

"I slipped; on the steps going down to the kitchen-garden." She wanted to add, "A humiliating performance," and go on to talk of something else, but she found that she had said, "God, I'm so miserable," coming almost to the point of tears.

"Is it hurting you? You look rather white. What fool strapped it up like that, anyway?" Michael asked, placidly sitting on the end of the long chair and examining the dressing. He laid gentle fingers on the swelling above and below the plaster. "I'll have to take all this off," he said after a moment. "We'd better go in. Can you manage with that stick or would you like me to carry you?"

She said, "Don't be kind to me, or I shall burst into tears. Saki's dead."

"Oh no. . . . What happened?"

"He got himself into a trap, poor darling idiot. And there sits Alencz's portrait of him and I don't think I can bear it."

Michael looked as though he were going to say something

sweet, then he glanced at her and said briskly, "You are having a gay day, aren't you?" He took the cat off the balustrade and put it in his pocket. "Where is everybody? Why are you alone? What have you done with la Haydon?"

"I sent her out for the afternoon; she gets so enormous when she's sympathetic."

"And your party? Alencz?"

"Alencz left; he doesn't respond well to trouble. The others have driven over to Rye. I trust they drown."

Michael helped her into the house. He had to carry her up the stairs, and this was humiliating also; to be carried and laid on her bed like a parcel. She thought she could bear the pain more easily than she could bear his thoughtful efficiency; she did not want to be glad that he was here.

The room felt cool, but her head swam, making it recede down watery corridors; the carved ceiling, the long yellow curtains and the cheval glass; the roses; the Utrillo street-scene on the opposite wall. She saw the maid, Louise, coming and going, bringing the things that Michael needed. She could hear the click of the scissors and feel the cold spirit trickling down. Michael's voice went on. "Good God, the amount of Barbola work he's put in. It shouldn't be strapped. You want cold water dressings on it until the swelling goes down. He ought to be shot. Take a deep breath, deep as you can; sorry, Mercedes, I've got to get it off."

The pain grew hot and ate inwards, becoming enormous, so that you no longer knew where it was, if you were drawing away from it or pushing at it with your full strength.

She heard Michael say, "*All* right." He got up and came to stand by the head of the bed, with his fingers on her pulse. She was cold and sick; the touch of those fingers was heavy; Michael's voice reached her ears through a beginning of deafness, with her own voice saying, "I am going to faint."

"Let's have the brandy," Michael said over his shoulder to Louise. "You think of everything," she muttered, vaguely observing the bottle, the Normandin brandy from the side-board downstairs. She had just enough energy left to be cross with herself while she let him hold the glass at her lips and afterwards bathe her face. He knew that this was a further humiliation; he sent the fussy Louise out of the room; his manner became every moment more paternal and matter-of-fact. He held her until the sickness and the shivering passed. She said, "Thank you. Better. I apologise, but you did hurt me. You can continue with your butchery."

"This part is quite gentlemanly," said Michael; he folded a towel under her foot and began to lay the cold compresses over it; he turned the sheet back tidily. "You'll oblige me by staying where you are until to-morrow morning; and then I'll drive you up and we'll have it X-rayed."

"X-rayed. Such a fuss."

"Well, you may have broken one of the small bones. What were you doing, playing football?"

She laughed. "I tell you; I was going down the steps to the kitchen-garden."

He stood beside her in his shirt-sleeves, looking down at her, still the doctor with the patient, she thought sadly.

"What I should like to do," he said, "is to give you some aspirin and see you try to sleep."

"Not yet; don't go."

(This is absurd, she thought; the old unanswerable words were coursing past as clearly as though she saw them written on the wall:

> "Now at the last gasp of Love's latest breath,
>   When, his pulse failing, Passion speechless lies,
>   When Faith is kneeling by his bed of death
>   And innocence is closing up his eyes;
>   —Now, if thou wouldst, when all have given him over,
>   From death to life, thou might'st him yet recover."

But this was only a revulsion born of weakness, of the moment, of the fact that he had been there to help her.)

"You don't feel like talking," he said.

"I think I do. Give me a little more brandy. Why did you come down to-day?"

"I got restless. I wanted to see you."

"What did you do last night?"

"Do you really want to know?"

"Yes."

"I dined at the French Horn," he said.

She was silent. Then she said, "I think I had better go away, Michael."

"Yes," he said, looking at the floor. "Probably you are right. But I'm not sure it is the best moment to discuss it." He went over to the chair where he had hung his coat; he put it on, taking the Alencz cat out of his pocket. "Do you want this where you can look at it, or does it make you sad?"

"Anywhere," she said and saw him fondling it for a moment, taking obvious pleasure in its beauty, before he set it down.

"You see, Michael, I can't go on doing this to you; as long as I stay, I am keeping you in doubt, making you believe that some day it will be all right again."

She had said this before; they had said it all before. Now he came to sit in the chair beside the bed; his self-control was very clear to her; if she painted this portrait, you would see patience in every line of it.

She said, "We have tried to compromise too long. If you would forget my scruples and divorce me——"

"I could have done that," he said reflectively, "five years ago; at least it looks as though I could, from here. But it is easy to acquire a perspective. I live more and more in the past."

She said, "We had bad luck."

"I wonder."

"Wonder what?"

"If the child would have made any difference."

"It would have anchored me. You know that," she muttered. He put his hand on hers. (Absurd also that after nine years the thought of the baby should still make me cry; that thing happens so often, to so many people, and still remains the saddest thing.) She looked back and saw, with the perspective of which he had spoken, that there had been two ways then; the way of acceptance and the restless way. "Ours," she thought, "is the most conventional story. For you the channelled, orderly life; the course that I embraced so eagerly and tired of so soon. And boredom opens the door to the devil more quickly than anything else I know. *'Come in, sir; sit down. I've been looking forward to your visit so much.'* " She shut her eyes.

"Yes; you're right. One acquires a perspective. It is easy to see now that the whole of our future depended on an act of will; an act that I couldn't bring myself to make."

"Oh, you tried."

"Not very hard."

"And this becomes untidy," he said, frowning abstractedly. "If I were an ascetic person, it need not; we could still go on in our polite way."

"So you want me to go."

He smiled at her.

"Yes," she said, "that was a stupid thing to say."

"As far as divorce goes," Michael said, "I can't see it. Marriage will always mean you."

This, too, he had said before. This talk was following the pattern of the other talks; it was no different. ("Except that it is the last. *Ora pro nobis.*")

1939

Mercedes came into the drawing-room of the Newells' house on Commonwealth Avenue and saw Michael waiting. He presented an untroubled profile; he was standing by the window, his shoulder turned to the wide sunny street, with the ripple of cars going by. He was reading a book.

"Hullo, there," she said at the door.

They had not met for nearly three years. He gave her the old impression of tranquillity; a more middle-aged tranquillity now; his hair was much greyer; she still had the feeling that she might have been looking at her own forehead. He shut

the book and said, "These are charming. Yours?" She saw
that it was the volume of verse by Sheila Wingfield.

She said, "Yes. The first one is the best. Odysseus Dying."

"I liked that and liked this; here——" He turned the pages.

> " 'Cease your wooing: you should know
>   Warm Daphne cannot be remade
>   Out of the dark laurel shade.' "

It was appropriate, she thought, to themselves and their
meeting; but he sounded extremely placid about it.

"You look very well," he said.

"I am. Apart from the harassing imbecilities of the company,
my life is peaceful."

"The theatrical company? You were never going to do
another piece of work for the stage."

"Well, you know me. I got carried away."

"Are you going to lunch with me?"

"I ordered lunch here. The Newells are out. Have some
sherry?"

"Your fondness for playing hostess in other people's houses,"
said Michael, grinning. "No thank you, my dear. I still don't
drink in the middle of the day."

"Nor do I."

"Here you are," he said, putting his hand in his pocket.
"I brought the cat."

"Thank you." She turned it over in her hands. "Beautiful
job," she said; "he had talent, that nasty little man."

She looked up from it to see Michael gazing at her. "What
made you want it suddenly? You, who have no use for
things." He appeared to put a capital "T" on the word.

"Oh, anything small," she said vaguely. "Anything that
one can carry. And I always loved this. Lately I've been
missing it."

"Whims," said Michael.

"Shall we go into lunch?"

The dining-room had dark-panelled walls; large, august
pieces of silver stood on the sideboard; there was a wreathed

and apparently snarling candelabra in the middle of the table. They talked his shop and hers until the servant had brought the coffee.

"Now," said Michael, lighting a cigarette, "you had better know, first as last, that I've no intention of letting Cold Ash become a refugee training ground."

"So you indicated in your letter."

"Let us get rid of it once and for all."

("I wonder, when he says that, does he remember, as I do, our writing the names with the diamond?") She said, "This would be getting rid of it once and for all."

"No, Mercedes, it wouldn't. They can't afford to buy the place. You'll be living in France. I refuse to have it dragging on, with myself acting landlord to an impoverished bunch of voluntary workers."

"Not very charitable, are you?"

He said, "I owe myself an occasional dose of consideration; as you pointed out to me, a long time ago."

"As I pointed out," she said, reflecting that on all occasions he could give these opinions back to her: "You taught me," "You said," "As you once phrased it." There was no blame implied; it was the obstinate avowal, the obstinate fidelity; tribute to the creator from the finished work. But this seemed to her no longer valid; it was long since she had grown tired of the creation; the work had gone on and finished itself.

He said, "You are happier in France than anywhere, aren't you?"

"It is the place where I must be, if war comes."

"Yes; I see that. And——" he hesitated, "you are at peace in your mind now?"

("As much at peace as I shall ever be; there was once a devil that plagued me, but he has been driven out over the years; exorcized in solitude and wisdom and indifference—but I do not say that to Michael. I say, Oh yes; and you?")

"Very much at peace." He took a walnut from the dish in front of him and cracked it; she watched his neat fingers

327

peeling the brown skin; he began to whistle softly; the hackneyed tune.

"Not only peaceful, but gay," she thought. "You like what
is on your mind."

"My dear," he said, "this is more difficult than I expected."

"Why is it difficult? I have heard—one does hear—one
can't help hearing—rumours. Are they true?"

"Yes."

She said, "Then the battle is over, isn't it?"

He said, "I told you that I would never fall in love again;
and that was true. This love came gradually. If I say that
what I felt for her in the beginning was an emotion that had
something fatherly in it, I suppose that you will retort, 'Un
brave petit coup d'inceste, quoi?' "

"No," she said, "I don't say things like that any
more."

"Or my professional love for looking after people. Call it
that if you like." ("I never wanted to be looked after; did I?")

He said, "I haven't behaved well about it. But this can't go
on. She is too important. And I have changed. I love her. She
has brought me as much happiness as I thought that I could
ever have. I want to marry her, Mercedes."

"Yes," she thought about it. "Well, I cannot stop you. I
don't want to; I've told you that you can divorce me any time
you like. I am the sinner. I refuse to assume a virtue and pretend to be a wronged wife. I fell out of love; I shut the bedroom
door on you. I broke up your home. I don't approve of divorce,
as you know. But I shall never marry again, in any case. It is
all right with me, Michael."

"But now," he said, "I am in your case. I refuse to assume
a virtue. The King's Proctor would intervene, anyway. I
couldn't divorce you now."

She said quickly, "I don't like this," and sat still, smoking,
watching him through the smoke.

"Does she know my views about it?"

"You are never discussed between us. You never have been."

"Isn't that a mistake?"

"It is a literal impossibility for me. You know me when I cannot talk; you should know."

Yes; I know; I drove you to those silences, she thought, looking at the shape of his head and shoulders against the window.

"I don't like this," she said again. "There are two things I don't like. The insincerities and subterfuges of the English divorce court are horribly unattractive to me. But I suppose I've lost the right to wince at them. The other thing, and this, I suppose, is not my business, seems to me dangerous for you both. You should be able to talk to her about me."

He shook his head, dumbly.

"Michael, it is foolish. You have let me become a haunt, an obsession."

"I know I have."

"It isn't worthy of you."

"No, my dear. In the last ten years I have done a number of things that are not worthy."

"Blaming me?"

"Of course not. I do not place my sins, to use your language, on other people's souls."

"Does she know that we are meeting to discuss this?"

"No; I haven't told her that you are in Boston. She knows I am going to the Mass General and that's all."

"But Michael, she isn't here, with you?"

"Yes," he said after a moment.

She was, to her own surprise, shocked. She got up from the table. "This is impossible; why did you do it?"

"I had to see you. I wouldn't leave her alone in New York."

"You could have told me that we couldn't meet here. You could have telephoned; written; anything."

She wandered to the sideboard and stood contemplating the silver pieces.

"You will tell her, at least?"

He said calmly, "I shall try."

She thought, "Why do I hate it so much? The honesty that you had; a long time ago. Did I debauch that, or have the

329

years debauched it? These years of drifting, maintaining my integrity and, apparently, damaging yours. While I refused to take the way that you offered me, in your persistence of quixotic chivalry, what was happening to you?"

She looked back at him; he sat watching her, with his chin on his hand.

"Very well, Michael. As the expedient way out of what seems to me now a very untidy business, I'll come to England and file my petition; on my way to France in June."

"Thank you." He looked at his watch.

"You're still in a hurry," she said laughing.

"I apologise. I have to be there at half-past two. One more thing."

"Yes?"

"Do you remember telling me that it wasn't necessary to like people; that it was only necessary to love them at a distance?"

"Simple Christian ethic," she said.

"I am learning to love you at a distance. And I always shall. Good-bye, Mercedes."

JUNE, 1939

She met Dennis in the smallest dining-room at the Berkeley Hotel, the little room with only a few tables in it, where Louis the tiny maître d'hotel, fussed over his cherished clients. The music was sounding from the ballroom through the alcove. Dennis at thirty-four, hawkish and benevolent, still recalled to her the velvety-eyed young man who had loved her once. He was saying, turning his long-stemmed glass in his hand.

"Well, dear, I couldn't begin to draw you an unbiased portrait of Caroline; nor give her a certificate of reliability as Michael's future wife. You see, I happen to be in love with her myself."

"I suppose the appropriate reply to that would be 'it's a small world'," she said at last.

"Damned small," said Dennis. " No room in it for Michael and me. Wherever I turn, he's got there first."

She did not want to revive the old, unfinished story. She said quickly, "At least you can tell me if she is a loving person. That is the only thing that seems to me to matter for Michael."

"I should say that her talent for loving amounted to an artistic gift," said Dennis bitterly. "The fact that I don't approve the place where she chooses to practise it is something else again."

"What does she look like?"

He laughed at her. Really, Mercedes. . . . And I always credited you with qualities above the average woman's."

"Any lady," said Mercedes, "would want to know."

"All right, dear. She has green eyes, curly hair and high cheekbones. Her mouth is too big and her legs are too long; she swears like a Billingsgate porter and she is without exception the most heavenly creature I ever saw. And I hope that she falls into a deep river, wearing heavy boots. Now it's my turn. Why are you two divorcing at last?"

"There comes a time——" she said.

"Too bad it didn't come before."

1948

The woman sitting alone by the fire saw the dead figures disappear. They were so greatly dead that all this might have happened a hundred years ago. A world had died since. She found that she was remembering,

> "*Quand vous serez bien vieille, au soir, à la chandelle,*
> *Assise auprès du feu, devidant et filant. . . .*"

"No," she said sharply to the echo, "I am not an old woman. I am simply a person who has gone through changes; who should have died, perhaps; because the only life that looks real to me now is the life that I led in France during the war. The rest of it, Michael and marriage, the eternal restless leisure of having enough money, enough time—all that seems to me like a story told by a spoilt child.

"Even such toys as a bottle of Normandin brandy, a personal maid, a black Rolls-Royce, a suite at the Carlton, a *soufflé-à-la-Mercedes*; they turn into historical annotations. Some time, not far ahead, there will be chroniclers who will find interest in recording these trivia; they will be as comically indicative as the wigs and patches of another century."

It was a tiring reflection; as tiring as the impact of the New World, when she woke before dawn and thought, in her half-dream. "Who killed me and reincarnated me here?" After a few minutes, she would become aware of the truth, of the life of the ranch outside the windows. She would know, rising to prepare her breakfast, that this was the factual present; that Mercedes Knowle was now a middle-aged woman in poor health; she had her niche in the Adams family, her uses as arbiter, children's companion, old friend.

It was a situation as comfortable as she could expect; it was fortunate. She would remind herself of the benefits, adding, "And you guaranteed your independence when you put what was left of your money into the ranch itself; achieving this roof and this much solitude."

"*What was left of your money.*" A startling phrase. She had had an endless purse, a glorious immunity from the sad, universal plague of counting the cost. At first it had been difficult to realise that the immunity was ended, to go down and explore the unknown regions where the inhabitants looked at prices before they bought. Now she had almost acquired the habit.

There was that unfamiliar thing. There was the sense of being on the wrong side of the map; hearing Europe spoken of as a poor sick relation who, mercifully, lived a long way off. Europe, a place that must be saved, that needed too much saving, that was subject to a mysterious political disease. (Nothing to do with war, of course; merely a plague; a plague called Socialism, whose tertiary symptom, Communism, would soon develop. This had slowed up Europe's production and made its efforts puny. This had presumably laid its towns flat, starved its land, weakened its children. Sometimes, when listening to American conversation, it was possible to think that Europeans had bombed themselves for fun.)

She was aware now that she had begun to think her morning thoughts at evening. You could only think that way before you remembered that you were now a part of the American pattern. She had detached herself from it as the other Mercedes came to life for a little while.

The other Mercedes. . . . And her successor who fought for France? Where was she, the tough crusader responsible for this wrecked body? Absent to-night. There was only the image of the younger person who had failed.

"Then on my tongue the taste is sour
Of all I ever did."

CHAPTER FOUR

It was like the country of a dream, Caroline thought, haphazardly beautiful. On either side of the road there were orchards, with avenues of flat brown earth running between the straight groves; the speed at which you travelled made these avenues flicker past your eyes, each avenue taking the past one's place, a narrow shaft with the sky at the end of it, and another, and another, moving like the spokes of a wheel. There were no leaves on the trees; but the blossom had begun to break. Where the irrigation-trenches were dug the sky reflected in the watery channels so that you saw narrow blue seas and brown islands. There was an orchard whose every tree was coloured aquamarine; it looked like an expensive fantasy in the window of a New York florist's; it was the magic result of a disinfectant spray.

The roads were straight and wide. The signs of human life were scattered, never crowding but always obvious; one-storeyed wooden houses, white or brown; gas-stations; huge, sudden advertisement-hoardings; tin mailboxes perched on posts; small notice-boards telling of eggs or dried fruit or dogs for sale.

The tallest things that came in sight were the graceful, ragged groups of eucalyptus trees; the palm trees were shorter and their growth of old leaves, turned into thatch below the waving green, suggested a dingy fur; more animal than vegetable. All the colours were sudden and violent; a yellow spread of mustard flowers; a border of Californian poppies, a low bush garlanded with blossom that was dark red; blazing oranges heaped on a stall; the gold fruit that hung from a lemon tree in a garden.

Caroline had left Monterey before nine; an early-morning drive that would end the pilgrimage at the awkward hour of eleven o'clock. No time to arrive, she thought; the worst time for joining on to somebody else's day. At evening you would dovetail in with drinks and dinner and conversation, and your hosts would have become used to the idea of you by the time that they woke next morning. "But at least this doesn't suggest that I expect to stay the night; I am on my way to San Francisco; that's my story and I stick to it."

The road turned westward now and the mountain became a barrier at the road's end. It made a green wall, a long horizon without peaks.

She could not yet take her rendezvous seriously; she was too much at company with the landscape and the enormous sky. There was a joy in this lonely drive that made the small things sharply important, beseeching her eyes to remember the look of the turkey-buzzard's wing-feathers as he sailed overhead; to keep the image of the brown dog running off the highway, to recall the slow-moving shape of the woman with the bundle, and the child who plodded behind her.

She came to the town. It was built on a hill. It was smaller than she had expected it to be. These streets met in a triangle, enclosing a little park planted with trees; a pompous white archway led into the park. There was the Fir Tree Inn, that was not an inn, but a tea-shop with tables set in the window. The little park intervened between this place and a garage opposite; she looked up the short Main Street, seeing a "Buy and Save" Market, a red-brown building that was a bank. She found it necessary to receive the impact of this place, to be aware of the cold wind and the sunlight, the triangle of streets, the green mountain-barrier rising behind the town.

"This is it; I am here."

She locked the car and went into the Fir Tree Inn; she sat down at a table near the window and ordered a cup of coffee. The waitress said that to get to Mrs. Adams' place, you drove up Main Street and turned right, on to the mountain road. It was about five miles away; you would see the name on the mail-box.

As she lifted her cup, Caroline saw her hand tremble and jeered, "Aren't you making this a little too important?" But the retort came from further inside her mind: "No. How could you be? It is important; it always was. You could say, if you liked, that there was a path you began to walk nearly five years ago. Shut your eyes and you can see the beginning of the path; the brown carpet on the floor of the officers' ante-room in Edinburgh. You can see your feet, in flat Army shoes, pacing the brown carpet while Mitchell brings you a packet of Players and a cup of tea with sugar in it."

"But it is absurd to think that the path has led to this place; or indeed that there is a traceable path at all. That was the beginning of my journey away from Michael. I had no destination. I wandered in limbo; a limbo conveniently framed by war. Gradually, time righted me to an acceptance of loneliness. Only a half-acceptance, perhaps. There was the moment when I thought that I could marry Dennis."

"You didn't really interrupt the pattern, even then."

"Because I had no time to interrupt the pattern; they killed Dennis first. I might have changed; had children; become a different me. As it is, I seem not to have moved since. Nor have I grown wise, nor learned anything new, except in my work. That is the only lively satisfaction. But I still have fun," she said, as though to reassure Dennis and Michael. "This is just a selfish piece of fun."

"Oh, yes? Is that why your hand shakes and you feel a little cold inside? You are coming to the Dark Tower."

"On a destined journey? All my eye. Nothing but my own obstinacy has set me here, in Saratoga, Calif., at a quarter past eleven on Saturday, February 28th, 1948; in a car that doesn't belong to me, and without a driver's licence. Ask Jay what he thinks about it. He'll have found my note by now."

She looked at the little park outside the window, at the white archway, at the garage on the other side of the street. The sense of a dream was over. The diminishing of her courage came quickly. "And Jay is right; this isn't an easy thing to do; or a wise one."

"You can still dodge it," she reminded herself. "Get back on to the Highway, drive down to Monterey; forget the whole idea."

She spoke aloud, "Budge says the Fiend. Budge not, says my conscience. Except that in this case, I don't know which is my conscience and which is the Fiend."

The waitress came hurrying from the other end of the room. "I'm sorry," Caroline said, "I was talking to myself; it is a habit of mine." She paid the check and walked out, standing still beside the car to light a cigarette and give herself a last chance. She quoted Jay; Jay arguing reasonably before he lost his temper. "Isn't this rather too artificial a complication to invite? As though you had built yourself a house and found peace in it, and now decided to see how it felt to pull the whole structure down on your head?

She said to that, "But, don't forget, the moment that I've gone back on the decision, I'll start seeing it again from the other side of the counter and wishing I'd held to it. That's the way it always goes."

"Come on," she said, "what's the worst that can happen anyway?"

She climbed into the car and drove up Main Street; it petered out quickly and became a lane of small houses, each in a garden. In some of the gardens there were lemon and orange trees; there was a white Catholic church on the left.

The road began to curve upward; it forked and there was a sign here, reading "Boulder Creek; Santa Cruz." That road went to the left; hers to the right. She passed a stone quarry, a big greyish wooden building like a mill.

Now the mountain wall on her left, the foothills on her right, began to close in; the crowding trees, groves of fir and redwood, some trees still bare and smoke-grey against the green, cut off the sunshine; the road crossed and recrossed a winding river. She came out of a tunnel of shade and felt her ears click from the height; going up, going on, she saw loops of road and the forest crowding; the white walls of another low bridge.

On the right-hand side of the road, just beyond the bridge, there was a metal sign reading, "State Highway 9," black letters on a white ground, with the black emblem, the Californian bear, above. Caroline braked here, looking ahead; at the bridge and the sign, the towering trees on either side, the short stretch of road before the next curve.

> " 'Burningly it came on me all at once,
> This was the place! . . . ' "

She drove past the sign and saw the mail-box with the name Wynstay Adams painted on it. The gate was set back from the road and behind the gate the drive went down steeply among the trees. She drove on, down the green tunnel, letting the words of the poem keep her company.

> "For, what with my whole world-wide wandering,
> What with my search drawn out thro' years, my hope
> Dwindled into a ghost not fit to cope."

It was a rough, narrow way, and after it had dropped, it sloped up again at the same steep angle. High up on her right, she saw a glimpse of rooftops through the trees, but the drive slanted away to the left. She followed it; it levelled out; on her left now there was a clearing, and a trail leading away through the trees.

Caroline leaned out of the car, looking down the trail; she thought that she saw a figure move on the pattern of branches and sunlight. Yes, there was somebody coming now, whistling as he came; he was whistling *Loch Lomond*.

In the middle of the trail, dazzled with light and shadow, she saw Michael coming towards her; a living man. He was walking with his head bent; she saw only the white hair brushed back, the sharp curve of the forehead, the set of his shoulders and the easy, youthful walk as he whistled his tune.

> "Oh, you'll take the high road
> and I'll take the low road——"

The tune broke; the figure halted in the clearing, turned to face down the trail and now whistled two long, calling notes. It was not a man; it was a woman wearing lumberjack's clothes, a dark blue shirt, trousers and heavy shoes. She stood still, waiting, with her back to the car and to Caroline.

There was an answering whistle; a boy and a girl dodged out of the trees, two children with fair untidy hair; all three turned towards the drive.

"Hullo," Caroline said.

Now she saw that the look of Michael stopped short below the temples; the woman had large dark eyes, a short nose and a small chin. For a moment her expression did not change; the whole face seemed stony and vigilant. Then she smiled.

"Can I help you? Were you looking for somebody?" The voice was impersonal; mellow and of medium pitch, with a British accent.

"I was looking for the house; for Mrs. Adams," Caroline said.

"Straight on and then left where the drive forks. Don't take the right, that goes all the way up the hill to the farm."

338

Caroline said, "If you're going to the house, would you like a lift?"

"No, thank you. We're going the other way."

ii

Lee Adams was sitting in the study working on the proofs of Wynstay's memoir, when Dan put his head round the door. He looked as though he were asphyxiating.

"Mother, *Caroline Seward's* here!"

"Say that again slowly," said Lee.

"Looking so stunning she'll knock your hat off. Gosh," he said, "she's even better in slacks than in orchids. What's the matter with you? You don't seem a bit excited. She's on her way to San Francisco and she's got nothing to do all day and she can stay to lunch."

"Well, isn't that perfectly fine? Do you happen to know where Mercedes is this morning?"

"I don't. With the children, I guess. Oh, come *along*; what does it matter where Mercedes is?"

"You'd be surprised," Lee said bitterly. She went out and found Caroline on the patio, playing with the police-dog. "Hi," she said, trying to sound pleased; Dan's enthusiasm was understandable. Caroline looked as an actress on vacation should look. (Miss Seward relaxes in a tailored suit of light green corduroy, with a primrose shirt and socks to match.) She held out her hands to Lee. "Do you mind? I saw Saratoga on a signpost and it was too much for me."

"Of course I don't mind. Glad to see you." ("And in a sense," Lee thought, "that's true. Your first impression is still endearing. But don't think I wouldn't love to wring your neck.")

"A drink?" Dan fussed: "What would you like, Miss Seward?"

"Oh, a soft one," she said, "Any thing you've got." He vanished and Lee said, "Now, did you come to see Mercedes?

Is that the idea? Because if you did, I warn you you're leading with your chin."

Caroline took a cigarette-case from her pocket, lit a cigarette and said, "Well; it was a temptation; and I tempt easily. I suppose you are angry with me."

"I'm too surprised to be angry. I didn't think you'd do this."

"Well, there it is. Before anything else, you'd better know I've seen her."

"The hell you have. Where?"

"In the drive."

"You would. Did you introduce yourselves?"

"No. But I knew." She lay full length on one of the long chairs. "Somebody might have told me she looked like Michael."

Lee stared at her. "Like Michael? Yes, I believe she does. More so, I guess, since her hair turned grey. Same pattern of skull. Well, what did that do to you?"

"It hasn't taken yet. For a moment it was violently disturbing; then it turned into a kind of dream."

Dan came back with a tray and glasses; he established himself as near to the long chair as he could. He kept his eyes faithfully upon Caroline, shooting questions at her; rhapsodising over *The Grape and the Vine*; using three matches to light every cigarette; stepping on the dog; asking about the Old Vic and expounding his passion for Shakespeare. Caroline, Lee admitted, was good with him. She talked to him on equal terms. At least success had given her no affectations of voice or manner. Watching her, Lee found the vulnerable young woman of no reputation who had lunched with her in Boston long ago. Nor did she look much older; her face in repose was a little thinner and a little more serious. She had acquired a placid and almost masculine assurance; a detachment that reminded Lee suddenly of Mercedes. "That's funny; no, it isn't. These people who lived in the middle of war, they'll differ from us forever," Lee thought, "and if Wyn had come back he would have been like them." She said, "Dan, I don't want to break this up, but since Caroline's here, I would like her to look at that English chapter in proof. Good idea?"

"Good idea——" he said reluctantly.

Lee took Caroline through the living-room into the study, waiting while Caroline looked around. "Heavenly room," she said—"All horns and hides. Couldn't like it more."

"Wyn liked it; he built it. Remember the study in the Charles River Square house? I've transplanted some of it." Caroline stood looking up at Wyn's portrait. "Dan's a ringer for him, isn't he?" Lee said; "Now; don't worry about the proofs for now; I'd love to have you look at that chapter later if you've time. But it wasn't really the point."

"No," said Caroline, "I didn't imagine it was." She perched on the arm of a chair and hugged one knee. She looked up, slant-eyed.

"Let's have it," she said.

"You oughtn't to try to see her, Caroline."

"Shan't we meet anyway, at lunch?"

Lee said, "No. She eats in her own house. She's got a standing invitation to come up here, but she doesn't make use of it unless I twist her arm. Which I don't propose to do to-day." She looked at Caroline, who continued to rest her chin on her knee; looking thoughtful and unconvinced.

"What's your motive, anyway? Sheer curiosity?"

"You might call it that." Her expression changed; she looked oddly frozen and guarded. It was a look that Lee did not know.

"But why? You weren't in the least curious about her last year; when we met in New York. You didn't even care to know why I have her living here. What's changed your mind?"

"Proximity." She raised her head and said in a rougher voice—"Why *do* you have her here?"

"I'll tell you. I owe her a lot; I owe her this place for a start. After Wyn died, I thought of selling it; then I tried to hang on because of the kids. By '46 I was well in the red. Mercedes offered to go in with me. She's put what remains of her capital in here; and taken the little house on the property in exchange. It's the only roof she's got; you knew she'd lost nearly everything?"

"I know nothing about her," said Caroline.

"Well, that isn't all. She got the two families, her refugees, to come and work here for next to nothing. They're French and German; so you can guess without my telling you how well they mix. Mercedes keeps all that under control; I couldn't. And she does a good job with their kids."

"How simply spiffing," said Caroline moodily.

"This place works now," said Lee. "It ain't no Shangri-La, but it works. I've been able to give my son-in-law a job running the chicken-farm; and a home to Marilyn and her babies. My brother Charles, who's still a problem child at forty-eight, keeps off the bottle managing the business-end of things here and doing odd jobs. And we're beginning to make money; we're a self-supporting unit; we market the fruit as well as the poultry and eggs. That means, among other things, that Jean can keep on at school and Dan can finish at Stanford. See? We've got something here. This place is our life, Caroline."

She stopped. She was conscious of the overtone behind her words; the warning note. "We're a happy family, keep out." She thought that it was also a little smug; she said hurriedly, "That's to give you a picture of the set-up; to show why Mercedes is important around here."

"I get it," Caroline said; her voice non-committal.

"And I don't know if you realise that she's still a sick woman."

"What is the matter with her?"

"Oh, she'll never be well again. They claim to have cured her of T.B., but I doubt it. And she has a tricky kind of anæmia; she gets a recurrent headache that lays her out completely and makes her no good for anything. Result of malnutrition and the other pretty experiences. They might easily have killed someone younger. She's fifty. She's tough."

Caroline slid off the chair. She said, in her most off-hand manner, "It's an imperial build-up. Know what it's doing to me? Putting me back to the days when I used to call her Rich Bitch and Spoiler-of-the-Fun." She paced the floor. "Funny. I haven't felt this coming over me for years. The mood is not unlike finding an old dress hanging in the wardrobe and trying it on."

"Don't try it on. Damn it, you're on top of the world at the moment, and it's a different story for her."

Caroline raised one eyebrow; her expression was comically disbelieving as though Lee had just said something too outrageous to be borne. Then there was the frozen look again. She said, "One thing more. Does she ever talk about me?"

"Never. Nor of Michael. Nor of anything that she's done in the last ten years. She's settled for this existence and she might never have had another. I figure she's got more that she'd like to forget than most people have."

"And those things would include me?"

"Well, possibly, they'd include you."

"I see."

"I guess I'm only asking you to have pity on her," Lee said.

"*Pity?* Would she thank me for that? Would anybody?"

"No," Lee snapped, "I meant pity in your heart. And, to descend from that high plane in a sharp, vertical nose-dive, you might spare a touch of pity for me. What kind of fun do you imagine I'd have introducing Michael's widow to the gal who got there next? My working knowledge of Emily Post wouldn't help me much."

Caroline giggled.

"And, postscript, I have to live with Mercedes afterwards. You don't."

CHAPTER FIVE

"You've got rather too much paint on your brush," Charles said. "See where all those drips are running down? Paint them out now or they'll turn solid. Here, I'll do it for you."

Caroline pulled off the gloves that were stiff with old paint;

she lit a cigarette. Charles bent meticulously to the task; he looked something like Lee, but all Lee's features had slipped a little and his forehead was excessive, his eyes prominent, his nose spoon-shaped, like a duck's bill. It was a cockyolly-bird's face; it might have been perched on the handle of an umbrella.

In front of him the liver-coloured chest of drawers looked odd, piebald with the beginning of its white shroud. So did Charles's own temporarily-deserted task, a dresser. Marilyn, Lee's elder daughter, was engaged upon the second of a row of three chairs. The garage-floor was spread with dust-sheets; the paint-pots and brushes were lined up on a trestle-table. Lee was doubtless wondering why she had let herself be enlisted for this chore. Caroline strolled out into the sunshine. She looked down at the orchard, guessing at the positions of the main house, the white guest-house and the pool. These were all out of sight; directly opposite her there rose the green mountain wall. She had learned that the new cottage awaited the Germans, that the cottage beyond the fence was the Dufaillys' property; there was one more thing that she needed to know. She turned back.

"No need to go on, if you're bored with it," Charles said.

"I'm not bored. It is the sort of thing I like doing."

"Mean that? Lee calls me a slave-driver."

"You're a perfectionist," said Caroline, "which probably amounts to the same thing."

She picked up the brush and dipped it more carefully, drawing it with long strokes across the brown surface. She made a casual work of saying, "Oh—tell me. Where is Mrs. Knowle's house? Up here or down below?"

"Down below. Have you been to the pool yet?"

"I know where it is."

"Well, the house is about two hundred yards east of the pool; no, nearer two-fifty. There's a gravel path that goes past the dressing-rooms. You follow that; then you'll see the house on your left. The path divides." He went on giving instruc-tions. Marilyn said lazily, "Uncle Charles has a passion for detail. He'll draw you a map any minute." Looking at her,

Caroline remembered the self-assured sixteen-year-old in the Boston drawing-room. Married and mother of two children, she did not look much more than sixteen now. She wore her fair hair long and she was dressed in a scarlet blouse and blue jeans. Charles strolled towards her.

"How's it coming?"

"I'll thank you to keep away."

"You don't seem to me to have enough undercoat on this one."

"Between ourselves, Uncle Charles, I don't have any at all. I forgot to put it on."

"You're no good," he said disgustedly. "Your husband did a far better job on the highboy."

"I was born without zeal," said Marilyn.

Dan came up through the vegetable-garden. He said, "Hi," and stopped in the doorway. Charles said, "You're blocking the light."

He came in and stood beside Caroline; the duplicate of Wynstay; he had the small neat body and short neck, the soft eyes and monkeyish grin. She expected him to talk about Dickens; he said breathlessly, "There's a long-distance call come through for you. It's Jay Brookfield," putting the name in capital letters.

"Retribution" said Caroline, "comes at last. Leaden-footed but iron-handed; as my nanny used to say. Please excuse me," she said to Charles.

"Calling from Pebble Beach," Dan explained.

"And in a very nasty temper, I shouldn't wonder."

They went down through the orchard. "Why should anybody be in a nasty temper with you?" Dan asked.

"You see, I took his car."

"Without asking him?"

"Not so much without asking him as after having asked and been refused."

Dan laughed—"Do you always do things like that?" he asked, looking more than ever like Wynstay; half disparaging and half tender.

"Not always. But this was important."

Dan said, "And look at the way we entertain you. Having you paint the servants' furniture; it makes no sense. I wish you'd stay longer. Can't you stay all night? The guest-house is empty. Do stay. Or do you have a glamorous date in the City?"

She said, "I have no date at all."

They were on the edge of the orchard now, above the lawns. The boy said, "Then why was it important?"

She looked at him ironically. "Just a thing."

"To get here? To see us? You knew my father, didn't you?" he said. "I remember your coming to lunch with us in Boston."

She nodded. They had come to a halt on the path beside the guest-house. "What's worrying you?" Dan asked. "Jay Brookfield's car?"

"That, too."

"You aren't a bit like an actress, are you?" he said comfortably. "I always expect actresses to be smooth. Look, if you don't want to talk to Mr. Brookfield, why don't I say I can't find you?"

"No," she said, "thank you kindly, but that's too simple."

The telephone was on the corner of the bar in the diningroom. Jay's voice crackled at the other end. She ignored it, saying, "Is that Detective-Inspector Brookfield? This is your man, Inspector." She accepted the blast of adjectives. "Insane; criminal; morbid; goatlike; and you do understand, my darling, do you not, that the tiniest incident on the highway would involve you in arrest for driving without a licence?"

"Yes, well. . . ."

"May I therefore urge you to let somebody else take the wheel when it occurs to you to return my stolen property?"

"Urge away, my love."

"Seriously, Caroline——"

"You still remind me of my mother, after all these years."

"If I told you what you reminded me of, the operator would have a hæmorrhage. Seen Mercedes?"

"No—yes."

346

"She can't have become as unobtrusive as that, dear."

Now Lee emerged from the study. Jay was crackling again; she said, "Look, I must go; see you soon," and rang off.

"Trouble?" Lee asked.

"In a sense. Lee, don't think me a bore, but I've suddenly gone tired; I think I got up too early or something. May I go and lie down in your guest-house and drive on a bit later?"

"Sure—stay to dinner, if you like. I'll keep our friend out of the way." She took Caroline's arm. "My son has fallen for you so heavily that I think it would break him if you left now." They went along the path to the guest-house. "You shouldn't have let yourself be corralled into that painting job," said Lee.

"I liked it; I've just gone tired."

"Well, relax—take a nap," Lee said. "I'll call you around six."

Caroline stood at the doors of the guest-house, looking across the lawn; she could see the end of the high hedge that surrounded the pool. "Two hundred yards to the east; say two-fifty. And the path divides. Thank you, Charles, for the directions. If Lee is coming to call me at six, I've got an hour and a half."

ii

This was the place where the path divided; Caroline took the path to the left and saw through the trees the cottage that belonged to Mercedes. It was a white frame cottage, with dark blue shutters; there was a small square lawn in front. In the flower-bed bordering the patio there were daffodils and jonquils, the spring flowers that looked out of place in California; they belonged to costers' barrows in a London street, to windy skies and English gardens.

It was suddenly cool with the beginning of evening; the sun was still above the mountain but there was a wind rising and the leaves rustled; it would be cold here after dark.

She went up the path beside the lawn; it ended below the

347

two steps at the corner of the patio. She had to repeat in her head one of the lines that brought courage: "Stand in the trench, Achilles, flame-capp'd and shout for me." There was a dark blue door, with a wire screen outside it. She put back the screen and knocked.

Mercedes Knowle opened the door and stood looking at her.

"How do you do. I hope you don't mind my coming to see you. I am Caroline Seward." She was glad of the actor's skill that kept her voice light and her manner easy; because Mercedes was not going to take this visit as a matter of course. The expression on her face was still vigilant; it was a sculptured face, like stone; it was a sculptured head; the short silver hair was smooth and shining. It grew exactly as Michael's hair used to grow, making a square about the forehead and temples. She wore a linen dress that was greyish-silver also; and this seemed to Caroline a contrived and affected choice.

"I know who you are. Do come in." She looked friendly now; but it was a look, Caroline thought, to be removed as easily as make-up; to be wiped off leaving something structurally handsome but entirely cold.

She followed Mercedes into the room; it was unexpected; its foreground was a small living-room; there was a brick fireplace set in one wall, a dining-table standing against the other, some low bookshelves; at the back the room became a studio, with easels and canvases, unfinished pictures, a dais; a screen hiding half these things. A plump young woman with dark hair scrambled out of one of the armchairs. Mercedes said, "À toute à l'heure " and introduced her to Caroline as Madame Dufailly.

"Did I drive her away?" Caroline asked.

"No, indeed. She has preoccupations with her children's supper. She only looked in to bring me some eggs." The voice too was impersonal. Mercedes made a gesture towards the chair.

"Would you like some sherry? Or a highball?"

"Thank you kindly; but I don't believe I want a drink."

"Cigarette? There are some beside you."

"Thank you. Do you mind my coming?"

Mercedes hesitated. "Perhaps it is a good idea," she said. She sat down in the opposite chair and there was the temptation now to stare hard, to look at her all over, at hands, body, legs and feet. It was impossible to think that this was in fact Mrs. Michael Knowle; that person had belonged to another life; she was dead. Perhaps the Caroline Seward who would have been interested to meet her was dead too; then the present intruder must have some modern motive for coming.

"What have we got to say to each other?" Mercedes asked; the question sounded half-amused and half-helpless.

"Well, it is possible that you may think I'm here out of straight curiosity; to get an impertinent close-up."

"And why not?" said Mercedes coolly. "It would be natural, wouldn't it? I own to a certain curiosity about you."

There was a moment's silence.

"To begin with," said Caroline, "it seemed foolish— when the two of us have suffered so much, and lost so much, not to meet; not to talk. For me to stay up at the house with the others, and you to stay down here. And when Lee fended me off, that made me crossly determined to come and knock on your door. That is part of it."

"Yes I understand. I think I expected you, once I had met you in the drive." (She sits as still, Caroline thought, as though somebody had posed her.)

"But you were rather brave to come, weren't you?"

"Why do you say that?"

"Well, I imagine that I was always something of a nightmare in your life." The detached note had returned; she might have been speaking of the affairs of two other people.

"Yes, at one time you were."

"I don't want to add to that," said Mercedes.

"How could you?"

"Oh, I think that if we talked for long, you would end by disliking me," and she sounded as though she did not care. Caroline felt the first hint of irritation.

349

"Why should I dislike you, Mrs. Knowle?"

"Because," said Mercedes, "our experiences are radically different. Michael's death meant comparatively little to me. That puts us far away from each other at once. I didn't mourn for Michael as you did."

("I believe that you are right and that I am going to dislike you. But it does not matter. You are the only person who can tell me what I must know."

"He would have hated to be old," said Mercedes.

"I know that."

"Yes, of course you do. I'm sorry if I sounded instructive."

Caroline said, "Silly of me to snap. I thought I had grown out of being truculent about Michael." She shook her head, appealing to the distant face. "You see how it is. After all this time, I meet you and automatically I revert; I try to stake my claim and feel as though you were staking yours."

"But that is natural too."

"No, it isn't, Mrs. Knowle. It is about as natural as a hangover would be if I hadn't taken a drink for five years. He is gone; we are left; and now it doesn't matter how much you loved him; or how much I did. Your Michael isn't mine, nor mine yours. And there was, I imagine, a Michael whom we neither of us knew." (Now I must say it; I must choose the words.)

Mercedes narrowed her eyes, looking down, to think it over. For a moment she looked like Michael when he was thinking about his work. Caroline felt the same violent disturbance that had shaken her when they met in the clearing. She did not want to go on seeing this likeness; she glanced away at the mantelpiece, just above her right shoulder, and found that she was staring at the Alencz cat. It was placed there by itself; there was nothing else on the mantelpiece; she saw the slender stone body, the precise paws and the triangular face.

"The cat——" she said, "you have it too. I always loved it," and then stopped.

"Oh?" Mercedes followed her glance. "Yes, I am fond of

that fellow. You know, it was a portrait," she said, "Alencz modelled it from a Siamese cat of mine."

"That is the original," Caroline said.

"Yes."

"Did you ask Michael to bring it to you in 1939, when he came to this country?"

"Yes."

"And you and he met in Boston, didn't you?"

"Yes."

She saw Mercedes looking at her with compassion.

"Don't," Caroline said quickly, "please don't say anything about that. There are too many things." She thought that she could feel them crowding in; Cold Ash in the summer afternoon, stripped and empty, with the vans of the door; the echo of Dennis's voice saying, "One person to whom he belonged entirely of his own free will," the frosty lettering of the two names written on glass. And behind these there was the grim question-mark that had begun to form in her mind as she sat in the coroner's court between Lloyd and Dorothy Knowle, hearing the evidence of the old man who kept the restaurant called the French Horn. (To find the answer to that question I am here. For that reason alone, I have come to the Dark Tower.)

The light was going out of this room. She was looking over Mercedes' shoulder; the shadowy easels and canvases did not seem to be there. She saw instead, stretching away in darkness, the whole hidden kingdom of his marriage with this woman, the times and the places where she was not.

She said, "There is something I must say to you."

iii

Mercedes waited, wondering whether the habit of conflict so clearly visible in this face were old or new. She could not imagine the face wearing a look of peace. In her mood of enforced detachment and withdrawal, she had been studying it only as an artist would. She was reluctant to open the door

351

to any of her old thoughts and this seemed the most intelligent thing to do; to sit and watch Michael's second love with artist's eyes.

These saw the contradiction between the upper and the lower half of the face. Looking at the curled head, you could, she thought, with little effort of the imagination, put vine-leaves in the hair, or two small velvety horns. The forehead, eyes and cheekbones made the faun's image appropriate, but it was denied by the blunt, gentle beauty of the nose and mouth.

Though Mercedes would have preferred to go on making observations, it now became impossible to keep Caroline Seward within visual limits; her silence was more demanding than her words. She had said nothing that mattered; the words had been alternately shy and violent; they were only lines spoken by an actress. This was over. Stripped of pro-fessional armour, she sat twisting her long hands together staring at the floor. It was disconcerting to be made so much aware of her pain, to be so completely without a clue to it.

"Please," Mercedes said, "you must say what you like; ask what you want to ask. Don't be afraid of hurting me."

Caroline Seward unlinked her hands; she rubbed the palm of one hand upward across her forehead; her mouth twitched. She said roughly, "All right. Michael committed suicide, didn't he? You know that."

Mercedes was so much startled that her reply came automatically, fatuously: "Suicide? Michael? What is this?"

"I haven't said it to anyone else," Caroline muttered; her face looked green.

"But—what do you mean? Were you with him?"

"No," said Caroline Seward, "he was with you."

"Forgive me; I don't understand."

"He went back to the French Horn. That was your place, wasn't it?"

"Yes. It was."

Caroline shut her eyes. "I knew that, you see; he went there before. That time he had the sense to give me the bottle." She seemed incapable of saying another word. Mercedes got up and stood by her, putting a hand on her shoulder.

"Listen—I don't understand; I can't understand unless you tell me. But if he did kill himself—and you may have a reason for thinking so—I know nothing about it. Please believe that."

"All right," said the rough voice again. "I'll believe it."

"But what did you expect of me? I wasn't there. I have his letter and that's all. It is a happy letter. If something happened afterwards; after he wrote——"

She felt the shudder that passed through Caroline Seward's body. She said, "It is cold now; I'll light the fire," and knelt and watched the flame eating through the paper to the pine branches; the beginning of the smoke. Above her head the rough voice said, "A letter? You have a letter?"

"Yes. He wrote to me that night, from the French Horn."

"Good God——" the voice went flat.

Mercedes rose from the hearth. She said, "He wrote to me once or twice during the war. Do you mind? How can you mind?"

There was silence.

"Letters were a habit with him, after all," Mercedes said.

"How could he write to you? For all he knew, you were dead by then."

"He didn't believe I was. He wrote care of my bank in New York; I found the letters when I got back. This one—please read it."

"Read your letter?" There was laughter behind the voice now.

"Oh yes. I don't know why you think he killed himself. But this would seem to disprove that absolutely. It doesn't look to me possible. Michael, of all people . . ." She found that she was still dazed by the suggestion; she could not find words. Helplessly, she stared at Caroline Seward. She saw that the conflict in the face was now increased; she watched a sequence of emotions there; sorrow, doubt, relief, and at last defeat; only a small rueful smile.

353

"Obviously you know something that I don't—" said Mercedes. She was unprepared for the savage tone of the interruption: "*Look*; I heard nothing from him, do you see? I know he was alone; that he had gone back to that place. I hadn't seen him for days."

"Then why?" Mercedes began. The movement of the hand silenced her. "Leave it. For five years I've lived with this. And you tell me he sat there and wrote you a happy letter." She shook her head. "My God, it's funny," said Caroline Seward. "You must see that it's funny." She stood up.

"All I need from you now," she said in a quiet, shaky voice, "is an assurance that he was all right; not tortured and despairing because he thought he wouldn't see you again."

"Why should he be? Only read the letter."

"No, Mercedes." The Christian name seemed to be spoken in an old context of hatred. "Yours, not mine," said Caroline Seward. "You got the last word—so, in one way, I've been painting devils on the wall. In another way, you've won again; you always did." She shrugged her shoulders, murmured mournfully, "What a thing . . ." turned towards the door and then turned back. "It was a sane letter, a gay one? You're quite sure that he was normal when he wrote it?"

"Quite sure. But, please——" Mercedes said, "let us stop this. Why suffer so much? Look at it; read it here."

"I'd rather die," said Caroline Seward. "Sorry, but that is how I feel. And I do think it's funny. Remember the end of 'Cyrano'? The log dropped from the window on his head? You just dropped it on mine. Good night."

Mercedes stood for a moment, hearing the footsteps die away. She went to the desk and took the letter from the drawer. The envelope was greyish, tattered along the edges; there were air mail stamps on it and the lower left-hand corner was censored with his signature and rank. The postmark was still clear 'London, W.C.1,' and the date of August 20th, 1943. Along the top of the envelope he had written "To Be Held Until Called For."

354

She unfolded the letter:

"DEAR MERCEDES,

"I still think that this, like the others, will reach you one day. Perhaps it is a superstition to go on thinking that I'll know the exact moment when you die. Or perhaps the present powerful certainty owes itself to a long day's work, to more drinks that I am in the habit of using, and to the fact that I am dining at the French Horn.

"I can see you looking exquisitely impatient already. Don't. I haven't come back to prove, or disprove, its echoes. I am going out to M.E. again shortly, and there is always the possibility that I shall be killed, the feeling that I might as well take a last look round. I couldn't leave this place out, could I?

"But I do not see here the enemy who hurt me once, nor the tiresome lodestar that I let you become after that. I see us at the beginning; just over there, in the corner, sits the young woman with the squarely-growing dark hair, the lively eyes, the short nose (like a cat's nose) and the bloom of a peach on a south wall. She is looking this way; but she doesn't see me; she sees the dull, dreamy young man who I used to be.

"I have come back here often; in rage, in sorrow, and once, it appears, in a state of near-amnesia, when I got drunk, just after you left England in '39. I haven't come before in a mood of detachment like this.

"I don't know where you are, nor how you are fighting your war for your beloved France (and it is comical, after all this time, to think that we are still under the shadowy dominion of the King's Proctor, who might take an active view of my letters . . .).

"Why do I write again? Because, I suppose, you will always haunt me a little. There is a reality, of which you know; and there is a shadow; who is you. With the reality, I share all that can be shared. I love and am happy. Between me and you there is only a strand pulling; the wisp of im-

portance attaching to you because you were the person who
ceased to love first.

"My dear, I am suddenly very tired; it occurs to me that I
have no place to sleep, having left my place of business
(security-precaution) and come to London on impulse after
mending some broken bodies. If I do find a bed I shall
certainly have nightmares. Yes, they go on and I am still
afraid of them.

"Good night, Mercedes. I pray for you, in my inferior
private way, to my unknowable God.

"If we don't meet again in this life, you must try to waste
some of your good eternity upon me in the next. I owe you
so much; I have, thank God, ceased to love you except at a
distance; and all the bitterness has gone.

" MICHAEL."

Mercedes folded the letter; she felt like a ghost again; as
she had felt a week ago when she drove deep into the past.
It was perhaps the ghost who was saddened by the sight of
Michael's handwriting, who felt the pathos of the last
message, sent off trustfully to wait for her. In three years it
had not accosted her like this. The small bundle of letters at
the bank had been merely another echo from a forgotten
world.

She tried to see what the letter would mean if she were
Caroline Seward, reading it for the first time.

"At least I should be sure that there was no thought of
suicide in the mind of the man who wrote it. And that,
presumably, is what she came here to find out. But why
should she have thought it of him? She couldn't have
known her Michael as well as I knew mine. 'Hers', 'Mine'—
what nonsense this is."

Her habit of solitude was so complete that she had no
difficulty in maintaining the conversation as though there
were still two people arguing beside the fire:

"Why did she say 'You won; you always won'?"

"Because she believed that Michael loved you more."

356

"Did he never tell her the truth?"

"Not about you."

"But what was secret about it?"

"Nothing. He told you that he couldn't make himself talk. You hurt him too much; he was too loyal."

"And if she sees the letter?"

"Then it will only prove to her that his last thoughts were of you."

"His last thoughts? No. He went off into his drugged dream and woke with a nightmare and put out his hand for the bottle. Neither Caroline Seward nor I was in his mind at that moment." She stretched her hand to the bookshelf. pulled down a book and glanced at the first page.

> "I think Odysseus, as he dies, forgets
> Which was Calypso, which Penelope."

She put back the book. She laid the letter aside and went through the studio into the kitchen. She was an expert cook, but to-night dinner seemed a waste of time, a foolish expenditure of creative energy; to cook a meal with care and taste, to set it on the table and then demolish the masterpiece. She laughed. It was in any case too early to eat; only six. She took a sketching-block and a pencil; she began to draw Caroline's head from memory. It was almost a likeness. As it grew under her hand, she was nagged increasingly by the sense of work left unfinished; not this idle sketch, but something human and important.

At the end of half-an-hour, she tore off the sketch and set it on the mantelpiece, propping it there with the Alencz cat. She narrowed her eyes and measured the proportions with her pencil. "No; it isn't quite right. It won't do." She tore it and threw it on the fire.

The work left unfinished.

"And after dinner she will go. "Where? Lee didn't say. Driving off into the dark, hating me and hating Michael. What was it that Dennis said of her? 'Her genius for loving; that amounts almost to an artistic gift.' Well, never having

357

had a similar talent (God forgive me), I can still imagine how that sort of love reacts to the wife, the deserter, getting his last word."

She thought, "Oh, but that love suffers only a temporary setback; at the moment she is a child with a bruise, asking, 'Why did you hurt me?' And what will she do with her bruise this evening? She will, if I know her, dress rather more extravagantly than she need, drink several cocktails too many and put on an act."

The work left unfinished.

Mercedes picked up her telephone, switching it through to the house extension. The mournful voice of Liesel Veit answered at once.

"Hullo; Liesel, this is Mrs. Knowle." She spoke in German. "If I came up for dinner to-night, would there be enough?"

"I understand from Mrs. Adams already that you would not be coming."

Mercedes said, "Exactly; but that is not the point. If I asked you to put on an extra plate for me, would there be enough?"

"Oh, we make enough," said the dirge-like voice.

CHAPTER SIX

LEE worked on the galley-proofs all the afternoon and it was a quarter to six when she went to call Caroline. The guest-house was empty. She waited a little while, then scribbled a note saying, "We eat at seven; hope you don't mind a quiet evening. The Germans raise hell every time I give a party."

Walking back, she decided that it was impossible to know whether Georg and Liesel were made more gloomy by guests or by the absence of guests. She herself felt fussed and disorganised by Caroline's presence here; she knew that she had not behaved like a good hostess and the evening ahead now seemed a dull offering for a star actress used to glamorous receptions. "I ought to have shopped around on the telephone; got somebody to meet her. Anyway, if the talk runs out we can play bridge," Lee thought; she took her shower, put on a short silk dress and went into the living-room to make the cocktails.

It was a shock to find Dan wearing his white dinner coat, dark red cummerbund and dress trousers; she had bought him these clothes last year for the fiesta in Santa Barbara. He was standing before the fireplace, critically tasting something from a cocktail glass.

"Get you; are you going some place?" his mother asked.

"Me? No." He overdid his casual act, saying, "I felt kind of sloppy; nice to change once in a while. Would you see if you like this cocktail? It's a new idea."

"Dan, you haven't invited anybody for dinner, have you?" she asked suspiciously.

"Only Pete; he called and I said to come along. I asked Liesel; there's plenty."

"Oh, yes? Plenty for Pete?" Pete Layman was the most tiring of Dan's college friends; a firework of enthusiasm, with blazing brown eyes, teeth that flashed, and an immense appetite.

"He's putting his car away," Dan explained. "He's almost out of his mind; he never met an actress before. Do taste this."

The odd-looking drink was checked on its way to her lips by a bellow: "Good evening, Mrs. Adams; wonderful of you to let me come." Pete flashed like a masthead light, she thought; he shook hands with a force that hurt. He looked enviously at Dan's clothes and mournfully at his own flannel suit. "Maybe you could lend me a better tie, Dan?" He fingered his tie, a disaster of scarlet and yellow lightning-flashes on a blue background. "Something gay?" said Pete, wistfully.

"Sure—go right along and help yourself."

"Dan," Lee said, "does this room seem to you to reek of perfume? Is it something you've put in the cocktail?"

"Why, no; that's my new hair oil."

"Oh, is it?"

"Nothing sissy about it," Dan snapped; "men only; says so on the bottle."

"And what is this drink?"

He looked at her in agony. "Don't you *like* it?"

"All I ask you is not to spill any; it might set fire to the rugs."

Pete rushed back, wearing Dan's most repulsive tie, patterned with nymphs and satyrs; a further blast of perfume came with him; obviously he had found the hair oil as well as the tie. He was followed by Liesel, carrying two plates of hors d'œuvres; she complained frequently of the time involved in making them; Lee had long ago told her that they were not necessary. They were highly ornamental; there was a design of chives on each mound of cottage cheese; each anchovy was curled around a stuffed olive.

"Why, thank you, Liesel; how good they look."

"I thought as we would be so many extra to-night you would like," said Liesel gloomily and stumped away; Lee stared after her: "What does she mean, so many extra? Is she crazy?"

"She means Pete," said Dan unkindly.

"Am I late?" Caroline murmured—"my watch stopped."

It was a stage entry; she halted just inside the glass doors that opened from the patio, leaning back her head. She was wearing a long dress of flame-coloured chiffon and the flame-colour was punctuated with gold; gold chunky sandals; a gold belt; a thick gold necklace; nugget earrings.

"Is that the most practical costume for driving up to the city?" Lee asked, sweetly.

"I'm sorry; I just thought I'd throw on something comfortable. So I got my things out of the car. That's how I missed you; I found your note."

Lee looked down at her own short dress, was automatically reminded of Peter begging for a gayer tie and looked up to observe the impact of Caroline upon the two young men. As she glided towards them, each became rapt after a different fashion, Dan speechless and Pete explosive. Lee took another swallow of the sulphurous cocktail. "So she's decided to give them the full treatment. *Throw on something comfortable;* of all the corny lines. I suppose it would include the more-than-professional make-up. Damn this cocktail." Her head was beginning to swim; she looked at the flaming shape of Caroline and the two male figures in profile, devotedly pointing at her, like gun-dogs.

"You know in some ways I'd call your play greater than Ibsen," Pete was crying.

"Ibsen," Caroline said, "yes, well . . . I have no education. I understand that Ibsen wrote a play called the *Master Gabbler* and qualified for the leading rôle."

The two boys doubled up with sycophantic laughter. Caroline bestowed a grin on each. "Other people's jokes are my stock-in-trade. Thanks to a verbal memory and no conscience, I get by——" She raised her glass to Lee. "What a wonderful cocktail this is."

"Hangman's Blood," said Dan.

"Such a sweet name."

"It's really a variation on Hangman's Blood. Port, gin, brandy, rum, limes and a dash of angostura bitters. Glad you like it."

"It's bliss," said Caroline, "isn't it bliss, Lee?"

"I wouldn't know what I think it is."

("And I wouldn't know what sort of an act you think you're putting on—dear heaven, here's Charles in a tuxedo. I don't believe I can bear it.")

"As for Ibsen," said Caroline, "hullo, Charles. How's the painting coming? As for Ibsen, I can never see why they all go mad or into the mill-race, can you? There was the Ibsen girl, though."

"Tomato-juice, Uncle Charles?"

"No," said Charles with his eyes fixed on Caroline at a level below her chin, "I'll take whatever you've got there."

"Who was the Ibsen girl?" asked Pete, "do you mean Nora?"

361

"It was a song," said Caroline. "I recall it distinctly."
She recited:

> "You wear a bored expression
> With a monumental curl,
> And you walk along with a dip in your back
> And they call you the Ibsen Girl."

Charles bellowed. "But, young lady, you aren't old enough
to remember the original, surely?"

She said solemnly, "My mother taught me; my mother
was a very remarkable woman. She weighed fourteen stone
in tights."

"How many stones in a pound? Was she on the stage
too?" Pete gabbled. "Guess she must have been if she wore
tights." He was spilling his cocktail.

"In a sense she was," Caroline replied. She looked disquieted. "As a matter of fact, she had a troupe of performing
seals." She sighed and held out her glass toward Dan for a
refill, "I suppose my low origins shock you. I don't really
care to talk about them; in fact I've been allergic to fish
ever since."

"Then you mustn't take these," said Pete strenuously,
"they're anchovies." He put two in his mouth.

"I'm losing my mind," thought Lee; she got up from her
chair. "Since you're all so elegant, I guess I'll change."

"Into tights?" said Charles.

"Oh, don't change, Lee; you'll make me feel terrible. And
the end of it was sad," Caroline said to Pete, "but the end
always is sad, isn't it? I mean after she died I used to go and
see them in the Zoo; they used to remember me and form a
pyramid when they saw me coming."

"Gosh; no kidding?"

"Well, but, don't let's talk about it."

"You can't change, Lee; there isn't time," said Charles
looking at his watch, "it's six-forty-eight and a half now."

"Never mind that," said Dan, "I told Liesel we wouldn't
eat till half-past."

"You did *what*?" Lee said.

"It was okay by her. Let me sweeten that for you." He held out the shaker. Pete was saying, "You must eat—meet all the most interesting people."

"Every one of them," said Caroline, "and they have the nicest faces. But of course I know far more dead people than live ones, beginning with my grandfather; after all, we must begin somewhere, mustn't we?"

"That's terribly true," said Charles. "Hey, Dan; I could do with a dividend, if you've got one."

"I'll make some more."

"Over my dead body you'll make some more," Lee said.

"Well, then, let me make them," said Caroline, "except that I have extraordinarily clumsy hands." She held them out in front of her. "How far away they look," she said. "Perhaps Lee's right."

"If you'll excuse me," Lee began; the doors from the patio swung open again. Dan cried, "Why, hello, Mercedes; I didn't know you were dining with us; that's wonderful. Now, who haven't you met?" "Not me," said Lee, advancing to greet her. "I'm just the cleaning-woman around here." Thanks to the cocktail, she had momentarily forgotten Caroline and was focusing upon Mercedes' appearance. She had seen the dress before. It was a plain black taffeta dinner-dress and its short jacket had silver lapels. It suited Mercedes well. "And why," Lee thought, "she chooses to go around all day in blue dungarees and no make-up, when she can look like this. . . . Well, you don't expect her to teach the kids and do the gardening in black taffeta, you dope." She said, "Dan has made us all high with a quite impossible drink." She had begun to say, "Now, may I introduce——" when the meaning of the occasion hit her.

Lee said to herself, "This isn't possible. I am about to introduce Miss Caroline Seward to Mrs. Michael Knowle. Ah, no; I see I am not; they are saying 'Hello' and smiling at each other. That I should live so long. . . . Maybe I got the story wrong and they're really mother and daughter. In which case Mercedes would be wearing tights, wouldn't she? Anybody mind if I go into my bedroom for a moment and scream? I could change my dress while I was screaming, couldn't I?"

Liesel beat the gong.

ii

The atmosphere of crackling insanity persisted in Lee's head as she placed Pete on her right and Charles on her left. Dan faced her at the other end of the table. Mercedes and Caroline faced each other across the candlelight; Caroline looked like Bacchante; Mercedes looked like an eighteenth-century roué; being the only person who had not drunk the terrifying cocktail, Mercedes, Lee concluded, would be glacial. "But glacial is not what she is going to be when she gets me alone. She'll think I did it on purpose; of course they did say 'Hello'; well, what do I expect them to do, clip each other on the jaw? Now here comes our opening move; Caroline's move; courteous inquiry from Miss Seward to her lover's widow. Mrs. Knowle doing any stage-designing these days? Sure she does; the opportunities on a chicken-farm are limitless."

"Not unless you count painting the backcloths for a children's production of the *Blue Bird*," said Mercedes, sounding sunny rather than glacial.

Caroline went silly again. "The *Blue Bird*; my favourite thing; my worst thing; my third-form triumph; I mean we did it at school."

"Sir James Barrie wrote the *Blue Bird*, didn't he?" Pete said, lunging towards her; at least, Lee thought, when he turns away I can get a bit of fresh unscented air.

"No. Ibsen," said Caroline. "I played Tyltyl," she added. "Nobody can take that from me."

"A strong dramatic rôle?' asked Pete. "I shall always see you playing strong dramatic rôles. What sort of a woman was Tyltyl?"

"A little boy. He wears a hat with a jewel; in my case it

was a red fez, though, from the winter term's production of *Ali Baba*."

("I don't know why Mercedes thinks that's funny; oh, British camaraderie, I guess; one touch of boarding-school.")

"Oh, and linings," said Caroline, "I wore two pairs of linings."

Even Mercedes looked baffled by this one. "Perhaps I shouldn't mention them," said Caroline to the circle of mystified faces.

"What are they?" asked Pete.

"Purely a technical matter," said Caroline. "We wore dark blue knickers under our school-tunics, and we wore white knickers under the dark blue ones; they were called linings."

"I get you," said Charles, "every gal wore two pairs of panties."

"Roughly, yes."

"Wouldn't that look sort of bulky?" asked Pete.

"It would. It did."

"Still," said Mercedes, "the whole idea has a certain antique charm."

"But why," said Dan, "did you have to wear two pairs as Tyltyl; two pairs of *linings*? I mean, I get it about the dark blue and the light blue; hell, no; you said white. What am I thinking of?"

"The boat-race," said Mercedes.

("And now Caroline thinks *that's* funny. What's the matter with these people?")

"You see," said Caroline, with the air of implanting a profound truth, "linings are tight-fitting. For Tyltyl I was supposed to have ordinary white knickers, small boy's knickers."

"Shorts?" said Charles.

"Yes, shorts; I seem to have got in a zone of knickers, don't I? Well, as it happened, both the gym mistress and the house mistress each lent me a pair of linings, because, being bigger, they would look more like real knickers, I mean shorts."

"Gosh, did the *teachers* wear them too?" said Pete.

"Certainly."

"Two pairs each?" said Charles.

"I suppose so. I don't really remember; what I do remember is that I was so much afraid of offending one of the kind donors that I wore both pairs."

"Maybe you'd got into the habit," said Charles.

"I don't honestly see how they'd have known," said Pete, "I mean the teachers; do you, Mrs. Adams? If she'd only worn one."

"I don't honestly see anything," Lee said, drinking ice-water. Caroline drank wine and said to Mercedes:

"What are you going to do about the bird itself? I must advise you against a pigeon. We had a pigeon; it was very old and fat and the child who played the part of Light of Joy or whatever she's called, had a thing about birds."

"What d'you mean, a thing?" Pete asked.

"She couldn't bear to touch them."

"That's an allergy," said Charles, "did she sneeze?"

"No, no; it wasn't that sort; it was a phobia."

"Birds are symbols," said Dan helpfully.

"Do go on," said Mercedes.

"Well, she couldn't bear to touch the bird, so I carried it and it got stage fright and wouldn't fly, which was quite irritating because the whole cast said 'Oh, he's gone' several times without waiting to see if it had gone and it was still there, with its eyes tight shut. I was terribly sorry for it, but I tried tickling it and giving it little pushes and absolutely nothing happened; so as the whole action looked like being held up indefinitely within one speech of the last curtain I decided to bowl it underarm. Which of course looked pretty silly, but still it was airborne and it just got up to the rail that held the curtain. And after that of course it wouldn't come down. So we sprinkled a lot of maize for it and coo-ed at it but it just sat there behaving unsuitably at intervals and we had to get a ladder."

("And what is so mysterious to me is to see Mercedes taking it. She must be drunk too; she can't be; she hasn't had a

TIME HARVESTED

drink. How do I know that she hasn't had a drink? Maybe
she and Caroline killed a bottle between them this afternoon.")

"I think," said Mercedes, "that you would be useful at our
rehearsals."

"Why not take the part again yourself?" said Pete. "What's
it called ? Tittle?"

"I'd rather play the cat," said Caroline, "I always wanted
to play the cat; the drawing-mistress made a wonderful head
for the cat, and when it rubbed against my legs in the forest
scene the head fell off and one of the little girls fainted."

("Did I say, some time, somewhere, a long, long time ago,
that we'd play bridge to-night?")

"Are all British schoolgirls neurotic?" Pete asked.

"Neurotic?"

"Having phobias about birds and fainting at cats?"

"It's the diet," said Caroline, "all that starch. Did you go
to an English boarding-school, Mrs. Knowle?"

("If we are going to have Mercedes' reminiscences I think
I'll tell Dan to make another cocktail.")

"I was at a French convent," said Mercedes, "but they did
put me into boarding-school for two terms once."

"What plays did you do?" said Pete.

"None—there wasn't time. I was expelled."

"You *weren't*?" Caroline's face was alight with honest
admiration.

"I was, indeed."

"What for?"

"Having a bad influence, as I recall. I believe that I read
Baudelaire to the dormitory after lights-out. But all that, of
course, was in the time of Disraeli."

Peter swung back to Lee. "Disraeli? Does she really mean
Disraeli?" he asked in an awed whisper.

"No," said Lee acidly, "it's just British understatement."

iii

Daniel Adams found that while the effect of the cocktail
departed, leaving his head clear, the effect of Caroline Seward

367

was cumulative; the moments continued magic and unpredictable, the last moments of a magic day.

He had been in love before. Since the age of fourteen, his emotional life had followed the prescribed pattern of dates and girls. As far as that game went, he obeyed the rules and knew the answers. For the future, he could see the pattern; he had observed his elders proving the point that the not-impossible-she was most often discovered to be living next door. Romance was a necessity. Even if you never found anything quite as good as the article advertised in print or celluloid, you could look forward to meeting the reasonably exact fascimile. And that was the signal for marriage, the end of the quest. Awaiting it, he divided his time between girls who looked as he wanted them to look, and girls whose conversation extended beyond a 'line.' Reviewing these young women now, with a backward glance across the distance that he had travelled to-day, he was not surprised to see them become two-dimensional; dolls cut out of paper.

"She does things to all of us," he decided; nobody, except Pete, was behaving as usual. His mother was on edge; Charles was off the wagon; Mercedes was human. And this last was the most remarkable change. Taking his eyes from Caroline, to spy upon the ivory profile beneath the curve of silver hair, he saw that the expression of the face was still gentle; he liked Mercedes the better for that. It puzzled him that Caroline should soften her so much. But Mercedes always puzzled him. Privately, he called her Medusa, he admired her for her achievements and left her alone because she held all approaches off.

Now he was flinging Shakespeare at Caroline and hearing the words flung back to him in the voice that made them come newly alive, the voice that could, he guessed, make a column of figures in a ledger sound like poetry. She could get drunk on words as he could. As though her looks, her wildness and her cock-eyed sense of humour were not enough, they had given her his passion for words. "I'll never be the same again," Dan thought. He was bewildered by the crescendo of her vitality; she had begun as a clown and was ending as a tragedy queen, with fire in her eyes and a pale forehead and the short curls of the endearing hair disordered ; every moment she became more noticeably tense; he saw that her hands trembled. He felt that she was stretched on glittering wires and that somebody was drawing the wires tightly and then more tightly until there would come a moment when they snapped.

He did not know why. He did not know why she had come here, unannounced and driving a stolen car, soon to shoot off into the dark. ("It was important." "Why?" "Just a thing.") There was a mystery behind her. He would never know. He said to her:

"Set me down this . . . that in Aleppo once——"

She went ahead of him, declaiming, with a flourish of the butter-knife and her face mutinous, exhausted, the face of a person about to die, the tragedian's face:

> "When a malignant and a turban'd Turk
> Beat a Venetian and traduced the state,
> I took by the throat the circumcised dog
> And smote him—thus!"

She turned the butter-knife with violence against the swathe of flame-coloured chiffon across her breast and said in an ordinary voice, "Ow: that hurt!" as though somebody else had done it. She giggled with him and was the clown again; but not for long. As Lee swept them up from the table and into the living-room where the fire was lighted, she wheeled on him like an avenging angel, "Play my game with me; one round and then I must change and go."

"Must you go?" he said, catching her by the hand and halting her beside the bar while the others went on into the long tunnel of firelight and shadow. Over Caroline's shoulder he saw Mercedes seating herself, a little apart from the rest, beside a lamp whose light made her two-colour design complete; the silver head, the white profile and the silver lapels above the severe lines of black. As ever, she sat very still; he saw the contrast between this figure and the blazing shape of Caroline standing taut beside him.

"Yes, of course, I must go," said Caroline.

"What is your game?" He took down the brandy-bottle from the bar-shelf and began to fill the liqueur-glasses.

"Quotation-battle. We toss for the opening. Whoever opens speaks one line; the opponent then has three chances; he can give the next line, if he knows it; in which case he scores five points; if he can't do that, he can give any other line that rhymes and scans with the first one, scoring three points. If he can't do that either, his last chance is a line that scans but doesn't rhyme; scoring two points. If in three minutes he can't get a line at all, the opener scores ten and opens again. Three tens wins the game."

"Okay. Let's go. But I'll take a beating," Dan said. Pete leapt on one of the bar-stools; Mercedes turned her head to listen; Charles was smiling vacantly in a corner and Lee had vanished, possibly to soothe Georg and Liesel for the outrageous time that they had taken over dinner.

"Flip a coin," said Caroline impatiently. "Time us, Pete." She leaned with her back against the bar. "Heads. I open . . ." She stared in front of her; she was still shivering a little and her eyes looked enormous. She spoke in a hushed and dreaming voice:

"I cannot see what flowers are at my feet."

"Nor what soft incense hangs upon the bough," Dan muttered, unable to take his eyes from her face.

"Five to you," she said, "your opening."

"Give me my scallop-shell of Quiet."

"My staff of Faith to walk upon," she snapped, "Five all." Still she did not look at him; she glanced toward Mercedes, grinned and raised one eyebrow; she spoke the line to Mercedes.

"I saw them, and I knew them all. And yet——"

"Got me," thought Dan. "If the worst comes to the worst I can scan with any blank-verse line; but, damn it, I must rhyme." She faced him, laughing. "Yet, set, wet, debt. . . .

Since Merlin paid his demon all the monstrous debt . . . too long; but what's the line before? Yes."

"Never on such a night have lovers met," he crooned. "God bless my pal Keats."

Caroline said, "Three to you. Five-eight. Your lead."

For a moment his mind went blank; Pete's strenuous concentration upon his watch was disturbing.

"Tell me not here, it needs not saying——"

"What tune the enchantress plays," said Caroline, smoothly, "putting me two up."

"I'll get you," he said.

"Try this for size," murmured Caroline—"What is love, I asked a lover?"

"Liken it, he answered weeping," said Dan with a bow; he raised his glass to her. They went on and finished it together.

"But the end of all is Sadness! Devastation! Desolation! Spoliation and Uprooting!"

Pete was growing restless. "Give me one; just let me try——" He went on burgling and pleading until Caroline turned on him with, "My mistress' eyes are nothing like the sun."

"Gosh," said Pete, "that's wonderful. That's telepathy. Gosh, you must be psychic; that's just what I wanted; wait for this; it's good.

"Oh Captain! my captain! our fearful trip is done!"

He repeated.

"My mistress' eyes are nothing like the sun.

O Captain! my captain! Gosh, what a bit of luck." He beamed at them both. Dan met Caroline's eyes; she wore a careful and embarrassed look, as she said, "Terribly good; aren't you clever; what a thing——" and that was not enough for Pete, who had to be congratulated and cajoled and deflected from spoiling the next round, and now Dan lost interest in the game because this was almost the end of the evening.

"Halts by me that footfall."

THE WILLOW CABIN

Caroline spoke softly. Dan's mind went blank again; he could see nothing but her head and the line of her neck and the long hand whose trembling fingers rested on the bar beside him. He was trapped. "Two minutes——" said Pete. . . . "Two and a half." (What is love, I asked a lover?) "You've ten seconds."

"I'm sunk," said Dan, meaning it. Over his shoulder he heard Mercedes' voices take it on.

"Is my gloom after all
  Shade of His hand, outstretched caressingly?
Ah, fondest, blindest, weakest,
  I am He Whom thou seekest!
  Thou dravest love from thee, who dravest Me."

"Good enough," said Caroline.

"But, you know," Mercedes added, "the scoring in this game has always seemed unfair to me. I think it is more difficult to rhyme and scan with a new line than to get the original."

There was the small clash of Caroline's glass set down with violence upon the bar; she whirled towards Mercedes. "You know the game? You have played it? But of course you have. How extraordinarily unintelligent of me to think otherwise. Yes, well . . . there it is," she said, smiling brilliantly upon them, "I *am* extraordinarily unintelligent." To Dan, the image of the stretched and glittering wires became clear again; in another second they would snap. She was goading him. "Get on, your turn, and this must be the last shot. I'm on my way." He blew her a kiss; he was suddenly worried about her; he wanted her to stop blazing and shivering. He intoned with solemnity.

"Let us bury the great Duke, with an Empire's
                                    lamentation."

Caroline swept her hair back from her forehead with both hands; she added coolly,

"It's a belly-laugh for the Duchess, who married above
                                    her station."

372

Pete crashed off the stool, hiccoughing with laughter; Dan giggled, trying to control himself and sound as cross as he had the right to be.

"You made that up."

"Certainly, I made it up."

"Well, it can't score."

"Who said it could?" She leaned towards him, pointing her finger. "If you can fill the unforgiving minute with beaded bubbles winking at the brim, *my* name is Ozymandias, King of Kings. Good night." She went smoothly towards the door.

"Oh, but look here, stop," he said—"this is crazy. You can't."

"Go she must," said Caroline, opening the door, with Pete running after her, "Gosh, Miss Seward; I'll never forget it; the seals and the Ibsen girl and the linings and everything; it's been swell. Do you really have to go?"

"Oh, yes. Into the boat-race; I mean the mill-race." The deep voice cracked. The curtains closed behind the flame-coloured dress. Dan said, staring about him, "I'll get mother. She'll want to say good-bye."

"Put your mind at rest on that point," said Mercedes, and he became aware of her now as an authority, tranquilly amused. "Caroline isn't driving to San Francisco to-night."

iv

She was cold. There was the little margin of light upon the patio; then the black garden with the crowding trees. She told herself that she must not cry yet; but it was difficult to keep from crying. "Only because all this has piled up too high; because you are tired. 'Old weariness with his rust-eaten knife.' None of it will hurt so much in the morning. It is the end of the nightmare and you know that he was at peace. You will have her image on your eyes for a time and that serves you right. As Lee said, you were leading with your chin. Thank God for being still a little drunk."

There were footsteps behind her.

"Caroline——"

"Oh, please," she said exhaustedly, turning back from the guest-house door. And now it was impossible not to weep. She sobbed, "Let me go. Don't talk to me any more."

"I won't talk to you." The voice was as gentle as Michael's. "Only to say that you're going to bed. Here. I'll unpack what you want. It is nonsense to drive up to the city to-night, my dear."

She was ashamed of herself because now that she had begun to weep, she could not stop; and there was reassurance in the feel of the arm holding her after she sat down upon the bed.

"Take it easy," said Mercedes. For a long time she said no more. Turning up the lamp, unpacking the suit-case, bringing a glass of water, she was familiar and anonymous as the companion in a dream, whose answers came to all your questions, whose face you could not see.

It was good to lie still; it was a comfortable bed. Drowsily she was playing the quotation-battle out.

"What will they give me when journey's done?
Your own room to be quiet in, Son!"

She struggled up to say, "But can I see you in the morning? Shall we have time to talk?" and heard the familiar voice replying, "All the time you want. Now rest." The last thing that she remembered was the black and white figure moving beside the lamp.

CHAPTER SEVEN

"Head up a little," Mercedes said.

"I'm sorry . . ." Caroline looked at her pleadingly. "May I get down and stretch? I don't want a real rest; it is just that I have become gnarled."

"Yes; get down if you like."

"Am I the worst model you ever painted?" Caroline asked, doubling up like a jack-knife and touching the floor with the palms of her hands.

Mercedes thought about it. "No, certainly not. When you do sit still, you sit very still. I'm not sure," she added, looking at the portrait, "that the pose wasn't wrong in the beginning. You seem to me to be sitting in a position that's anatomically impossible."

"That is how it feels," said Caroline, rubbing the back of her neck. She returned to the dais and at once the work under Mercedes' hand looked thin, a mere guess at the awed, vivid head and the flying lines of neck and shoulder. She thought that she would never capture them. After six days she might as well settle for the guess. Caroline would be here only four days more.

"What shall I remember of her?" Mercedes wondered, aware that if she knew the answer she might be painting a better portrait. Certainly, the picture fell short of the truth, but what was the truth? Since her capitulation Caroline had told everything; obviously she was most comfortable keeping all her emotions on the top. But she was as variable as a stream reflecting images while it flowed; the liveliness and ardour changed their source continually, and she changed with it. In Dan's company she became as young, as moon-struck as he; their dialogue was half-finished and excited, poetry and philosophy and observation tangled together. Talking to Lee, she became tough with bereavement as Lee was, and oddly combined the qualities of war-veteran and war-widow. Under Charles's meticulous direction she was a labourer with a practical eye and a willing hand. With the children, she was an older child, picking up their wave-length at once, knowing their differences, as she coached their rehearsals for the play that she would not be here to see.

From every encounter in the day, she emerged wearing some of the colour of the person whom she had met, until the next meeting changed her mood and manner again. It was impossible to link the various Carolines; one might say

375

that she was insincere, only an actress after all. Or that her unprotected energy and warmth made her so much available to every one of them that their preoccupations could, enter her bloodstream at any time.

"Never was there a person who fitted in so effortlessly. She might have been about this place for years," Mercedes thought, deepening the shadow at the base of the throat.

There was one encounter whose influence she could not assess; the encounter with herself. It was impossible to step back and look at their relationship in perspective, as she could step back now to see the person on the dais. Caroline had stirred the waters of the past; she had stirred them so thoroughly that this week had renewed Mercedes' acquaintance with Michael. But it was another Michael. They would never establish a true line of communication there. Michael, for Mercedes, was the lonely boy whom she had turned into a deceived husband, in retrospect sweet and a little dull and greatly wronged. Michael for Caroline remained the light that never was on sea or land, the light put out forever. And all the colours that she let the crowd impose upon her now were superimposed on his. He was the beginning. He was still so important to her that she wanted to gather up in her hand every tiny thread of the past pattern; the pattern that she had not seen. Her curiosity was endless and inoffensive. She listened and gave no judgment. "She judges nobody and nothing," Mercedes thought. "She is incapable of moral indignation except where cruelty is concerned. She is a believer who cannot identify her God; she has simply the habit of loving."

With Michael dead, it would inevitably become that and no more; a spark that could now blaze up for anyone, where once it had been a flame on a single altar. The refractions of the flame touched all the different people in the story; when Caroline talked of them they lived. She re-created the austere shape of Dorothy Knowle. Vera Haydon behind her table in the drab Ministry, Dennis on his last leave. She brought back the dead; she brought into this room also the living

376

whom Mercedes did not know: Jay Brookfield in his forties; Joan Hellyar, who was Caroline's oldest friend; Army figures and stage figures; the few who came under the heading, "A chap of mine; nobody important, just a chap."

It was disturbing, this vividness, this ability to put herself inside the skin of every man or woman whom she described. Each might have given her something palpable to carry away from the acquaintance, as she carried Vera's silver knife. And there were several bygone versions of Caroline keeping the lively ghosts company, actors who had been among the audience; less from self-consciousness than from an un-controllable detachment.

It was futile, Mercedes decided, to expect that these bewildering facets could appear on the canvas. But there was still something missing that should be there; that it should be possible for her to capture. She tried to see what it was, looking at Caroline with her eyes quite differently from the way that she was reviewing her in her mind, using only the fixed medical stare of the artist. She dabbed the brush on her palette, then wiped it against the sleeve of her white coat, "And another trouble; you are getting too brown for my colour-scheme."

"Disadvantages of the drought," said Caroline. "Artists' models all over California are drying up and turning black."

"We'll have coffee in a minute," Mercedes said, seeing the pose become strained. "Just let me get the tone right."

"May I see it this morning?"

"No."

"When may I see it?"

"I've told you; when it is finished. And that won't be to-day. I lose you to-morrow, don't I?"

Caroline shuddered. "Don't mention to-morrow. I've almost decided that I can't face it."

"Can't face Jay? I cannot see Jay as an intimidating circumstance."

"You never pinched his car without asking. Besides——" She bit the sentence off.

"Besides," said Mercedes, painting smoothly, "he didn't approve of your coming here to find me. Well, you can tell him with my love that it's none of his business. As to the car, it is of no importance, that. Why are you laughing?"

"It always gives me pleasure when your English sentences come out in French."

Mercedes thought, "I wonder if Michael found your talent for personal observations a little overwhelming?" She laid down her brush. "You are now released."

"And it is time for your second cigarette," Caroline said. "Do you want to keep it until the coffee? I'll get the coffee. You sit down. You do not rest enough." Mercedes said, "Nonsense," but she went to sit in the armchair beside the brick fireplace. She felt a certain cloudiness behind her eyes that might be the earliest stage of the headache. Caroline came back with the tray. "You know," she said, as she placed it on the low table—"if I had to use an American kitchen for too long, I should become homesick for a dirty London kitchen in a basement, with an old black range and no refrigerator."

("As I, for the kitchen on the farm; whose door opened on to the crooked apple tree with the mountains behind. I can see the black pot, corroded by centuries of soup, the hens running in from the yard.") She took the cup from Caroline and drew on the cigarette with sharp enjoyment.

"Are you staying the night at Monterey, Caro?"

"Probably; Jay said he could get me a lift back here in the morning." She dropped on to the floor, cross-legged. "That means I miss a rehearsal, though."

"You needn't exercise yourself about that. They are capable of carrying on now."

"Still worried about Franz," Caroline muttered.

"Worried?"

"Lucien and Marie-Therese are demons, but it's all on the top; all visible."

"Only too visible," said Mercedes. "You heard they drove the two goats into the Veits' garden yesterday?"

378

"I did; I'm on their side. I can't take the Veits. And Franz is a sinister little boy; he hates, deep down."

"He adores his mother," Mercedes reminded her.

"Too much," said Caroline. "Nikki is the nicer of those two brats; doesn't give a damn; he's much more American than Franz. And he's quite independent of Liesel."

"In your philosophy," said Mercedes, "mothers are all villains."

"Yes, well; you should have met mine." She got up to pour some more coffee; she stood looking down the room into the studio, back to the glass door framing the bright garden. "I shall remember it," she said abruptly.

"I hope you will."

She shook her head and laughed. "It is still like a dream; and I wish it wouldn't be; I don't want time to close over it— hell, I wish I hadn't got to go to Monterey to-morrow."

"To-morrow," said Mercedes, "is going to be a peaceful Sunday; if the children behave. Nobody here."

"Nobody," said Caroline; and added, "You're never lonely, are you? I see that when I look at you walking alone. It reconciles me for the way Lee and Dan and Charles go off and leave you."

"There is nothing," said Mercedes, "that I like less than a long motor ride. If they went on their knees to ask me to accompany them to Belvedere, I shouldn't play."

"And you won't come to Monterey with me?"

"For the same reason." She did not add, "Because driving shakes my head into action." Foolish to be so much ashamed of that. She said, "Come on, idler; you've had your coffee."

Still Caroline stood, looking up and down the room. She said, "The summing-up."

"The summing-up?"

"That is what happened here."

"You, unlike Mr. W. H. Davies, have no time to stand and stare. That is, if I'm ever to get the portrait finished."

Caroline said, "How I hate things to stop," as she went to the dais. "That is like Dorothy Knowle," she added, climbing

379

into her chair. "I used not to. I used to like moving on. But I want to stay here a long time. Perhaps I could break my leg—I always think that sort; but it never happens, does it? I go on hoping it will one day."

"Too sad," Mercedes murmured, "to go through life longing for a broken leg."

"Well, you know what I mean. What my mother used to call Not Facing Issues."

"If by that she meant that you took things when they came and lived in the moment, she should have had no complaints."

"She always had complaints."

Mercedes said, "I think it is only the habit of not facing issues that has enabled me to cope with them. I may be wrong, but I believe that the congenital issue-facer always ends up by dodging. I see him with the sweat standing out on his calculations, squaring his shoulders, thrusting out his jaw, stepping back to get a pace on the jump and then suddenly saying, 'Oh dear no. Not worth the risk.' "

"You are like Michael to-day."

Mercedes paused, with the brush half-way to the canvas; decided that the remark needed no comment and said, "The advance-arithmetic has always seemed to me a waste of time."

ii

Caroline went up from the white frame cottage with a long-forgotten, recently-remembered phrase in her head. It had been spoken originally by Hellyar; the perplexed young officer standing on the staircase at Cold Ash, saying, "When I fell in love with Joan, I feel in love with a bit of you."

It was impossible not to be reminded of this. So much that she had loved in Michael and learned from him had its origins here; in the mind of the woman who looked like a tired marble statue. Logically, Caroline supposed, it should diminish Michael in her own mind, but it did not. The pattern seemed complete in this place, where the ghosts of Michael and Wynstay kept company with the shadow of Europe; it was a survivor's place and it seemed inevitable that she should have met Mercedes here and nowhere else. The Veits and the Dufaillys were not the only refugees.

She came up across the lawn and saw Dan reading on the porch, with the police-dog beside him. He looked up, half-drowned, and loved her with his eyes and bowed his head over the book again. She went on through the living-room into the study.

Lee was sitting behind Wynstay's desk, with the galley-proofs spread around her.

"Hi," said Lee, "all yours." The galleys were now disfigured with savage crosses that deleted entire paragraphs; there were typed additions pinned to the galleys.

"Lord it makes me tired."

"All of it?"

"All of it. They dress the guy up. Wyn wasn't a hero and he wasn't a genius. He was a painstaking craftsman with a New England conscience." She ruffled her hair with both hands. "Half an hour on this and I get to wondering who it was I married."

The London chapter brought back memories; but it was riddled through with the usual American complaints of military autocracy. "No American G.I. who didn't hate his senior officer more than he hated Hitler," Caroline quoted.

"Well," said Lee lazily, "we're a civilian country. You've something called a military tradition. We don't want any part of it."

There was no right or wrong about that; there was only a difference in geography and history. Yet it was bewildering to her and she forgot the galleys, thinking, "There is something lost and long-ago. Something that was the privilege of tired people in ugly uniforms, on an island under fire. My privilege and Michael's; and all that I have done since, my work, my fun and my travel, are in the nature of a postscript. Does Mercedes feel like that? That the present and the future are not ours; they belong to Lee and Dan; to America. We have only the past."

For a moment she felt like a ghost and it was a relief to fold up the printed pages where Wynstay was inaccurately remembered, to leave his memorial room for the porch where his son was playing with the dog.

iii

Sunday morning was fine. More, it was an afternoon that promised leisure. The Adams family had eaten a late breakfast and departed for Belvedere; they would not be back to supper. The children were down at the barn with Mrs. Knowle. Liesel Veit was doing the last of the housework with Georg and Renée Dufailly; they had left it until after lunch, by common agreement.

"*Enfin*," said Renée, with her hands on her hips. She looked round the L-shaped kitchen, with its impressive equipment as though she liked it and were sorry to leave it. She was a sentimental creature, Liesel thought: all colours and curves and perspiration. She was forever disorganised; she was saying now that there was still a consignment of laundry to be washed and that this would be a good moment to do it. She departed happily to the washing-machine.

"Really, I have no time for her," Liesel said to Georg, "she could have finished the laundry yesterday afternoon."

"That, my dear, is her business," Georg said.

They went out of the kitchen together. Liesel took his arm and they began to walk slowly in the sunshine. They went up through the orchard and as they came to the border of the vegetable garden, both stood still to look at their house. The cottage was still a new toy; with its clean white façade, the dotted Swiss curtains blowing, the window-boxes of red geraniums, the neat brown earth before it and the little trees.

Liesel glanced at her husband's dark profile and saw that he was content, placidly taking pride in the new toy; for her it was more than a house; it was a victory. Renée Dufailly had hoped up till the last minute that Mrs. Adams would let her have it. Liesel gazed contemptuously at the older cottage; it showed typical signs of Dufailly habitation; a window curtain that drooped; copious laundry strung on a sagging line; the lawn was dried and patchy, the path green with weeds. The garage, standing open, showed a curious collection of old cardboard boxes, tin cans and other unidentifiable junk piled in corners. Liesel turned her eyes away.

Behind the house, the hill was dry and golden; rain had not fallen yet. She could see the goats' pen, the two nanny-goats feeding at their wooden trough; the kids were out of sight. A hawk was hovering above the hill; poised as though caught in an invisible web.

Georg said, "What would you like to do, my dear?"

"First I will rest; and listen to the radio; there will be the symphony already," Liesel said, looking at her watch.

He smiled at her; Franz had the same smile, gentle and melancholy. "I shall make myself busy in the garden for a little while," he said. He went towards the garage to fetch his tools.

As Liesel came to the front door, she heard a scuffling thump from inside. "So; the children here. Why are they not down at the barn? Nikki—Franz——" she called, opening the door.

A half-grown kid stood looking at her humorously from the hearthrug; he had a leaf in his mouth. The plant from which the leaf had been pulled was on the floor, its rose-china pot smashed in pieces, the earth scattered. A chair lay on its back; the pale carpet was dotted all over with proofs of the goats' visit. She heard a crash in the kitchen and a slithering noise on the oilcloth. The other kid rushed in, scared and off-balance. He skidded on a rug; he lifted his tail and added his excrement to the mess. As he charged, his brother caught the panic and they both began to race round the room, clacking and capering, hopping and cannoning against the walls. Their little feet left wet tracks. She tried to save the spindle-legged table with the photographs on it;

she caught it as it fell, but the photographs smacked into the hearth with a splintering of glass. She saw that one kid was hurt; blood trickled from his soft nose. Now they were both bleating pitifully as they ran.

"What the devil?" Georg shouted at the door. The two kids went through on either side of him. Reaching the garden they calmed down; they trotted across the new earth, bleating a little and headed for the vegetables. Georg said, "We must catch them. How did they get in here?"

"No need to ask," Liesel said. "Lucien and Marie-Thérèse." She turned away and went into the kitchen. On the white table a bowl of fruit had been upset; half-eaten apples lay squashed on the floor. The flour bin had overturned and poured a white cascade across the oil-cloth; the flour was scattered to every corner; here and there it sparkled with broken glass from the wreck of the coffee-pot. Everywhere there was the mess; little marks of blood, little balls of black excrement, a dish-towel soaking in coffee-dregs, coffee-grounds mixing with the flour.

She was conscious of Georg's hand upon her arm, of his voice saying gently, "Liesel, it is not very bad. We can soon put it tidy; I will clean up this mess; but first I must catch the kids or they will eat all the vegetables." She did not often swear, but now she heard herself begin to swear; she swore as she ran.

iv

Mercedes drew the last bird on the last programme and carried it to the table, where Lucien and Marie-Thérèse sat side by side, dipping their brushes in blue paint, carefully filling in the colours of the bird and the lettering upon the outlines that she had made. They were unusually quiet this afternoon. For the last half-hour she had seen them exchange glances every few minutes, one angel-profile turned towards the other, with the beginning of a giggle.

"What's the joke, Lucien?"

"Nothing, Mrs. Knowle."

She thought that she would leave them now. She was half-stunned with headache and she kept putting her hand to her temple to warm the cold pain. It was not developing; there were days when it hung around, a bearable handicap. But it would be intelligent to lie down.

"Look——" Nikki said; he was sitting in the middle of the floor, carving a boat from a piece of wood that was too soft; the shape of the boat was beginning to appear. She bent over him and praised it, approved Suzanne's lumpy clay doll and glanced at Franz, isolated, half a world away, as he sprawled on the battered divan with his book.

"That is such a bad light, Franz; can't you pull the couch over nearer the door?"

She had to say it twice before he heard her.

"It's okay," he said; but he got up unwillingly; she was surprised when Lucien came without being asked, to help him move the divan. There had been a cold war between them ever since Caroline had given the verdict that each should play the part of Tyltyl in a different scene. "Which only proves once again," Mercedes thought, "that compromise is not necessarily a solution."

For a moment she found in the small, divided group a likeness to another awkward company of young people, met in secret and agreed only upon the fact that they were in danger of death. Always when the headache began she went back to there; to the meetings after dark in the back-room of the dingy café; to the years of terrifying hide-and-seek among the mountain villages. In retrospect it looked impossibly dramatic, as improbable as the radio-serials that the children loved. But the poor heroes, she thought; not Buck Ryan nor the Lone Ranger, merely frightened young men who quarrelled among themselves; matched against the cunning louts of the Pétain Youth, their own blood-brothers. It was a band of the Pétain Youth, not the Germans, who had burned the farm. Frenchmen, she thought, and stopped her mind there as though she braked a car.

"Ow," said Suzanne, "her arm's come off." Could you fix it, Mrs. Knowle?"

Bending over the clay she felt the pain slide forward, making a bar above her eyes. She straightened herself; when this began to happen, it was time to go.

"So long," she said to them. "I'm going to rest. If I don't come back at four o'clock will you leave the place tidy?"

"Yes, ma'am," said Lucien.

"Hey, here's mother——" said Nikki, looking towards the door.

With one accord Lucien and Marié Thérèse flung down their brushes. As Liesel rushed into the barn, they dived under her arms. She grabbed at them, but they pulled free; she struck downward with her clenched fist at Lucien's head.

"Stop that," Mercedes said. The boy had dodged the blow; he caught his sister's hand and they raced away through the trees. Liesel did not attempt to follow them. She stood raging in the doorway. Anger had changed the face that was by habit set in dignified melancholy, making a purple, weeping distortion of it; the sounds that came out of the face were all hoarse and uneven. Franz was clutching at her, but she paid no attention to him. Nikki sat quite still, with his boat in one hand, his knife in the other. Suzanne went on modelling the doll.

"Come and see," Liesel was repeating, "come and see the swine ; the dirty, wicked, damnable little swine."

"Not that language, please," said Mercedes, speaking in German. "Pull yourself together at once." She put a hand on Liesel's shoulder and kept it there. " Quiet. *At once.*"

Liesel gave a last sob and was quiet.

"Nothing whatever," said Mercedes, "is gained by making all that noise. Come with me." She turned Liesel about and marched her through the door. "Stay behind, Franz, please. I want to talk to your mother." Still he clung to Liesel; his face was white and set.

"If your house had been wrecked, made filthy——" Liesel raged.

"In my time," said Mercedes, "I have had my house burned to the ground. I didn't behave like a maniac." She knew that this was unfair, that even if it were fair, she should not rebuke Liesel in front of her son. "I agree that it is intolerable," she said quickly, "and the children must be punished. Not by you, though; by Renée. If you'll wait while I get into some other clothes——"

"What are you going to do?"

"Find Lucien and Marie-Thérèse and start them on cleaning up the mess. But I must change first. Will you wait for me?"

Liesel said nothing.

Mercedes went down to her house; wearily she took off her dress, put on her blue dungarees and returned to the barn. Nikki was still sitting on the floor, carving his boat; alone.

"Where did your mother go?" she asked. He shook his head; he looked as placid as usual. He said, "There's always trouble going on around here." The words might have been spoken by a man, not a seven-year-old boy. Nikki smiled at her.

"Trouble?" she said.

"Doesn't happen when you're with us," he explained, and added, "if Lucien called me a Boche, I'd sock him. Franz doesn't sock him. Why didn't you let Mother sock Lucien?"

She said, "Because he is smaller than she is."

"He'd have kicked her. I saw him do it before," said Nikki, "he can kick good and hard." He went on carving the boat. Mercedes stood, looking down at him, uncertain whether to leave the argument there. The pain in her head made it difficult to think.

"Nikki, old boy, as you grow up you'll find that you can't put things right by socking people."

"Why, grown-up people always do it on the movies," said Nikki.

She let it go. "Do you want to stay there and go on carving?"

He nodded.

"All right; leave it tidy when you're finished. And you'll go up at four, won't you?"

He nodded again.

She walked, feeling the jerk of pain behind her eyes at every step. She knew where to find the children; they would be hiding in the 'cave,' the tent of sacking and branches built at the side of the trail that came out into the driveway. She was surprised by her sense of cold desolation; she felt no anger on Liesel's behalf, no particular wrath with the Dufaillys, no wish to take sides. There was only a remote, tired sadness as though she saw them all condemned to death. When she came to the clearing, she began to whistle; she did not intend to take them unawares. She saw the tent; the sacking quivered; a head bobbed round the plaited branches.

She called, "Better not run away."

They came out of hiding; they stood still, with their chins lifted; they looked dignified and prepared for doom.

"Come along," she said, "we have to go and clear up the mess in Liesel's house; that is the first thing."

"Will she be there?" Lucien asked.

"But naturally she will be there."

"You'll stay with us?"

"Yes. Till we've cleaned up."

"That's good," said Marie-Thérèse.

"Did you know," Mercedes said as they walked, "that one of the goats was hurt? It cut itself on the broken glass."

"We didn't break any glass."

"Is it badly hurt?"

"Perhaps. I don't know. We shall see. I thought you liked the goats. And it is no use weeping, Marie-Thérèse."

At the edge of the orchard they hung back reluctantly. She held out her hands to them. "Come along now; have a little courage. Let's get this over."

v

Caroline said, "The gate is on your right; just past the bridge." She knew that the young man at the wheel of the car was still finding her good fun and she wondered whether

388

he would expect a drink. He had said that he wanted to be in San Francisco by half-past five and it was a quarter to five now.

"Nice place," said the young man, as they came out of the trees and saw the long dark façade of the main building, the pool of lawn in the middle of the forest. The police dog rose from his sad vigil on the porch and came leaping up to the car. Caroline quieted him.

"Where shall I take your bag?"

"Oh, leave it here. I know you are in a hurry," she said ingeniously; he stood smiling down at her; she knew that he was still puzzled by her decision to take a ride with him instead of staying at Pebble Beach. He had heard some of Jay's carefully-chosen expletives.

"Well, glad to have met you," he said, holding out his hand.

"Thank you kindly for the lift."

"You're very welcome," Still he prolonged it: "Hope you have a good trip back to England."

"Thank you."

"You'll be paying us a visit again, I hope?"

"Oh, yes. Next year, I shouldn't wonder."

"Well, you know where to find me. If you lose my card, you'll find the number in the telephone directory."

"Thank you. I won't forget."

She watched the blue Cadillac circle the gravel and shoot away downhill through the trees. "The majority," she thought, "says good-bye that way; and the majority includes me. Michael is still the only person who could get it over in thirty seconds." She stood, stroking the dog's head. "Now that I've done this, I feel rather a fool," she said to him.

She looked behind her at the long day; the two-hour drive in the morning; lunch with Jay at Pebble Beach; the sudden panic that had come upon her while they walked by the sea. ("Look; I must go back; I don't know why.")

"Jay ought to be used to that sort by now," she told the dog: Jay had frozen her with his chilly sermon. "You have brought doing as you like to such a fine art that it has ceased to be funny or admirable. You are becoming an eccentric; and nobody under forty-five can take out a licence for eccentricity. May I remind you, my little weather-cock, that we have a date for drinks and another for dinner." He would not forgive her easily for finding the young man who wanted to be in San Francisco by half-past five.

It had been a hunch; it had petered out now that she was here. She picked up her suitcase and walked along the path to the guest-house, with the dog at her heels. She stood in the living-room that felt like home after seven days' tenancy; as much like home as her own flat, the two rooms in Montpelier Terrace, walled with Michael's books.

She took a shower and poured herself a drink while she was dressing. She went down across the lawn to Mercedes' house. She knocked; there was silence. "Did she go to Belvedere after all?" Caroline wondered, having explored. She was tempted now to look at the portrait; the easel was turned to the wall. "No; my alleged eccentricity does not include that type of behaviour, Jay, you'd be surprised." She touched the Alencz cat on the nose and went out; she went down towards the barn. But Franz Veit, stumping through the trees with his hands in his pockets and his head lowered, said that there was nobody in the barn. He looked pale; his eyes were red.

"Where is Mrs. Knowle?"

"Up at my mother's house, I guess."

"What's wrong, old boy?"

"Nothing, ma'am."

"Yes, there is something. Did you hurt yourself?"

He shook his head.

"Well, I'll go on up, I think. Coming my way?"

He shook his head again. He stared past her with tears in his eyes. She did not like to leave him, but he dashed away suddenly, back in the direction from which he had come. "By the pricking of my thumbs," said Caroline, looking after him.

As she came out of the orchard she could see heads over the top of the Dufailly fence; old Paul Dufailly's head and

Georg Veit's head. She could hear their voices. She walked up the path between the beds of vegetables and came to the gate. Mercedes was with them. Mercedes was saying, "That will be quite enough, from both of you. I cannot listen to any more." She turned. With the sensation of having entered on the wrong cue to speak somebody else's lines, Caroline called "Hullo."

Mercedes came out of the gate; she wore her blue dungarees. She looked dusty and ill and tired. She said, "Hullo; the last person I expected to see." There was a blurred film over her eyes and she held her hand to the side of her head.

"What pretty thing goes on?"

Mercedes said nothing; she put one hand on Caroline's shoulder to steady herself as they went down through the orchard. "I must find Franz," she muttered.

"He's not far off. I saw him just now. You're all in, Mercedes. What have they been doing?"

"Fighting. Lucien and Marie-Thérèse shut the kids in the Veits' house. Liesel has gone to bed and Renée has had hysterics; since when I have been organising the clean-up, reducing the tempo at which Paul prefers to beat his grand-children and refereeing the usual Franco-German brawl. Pay no attention. Do you think we'll find Franz in the barn?"

"He went that way."

"He started kicking Lucien, just to add charm. I pulled him off and he ran. He's in a bad way."

"Is your head worrying you?"

"A little, yes."

"Well, don't bother about the dreary Franz, for God's sake. Come into the guest-house and I'll give you a drink."

"No; I must get down there."

They came to the door of the barn. It was empty. On the stage they saw the remnants of the painted screens, the cloud-and-castle designs for Maeterlinck's "Kingdom of the Future." These were now merely frames of torn, hanging paper.

For a moment Caroline forgot the woman by her side. She

remembered looking at the screens while she rehearsed the children, staring at them again and again, moved by their loveliness, saddened and perplexed that this talent, this professional skill once recognised, should be put to so small a use. She said, "Good God, what's happened to them?"

Mercedes, with her hand still curved about her temple, said, "Franz. He gets these rages. This means it's over. He'll be all right now. And very penitent." She sounded casual; she turned away.

"The little——"

"Don't, Caro. I can't take any more words like that."
She stood still; frowning, looking as though she were trying to focus her vision. "Do go; leave me, will you, my dear? I must lie down."

"I'm not leaving you."

She expected Mercedes to argue, but there was silence; the face contracted with pain, the eyelids drooped and the hand came down heavily upon her shoulder. Once more, inside the living-room, she said, "Do go. Do leave me."

It was a long time since Caroline had seen anybody so ill and in so much pain. Small, forgotten scenes out of the war came back to her; people came back; the fat corporal who broke a wrist, the girl with serum-sickness, the orderly who cut the top off his finger. She remembered that when she was younger she had felt disgusted and frightened by such things, wanting to run away. The years had taught her to make the mental and physical effort; to go all the way with the thing that was happening, until the performance of repulsive tasks became automatic and comparatively easy.

At first, beside the bed in the darkened room, she saw most clearly the reason why Mercedes begged to be left alone. This was, above all, ugly. It was the humiliation of pain that brought from a human being the groans of an animal, that took the mind away and left the body in command. She thought and hoped that Mercedes was becoming gradually unconscious of her presence, anæsthetised by pain and nausea. For the time being, it was impossible to give her the pills that

would stop the pain; it was only possible to perform the
menial services, to hold her hand, to talk to her soothingly
as to a child.

With a sense of bewilderment she saw the racked body and
thought, "This is Mercedes; the person whom once you hated
so much." She began to remember the old quest for Mercedes;
the hints and half-shares of information that had come her
way; how to one she was cold, to one possessive, to another
a martyred heroine. Jay had called her an eccentric; Dennis
had seen her as an escaping truant. For Michael she had
made the rain and the fine weather. Now, as Caroline bent
over the bed, she thought of all the people guessing at that
marriage; making their versions of it; the curious people,
whose curiosity was never satisfied, whose guesses were wrong.

"And you with them," she told herself. "You were a little
right, but far more wrong. You came here stridently, with
your dread that was unjustified, your mystery that she took
away. How can you ever repay that debt to her? Least of all
by the things that you are doing for her now; she isn't here
to know about them."

And that was true. This body was all that was left. The
person whom she had come to meet, the enemy whom she
had tried to fight, the friend whom she had found, these were
gone. The sick creature that she nursed was not Mercedes.
She recalled Michael's quotation from the statement defining
the body as a bandit that could at last destroy its owner
absolutely. It seemed, for the moment, to be valid. It was
painful to her; she was so well-acquainted with death that
the sense of loss became exaggerated. She found that she
was trying to picture Mercedes well and in command of
herself, the cool, authoritative person who had been here
yesterday. "I can remember what she said to me when she
wiped the painted devil off the wall: 'You buried this too
deep. If you had let yourself talk, no matter to whom, it
would not have become a haunt. You were too loyal.' And
after that; 'Silence can be as dangerous as speech. There are
thoughts that must be taken out into the air.'

393

"It surprised me to find how much she liked to be made to laugh; how quickly she tuned in to any silly mood of mine. That was unexpected.

"There was the morning when we drove into Saratoga and sat there for an hour and a half drinking coffee in the Fir Tree Inn, talking of France. It seemed to me then that she starved for Europe.

"She has only a little money now. I keep thinking about that, wondering how much she minds. It seems so unnatural for Mercedes to be poorer than I am.

"I can see her on the hill, with the grey goat trotting to meet her. She stands there, ready to play his game with him; she likes doing that.

"What shall I remember of her most clearly? Yes; the look of her walking alone, without touching my heart as others have, all my life, when I see them walking alone. If she were dead, I should see her walking, free and whistling Michael's tune, content. Content with what? What has she to be content with, after all? Her faith? Her knowable God? Look what He does to her."

Now Mercedes seemed to return to life a little; there came the signs of the spirit in charge of the seemingly omnipotent body, a muttered apology and a broken smile. These made her pathetic, as she would not wish to be.

Idle, Caroline thought, to be angry with God for it; easier to be angry with the German family and the French, with Lee Adams and her sulky son-in-law, with all those who took from this person and gave her nothing in return. She saw the persecutors as she saw the pain. She was ranged on Mercedes' side against them. One of them, at least, was growing weaker and though Mercedes could not speak, Caroline thought that she could swallow. She held her up and gave her the pills one by one; there was a sudden, impatient strength in the hand that took the glass from her and tilted the water down three times.

"All right," Mercedes said in a whisper. She lay back and began to be quiet. Now it was possible to relax from the last furious tension, to cease to fight on her behalf. Caroline settled the pillows beneath the heavy head. She rose, feeling that her knees trembled; it was an effort to put away the things that she had needed, to make all tidy and clean. The calm that she had known was used up now; it left behind it a cold anger.

She came back to pull up a chair beside the bed and sit there for a while. She watched the shape of the crucifix upon the wall recede in shadow, the mountain picture fade, the twists of the pale flower-petals become a faint frieze against the curtain.

Still she was angry. She was angry with every person in this place; she needed, she thought, take only one more step in her mind to turn the anger on Mercedes also. The part that she played here seemed now pointlessly self-destructive, a deliberate mortification like the wearing of a hair shirt. When she shut her eyes she could still see the wreckage of the painted screens.

She stormed at Michael. "You can't agree to this. You who would have looked after her and cared for her, as you did for me. And yet she says that she doesn't want that, never wanted it, because she had to be alone and free. Free. This is the worst and most futile bondage; the act of sacrifice for worthless people and useless things." She was warring again on an old battlefield, raging against the Spoilers-of-the-Fun. "Bunch of bastards. There isn't one of them who doesn't owe her a debt. And they imprison her. In a creditor's prison, get it."

Presently she rose and went into the living-room to smoke a cigarette. It was cold here now, with the curtains drawn back, the dark garden standing at the window. She turned up the lights, drew the curtains and lit the fire.

At once she was aware of the room; the room where the summing-up had taken place. Here she had read Michael's letter; here she and Mercedes had exchanged their memories, that fitted together the two halves of his life. In this room she had seen the end of her perplexity, known that there was nothing left to fear. She looked from the stone cat upon the mantelpiece to the titles along the bookshelves; up to the shadows now fallen upon the studio end, the ghostly easels and canvases. Here they had laughed; here they had come to know and value each other.

She felt her tired body relaxing still more, her head becoming light, peace dropping upon her. The room was so comfortably not her own; always she had been content to sit beside somebody else's fire. She chanted, just above her breath,

> "Come! let us draw the curtains,
> heap up the fire, and sit
> hunched by the flame together,
> and make a friend of it.
>
> Listen! the wind is rising,
> and the air is wild with leaves.
> We have had our summer evenings:
> now for October eves!"
>
> The great beech-trees lean forward
> and strip like a diver. We
> had better turn to the fire
> and shut our minds to the sea,

She said, "Yes. That is the way it ought to be for her, but not alone. Not by the fire alone, with her memories. There should be two people turning to the fire.

> "Come! let us draw the curtains
> and talk of other things,
> and presently all will be quiet—
> love, youth, and the sound of wings."

vi

She wondered how long she had been sitting here. She looked at her watch and saw that it was nearly ten o'clock. She got up and pushed open the bedroom door that she had left standing ajar.

Mercedes' voice spoke out of the dark, sounding cloudy and far away. "That you, Caro?"

"Yes. Did I wake you?"

"'Crois pas," said the cloudy voice: "Were you with me all the time?"

"Sure." She went to the side of the bed. Mercedes turned on the lamp as she moved. The face was changed, still white but smooth and washed-looking. The eyes were luminous, the lids heavy; this was a drugged and peaceful person now.

"You were with me all the time, weren't you?" Mercedes repeated.

"Yes."

"I thought you were. I am so sorry."

"Please don't be an ass," Caroline said inadequately.

"Pretty business, what? You are good. I do hate it." She blinked at the light.

"How does it go now?"

"All right, bless you."

"Anything you want?"

"Water," she said drowsily, "about six gallons of water. And the scent off my dressing-table—bottle with the gold stopper. Thank you." She splashed her hands and face with scent; she drank three glasses of water. Again she said, "Thank you. What is the time?"

"Getting on for ten."

Mercedes said, "What time was it when we came in here?"

"Around five-thirty, I think."

"How much dope have I had?"

"Three pills out of that bottle."

"Only two more, then." Her hands were steady, taking the pills from the bottle and raising the glass. She said, "If I can look you in the face to-morrow after this performance, I shall be very much surprised. At the moment I am only half here. You are good."

"Shut up."

"Have you had any dinner?"

"No."

397

"Then you must be starving. I hope you had a drink?"

"No."

"Do have one."

"In a minute. Mercedes——?"

"M'm?"

"How often does it happen?"

"Every two or three weeks."

"And do you always go through it alone?"

"Hardly a thing one would issue ringside seats for, is it?" The voice had turned bitter. "In fact it was my fault this time. I made it worse by keeping going all the afternoon. If I take the stuff in time it is quite simple. Liesel forestalled me."

Caroline said, "It would give me the purest pleasure to see both those families dead and buried; and that goes for the Adams family too; every one of them." She strode out of the room. She poured herself a whisky and made a sandwich. Mercedes called her as she came back to the fire. She went in, with her glass in her hand. There was another change in the face; the eyes were brilliant, the expression wholly satirical, that of the eighteenth-century roué.

"*Il ne faut pas exagérer*," Mercedes said, pointing a finger at her.

"Meaning?"

"Nobody, on the long haul, does what he doesn't want to do."

"Drains to that. These people use you."

"They couldn't, unless I let them."

"So?"

"There are worse things. There is the feeling that one's hands are tied, that God's mercy can dry up for His children most in need of it." She stared at the cross.

"Tell you a story," she said, sounding more deeply drugged than ever. "There was an afternoon in Lisbon, nearly four years ago. I was out of hospital. I was sitting in a small, dingy writing-room, half underground, at the Hotel Borges. It was dark and there was some kind of small stinging insect

398

buzzing about. I kept slapping at it. I was trying to write a report and not getting far.

"It was so shadowy that when the old lady came in I didn't see her; and I don't remember hearing her. I suddenly became aware that she was standing in front of me, holding out a piece of paper. She was squat, near the ground, wearing a black dress; she seemed to be part of the dismal room. I wouldn't have been surprised if she had been a ghost. But she talked. She asked me if I spoke German.

"When I said yes, she pointed to the address on the piece of paper and asked if I knew this place, if I thought that she could get a cheap room there; she couldn't afford the room that she had now. She was waiting for a passage to the United States.

" I asked her how long she had been waiting and she said for months. Her husband and two of her children had died in a concentration camp; there was one surviving daughter who lived over here. Her visa had come through at last and the poor silly old thing had thought that this meant a place on a boat. So she packed up and went down to the harbour on the day that one of the Portuguese ships was sailing. I don't know if you heard about those ships. There was a waiting list of thousands, they sailed with people sleeping on mattresses along the decks. Naturally she had no ticket, no reservation, nothing but the visa. And the man at the gangway laughed at her and sent her back. She didn't know how long she would have to wait.

"She told me this. Then she began to cry. She stood there crying and saying, '*Unser kinder; unser kinder*' and '*Ich bin so alt; ich bin so alt.*' I think that of all the human sounds I ever heard, that was the loneliest. I remember putting my arms round her; she felt very small and knobbly.

"I didn't think at that time that I could be much hurt again by anything; but I revised the opinion. Then she looked at me, with the tears still on her face and said, 'You are English? American? You are killing them? Bombing them?' I said, 'Yes.' She said, '*Gut; gut,*' and she turned both her thumbs up, like a British soldier in a newspaper-photograph and she bobbed out of the room.

"It seemed darker after she had gone, and the thing that I was writing appeared to make even less sense."

The voice had become slow; it ceased. Caroline waited through the silence, puzzled and alone. She could see the incident clearly, but not the point in the telling; unless Mercedes meant to prove that here in this place there was at least something that she could do. Surely to-day had proved beyond doubt that there was nothing within her power to do that would not be thwarted? "But now she is seeing something that I do not understand and cannot see. She is a different person from the friend that I conjured by the fire."

"Are you there?" she asked softly. When there was no reply, she turned out the light and went back to the living-room. She was suddenly heavy with sleep. The whisky had taken the edge off all her thoughts; she went to the sofa and lay down there, saying, "Here if you want me," more to the imagined friend than to the deeply-drugged storyteller with the bright eyes.

vii

Mercedes woke at seven, to the lucidity and peace of the day after the headache; to the feeling that her brain had been washed and that she had been given a pair of new eyes. She was thirsty; while she took her shower, her skin seemed to be drinking.

Since it was Monday morning, old Paul would be driving the children to school. She thought that she might finish Caroline's portrait to-day. She kept moving away from the blurred recollections of last night. Caroline had been there at the beginning. She remembered Caroline coming back, later, with a glass in her hand. Mercedes thought, "However it was, she will be tactful; and still I cannot bear it."

She went into the living-room. Caroline was sprawled on the sofa; she looked flat and comfortable. She had not undressed; she had taken off her shoes and unbuttoned her

400

shirt. Mercedes did not know why the sprawled figure in shirt
and trousers should make her think at once of war. The face
was innocent and unwary with sleep; one hand was folded
below the cheek. "For no definable reason, you can see that
this is somebody well-used to responsibility; to being on call.
Did I ask her to stay? No, I do not believe that I could do that,
even under dope. Really, she is the kindest of creatures,"
Mercedes thought, walking softly past the sleeping figure
towards the kitchen door. As she began to squeeze the oranges,
she heard Caroline stir and say loudly, "What a thing . . ."
Then she was framed in the doorway, looking benign and
guilty.

"Good morning. Are you all right? Anything you want?"
She blinked and leaned against the lintel. "But you look better,"
she said, "than I have seen you look for a long time."

"Always . . . on the day after," Mercedes heard the abrupt
note in her own voice and Caroline said quickly, "Are you
going to give me a rocket?"

"A rocket," said Mercedes thoughtfully, "a rocket? I was
going to give you some breakfast."

"It is an Army vulgarity, meaning are you cross because I
slept on your sofa?"

"Cross? It was most sweet of you. You must have been
horribly uncomfortable."

Caroline shook her tangled head.

"Could you give me a toothbrush?" she asked in a deeply
urgent, supplicating voice.

"Certainly. There are two new ones in the bathroom
cupboard. Help yourself to whatever you want."

"We talk of toothbrushes," said Caroline and faded away
round the angle of the door. Mercedes had prepared the
breakfast by the time that she came back, now wide-awake
and uncrumpled.

"How would you like your egg?"

"We talk of eggs."

"Do you always wake up as inconsequent as this; or is it
the effect of the abominable sofa?"

Caroline said, "I have woken up in the same mood that I was in when I went to sleep; which makes one feel wise.

They faced each other across the white kitchen table in the chilly sunshine. Mercedes made the effort. "Caro, my memories of last night are, *grace à Dieu*, very vague. But I do know that it must have been hideous for you."

"Oh, please——"

"I do apologise; and I do thank you. And may we never talk about it again?"

"The details," Caroline said, "shouldn't worry you so much. They didn't worry me. I only minded for you."

Mercedes grimaced. "It is my worst, that. Absurd to feel like this about it. Perhaps if one were young;—no, I was always the most unwilling and intractable invalid."

"Like Michael," Caroline murmured, looking out of the window.

"Yes. We had it in common. I remember a time when we both had influenza at the same moment; very badly. We had one nurse and between us we nearly killed her. Vera Haydon was with us then. I threw a bowl of blancmange at her; I trust it was only the blancmange and not the bowl, but I can't be sure."

Caroline said, "Types like V. Haydon are natural targets. For blancmange as for bombs." The tone of the brutal speech was compassionate. After she had lit their cigarettes, she poured herself a second cup of coffee, returned to her chair, propped her elbows on the table and looked steadily at Mercedes.

"Will you do something for me? Will you come home soon? To Europe? I can look after you."

"Oh, darling." It was not a word that came naturally to her. "Are you serious?"

"Absolutely."

Mercedes blew her a kiss. The watchful look on the face did not change.

"No, I can't, Caro. Ever."

"You couldn't come home and live with me? Last night I thought you might like it."

The simplicity was touching. The only way to treat it as honourably as it deserved was to say with equal simplicity, "I should like it, but it won't do. Listen, my dear; leaving all question of my health out of the argument, I'm a person who left every job I ever began unfinished. Even the work in France; I had to desert there, too."

"For your life."

"I ought to have stayed and died."

"No."

"I think so," said Mercedes. "And here at least, I have begun something that I must finish."

"Regulate servants' brawls? Paint beautiful screens to have them smashed by a disgusting little boy? Suffer agony, as you did last night, with nobody to help you? Live in America when you only want to be back in Europe?"

"Some of those things," Mercedes said, "one can offer up."

Caroline frowned. "I don't understand the line, as you know. I mean, I'll take it from you that one does." She rose from the table and began to pace. "All right. You make your sacrifice and cut yourself off from what you want."

"No. I find much that I want here."

"I don't believe you." She paced like a tiger, turning back and frowning and turning again.

"You must believe me. Come here." She took hold of the restless hands. "You love people," she said, "you should understand. You love on a wide scale; you make people love you. Perhaps I love in a different way. If I talk to you about the Mystical Body I shall only increase your irritation. But this group here, those who seem to you unimportant. They aren't unimportant. Nobody is."

Caroline said, "Hell—look at them. Look at yesterday."

"Yesterday didn't disprove anything."

"To me it did. I can't understand why you shouldn't feel as hopeless as you felt in Lisbon, with the poor old German woman."

Mercedes let the two hands go, "When did I tell you that story?"

"Last night."

"It comes to the top of my mind repeatedly . . . I don't know why. No, I assure you, I never feel that hopelessness here; or not for long. There are things that I can do. To you, I suppose, they must look silly and small."

"No; they just look tough and unkind."

"Think for a moment. I can make these people work together. They do work together; always they climb down at last, because they know I'm right and they trust me. More than can be said for any of the men in the world who ar⁻ trying to reconcile Jew and Arab, Right and Left; isn't it?"

"But why do they matter to you?"

"As people; people with homes and families and lives of their own."

"Their own. You want nothing of *your* own?"

"No, my dear. I was born deficient in a sense of property."

Caroline sat on the edge of the table, swinging her legs; she looked mutinous and baffled.

"Caro; try to get under my skin, see it through my eyes. You're so good at that. Don't look at it as though you were called upon to do these things. I am years older than you I am infinitely less vulnerable. And I always was. I haven't your size heart, nor your warmth. When I was young I only needed me. Now I'm getting old I only Need God and me."

She saw the quick turn of the head, the stare and the lifted eyebrow, as though Caroline recognised a familiar quotation.

"Only God and you." The voice was awed: "You look forward to this for the rest of your life—alone."

"But naturally, alone."

There was silence.

"I do have pipe-dreams about going back," Mercedes said, trying to sound intelligible, "but that is all they are."

"Is it . . ." Caroline lit one cigarette from the stump of the other.

"Is it what?"

"Is it just that you won't admit to being lonely; or that you really need nobody? That I must know."

"Lonely?" Mercedes looked up, startled. "I promise you that I have never fully understood the meaning of the word."

Caroline's shoulders drooped. It seemed impossible to comfort her; she had become all at once a person poorer and less certain than her gifts warranted. "Look here," Mercedes said, "you have been alone since Michael died. Everybody matters to you a little; nobody matters supremely. You have work and fun and the illusion of company."

Caroline slid off the table. She straightened herself and stared away through the window, with an expression that Mercedes had not seen before. It was at first a sorrowful smile, a recognition of loss, as though she were about to weep; then the face changed, became alight with a certainty that challenged the grief and threw it down.

Caroline turned, drew a long breath and said in an ordinary manner, "All right. Do you want to start work now?"

Mercedes went into the studio. For a moment she tested her eyes, looking first at the nearest things; it was a pleasure to see so clearly. She uncovered the easel; there was little left to do. She could finish to-day.

Caroline climbed on to the dais. Now Mercedes saw what was wrong with the portrait; not the pose, not the colour, only the look on the face. She had caught the slanting laughter, but not the look of dedication. It was palpable this morning.

EPILOGUE

"The soldier's pole is fallen; young boys and girls
Are level now with men. The odds is gone
And there is nothing left remarkable
Beneath the visiting moon."

Caroline's eyes had moved away from the book on her knees and she was speaking Cleopatra's words from memory. The actor who was to play Antony went on staring at her in silence. He wore the beard that he had grown for his most recent picture. He had a brown tweed suit and he could not have been less Antony. Moreover he was sitting on a chintz sofa. The stage was still dressed for the drawing-room comedy that would close here next week. There was another dimension, though; the little stir of the air created by the words; she lived there until the producer said from the stalls, "That was lovely, Caroline," and the air was changed. The actor stood up smiling at her; he shook his head as though bewildered and kissed his hand to her.

She came back into time. It was four o'clock; they would break now. He was saying something, the lion with the beard, but she missed it because the impact of the theatre had begun to press in upon her; all theatres were haunted by an identical ghost, she thought, studying the gilded bulges below the stage-box; she would always recognise its presence and never see it. She began to collect her miscellany from the front row stall where she had placed it; her fur coat; a bunch of tulips, an egg in a paper bag, a copy of *Punch* and a blue china clock. "Why the clock?" the lion asked, towering above her.

"I took it to be mended in September," she said, "and I felt awful about not having gone back; it was in Tottenham Court Road. But I needn't have bothered because they say it is unmendable. The egg seems to me more of a problem."

"And equally unmendable. Do let me carry something for you."

"Thank you kindly. If you would take the tulips."

The producer went up the stairs with them. It was odd to be directed by somebody who was not Jay; who was gentle, complimentary and a stranger. "But I believe I am going to miss our nightly wars-to-the-death," Caroline said to herself, "and I don't really go for Cleopatra. All this 'my-women' stuff has an A.T.S. connotation." She remarked upon it to the lion, who laughed and went on looking at her.

"Have you a car, Miss Seward? Then let me drive you home. I should hate to see that egg in trouble."

They went through the shadowed foyer, the deserted place where nothing would happen until the evening. As they came down the steps Caroline saw four things at once; a coster's barrow white with narcissus, the fat face of a woman who recognised the actor and appeared to suffocate instantly, the sunlight on the street and the man with the monkey; the man wore a velvet jacket; he played a harmonium and his monkey sat on the top. She rushed across the pavement.

"It is the same monkey; I've known it for years. I used to worry about it in the blitz," she explained to her august companion as she put sixpence in its small cold hand. It was yellowish in colour and had the face of a crone. It climbed on to her shoulder; she smelt its Zoo smell; it pulled her hair. She would have been content to stand here and play with it, but she was keeping the actor waiting. She lifted it down.

"Surprised," the actor said, "that you aren't taking that home, too."

"I should like a monkey," said Caroline, climbing into the open, low-slung car. The actor put her various property in the back seat, with the exception of the egg which he implored her to hold. He drove furiously; his head, beard and shoulders looked enormous on the shifting background. He drove across Trafalgar Square and under Admiralty Arch.

He was talking all the time and she liked his atmosphere. She forgot the importance of her private vision, the vision

407

that had only a little time to run; it lasted, she had discovered for the first few days on any return to London; it was sharpest on a return in the spring, when you felt that you took the city unaware and saw its heart.

There was no bomb-shattered corner, no new-painted satiny façade, no grimed wall of brick and no flowering tree that did not expound this knowledge.

"What most people cannot realise about Shakespeare," said the actor, treading hard on the accelerator, cutting in past the fat red haunches of a bus and roaring across Stanhope Gate, "is that he dashed off every play with a quill pen in a hurry, carried it round to the Globe, threw it at Burbage and never took a second look at it because Burbage wanted another by Friday. All these scholar detectives chasing clues as to what he really meant seem to overlook that fact. *Dear* lady ——" he groaned after the scuttling shape of a woman whom he had just failed to mow down—"if you would *only* look to your left. Now where did you say you lived?"

"Montpelier Terrace. Couldn't he have made corrections at the theatre, during rehearsals?"

"What—and never blot a single line?"

"Yes, well . . ."

She studied this profile, trying to re-establish him without the beard. She said, "Are you going to keep it?"

"Keep what?"

"Your beard."

"Were we talking about my beard?" he asked, and interrupted himself with a bellow: "Oh, my good man, if you *will* drive in the middle of the road—sorry. What about my beard?"

"I said are you going to keep it?"

"Well, I don't know. (*Look* at that fool on that bicycle.) What do you think?"

"I couldn't not grow one, if I were a man," said Caroline, "I'd have to know how it looked, even if I cut it off afterwards. I couldn't die not knowing."

He said, "I once worked out that in a life of sixty-five

years I could save three weeks if I didn't shave. Did you say Montpelier Square?"

"Terrace; south side. It is this house," she said. "Thank you so much."

"You can't manage all that." He came after her with the clock and the tulips. She tried to find her latch-key. Her ration book and the last packet of American cigarettes fell out on to the path. The actor picked them up. He followed her into the hall and into the room that was furnished with Michael's possessions. It was still, after the months of travel, unfamiliar and pleasing to her eyes. It made an impact; the trouble was, she thought, that the impacts came too quickly; in a moment something else would overlay this sense of home-coming, that was already blotting out the coster's barrow, the yellow monkey, a picture of Shakespeare hurling his manuscript at Burbage and the statistic of time saved by growing a beard.

"Interesting portrait," the actor said, looking up at Michael in the white coat. . . . "Well, see you to-morrow. No, I won't have a drink, thank you. I'm late as it is. God love you."

She stood at the door, watching him go down the path. He waved and vanished, a beard and a roaring engine. She looked at the street; she went back into the house.

She tried to assess the magic quality in the empty room; the sharp excitement deriving from the fact that you were you, standing here in silence. Ahead there lay only the short track of immediate tasks, putting the flowers in water, setting the blue clock on its shelf, placing the egg in the kitchen for to-morrow's breakfast.

She looked at her watch. It was half-past four. She found herself subtracting eight hours; it was only half-past eight this morning in California.

She stood still in the middle of the floor, with the tulips in her hand. Her palm pressed the creaking smoothness of their stalks; her eyes stared at Mercedes' portrait of Michael. But it seemed that it should be easy to nudge time and space aside with her shoulder, so near and vivid was the dry gold hill. Below it there stood the two cottages on the brown earth, and downward from their fences there sloped the beds of the vegetable garden, after that the terraced orchard. Now she came to the pool of lawn, with the trees all round ; the long dark façade of the main building, the guest-house with the magnolia growing beside it. At this hour, all was made sharp and fragile by the chilly sunshine, the pale shadows.

She went on down the path, beside the high hedge that hid the swimming pool; she came to the white frame house with the blue shutters. She stood for a moment on the patio, looking in at the room with the brick fireplace on the right and the studio at the end. She saw the small tawny shape of the stone cat on the mantelpiece.

Half-past eight. Mercedes would walk out on to the patio, wearing her working clothes; would pause and look up at the sky, watching for rain. Perhaps rain had come now and the drought was ended.

But that was impossible to see; she could not imagine the hill when it was green instead of gold, nor the sky overcast; she could not guess at the sound of rain falling on the leaves of those trees. She would see the place always by the light of that unseasonable sun. Just as she would see the figure always walking alone and whistling Michael's tune.

In such a moment of solitude as this, she could feel accompanied by every joyful adventure that she had known, every person whom she had loved. She brought into the empty room the crowd, of whom she was made.

THE END

VIRAGO MODERN CLASSICS

The first Virago Modern Classic, *Frost in May* by Antonia White, was published in 1978. It launched a list dedicated to the celebration of women writers and to the rediscovery and reprinting of their works. Its aim was, and is, to demonstrate the existence of a female tradition in fiction which is both enriching and enjoyable. The Leavisite notion of the 'Great Tradition', and the narrow, academic definition of a 'classic', has meant the neglect of a large number of interesting secondary works of fiction. In calling the series 'Modern Classics' we do not necessarily mean 'great' — although this is often the case. Published with new critical and biographical introductions, books are chosen for many reasons: sometimes for their importance in literary history; sometimes because they illuminate particular aspects of womens' lives, both personal and public. They may be classics of comedy or storytelling; their interest can be historical, feminist, political or literary.

Initially the Virago Modern Classics concentrated on English novels and short stories published in the early decades of this century. As the series has grown it has broadened to include works of fiction from different centuries, different countries, cultures and literary traditions. In 1984 the Victorian Classics were launched; there are separate lists of Irish, Scottish, European, American, Australian and other English-speaking countries; there are books written by Black women, by Catholic and Jewish women, and a few relevant novels by men. There is, too, a companion series of Non-Fiction Classics constituting biography, autobiography, travel, journalism, essays, poetry, letters and diaries.

By the end of 1988 over 300 titles will have been published in these two series, many of which have been suggested by our readers.

Also of Interest

RUTH ADAM
I'm Not Complaining

PHYLLIS SHAND
ALLFREY
The Orchid House

ELIZABETH VON
ARNIM
Elizabeth and Her
German Garden
The Enchanted April
Fraulein Schmidt and Mr
Anstruther
The Pastor's Wife
Vera

ENID BAGNOLD
The Happy Foreigner
The Squire

SYBILLE BEDFORD
A Compass Error
A Favourite of the Gods

ELIOT BLISS
Luminous Isle
Saraband

ANGELA CARTER
The Magic Toyshop
The Passion of New Eve

BARBARA COMYNS
Our Spoons Came from
Woolworths
Sisters by a River
The Skin Chairs
The Vet's Daughter
Who Was Changed and
Who Was Dead

LETTICE COOPER
Fenny
The New House

JENNIFER DAWSON
The Ha-Ha

E.M. DELAFIELD
The Diary of a Provincial
Lady

MAUREEN DUFFY
That's How It Was

DOROTHY EDWARDS
Rhapsody
Winter Sonata

RADCLYFFE HALL
Adam's Breed
A Saturday Life
The Unlit Lamp
The Well of Loneliness

WINIFRED HOLTBY
Anderby Wold
The Crowded Street
The Land of Green Ginger
Mandoa, Mandoa!
Poor Caroline

STORM JAMESON
Company Parade
Love in Winter
None Turn Back
Women Against Men

ELIZABETH JENKINS
The Tortoise and the Hare

F. TENNYSON JESSE
The Lacquer Lady
Moonraker
A Pin to See the Peepshow

SHEILA KAYE-SMITH
Joanna Godden
Susan Spray

MARGARET KENNEDY
The Constant Nymph
The Ladies of Lyndon
Troy Chimneys

BEATRIX LEHMANN
Rumour of Heaven

ROSAMOND LEHMANN
The Ballad and the Source
The Gipsy's Baby
Invitation to the Waltz
A Note in Music
A Sea-Grape Tree
The Weather in the Streets

ADA LEVERSON
The Little Ottleys

ROSE MACAULAY
Told by an Idiot
The World My Wilderness

OLIVIA MANNING
The Doves of Venus
The Playroom

F.M. MAYOR
The Rector's Daughter
The Squire's Daughter
The Third Miss Symons

BETTY MILLER
On the Side of the Angels

EDITH OLIVIER
The Love Child

MOLLIE PANTER-
DOWNES
One Fine Day

MARY RENAULT
The Friendly Young
Ladies

E. ARNOT ROBERTSON
Four Frightened People
Ordinary Families

VITA SACKVILLE-WEST
All Passion Spent
The Edwardians
Family History
No Signposts in the Sea

MAY SINCLAIR
The Life and Death of
Harriett Frean
Mary Olivier: A Life
The Three Sisters

STEVIE SMITH
The Holiday
Novel on Yellow Paper
Over the Frontier

G.B. STERN
The Matriarch

LAURA TALBOT
The Gentlewomen

ELIZABETH TAYLOR
The Blush
The Devastating Boys
A Game of Hide and Seek
In a Summer Season
Mrs Palfrey at the
Claremont
Palladian
The Sleeping Beauty
The Soul of Kindness
A View of the Harbour
The Wedding Group